When Love Hurts

A Novel

S. J. Greene

Book One of the Fresh Start Series

To all who believe in

Love.

To all who have been

Hurt.

To never losing

Hope.

CHAPTER ONE

Decisions

Late April

*L*onely cat lady. *That's what people will call me,* Natalie Roberts thought as she sat on the floor of her living room, vigorously wiggling a satiny ribbon in front of her energetic kitten. Tux, as she had aptly named him, was a black cat with a white belly, white paws, and lime-green eyes. She had opted for him instead of a calico at the advice of her best friend. "Pick him. He's all alone," Jessica had said.

The calico kittens at the animal shelter were all together in a large cage, perhaps from the same litter; whereas the small tuxedo cat had been isolated, hanging from his cage doors as if saying, "Please get me out of here!" Of course, she couldn't say no to that. But in hindsight, it should have been her first sign that he was a wild one.

His energy radiated throughout the room as he planned his attack on the ribbon. Natalie imagined it would be another night of Tux bouncing off the walls while she attempted sleep, same as every other night in the six months since she first brought him home. *Nick had been allergic to cats*, she thought as her cell phone vibrated against the hardwood floor.

"Hi, Mom," Natalie answered cheerily, trying to disguise the exhaustion she felt. After another twelve-hour day in the office, she was still wearing her gray pantsuit and a floral-print collared blouse that had ruffles down the front. Her favorite suede pumps with ankle straps, which she owned in multiple colors, laid next to her on the floor where she sat. That day's pair were a shade of dark pink that exactly matched the flowers on her blouse. "What's up?"

"Oh, nothin'," Linda said in her usual laid-back drawl. "Just callin' to see how you're doin'. You're all alone out there in New York now. You should move back home to California."

This was not her mother's first petition to have her move back, nor did she need to be reminded that she was alone. The takeout containers overflowing her trash were a reminder. The large king-size bed she slept in diagonally to fill the void was a reminder. *Not to mention being a lonely cat lady now.*

"Mom," she said with an eye roll, "I already told you I don't want to move back. I have a job here, an apartment, friends. Too much has changed already."

Her Manhattan apartment was larger than average but hardly spacious. Its gray walls, trimmed with thick moldings that enclosed the space further, suddenly seemed to be closing in on her. The truth was that she hadn't seen any of her friends in months and was working insane hours at a job she hated—both by choice. Work had been a welcome distraction. Whether or not it made her a workaholic, she had gone back only a week after Nick's funeral.

Linda jumped to the next subject without skipping a beat. "So, apparently, your dad's new little wife got a boob job. Your Aunt Teri ran into 'em at the grocery store last week and called me up. That bastard better not have paid for 'em. I bet he did, though. My alimony check is over a week late already. I went to my PO box again tonight, and nothin'."

Natalie was now sliding the ribbon across the floor in a zigzag fashion, inciting Tux to pounce. She mentally cringed at the mention of her father, still not believing he had the nerve to get remarried, but it was best not to dwell on that. "Do you need some money to cover your rent? I can make a transfer into your account, Mom. It's almost the first."

"Oh, no, no, thank you," Linda replied. "I'm sure it'll come any day now. I'll keep ya posted."

Natalie knew too well what that meant. She'd likely get a text from her mother on the fifth of the month, the last day that rent could be paid without a late fee, asking for a rush transfer to her account to cover the check she had already written that morning. Having always been financially responsible herself, it frustrated Natalie that her mother lacked any capacity for planning. *But that was Linda*

Blackwood. She lived her life day-to-day, paycheck-to-paycheck. Heaven forbid she paid her rent on the first of the month when it was due.

"I'll transfer some money into your account tomorrow, just in case. I gotta go now, though. Early morning. Love you." Natalie hung up the phone before Linda could reply and then let out a deep sigh.

The loneliness that she was feeling had been Linda's to bear for more than a decade. Still, Linda had stayed married to Natalie's father, Frank Petrov, far too long due to her financial dependence and, as she often rationalized, *for the sake of the children.* Even if the years since the divorce had been turbulent, her mother was better off alone, Natalie reminded herself.

Her mind then wandered back to her work as she rose from the floor and headed toward the kitchen. The lucrative corporate finance job she landed soon after moving to New York had been her dream job when she first started. Besides the high salary, it enabled her to work in a high-rise building with a view and wear power suits every day. Fancy clothes and tall office buildings were secretly why she had chosen to major in business in the first place, and that decision had made her happy for a while.

She had worked hard and raced up the corporate ladder, taking on a management role within her first three years. Her company often flew her all over the world for business meetings, where she'd stay in swanky hotels and eat extravagant meals on a corporate account. The glamour of it all had eventually gotten old, though, and she grew to dread the long flights and even longer work hours—especially after she had met Nick.

It wasn't rare that she had to cancel dinner plans with him after getting stuck at work late or delay taking a romantic vacation until "things calmed down at work." But they never did calm down, and now all she could think about were the missed opportunities to spend more time with him. Precious hours and days had been wasted.

Guilt pangs crept up on her—as they often did—when she thought about all the times that she wasn't there for Nick, including the weekend he died. The *should have, would have, could have* thoughts tortured her, and she imagined they always would. She couldn't possibly know if her being there would have somehow changed the outcome. Barring the invention of a time machine, nothing could change the fact that she was thousands of miles away when her husband took his last breath.

Natalie poured herself a glass of red wine and then headed into her bedroom to change. Tux followed closely beside her, pouncing on her bare foot after every step she took. His razor-sharp kitten claws nicked her when he forgot to retract them, but she hardly noticed. The physical pain was insignificant to the anguish she felt inside.

A widow. At thirty-three years old, Natalie could not believe that she was now a widow. She had always associated that term with white-haired women adorned with jewelry from years of marriage. Old women, with lots of cats, who took frequent trips to Vegas to spend their late husbands' money with their other widow friends. Jessica and she had jokingly planned to do just that someday. It didn't seem like such a terrible life when it was hypothetical and far into the future. *Everything was different now.*

After changing from her work clothes into comfy sweats, she stood surveying the bedroom that was still filled with Nick's belongings. Removing anything would first require her to admit he was gone. *Forever.* She shook her head as if the room had asked her a question. *No, she was not ready for that yet.*

She walked over to his nightstand, opened a wooden box, and picked up one of several expensive Swiss watches that lined the inside. She shook it back and forth to keep the automatic watch working. Another one had already stopped moving, so she wound the mainspring manually by turning the crown and then reset the time.

The next watch Natalie picked up was one she had bought for him as an anniversary gift a couple of years prior. It had a sapphire blue face, brushed stainless steel band, and more gizmos on the dial than she could ever understand. Nick had loved it.

She remembered his face the day she had given it to him. First, surprise and feigned discontent over her having spent too much. Then, after telling him she had gotten a great deal, his face had lit up like a small kid's on Christmas. It was the watch he had worn most days thereafter, including his last. Remarkably, it didn't have even a scratch after being returned to her with his other personal effects.

As she stood there watching the hand slowly glide ahead to the next minute mark, she contemplated, more than ever before, the passing of time. *What was she doing with her life?* She remembered a younger version of herself, pumped up and eager to make a positive impact on society after grad school. *But who had she helped in all the years she had been working?* She told herself that she was helping to "stimulate the economy" whenever she went out shopping, but it was far from altruistic.

She should be doing something for a living that helps others. Certain of that, but unsure exactly what to do about it, she decided she would call Jessica later as she put down the watch and guzzled the rest of her wine. Jessica always seemed to know what to say. She'd offer advice and encouragement, and somehow everything would be okay. Natalie reassured herself of this while getting ready for bed, and then she fell fast asleep.

The next day, Natalie did something she hadn't done in years: she took the day off. Figuring out what to do with the rest of her life sensibly took precedence over the multitude of meetings she had scheduled on her work calendar. Her phone buzzed incessantly with incoming emails, but she resisted the urge to check them. Work would have to make do without her at least one day, *maybe even the rest of the week.* Then she decided to do something else she hadn't done in a while: she put on workout clothes and headed to the gym.

Around the corner from her apartment, a police car sat double-parked in the street with its red and blue lights flashing. The siren was silent. Natalie stood and observed as a young man that appeared drunk or high, or both, slurred profanities while being handcuffed. Ten o'clock in the morning was a bit early for that, she thought, but then again, New York was known as "The City That Never Sleeps." His night may have never ended.

The officer began reciting the Miranda warning to the man, who continued to curse incoherently as he was carefully assisted into the back seat of the cruiser. A young woman, probably in her early twenties, sat on the steps of a nearby building, sobbing hysterically, while another officer tried to soothe her and take down her statement. Her face was swollen and red. There had most likely been an altercation of some sort between her and the young man in cuffs.

Passersby on the busy city sidewalk hurriedly went about their business, hardly even noticing the scene. Natalie found it impossible to look away. She had empathy for the young woman on the steps and for the officer trying to calm her down. She imagined it was an incredibly difficult job to protect and serve the public. When the white cruiser with NYPD in large blue letters finally pulled away, she finished her walk to the gym at a brisk pace.

She made it just in time to a group yoga class, which was exactly what she needed to clear her mind and focus on determining her new life goals. Her body needed the strength training as well, which was apparent when her muscles trembled holding various power poses. She worked up a moderate sweat during a series of planks and Sun Salutations. Then, about halfway into a five-minute restorative pigeon pose, as if having an epiphany, the career path she should follow felt suddenly obvious to her.

Eager to share her news and work out a plan, she tried calling Jessica immediately after the class. It rang unanswered, so she left a message to call back as soon as possible and then started her walk home from the gym.

The sights and sounds of the city were especially vivid on the way back. Car horns blared at the busy intersection she crossed. The street she walked along was lined with scaffolding and construction workers, whose unwelcome whistles and cat-calls were muted by the screaming siren of a passing ambulance. The air smelled faintly of the garbage bags that dotted the sidewalk. While none of this was new to her, she took it all in with a fresh perspective instead of mindlessly blocking it out.

For over a decade, she had loved living in the bustle of New York City, with the endless opportunities and entertainment it afforded. It was the place she had met Nick and where they had built their life together. But sadly, that life was over now, and it dawned on her that a fresh start would require a fresh city as well. While she would certainly miss Manhattan, the thought of exploring somewhere completely new was invigorating. As she focused on all the loud noise and pungent odors around her, she grew even more excited about the impending change.

Once back home, Natalie got on her computer and began researching the requirements for her new career. The good news was that she could complete the initial training in less than a year, but it would still require considerable preparation without pay. Between the insurance money, Nick's generous estate, and her own amassed savings, she *technically* didn't need to work another day in her life. She could live modestly off the interest alone from all the investments Nick had left to her, but that wasn't an option in her mind.

Her personal drive, and perhaps pride, necessitated working for a living. So, she also began devising a strategy to earn an income while she trained for the new job. Having made many contacts over the years, she could consult for private equity investors remotely, carefully choosing which projects she took on to leave her schedule flexible. *It would be perfect.*

Natalie answered her phone right away when it rang. "Hey, bestie, thanks for calling me back."

"Is everything okay? Your message sounded important." Jessica's voice oozed with concern.

"Yes, everything is fine. Sorry if I made you worry! I called because I have important news to share. But first, I have a question for you."

Jessica's tone lightened and was now bubbling with excitement and curiosity. "What is it?"

"Your Uncle Victor, how's he doing?"

"He's doing well. Why?"

"I was hoping you could give me his contact information so I could reach out to him for some advice."

"Sure, but why? Are you in some type of trouble?" Concern returned to Jessica's voice.

"No trouble. It's just… Well, this may sound a little crazy, but… I've been doing a lot of thinking, and I want to switch careers. I want to help people."

"*Okay*," Jessica replied, dragging out the last syllable. "That doesn't sound crazy, but I still don't see how my uncle fits into it."

Natalie took a deep breath. Saying it aloud would affirm her decision. "I thought of him since he's a police chief, Jess. I want to become a police officer."

CHAPTER TWO

#1

Early June

Death. Dealing with it never got any easier. Detective Derek Hartmann's unsettled stomach tightened at the sight of blood pooled around the victim's body. He stood observing her for a moment. Despite the onset of rigor mortis, it was apparent that she had been a beautiful woman with soft facial features, blond hair, and a slender but curvaceous body. *Someone he would have likely taken back to his place for the night.* His gut clenched even more. It was always bad news when he got called into work at three in the morning.

"What've we got, Carl?" he asked the medical examiner, who knelt over the bloodied body of the young woman.

"Nicole Brook, age twenty-nine, multiple lacerations and bruises, no sign of sexual assault. A vagrant found her body behind this dumpster just before two this morning. I'll have a better estimate for time of death once we get an autopsy, but the cause was most likely massive blood loss.

Both carotid arteries were severed when her throat was sliced from ear to ear." Carl motioned with a latex-covered hand over the victim's neck. "Murder weapon appears to be this box cutter."

Wincing, Derek pulled on a pair of latex gloves himself, bagged the box cutter, and handed it to an officer who approached from behind. "Jones, have forensics run this for prints. I don't expect to find any, given it was left at the scene, but we have to be thorough."

"Will do, sir." Officer Rhonda Jones grabbed the evidence bag he handed her and then disappeared into the blur of forensic activity.

Derek looked around the bleak alley. It was the perfect place to dump a body. No streetlights or security cameras. The only business with a door to the alley was a dental office that would have been long closed that night. Shaking his head, he walked over to the officer who was first on scene to get a detailed statement. Everything came down to the details in his line of work.

A forensic photographer circled the perimeter, taking photos of the body at various angles. He also operated a special 3-D scan station to capture 360-degree images of the crime scene that could be reviewed later. Other members of the forensic division buzzed around procedurally, taking notes and bagging evidence. It was like a well-rehearsed dance being performed on opening night. Each knew the routine so well they could do it in their sleep, but there was a nervous tension in the air now that the stakes were higher.

Another unmarked police vehicle came to a stop in front of the yellow tape barricade. A man in his early fifties, wearing a charcoal suit that complemented his salt-and-pepper hair, stepped out of the passenger side of the large SUV and marched onto the scene with a sense of authority.

Derek finished writing the statement of the first responding officer and then turned in surprise at the sight of his boss. "Captain, sir, what brings you down here at this hour?"

"Morning, Hartmann. The chief requested special attention to this case. I need to speak with you… privately." He motioned toward the blacked-out SUV he had arrived in, and both men slid into the back seat. Once they were alone, he handed Derek a manila folder. "This was found on the body."

Inside the folder was a plastic evidence bag containing a note that read: #1.

As if he had seen a ghost, all the blood rushed from Derek's face as he quietly stared at the note. Captain McCarthy continued, "We had forensics bag it immediately. Officer Marks, first on scene, has already been instructed not to discuss it. We need to keep a tight lid on this. Keep it out of the press."

Derek nodded his agreement but remained silent. It wasn't necessary to speak of what they both understood well. The number one on the murder victim implied there would be others to follow. *This was not a typical homicide.* A neighboring county had experienced a series of murders many years prior, where the killer had also numbered his female victims. Those cases remained unsolved, and Derek couldn't help but wonder if this murder was connected.

"I want you to head up a special task force," Captain McCarthy continued, "with Jones, Gibson, and whoever else you need. Other detectives, outside specialists, the entire bureau is at your disposal. Let's make sure we catch this SOB."

"Yes, sir. Thank you, sir." Derek then handed back the note and exited the vehicle, fairly certain he might get sick if he sat there any longer. He had to remind himself that cases like this were exactly why he had joined homicide detail in the first place. *To find answers for grieving families. To take murderers off the streets. And hopefully, to save innocent lives by doing so before the killer could strike again.*

It was the last part that weighed heavily on his mind. He had prepared his entire career to take on a serial murder investigation. But this was his first, and *what if he didn't have what it took to close the case? How many more lives might be lost?* A dull ache grew in his chest, making it difficult for him to breathe. Past pain mixed with worry in a torturous whirlwind inside him.

Being the professional that he was, though, it only took a couple of minutes for him to regain composure and jump back into the investigation. He continued taking notes and gleaning information from the forensic team that worked tirelessly to secure the scene. He would spend the rest of the day interviewing friends, relatives, colleagues, and anyone who knew or saw the victim while she was still alive.

Many hours later, Derek plopped down onto his oversized leather couch and kicked his feet up on the coffee table. The long day had produced *zero leads*. Feeling defeated, he opened a beer and turned on the late-night news. His only company—a white cat covered in patches of brown, orange, and black—curled in his lap while he looked around his condo.

Tastefully decorated with modern art and warm-hued furniture, the spacious living room separated dual master bedrooms. The mahogany wet bar in the living room perfectly matched his four-poster mahogany king-size bed. He considered both essential for entertaining his many, albeit infrequent, female friends.

No attachments. *It was better that way*, he reminded himself. His mind traveled back to earlier that day when he had broken the news of Nicole Brook's murder to her boyfriend, who apparently had plans to propose to her later that summer. The utter agony that had spread across his face was difficult to forget. It was clear that he had loved her. And equally clear that the helpless despair that followed would linger for years.

Derek knew much about death and loss. *Too much.* After four multi-year tours in Iraq and Afghanistan, followed by almost ten years on homicide detail, he had seen more than his fair share. He had also delivered more bad news than he cared to remember. Despite all that, he was no more immune to the horror of it than when he first laid eyes on a dead body. It kept him awake most nights, and as it was likely to be the case again, he picked up his phone to text a friend.

He tuned in when the reporter on television spoke of the murder of a young woman whose identity had yet to be released by police. The news report extensively covered the location where the body was found: an alley off Southwest Eleventh Avenue in downtown Portland, near a dental office and public library, in an otherwise peaceful area. It included interviews with residents of a nearby apartment building who were concerned with this discovery so close to their homes. *There was no mention of the note found on the body.* Only somewhat relieved, Derek turned off the TV and went to answer the knock at his door.

CHAPTER THREE

The Bureau

Just before dawn, Derek awoke to a sea of red hair haphazardly spread across his bare chest and face. He sputtered a few rogue tresses out of his mouth and slowly rolled away from their owner. It would be another long day of searching for answers in hope of sparing the next inevitable victim. He rose from bed and effortlessly dressed in the dark, eager to get to the station. Hopefully, forensics would have something for him, and if not, he would continue to scour the evidence to make sure nothing was missed.

His bed guest would wake in several hours, help herself to the coffee he had brewed, and then leave without questioning where he had gone. The door would self-lock, and his security system would arm upon her exit. It was a routine they had perfected over several months of casual encounters. She had agreed to the no strings arrangement. His good looks certainly helped him, but he made no promises to seal the deal. He didn't believe in leading women on under false pretenses. *What they had was honest and uncomplicated.*

Later that morning, Derek sat at his desk, reviewing images of the crime scene. Although he had been one of the first into the station, it now bustled with busy detectives, officers, and staff members. Phones rang persistently. Several people huddled around an outdated Xerox machine, anxiously waiting to collect their print jobs, send faxes, or make copies. Dreaded but necessary paperwork dominated most of their workdays. Nothing was worse than having a case dismissed for inadequate documentation.

Derek's newly appointed partner and trainee, Officer Rhonda Jones, sat at the desk directly across from him. He usually preferred to work alone, but Rhonda showed great promise. *And frankly, he could use all the help he could get right now.* She had graduated first in her class from the Academy, had a naturally investigative mind, and was as sharp as a tack. More importantly, she didn't take crap from anyone.

"Jones, have you heard from forensics on the box cutter yet?"

Rhonda was sipping her first cup of morning coffee. Her deep brown eyes looked up at him in slight annoyance. "No, Detective… unless you heard me on the phone already and I somehow missed it… but I intend to call the lab right now."

Unfazed by her attitude, Derek continued, "Good. We should have the results of the autopsy later today to confirm the time and cause of death, but I'm looking to get any possible leads before our first task force meeting at oh eight hundred hours. After that, you can shadow me at some more interviews today."

"Thank you, sir."

Training to become a detective herself, Rhonda appreciated any hands-on experience she could get and knew that her newly appointed partner was the best from whom to learn. Detective Hartmann didn't just do the job; he lived and breathed it. Still, she resented being treated differently.

Derek had *spared* her from the prior day's initial round of informing and interviewing everyone close to the victim. Much to her chagrin, he believed she wasn't yet ready to handle the emotional pain of communicating such news. Even if he were right, *which he wasn't*, it wouldn't make her any less pissed. As one of few women on homicide detail, and the only African American woman in the department, she had fought hard to earn her place on the male-dominated police force. And she would continue fighting if necessary.

After leaving a message for the forensic team, Rhonda hung up her phone and noticed a tall blond woman wandering through the station. She somehow looked simultaneously lost and like she owned the place. Her outfit, also a contradiction, was both conservative and thought-provoking. She wore a nude-colored mock turtleneck top that hugged her chest and ultra-slim waist. Formfitting navy slacks that equally hugged her generous derriere caused Rhonda to do a double-take. She wasn't normally attracted to blondes, but this one was exceptional.

At that thought, Rhonda looked over at her partner and saw that he had made the same observation. His attention seemed fixed on the woman's chest. Rhonda rolled her eyes. *Typical male, obsessed with breasts.* Sure, she had objectified the mysterious woman as well, but Derek didn't need to know that. "She has a pretty face too, you know."

In a daze, Derek responded to Rhonda without moving his eyes off the woman. "I'll be right with you."

Rhonda laughed, but he was too preoccupied to care. *Who was she, and what was she doing there?* He had spotted her as soon as she entered the station, and she now stood about ten feet away, speaking to the receptionist who had walked over to assist her.

The color of her sweater perfectly matched her lightly tanned skin, leaving little—or much, in Derek's case—to the imagination. A ripple in the fabric teased him further. *Was she cold or just wearing a lacy bra?* She seemed like the type of woman who would wear lacy underwear, probably black, he mused. Further imagining her in nothing but such underwear, he suddenly felt constricted by his own. The sensation jarred him from his reverie long enough to glance sheepishly around the room, half expecting all eyes on him.

No one was looking at him, though. The entire department appeared equally fixated on the mysterious blonde. Activity halted; phones rang unanswered. When Derek looked back in her direction, she had walked away and was entering the captain's office. *Why was she meeting with the captain?*

Deeply distracted, it startled him when Rhonda spoke. "Forensics called back about the box cutter. No prints, but they found a black fiber, probably from the gloves our perp was wearing. I asked them to run further analysis on the material, but it's not much of a lead."

Derek cleared his throat. "Okay, thanks. Let's hope they have something better for us from the other evidence. I'll check in with Carl on the autopsy." Picking up his phone, he glanced at the time. The task force meeting would start in less than thirty minutes. He hoped that was enough time to get a lead to share… and to calm himself down.

***

Morning came too soon when her alarm buzzed at five o'clock. It was a general rule of Natalie's not to get out of bed before sunrise, but Leah had talked her into a "quick run" before her seven-thirty meeting. She moaned as she hit off the alarm but supposed she would need to get used to an early schedule.

Leah Banks was an avid rock climber and marathon runner who would also be joining the Academy that fall. When Leah had posted an ad to find a rock-wall companion, Natalie had jumped at the opportunity—even though strength training was an activity she dreaded possibly more than running. With Leah, she had suffered through both for the past few weeks.

She rolled out of bed with apprehension, knowing that "quick" to Leah likely meant running at a faster pace rather than a shorter distance. Thanks to their daily runs, Natalie had worked up to running three miles without stopping, or in her case, without hunching over in pain from a side cramp. She knew that three miles wasn't much for most runners, but to her, it was a huge accomplishment.

Leah apparently agreed and had recommended that they go out for drinks later to celebrate her milestone achievement. It was one of the many things that she appreciated about Leah. Despite being *far superior* athletically, Leah never made her feel inept and was constantly providing positive reinforcement to help her stay motivated. She felt truly fortunate to have made such a kind and supportive new friend.

While finding running clothes to wear, Natalie sidestepped the many partially unpacked boxes that cluttered her new apartment. Although she had moved in a month prior, she was merely taking items out of boxes as needed. *Why finish unpacking when you can procrastinate and mentally beat yourself up about it instead?* Natalie shook her head at herself and continued pulling clothes out of a box labeled "workout."

Once dressed, she headed toward several large boxes marked "shoes" near the walk-in closet and made a mental note to buy a shoe organizer. She stopped with a jolt and screamed when the box nearest her popped open. A moment later, Tux poked his ridiculously cute head out of the box. Natalie laughed at herself and picked up the curious kitten. "Oh, Tux, what would I do without you in my life?"

Half expecting him to answer, she waited a moment before putting him down and fishing out her running shoes. *Another sign she had become a lonely cat lady*, she thought. Right on time, Leah knocked at the door just as she finished tying her shoelaces.

Natalie rushed to greet her. "I'd say good morning, but there ought to be a law against having to run this early."

"Aw, it's not that bad. This way you'll go to your meeting energized with a fresh batch of endorphins!" Leah, clearly a morning person, said this with a cheery smile on her pretty, caramel-colored face.

Natalie forced a smile in return. "I'll let you know if those ever kick in for me. About this quick run, I've been thinking, how *quick* are we talking?"

Leah's pearly-white smile widened. She replied with a deep chuckle, "It depends. How fast do you think you'll run your three miles today?"

"I was afraid of that," Natalie said as they exited her apartment building. "You know, if you weren't such a nice person, I'd think you get some sort of twisted pleasure out of torturing me."

Three miles later, Natalie returned to her apartment, winded and sweaty. At just under eight-minute miles, it was her best pace yet. Those so-called endorphins remained elusive to her, but she had to admit that she felt wide awake when she hopped into the shower to get ready for her big day.

As a time-saving strategy, she had picked out her outfit the night before. Much like her, the outfit chosen was modest yet feminine, professional yet fashionable. She paired it with comfortable nude-colored, faux-leather pumps and headed on foot to the Portland Police Bureau.

After the short walk, Natalie leisurely strolled around the station, which smelled of burnt coffee and cleaning products. Jessica's uncle, Police Chief Victor Serrano, was unfortunately not available to meet with her this visit, as he had explained on the phone, but they had scheduled another meeting for the following week. He had been more than accommodating when she called him months prior to inquire about opportunities in law enforcement. In fact, he had insisted that she move to Portland over the summer to meet with several of the department captains and get some experience before joining the Academy.

Her upcoming meeting was with Captain McCarthy of the homicide detail. Not knowing what to expect made her feel both nervous and excited. She stopped pacing the floor and stood there for a few moments, letting the realization of her major life change finally sink in. Goosebumps covered her bare arms. Whether they were from the cool temperature or nerves, or both, was unclear to her. Finally, a young woman with blond hair two shades lighter than her own approached.

"Ms. Roberts?" she asked and then continued without waiting for a response. "Captain McCarthy will see you now. His office is right over there."

"Thank you." Natalie stepped into the office that the receptionist pointed toward.

Captain McCarthy sat behind a large wooden desk. Plaques and pictures covered his office walls. His coffee cup was nearly empty, and he wore a scowl on his aged yet handsome face. He hardly glanced up when she entered, and Natalie could tell instantly that her presence was a nuisance.

"Good morning, sir. I'm sorry to disturb you, but I greatly appreciate you taking the time to meet with me today. Chief Serrano says you and your team are the best on the force, so I'd be honored to hear any advice you may have for me. I'm Natalie Roberts, by the way." She extended her hand and was suddenly aware of how cold and moist it was.

Luckily, he nodded across the desk rather than shaking her clammy hand. "I know who you are. The chief says you're a VIP. So, let's cut right to the chase. What are you hoping to get out of this meeting?"

Being accustomed to tough interviews, she was undeterred by his directness. After awkwardly lowering her hand, she matched his tone and responded confidently. "Ultimately, some hands-on experience to better prepare me for the Academy. From this meeting, I suppose insight into a typical day in your department would be helpful. I'm also willing to roll up my sleeves, metaphorically speaking, and help in any way I can. I'm sure there's a lot of work on your plate."

His scowl then crept into a smile, and she couldn't tell if her response impressed or amused him. She soon got her answer. "Have you ever seen a dead body, Ms. Roberts?"

"Um, no, sir." She gulped, unsure what the right answer would have been to him.

He picked up his phone. "Mandy, please call the medical examiner and let him know he will have a visitor at the county morgue today." The phone clicked loudly as he placed it back down on the receiver. "You want to know what a typical day in my department is like? Go spend a day around dead bodies and then let me know if you're still interested." He pushed himself up from his chair and Natalie followed suit. "Now, if you'll excuse me, I have another meeting to attend."

"Of course. Thank you again for your time." Natalie exited his office and was immediately greeted by Mandy, the bleach-blond receptionist.

CHAPTER FOUR

Pete's Bar

Only two blocks from the bureau, Pete's was a popular hangout for local law enforcement. Straddling the line between grungy and classy, it interestingly had all the best elements of both a local dive-bar and an upscale lounge: cheap drinks, bar games, and a laid-back vibe; but also stylish furniture, signature cocktails, and modern pop hits playing on the sound system.

Unsure if Leah would show, Natalie scrolled through her phone to feel less alone while sitting at a table near the bar. Friend or no friend, she had needed to get out of the house. She checked her text messages again. Still no reply, but the text she had sent Leah an hour ago stared back at her: *Drinks at Pete's in 30 mins? I need to blow off some steam.*

Her stomach fluttered with worry and self-doubt. Feeling weird about drinking alone, she nervously tapped her fingers on the glass in her hand and scanned the room. A few men clinked beer glasses while playing pool in the back corner of the bar. Near them, two other men played darts. Although inaudible over the bar noise, she inferred that curse words were flying from one man's mouth as the dart struck the outer edge of the board.

Closer to her, a young man and woman sat in one of the posh booths, leaning into each other to engage in conversation over the music. Based on their slight awkwardness, Natalie assumed they were on a first or second date. Maybe one that originated through some online dating app. She smiled at the idea but dismissed it as an option for herself. Dating was the last thing she needed right now. All the men in her life had only brought her pain.

She thought about Nick. He had been the saint among them all. His only fault, for which she couldn't blame him, was dying prematurely. It hurt, nonetheless. Natalie ordered another vodka with soda when the server came over and then returned to her thoughts once she was alone again. *It wasn't that bad being alone. Much better than getting hurt again.*

Natalie downed her second drink of the night and thought about leaving. *Who was she kidding? Sitting alone in a bar on a Friday night sucked. Being alone sucked.* Then a tremendous rush of relief spread through her when she saw Leah walk into the bar. She waved her arm to motion her friend over. "Leah, you came!"

It had taken some time for Leah to muster the courage to show up at the bar. She wasn't even sure if Natalie would be there. But as soon as she saw her sitting at the table alone, so excited to see her, she knew she had made the right decision. She sat down in the quilted-leather booth to face Natalie, both literally and figuratively.

The server came over again and took both of their drink orders. When he removed Natalie's empty glass, Leah wondered how many rounds she had already had. "I'm sorry I'm late."

"Don't worry about it! I'm just glad you're here." Natalie smiled warmly and then added, "You will *not* believe how I spent my day." She then proceeded to tell Leah all about her day at the county morgue and the striking resemblance she shared with a murder victim. "Her neck had been sliced with a box cutter. *A box cutter.*"

Leah could tell that Natalie was distressed and could use a friend. *But did she want more than friendship from her?* Desperately wanting to believe that Natalie also felt the strong connection between them, she reached across the table and rested her hand atop Natalie's while she continued to talk. Natalie seemed unaffected by the gesture, which only left Leah more perplexed.

"It doesn't help that Captain McCarthy had only sent me there because he didn't want to talk with me," Natalie said. "At least the medical examiner, Carl, had been nicer, though… even if a bit creepy. I couldn't tell if his stare said, 'I love you and want to have your babies,' or, 'I'm a vampire and want to suck your blood.' And frankly, I'm not sure which would be worse." Natalie's nervous laughter only amplified the anxiety Leah was feeling.

When Leah eventually pulled her hand away, Natalie stopped talking and looked at her with concern. "Is everything okay with you, Leah?"

At first, Leah was shocked that Natalie had even noticed. Then hope crept in, empowering her to be bolder in her response. "I care about you, Natalie." She then backpedaled by adding, "It sounds like you had a rough day, so I'm concerned for you."

"That's sweet, but I'm a jerk. I've been blabbing on about my day ever since you sat down, and I never stopped to ask how you're doing. You seem upset or distracted or something… Are you sure there's nothing else going on with you?"

Leah knew that this was her chance to be honest with Natalie, but she didn't know how. "Um, well, it's hard for me to open up sometimes, but you're right that I'm distracted. I guess… I guess I'm a little intimidated by you." *Not a total lie*, she rationalized.

"What? Intimidated by me? That's craziness! First off, you're gorgeous, Leah, and strong, *so strong*. If anyone should be intimidated, it's me! Also, I know we haven't known each other for long, but I feel like we've developed a solid relationship these last couple of weeks. I hope you know that I'm here for you if you ever want to talk."

Leah noted her word choice. Not friendship, but *relationship*. She also thought back to earlier that evening on the phone when Natalie had told her she had just gotten out of the shower and was dripping wet. *Clearly, she would only say something like that to arouse her.* The pieces of the puzzle all seemed to fit together now.

With her confidence lifted, Leah took a long sip of her dirty martini and then responded. "We should take a trip. You know, get out of the city together for a few days. Maybe rent a cabin in the woods somewhere, go on some great hikes, spend some quality time."

"Oh my gosh, Leah, that's an amazing idea! Ever since I moved to Portland, I've been wanting to connect more with nature, the trees, the mountains, the fresh air…"

Natalie continued to ramble on about how incredibly beautiful the Pacific Northwest was for about another ten minutes, but Leah didn't care. She had completely tuned out after Natalie had said yes to her idea. All she could think about was the two of them alone in a cabin. There, she could finally open up and hopefully take things to the next level. Leah daydreamed while Natalie gushed about the great outdoors. Then someone else caught her eye.

Rhonda Jones was leaning up against the bar with a beer in her hand, looking directly at them. Leah gulped, knowing there was no way she was getting out of there without a confrontation. Unlike her, Rhonda never held back when it came to speaking her mind.

***

Derek was mentally and emotionally exhausted after another long, unsuccessful day of trying to crack his case. Rhonda and he had spent the bulk of the day visiting everywhere that Nicole Brook's friends and family said she sometimes went, but not a single person seemed to recognize her photo or have any idea if she was there on the night of her death. The autopsy confirmed the cause of death and placed its time around eleven the previous night. Other than that, there was no new information.

It tormented Derek to know that the killer was still out there, able to strike again—at any time, at anyone. He sat at his desk studying the same crime scene photos he had already reviewed for hours, hoping some clue would magically pop out if he stared long enough. He was startled by a large hand on his shoulder.

"Go home, kid. Tomorrow's another day." The raspy voice belonged to Marty Thompson, a retired detective and Derek's lifelong mentor. He was now also a member of the task force Derek had assembled.

"Easier said than done, which obviously you understand since you're still here too." Derek let out a long breath. He didn't like the thought of going home without making any progress, and the thought of going home alone was even less appealing. But calling Amber from the night before would break his no attachments rule, so he'd need to meet someone new tonight. "Hey, Marty, let me buy you a beer at Pete's."

Marty chuckled, clearly attuned to Derek's plan. "A young stud like you doesn't need an old cripple as a wingman."

"Don't talk about yourself like that. I may not need a wingman, but I sure would appreciate your company."

Derek meant every word. He held Marty in the highest regard and, in some ways, saw him as the father figure he'd never had.

"Oh, all right. One beer and then it's bedtime for me, though." He winked at Derek as both men shrugged on their coats and headed for the door.

Once at Pete's, Derek ordered two beers and helped pull Marty's stool out for him, holding his cane so Marty could grip the bar with both hands. Both men then plopped down onto the oversized upholstered barstools.

"Thanks for that." Marty rapped his cane against his right leg, which, as Derek well knew, had been wounded on the job years ago. The injury had forced his early retirement. And since Marty didn't like to talk about it, Derek had learned to avoid the subject.

He waved his hand. "No problem. Thanks again for coming out with me tonight."

The beers soon arrived, and Derek took a long swig of his as he glanced around the room, instinctively scoping out prospects. It didn't take long for his eyes to land *hard* on the mysterious blonde from earlier that day. She had changed into a black sweater instead of the nude top that he still couldn't get out of his head. And she appeared to be there alone. It didn't make sense that a woman as gorgeous as her would be at a bar without a date, but he hoped that meant she was available—for the night, at least.

When his stomach started doing flips, he realized the idea of approaching her oddly rattled his nerves. Talking to women came naturally to him, but something about her made him uneasy. He turned his attention back to Marty and took another swig of his beer, which he intended to finish, and perhaps a couple more, before even thinking about going over there.

Marty didn't miss a thing. "It's not like you to need liquid courage to go talk to a pretty blonde." He flashed Derek a confident grin. "If I was about twenty years younger, I'd go over and talk to her myself."

Derek eyed Marty, who was well into his sixties. "I'm not afraid to go over there. I'm just pacing myself."

Marty's forced laughter came out in the sound of a cough. "Tell yourself what you need to, but I'm still out of here after this beer." He lifted his glass, and Derek obliged by doing the same.

Out of the corner of his eye, Derek noticed another beautiful woman walk into the bar. She looked like a runner. Tall and thin, with lean muscles that were covered in silky golden-brown skin. He imagined he could easily strike up a conversation with her about the last triathlon he was in and invite her back to his place. The new woman then walked over and sat down across from the mysterious blonde.

Of course. He couldn't catch a break. Derek uncontrollably gawked at the blonde again, who now had a radiating smile on her face. It was the type of smile that he could tell was rare for her. Somehow, he felt like he knew her, even though he was certain they had never met.

His trance was broken by the sound of Rhonda's voice. "Hey there, Detective, drinking alone?"

Derek wasn't sure how much time had elapsed, but it had been long enough for him not to notice that Marty had left. He looked side-to-side over both shoulders and then responded, "Not anymore. Can I buy you a beer? It was a tough day, but you handled yourself well."

Rhonda accepted his offer. They briefly discussed the day, and then, after her beer had arrived, she swiveled around to check out what Derek had been drooling over. Her jaw practically dropped to the floor when she saw Leah talking with the blonde from earlier that day. She couldn't begin to understand how they knew each other, let alone imagine that they were a couple. Her blood boiled at the memory of how coldly and easily she had been cast aside by Leah. *Was the blonde the reason?*

A few minutes later, Derek excused himself to the restroom while Rhonda strategized her attack. She knew she would need to approach them with a cool head and a plan. Maybe she would hit on the blonde to test the waters, see how serious they were. If nothing else, it would at least make Leah uncomfortable. She leaned against the bar and took a long drink of her beer. When she came back up for air, her eyes locked on Leah's.

There was no turning back now. Rhonda placed her beer down on the bar and walked to the booth where they sat. She forced herself to speak in a polite, albeit fake, tone. "Hi, ladies, I'm so sorry to interrupt," Rhonda said, focusing her gaze on Leah's date, "but I couldn't help but notice you were in the station earlier today. I'm Officer Rhonda Jones. Are you new in town?"

"Oh, hi, Officer…"

"You can call me Rhonda."

"Hi, Rhonda. Yes, I just moved to Portland about a month ago and plan to join the Academy myself in September." She then motioned across the booth. "Leah and I both are, actually."

Rhonda casually turned to Leah, whose flushed expression was priceless. "Is that so? Well, it certainly will be nice to have more women on the force."

Seemingly eager to make a new friend, the blonde replied, "It would be nice to pick your brain sometime about what it's like for you as a woman in law enforcement, if you don't mind. Leah and I were just talking about planning a trip to go hiking. Maybe you could join us, too. We'd make it a girls' weekend!"

Leah shot her a shocked look, and a smile crept onto Rhonda's lips. This was going even better than she could have imagined. "Oh, how nice of you to invite me. That would be fabulous!"

Leah finally found her voice but was at a loss for actual words. "Um, uh, I, um…"

"Wouldn't that be so great, Leah? To get another female's perspective about the bureau?" the blonde asked, blissfully unaware of Leah's torment.

"She doesn't know, does she?" Rhonda directed at Leah after relishing a moment of her stunned silence.

"Know what?" Leah's clueless date asked.

Derek returned from the restroom to find himself deserted at the bar, again, with Rhonda over talking to the two women he had been eyeing. *How did they know each other?*

He strolled over to make introductions. "Good evening, ladies," he said with an extra dose of swagger. Unacknowledged, he stood there confused as the three women passed around inquisitive glances at each other. *Okay… what had he interrupted?*

Unsurprisingly, Rhonda was the first to speak. Her eyes did not move from the two women. "Detective Hartmann, great timing. These are my new friends, Leah and… I didn't catch your name."

"Oh, it's Natalie. Natalie Roberts. Nice to meet you, Detective." She hardly glanced up at him. Her tone was flat and absent-minded.

"Please, call me Derek."

Rhonda carefully examined their exchange, searching for evidence of attraction. She reasoned that any straight woman would likely turn to mush in front of Derek. However, Natalie seemed unaffected. She would need to prod further. "So, Natalie, how do you and Leah know each other?"

The reaction Rhonda was seeking was finally stirred in Leah. "You know, Rhonda, it's been a pleasure and all, but I think it's time you leave now. We were having a private conversation."

Rhonda saw Natalie look at Leah in utter confusion, and her devilish grin was unmasked. She no longer cared about her charade or keeping cool. "Does your girlfriend know that you have a problem with intimacy?"

"Girlfriend?" Natalie muttered, suddenly a lot less confused.

Rhonda replied snidely to Leah, "Oh, *I'm sorry*, was that *not* part of your private conversation?"

"Leah, I'm really sorry for any misunderstanding. I thought we were just friends." Natalie uncomfortably reached for her purse. "I should probably go."

Rhonda snickered as Natalie rose from the booth. "Smart girl to play it straight and side-step this land mine," she said while motioning at Leah. "Trust me. It would've ended badly anyway."

"I'm not *playing it straight*. I am straight." Natalie's heart began to ache when she saw the distress on Leah's face. She hadn't meant to hurt anyone, especially a friend she greatly appreciated. "But if I wasn't, I'd be lucky to have someone like Leah."

Natalie's heartache soon grew to anger when Rhonda spoke again. "Ha, prove it."

"*Excuse me?*"

"I said prove it. Straight women usually find this guy attractive." Rhonda pointed to Derek. "So, go ahead and kiss him."

Derek was noticeably flustered. "Uh, Rhonda, isn't this getting a little crazy? Not that I would object," he added, looking at Natalie with an apologetic smile.

"Unbelievable!" Natalie swiveled around to be eye-to-eye with Rhonda, her temper fully aroused. "I don't need to kiss some guy in a bar to prove anything. Did it ever dawn on you that maybe I'm just not interested in anyone right now? That I'm perfectly happy to be alone?"

"Bull. No one *chooses* to be alone. So, what happened?" Rhonda challenged, her brown face flashing traces of red.

"You know what? I don't have to take this. You're clearly trying to cause trouble here." Natalie turned to face Leah and forced herself to speak more calmly. "Leah, again, I'm very sorry and truly hope we can still be friends."

"Notice that she didn't answer my question," Rhonda rudely declared. "Maybe she's got intimacy issues too."

Natalie spun back around to face Rhonda. "Not that it's any of your business, *whatsoever*, but what *happened* is that the husband I loved dearly is dead now. How does *that* answer your question?" Her throat constricted at the promise of oncoming tears. She hadn't meant to blurt out such personal information, to a total stranger no less, but she had been provoked. And now she needed to get out of there.

Without hesitation, she darted to the exit, holding her head high on the way out to salvage what little pride she felt she had left. The cool night air hit her flushed face like a gratifying barrage of tiny ice daggers, bringing both sensation and relief to her superheated skin. She took a deep breath and headed toward her apartment with blurred eyes.

Derek ran out after her. "Wait up, wait up. I'm really sorry about what happened in there."

Natalie increased her pace to stay several yards ahead of him. Tears burned down her cheeks. "Why are *you* sorry? You didn't do anything. Besides, I'm fine." She quickened her pace yet again so he couldn't catch up and see that she wasn't.

Derek increased his pace as well but kept a respectful distance. "Well, Rhonda's my partner, so I kind of feel responsible for her. She took things too far tonight, but I promise she's not normally like that." As Natalie walked full speed ahead without responding, he continued, "Plus, she knows I think you're cute, so she was probably just trying to help me out."

She wiped her face and scoffed. "Please! I can't believe you're seriously hitting on me right now. I'll save you some time. I would never go for a guy like you."

"A guy like me? What's that supposed to mean? Hey, slow down." He felt his voice rise unintentionally.

She stopped and turned to face him, gesturing as she spoke. "It means that I know your type—big muscles, charming, think you can get any girl you want into bed— well, I'm not that stupid." She looked him up and down and then added, "Military background?"

"Marines. Why? You've got something against the military?"

"It figures. That's all." She turned and started walking again. "My place is close by. I just want to be left alone, please."

"I understand, and I'll be quiet, but I'm going to make sure you get home safely." Derek slowed his stride to fall farther behind. He understood her need to be left alone. He understood the pain of loss far too well.

The two walked down the dimly lit sidewalk in silence for a couple of minutes, and then Natalie stopped abruptly and spoke without turning around. "I don't need an escort just because I'm a woman. That's sexist, by the way. I'm training to be a police officer too, and I can take care of myself."

Derek stopped several feet behind Natalie. "Are you packing a weapon?"

"No, I don't have one yet, but…"

"Then you aren't safe alone," Derek interrupted. "And no, I'm not being sexist. The unfortunate truth is that predators *are* sexist. And cowards. They tend to prey on women, especially attractive women such as yourself, who are alone and seem like an easy target." His voice, which had been calm, now rose. "So, I'm sorry, but I *won't* leave you alone—especially with a serial killer at large right now."

Natalie spun around. "A *serial killer?*"

He hadn't meant to let that sensitive information slip, but in that moment, he didn't care. "Yes, there was a murder this week. I'm on the case. She looked a lot like you, actually." He said this matter-of-factly, but knots formed in his stomach at the thought.

"I saw her… at the morgue today. It was awful, but I didn't realize it was a… Wait, doesn't serial murder require more than one victim?"

"We have reason to believe there will be more. Unless, of course, I can catch the bastard." Derek's voice cracked, and he realized he had shared too much.

"Oh," Natalie said remorsefully as she slowly turned back to walk again. "I appreciate you walking me home."

She stared blankly ahead as they walked in silence again, this time with Derek at her side. Several minutes had passed before she spoke again. "He was killed in a head-on collision by a drunk driver that entered the highway going the wrong direction. The young college kid who thought he was 'okay to drive' after an afternoon of beer pong with his fraternity brothers only sustained minor injuries and will spend up to five years in prison."

"Such a preventable waste of life, on both counts. I'm sorry."

"Don't be sorry," she said coolly. "Everyone is always sorry, but it doesn't change things."

Derek let a few more moments of silence pass, then asked, "Is that why you want to become a cop?"

She slowed as she thought about the question and then stopped in front of the granite steps leading to her building. "I think it's a factor. To be honest, I didn't put that much thought into my decision. I knew I wanted to do something with my life to help people, and law enforcement was the first thing that came to mind."

"It was a brave decision." His wide hazel eyes, full of sincerity, were fixed on hers.

Under the streetlight where they stood, she could see flecks of light green in his piercing gaze. Her pulse raced as she allowed herself to look closely at him for the first time. His jawline was strong and chiseled, as she now imagined his body was under the gray T-shirt that clung to his muscular chest. The veins on his biceps and forearms bulged from his perfectly tan skin. His arms, not overly bulky, were lean and sculpted like the rest of his body. His build was undeniably that of an athlete or soldier. *Trouble as far as she was concerned.*

"Well, this is me," she said, motioning toward her building. "Thanks again for making sure I got here safely, and sorry about before."

"No problem." He flashed her a winsome smile that made her heart beat a little faster.

She forced herself to look away. A light breeze from a passing car carried the woody scent of his cologne toward her. It was warm, fresh, and sensual. *Tantalizing,* she thought. Fearing her senses would betray logic if she stood there any longer, she dashed up the steps and attempted a casual farewell, but her voice came out sultrier than she had intended. "Good night. *See you around.*"

"I hope so," Derek replied with a smirk, right before she quickly closed the door behind her.

CHAPTER FIVE

Mentally F***ed

See you around? Were you seriously flirting with Detective McSteamy? Natalie scolded herself as she walked down the long hall that led to her unit. Bright lights illuminated artwork that hung on the walls. It was an upscale apartment building, but what had drawn her to it in the first place was its proximity to the bureau, the waterfront, and shopping. She had everything she needed within a few blocks and loved the walkability of her neighborhood. *Except now, it was only safe with an escort.*

Sighing after entering her apartment, she took off her heels and laid them next to three other pairs casually strewn by the front entryway. She made another mental note to buy a shoe organizer for her closet, and then her thoughts quickly shifted back to Derek. Those hazel-green eyes, those muscles… *Oh, those muscles. Why did he have to be so gorgeous?* Having vowed to never again let looks like his corrupt her judgment, she knew she needed to stay as far away from him as possible.

Still, there was no harm in fantasizing. She walked across the living room into the bathroom, turned on the water, and began undressing. It was her second shower of the evening, but she rationalized she needed it to unwind. Steam had filled the entire room when she stepped into the stall. The hot water ran over her already aroused body. She closed her eyes and pictured Derek there with her.

Water dripped down his smooth, muscular chest. Those intense eyes pierced into her as he leaned in to take her mouth with his. She envisioned his flawless body pressed firmly against hers as she slid one hand over her breast and the other between her legs. He'd gotten her so hot and wet already, making it effortless to glide her fingers back and forth across the ultra-sensitive flesh.

As pleasure mounted inside her, she tipped her head back, letting the water drench her hair. Her legs weakened, but she wasn't done yet. She gripped onto the shower wall with one hand while the other went to work, thrusting in and out as she imagined he would.

Her muscles tightened and relaxed with each stroke, a low rumbling forming in her belly. Derek's name escaped her lips with a groan as the most intense orgasm she could recall having in years rippled through her body. When the sensitivity had become too great and her knees finally buckled, she quickly withdrew her hand and pressed it against the opposing shower wall to steady herself.

Then, stumbling out as if drunk, she clumsily dried off and made her way into her bedroom. It had been too long since she'd indulged like that, and even longer since she'd had *actual* sex. Eight months since she had lost Nick, she reflected, but if she were being honest with herself, their love life had never left her skyrocketing. It had been safer that way. But now, her body yearned for more.

Exhausted from the day and warmed by the shower, she slipped on her favorite boxer-style sleep shorts and a comfy tank and slid into bed. The feeling of the cool, silk sheets had her picturing Derek's legs intertwined with hers. That thought alone made her ache, but she couldn't possibly do that… again. *Stop thinking about him; it's that simple.* She tossed and turned for several minutes before realizing it was hopeless. She needed to feel that pleasure again.

And why shouldn't she? She was a grown-ass woman, after all. One with needs, a dead husband, and the image of Derek's action-figure body currently "Magic Mike-style" dancing in her mind's eye. She knew better than to ever sleep with Derek *in real life*. It was just mental sex— *and that was the safest type.* Sufficiently convinced that she wasn't doing anything wrong, she finally relaxed and slid her hand under the band of her sleep shorts.

This time she imagined Derek's tongue gently licking and teasing, slowly building momentum as his need to taste her grew stronger. The thought of his strong jaw between her thighs caused her to spread them wider, and then she began thrusting her hips at the sensation of his tongue entering her. It didn't take long before she was bursting, her muscles involuntarily contracting and spasming until completely calm. Thoroughly satisfied, she rolled onto her side and drifted into a restful slumber.

An hour passed before she sat upright in her bed, gasping aloud in terror. Her heart raced as if a horrible nightmare had woken her; only she didn't remember dreaming. She took a minute to catch her breath, and when she did, a chill in the room sent shivers down her spine. It was a cool, crisp night outside at fifty-five degrees. But, being from Southern California, Natalie never let the temperature drop below seventy-two in her apartment. *Why was it so cold inside?*

A fleeting thought to go double-check the thermostat was interrupted by the sudden realization that Tux hadn't greeted her at the door in his usual fashion when she first arrived home. Normally that would mean that he was curled up asleep on her bed, but he was nowhere to be seen. As panic built inside her, she sprang from her bed to go look for him in the living room.

"Tux… here kitty, kitty… where are you?" She tried to keep her voice calm, but it trembled. *Why was she so afraid?* She was sure Tux was around somewhere. But there was something else. A feeling. That spine-tingling, stomach-clenching sensation normally only felt while watching a horror movie in the dark.

She quickly reached over to the wall switch and turned on the light, expecting to see someone standing there with an axe or chainsaw in their hand. She then audibly sighed a breath of relief at the sight of her empty living room. "I'm being ridiculous," she mumbled. It was only nerves, probably brought on by learning there was a serial killer loose in the city. That would frighten anyone, she reasoned, so she shouldn't chastise herself too much.

The question of Tux's whereabouts remained, though. She surveyed her living room. Although it was littered with moving boxes, nothing seemed out of place. The book she had been reading still sat atop an ottoman that she used as a coffee table. A black-and-white fleece throw she had used earlier that week laid heaped atop her gray suede sofa. Hoping to find Tux nestled under it, she went over and picked it up, but he wasn't there. She folded the throw, placed it down, and then kneeled to look under the sofa.

When he wasn't there either, she also looked under the oversized, cream-colored chair she loved to sit on when she read, which was covered in gray script bearing the names of various cities in France. The cream-colored shag area rug that laid on the hardwood floor in front of the sofa and chair cushioned her knees as she pressed back up to standing. After checking inside several moving boxes as well, she made her way into the kitchen.

"Tux… where are you?" Her voice was laced with worry rather than fear now. It was a small kitchen with an open layout. There weren't many places for him to hide. She peered under and on top of the barstools that separated the kitchen from the living room. She even looked in a few of the bottom cupboards. *A treat should draw him out*, she thought, as she walked over to the refrigerator to retrieve an open can of tuna.

With the stainless-steel door open and her back to the rest of the apartment, a chill crept up her spine once more and her heart began to race. *There was that feeling again.* She quickly swiveled around on her heels, can of tuna in hand, with a sickening suspicion that she was *not* alone. But she saw nothing. She closed the refrigerator door, keeping her back against it, and tried to steady her breath so she could listen for any sounds. A moment later, her heart jumped into her throat when she thought she heard a floorboard creak.

Was it just her imagination? Considering it better to be safe than sorry, she kept her back against the kitchen counter and slid toward her Cutco knife block. She knew a sharp knife wasn't the best weapon, since an attacker could easily turn it against her, but lacking alternatives, her need to feel protected trumped logic.

Out of habit, she grabbed the medium, non-serrated knife she used the most and waved it in the air. Soon after, her eyes were drawn to another open slot on the knife block. The small paring knife that she rarely ever used was missing from the bottom right-hand corner. Why would *that* be missing?

Blood pumped hot and fast through her earlobes. She could hear her own heart beating in her chest. Her vision blurred, and she fought to take deeper breaths. She had never had a panic attack before but supposed one would probably feel a lot like how she felt now. *Oh no, was she having a panic attack?*

Some cop she would make, freaking out under pressure, she thought disappointingly. She sat the can of tuna down on the kitchen counter, and deciding it was probably best, she also laid the knife down with a shaky hand. There was a movie, she remembered, where naming U.S. Presidents out loud was used as a remedy for panic attacks.

"George Washington," she started. *Who came next? Ugh.* She hated U.S. History. "Come on, Natalie, they don't have to be in order. Just name some," she scolded herself aloud. "Andrew Jackson. Abraham Lincoln. John F. Kennedy." *Great. A bunch of dead white men, and the last two were assassinated. This wasn't helping.* She tried the alphabet backwards instead. "Z, Y, X, W, V, U…"

She was interrupted by a loud thud coming from her bedroom and froze in terror. It sounded like something had fallen onto the ground. After taking a deep breath with conscious effort, she picked the knife back up from the counter and headed slowly toward her room.

When she got to the doorway and turned on the bedroom light, Tux was standing in the middle of her bed as if he had just hopped up there. A book from her nightstand laid on the mahogany floor, presumably knocked down by Tux. Relieved, she walked over to pet him but froze again when she noticed that her bedroom window was halfway open.

She didn't recall opening it, nor did she notice it open when she went to bed. But then again, she had been distracted. *Oh god, had someone been in her apartment earlier? Was someone still in her apartment now?*

Kitchen knife still in hand, she walked over to close the window and then began searching the entire apartment. She checked the closets, the bathroom, behind all doors, and even under the bed. There wasn't anyone there. *But had there been? Or was she going crazy?*

She was still adjusting to living alone. Before Nick passed, they had lived together for nearly seven years. And before that, she had always lived with either a boyfriend or roommate. Even though it would've been nice to have a roommate now, she figured no one should have to live with a grieving wreck like her.

Not wanting to go back to bed, she headed to the living room with Tux to binge-watch one of her favorite shows instead. A few episodes of *Friends* would help keep things lighthearted, she decided. A full season of jovial banter later, she finally fell asleep on the sofa with Tux curled up at her feet.

CHAPTER SIX

The Unfortunate Incident

Dreading the task ahead of her, Natalie reluctantly laced up the hot-pink running shoes she had been compelled to buy. As much as she hated running, she knew she needed to work on her endurance if she was ever going to pass the physical ability test. Her goal today of five miles would be the farthest she'd ever run continuously, assuming she could do it.

The racerback tank top she wore was heather blue with a picture of a cat's face sandwiched by text that read, "Check Meowt." Since the cat was wearing a hot-pink headband, she'd had no choice but to pair the top with hot-pink cropped leggings. Hence, the matching shoes.

Her breakfast had consisted of two scrambled eggs, one slice of dry toast, and a small fruit smoothie. Enough to give her the energy she needed for the run, but not too much to make her feel like she wanted to puke; she hoped, at least. Her nerves were still frazzled from the night before, which made her already sensitive stomach uneasy. Some fresh air could only help. She did a few quick stretches in her living room to warm up and then set out for her run.

A white van that sat parked in front of her building started its engine as Natalie began her jog toward the waterfront. After a few short blocks through her neighborhood, she picked up her pace on one of the many running trails that followed the Willamette River. The cerulean sky was clear for as far as the eye could see, with bright sunshine replacing the gloomy clouds that were typical in June.

If there were ever a right time to add running to her routine, she figured this was a great place to do it. Portland was a runner's paradise due to its many trails and amazing vistas. Running along the river, she gazed in awe at the gorgeous view of Mount Hood in the distance. Its snow-covered peak was a refreshing contrast to the heat of the long summer days.

It was a hot day already, Natalie thought as she wiped sweat from her brow. This did not bode well for her long run. She supposed she should have woken up earlier to beat the heat. But after the night she'd had, getting up at all had been an accomplishment. Less than a mile into her run, she debated turning around before she heard her name.

"Hey, Natalie!"

She slowed to a jog, and, in the few seconds it took her to recognize the voice, Derek had already caught up and was jogging beside her. He had evidently been running for a while, since his sweat drenched T-shirt hung over his shoulder. His bare chest and arms glistened in the midday sun, and she couldn't help but take more than a few glances at his sculpted pecs and abs. She counted an eight-pack. *For the love of all that is pure and… Why? Why did he have to be shirtless?*

Heat rose in her cheeks. "Are you stalking me or something?"

A sly grin grew over Derek's face. "It depends. Do you want me to be?"

"No, of course not," she blurted, perhaps too defensively. He was obviously flirting, and she needed that to stop. "I didn't expect to see you again is all, and I prefer to run alone."

"Sorry to intrude, but I saw you running and thought it would be nice to chat. I feel like we got off on the wrong foot last night." The sincerity in his voice had her feeling like a jerk.

"No, we're fine. Everything's fine. Let's just forget about last night." *She wished she could.*

"Great. So, you don't mind if I run with you, then?"

Oh, he was a clever one. If she said no now, it would imply she was holding some type of grudge. "Sure, whatever," she replied as casually as she could.

"Nice outfit, by the way," he said.

"At least I'm wearing a shirt." *Was that all she could think to say?* She needed to work on her comebacks.

His ridiculously charming grin widened. "It's a hot day. I'm on my eighth mile. How about you?"

"I've got a few less behind me, but about four more to go, if you can hang."

"Oh, I can hang."

Ugh, he was one of *those* people that loved running long distances. And probably competitive, too. At least that would force her to complete her goal today. *A silver lining,* she figured. She increased her pace, which he immediately matched.

Natalie focused on controlling her breath as they ran in silence for the next mile. Her lungs usually quit on her long before her legs got tired, which she supposed was from years of avoiding cardio. Derek was barely breaking a sweat now. This was a cool down workout for him, she realized. It was nice that he let her set the pace, never speeding up or pressing her to go faster.

Her face warmed as her mind wandered to thoughts of her pleasure fest the night before, with him as her inspiration. The guilt of that little secret, paired with her proximity to him—shirtless—made her insides squirm. She wondered if he somehow knew and then forced her brain to change the subject. They had been running for a while now. *Was it time to turn around and run back?*

Distracted by her own thoughts, she again traveled back to the previous night. Except this time, she thought about the window she didn't remember opening and the feeling that someone had been in her apartment. She wondered if she should tell Derek; he was a detective, after all. *But what proof did she have?* She knew enough about the law to know that a crime couldn't be investigated without evidence.

Finally, she decided to keep it to herself but broke the silence to stop her mind from swirling. "My outfit was a gift, by the way, from my best friend. She knows I don't like working out. Plus, I have a cat, so I guess she thought it was appropriate."

"Why would she get you workout clothes if she knows you don't enjoy working out?"

"Motivation."

"I see. What type of cat do you have?" His voice reflected genuine interest.

"A black-and-white tuxedo cat. I named him Tux… I'm not very creative," she quickly added.

"Well, I named my calico cat Cal, so I guess that doesn't make me creative, either."

"*You* have a cat too?" She gaped at him in disbelief while struggling to maintain her speed.

He let out a casual laugh that seemed fitting for him. "Yeah, why does that surprise you so much?"

"I don't know. I guess you don't strike me as the type of guy that would have a cat." As she said that, she realized she didn't know anything about him.

"There's that 'type of guy' thing again."

"Excuse me?"

"Last night, you said you'd never go for a guy like me, or my type."

"Oh, that."

"And I know you said to forget about last night, but the thing is, I can't get it out of my head. Why does it matter that I'm a Marine?"

"It *doesn't* matter. Can we please forget it?"

"It matters to me. I'm proud to be a Marine, to have served my country. I just want to understand why that would bother you."

"Honestly, I didn't mean any disrespect. I think it's great that you served our country. *I really do.* I just say stupid things when I get upset sometimes. I'm sorry if I offended you." An anchor settled in her chest. Running, talking, and breathing were proving to be three things she couldn't manage simultaneously.

He seemed to ponder her response for a moment before shrugging his shoulders. "Okay, no offense taken."

She was now completely out of breath and seeing spots. The sharp pain radiating through her upper back had her gasping for air. Decelerating to a slow walk, she put her hands on top of her head and attempted deepening her breath.

"Natalie, are you okay?"

Unable to verbalize a response, she held up a hand to say *hold on.* Her heart was pounding outside her chest; all its effort focused on forcing more oxygen into her lungs. Eventually, she caught her breath enough to spot a nearby bench down by the water. She walked over and sat down, feeling queasy again.

Derek joined her, again asking if she was all right. Before she could reply, she was hunched over, reliving her breakfast in reverse.

***

Mortified. Absolutely mortified. Natalie laid in bed at almost noon the next day, replaying that moment again and again. It was like a bad dream, except it had happened. It could have been worse, she told herself. She could have gotten sick *on* Derek. The fact that he had been a couple of feet away hardly made it seem any better.

He had been kind enough to offer to walk her back home after the *incident*, but she insisted on returning alone. Walks of shame are always best solo. On the bright side, she had wanted him to stop flirting with her. Projectile vomiting seemed an excellent solution for that.

Her cell phone rang, and it was the exact person she needed to talk to in order to get her head on straight. "Hey, Jess! I've missed you! How's it going?"

"Hey, chica, it's good. We just got home from church a bit ago. The kids were going *crazy*, but Brad offered to take them across the street to the park. So, I thought I'd take the opportunity to call my bestie and catch up! How's all the fitness training going?"

"Not good." Natalie groaned as she sat up.

"Oh no! What happened? And are you still in bed?"

"Maybe, but I'm getting up now, I swear. Anyway, I went for a long run yesterday. Or it was *meant* to be long, at least. I was wearing the cute outfit you got me, by the way. Long story short: I think I ate too much breakfast or something, and after three miles of running in the heat—two short of my goal, mind you—I got sick and threw up all over the place."

"Oh no! Nat, that sounds awful!"

Natalie finally dragged herself out of bed and began pacing her bedroom floor. "Oh, wait, it gets worse. I wasn't alone because I bumped into this cute detective guy that I had just met, and he saw the whole thing."

"Um, back up, please! What about this cute detective guy? How did you meet him?" Jessica's voice increased to a pitch that Natalie imagined only dogs could hear. "I can't believe I didn't know about this before. I want all the details!"

"Calm down. Nothing happened, *nor ever will.* And you didn't know about this before because I literally *just* met him Friday night." Natalie inserted her wireless earbuds and moved into the kitchen to pour a bowl of food for Tux.

As expected, Jessica was not backing down. "So, how did you meet? And what does he look like?"

"I was at a bar with my friend, Leah. I think I told you about her. Anyway, I left the bar upset. That's a longer story, but I met Derek because he insisted on walking me home. Something about it not being safe for a woman to be walking alone at night."

"Well, it's not, and I like him already. His name is Derek? That's such a cute name!" Jessica's excitement bubbled through the phone. "What color were his eyes?"

"Hazel, I think. It was kind of hard to tell." *A total lie.* She vividly remembered the tantalizing flecks of green that danced in his hazel irises.

"And?"

"And… he's about six feet tall. Dark hair, cut short. Nice tan. Nice smile. I don't know much more than that."

"Ooh, tall, dark, and handsome. That's your type!"

"That's everyone's type, Jess. Besides, it's never going to happen, like I said."

Jessica then went into *mom mode*, which was generally endearing even if sometimes annoying. "First off, why is it *never* going to happen? You're still young, and you deserve another chance at love. Secondly, why haven't you described his body to me yet? You're withholding details."

"Did you miss the part where I told you I threw up in front of him?" Natalie let out a sigh. "Okay, his muscles are amazing. I saw him without his shirt on, running yesterday, and I almost died. But that's kind of the problem. You know how I get around gorgeous guys. I can't think properly, and if I can't think, I can't trust myself not to get into a bad situation."

"Don't give me that. You're a lot smarter than you give yourself credit for, and you've learned from your past mistakes. That's not a good reason to not give Detective Gorgeous a chance."

"I've been calling him Detective McSteamy, in my head."

"*Ooh*, I like that better. But seriously, Nat, give him a chance."

"He was in the Marines, Jess. And I know, they're not all the same, but I'm telling you, my intuition is telling me that this guy is trouble. At a minimum, I know he'd break my heart. I can't ignore that."

"No, you can't," Jessica said, her tone softening. "But just promise me you won't block yourself off from *all* guys. And keep me updated on McSteamy. Oh boy, the kids are back, so I better let you go. Love you!"

"I promise. Love you too!" Natalie hung up the phone right as the sounds of Jessica's shrieking children entered the receiver.

Her shoulders reflexively lifted toward her ears. When they relaxed, she let out a long breath. She'd keep her promise to Jessica by being open-minded if another guy came along. *But Derek—being too damn hot for his own good— was off-limits.*

CHAPTER SEVEN

The Ride-Along

At a modest three inches and well broken-in, her favorite suede heels in a royal blue that matched the blazer she wore were her most comfortable pumps by far. Similarly, the black dress pants she had selected felt more like comfy leggings, thanks to their stretch cotton blend. Since she had no idea what the day might entail, comfort was key.

When she arrived at the bureau Monday morning, she told the receptionist, Mandy, that she was expected by Chief Serrano. The cheery blonde politely asked her to have a seat and then buzzed his office. Natalie peered carefully around the station while she waited. There was no sign of Derek, which was for the best. She imagined he was probably off working a case somewhere. A few minutes later, the chief poked his head out and waved her into his office.

Victor Serrano was a broad man in his early sixties, with gray hair, tan skin, and a congenial nature. His accomplished career was surpassed only by his zest for life. He stood by the door to greet her as she entered his office.

"Natalie! Look at you all grown up." He wrapped her in a warm embrace as he spoke. "I haven't seen you in years! Jessica kept me updated about your life in New York, though. I was very sorry to hear about your husband."

"Thank you, sir." Once released from the chief's bear hug, her heart immediately sank when she saw Derek sitting across the room.

The chief continued, "Natalie, I'd like you to meet Detective Hartmann and his partner, Officer Jones."

Before Natalie had time to react, Derek had risen to his feet and extended his hand. "Nice to meet you, Natalie. I'm Detective Hartmann, but you can call me Derek."

She shook his hand in grateful understanding. "Nice to meet you."

Rhonda played along as well by extending her hand. "I'm Officer Jones. It's nice to make your acquaintance, Natalie."

"You as well," she said with a half frown.

The chief then chimed in again. "I was just explaining to Hartmann and Jones that you're my niece's best friend and practically family. You'll be riding along with them today. They're the best on the force, so I know you'll be in good hands."

"Oh, no, that won't be necessary, sir. I don't want any special treatment, and I'm sure they've got better things to do with their time. Surely I could ride along with a less experienced officer today."

"Well, you're in luck there, too. Officer Jones here is the newest member of our team. She graduated from the Academy last year, top of her class. She'll be a great resource for you when you join in September."

"I see. Thank you, sir," Natalie said, feeling defeated.

As the three of them headed out of the office, Chief Serrano bellowed, "Hartmann, I need to talk to privately for a minute."

Rhonda and Natalie exited, while Derek stayed behind and closed the door. "Yes, sir, what is it?"

"Hartmann, you're the best damn detective we have."

"Thank you, sir."

"But you've also got a reputation with the ladies. So, I'll be blunt. Natalie's a good girl, and I want to make sure you keep things strictly professional with her. Do you understand?"

"Yes, sir, loud and clear." Derek left the chief's office and joined the women waiting for him in the lobby. *Forbidden fruit, seriously?* He knew it was immature, but that only made him want her more. It was bad enough that he hadn't been able to get her off his mind since that first night they met, and the image of her in those tight pink running pants certainly hadn't helped. Sure, watching her throw up hadn't been sexy, but even that hadn't put him off. And now he had orders to steer clear.

Once they left the station, Natalie was the first to speak. "Thank you both for what you did back there, and for letting me ride-along with you today."

"We didn't have a choice on that second part, but you're welcome," Rhonda blurted and then, upon receiving a sharp glare from Derek, added, "I'm really sorry about the other night, by the way. Leah and I have a *history*, and I let that affect my judgment. I was out of line."

"Thanks, but let's just forget it." Natalie then turned to Derek as they approached the squad car. It was a navy-blue SUV with the words "Sworn to protect" and "Dedicated to serve" separated by a red rose on the white wrapped doors. Appropriate for the *City of Roses*, she thought, full of unwarranted pride. "What's on the agenda today?"

"Are you feeling okay?" Derek asked with a grin.

Heat rising to her cheeks, Natalie hoped that Rhonda's confused face meant he hadn't told her about *the incident*. "Yes, why?"

"Good, because our first stop involves food."

Less than ten minutes later, they arrived at a trendy doughnut shop. "You've got to be kidding me, right?"

Derek flashed a mischievous grin. "I would never kid about good doughnuts. You're going to get the full cop experience today."

"A little stereotypical, don't you think?"

Derek laughed. "Consider it an initiation."

The line wrapped outside the door, but Derek pushed through the crowd and headed in straight toward the front counter. A young woman—maybe nineteen or twenty in age, with auburn hair and freckles—blushed as he approached. "Good morning, Detective Hartmann. Will you have your usual today?"

"Hi, Heather. Yes, please, times three." He flashed a winsome smile that Natalie assumed came easily to him as he gestured toward Rhonda and her. "I have a couple of colleagues with me today."

"Coming right up." The blushing girl dashed off and then returned moments later with a box and three cups of coffee.

"What's the usual?" Natalie whispered to Rhonda while they waited, but Rhonda merely shrugged.

More than that, Natalie wondered how this lean, muscular man with presumably no body fat could be a regular at a doughnut shop. Another one of life's cruel inequities between the sexes, she supposed. His muscle mass alone probably burned enough calories at rest to offset a doughnut. She, on the other hand, would need to up her running game if her new routine were to include pit stops like this.

Derek paid another blushing young woman at the register while making easy small talk and then turned back to Rhonda and Natalie. "Shall we?"

He motioned toward a booth in the corner, and the three sat down. Natalie frowned down at her coffee. She preferred tea, but it felt more polite not to say anything.

"What's wrong?" Derek asked.

"Oh, nothing. I'm dying with curiosity. What's in the box?"

"Well, first, I just have to say that if you don't love what I'm about to share with you, then we can't be friends."

"Love is a strong emotion. What's in the box already?" Natalie demanded.

"Little Miss Skinny Pants probably won't eat it anyway," Rhonda chimed in, earning her one of Natalie's infrequently used death stares. "I'm just sayin'. Anyway, are you going to open the box or not, Hartmann?"

"Tough crowd. Okay, voilà!" The open box revealed three round doughnuts topped with vanilla frosting and Captain Crunch cereal.

Natalie and Rhonda exchanged skeptical glances. "They look, um, interesting," Natalie began politely.

Rhonda was less tactful. "What are you, like, *five*, Hartmann?"

Derek picked up one of the doughnuts. "Don't knock it 'til you try it, Jones. *These are delicious*." He emphasized each syllable before taking an exaggerated bite.

Natalie sat quietly, pondering her options for a moment. If she chose not to eat it, Rhonda would be proven right, and that wouldn't do. She reached for a doughnut, took a bite, and was pleasantly surprised by the mixture of flavors and textures. The soft, cake-like base melted in her mouth, while the buttery flavor of the crunchy cereal blended well with the sweetness of the vanilla frosting. "Mmm… This is amazing!"

"I'm glad we can be friends," Derek said with an ear-to-ear smile that forced one onto her face as well.

Rhonda eventually caved, and although she didn't admit it, she seemed to enjoy her doughnut as well. The three sat, ate, talked, and laughed for about fifteen minutes, and then it was time to get to work. As they got back into the car, the radio dispatcher was requesting police assistance for a noise complaint and possible domestic disturbance in the area.

"Northwest Second Avenue, that's only a couple of blocks from here. We have to go!" Natalie bounced in her seat, unable to conceal her excitement.

"We're homicide. One of the patrol officers will take the call," Rhonda stated nonchalantly.

Natalie ignored Rhonda and looked sternly at Derek. "If someone doesn't get there quickly, it could turn into a homicide. Isn't preventing death more important than investigating it?"

Derek didn't dare argue with her on that point. He responded to the dispatcher that they were on their way and then drove toward the address provided. Rhonda scoffed, and Natalie quietly celebrated the minor victory. It was her first ride-along, and she was headed to a call that mattered. She desperately wanted to make a difference, to help someone in need. Several minutes later, they pulled up in front of an older, somewhat run-down apartment building.

"Stay here," Derek instructed Natalie as he and Rhonda got out of the car.

"What? No, I'm here to help."

"You can help by staying safe in the car so we can focus on the situation at hand." His tone was serious and made it clear the issue was not up for debate.

Natalie expressed her annoyance but agreed to stay put. *Some ride-along this was turning out to be. A doughnut stop and waiting in the back seat of the car. No action.*

Rhonda and Derek approached the door of apartment 104. Since she was in uniform, Rhonda stood in front and knocked. The scruffy man that answered was an average-height white male in his early forties, with sandy-brown hair and an unshaven face.

"Good morning, I'm Detective Hartmann and this is Officer Jones. We received a report of loud noise coming from your apartment and want to make sure everyone here is safe. Is anyone else home with you?"

"Uh, nah, man. My wife sometimes forgets and leaves the TV on real loud, you know, but everything is fine here."

"Is your wife home right now? We'd like to speak with her too," Derek said.

Before the man replied, a woman in her early thirties appeared a few feet behind him in the doorway. "What's going on, Irvin?"

"Hi, ma'am, I'm Officer Jones. We heard there was a disturbance of some sort. Are you okay, Mrs.…? I'm sorry I didn't get your name."

"P-p-porter," she stuttered. "I'm Sylvia Porter."

This earned her a sharp glare from her husband, who was now visibly agitated. "Look, I already said everything was fine here, so unless you have a warrant, I think we've talked with you enough today." Irvin went to close the door, but Derek blocked it with his arm.

"I suggest you cooperate, unless you want to continue this conversation down at the police station," Derek asserted as he pressed the door farther open. "We still haven't heard from Mrs. Porter. Ma'am, are you all right?"

She looked around nervously and then nodded. "Yeah, I'm fine. Everything is fine here."

"See, just like I said, now if you don't mind, we have things to get to." Irvin tried to close the door again.

"Not so fast," Rhonda blocked this time. "I will determine when this conversation is over, not you. Do you understand?" When he nodded, she added, "Good. Now, Mrs. Porter, I notice your face and neck are awfully red. Do you mind telling me how that happened?"

"She has rosacea, for Pete's sake! Do you want to know her whole damn medical history too? This is police invasion of privacy. I'm gonna sue!" Irvin's face flared to a beet-red color that matched his wife's, but Rhonda did not back down.

"Sir, I'm going to need you to calm down and step outside so I can speak with your wife privately."

"Like hell you're kicking me out of my own home! You have no right. I haven't done anything wrong."

Derek stepped in to de-escalate the situation. "No one has accused you of any wrongdoing, sir. We're just doing our job. The sooner that we get a statement from each of you, individually, the sooner we can be on our way. Please follow me over this way, where you and I can chat in private. It'll only be a moment of your time, I promise."

Irvin hesitantly stepped out of the apartment and followed Derek away from the building to a grassy area shaded by trees. Rhonda then continued questioning Sylvia about the redness and what had happened, but she corroborated her husband's story. Everything was fine. She had rosacea, and the loud noises heard by the neighbors must have been the television. Rhonda could tell Sylvia was scared, and probably lying, but she couldn't get her to change her story.

With no evidence or complaint, there was nothing they could do. Once Derek wrapped up his basic line of questioning with Irvin Porter, he and Rhonda walked back to the cruiser.

The sight of them returning empty-handed had Natalie springing out of the car. "Why are you back already? Where's the guy?"

"It's nothing but a noise complaint, which both parties claim was the TV and that everything is fine," Derek replied calmly. "Get back in the car."

"No." Natalie felt her heart rate rise. Everything in her body told her that something was wrong. "Now he's going to think she called the cops on him. Of course, she would say everything is fine *in front of him*. We have to go back and help her!"

"We questioned them separately…"

"We shouldn't even be here." Rhonda interrupted Derek and then turned to Natalie. "You may be friends with the chief, but you don't call the shots here. We know how to do *our* job."

Natalie ignored Rhonda and kept her eyes locked on Derek. Desperation filled her voice. "Please, Derek. She's in trouble. I know it. I can't explain how, but I just know."

Then, instead of waiting for his reply, she ran full speed toward the apartment building. Her suede heels dug into the moist grass, almost causing her to trip, but she pushed herself to run faster. Derek and Rhonda were only seconds behind her.

"Natalie, stop!"

She flinched at the authoritative sound of Derek's booming voice, but it didn't stop her. Nothing could. It was fight-or-flight mode, and she was prepared to fight. When she reached the apartment, she lifted both fists, ready to bang on the door. Two strong arms wrapped around her from behind before she could knock, restraining her wrists against her own chest. Derek's heat radiated through her body as it writhed to break free, and then, after expending all her energy, she went still in his tight embrace.

Mustering the strength for another escape attempt, she was taking in a deep breath when a loud crash came from inside the apartment. Before she could even register it, Derek had moved her away from the door that he then kicked open.

Inside, a broken lamp laid next to the couch where Irvin knelt over his wife. She gasped for air once his large hands were startled into releasing her neck. Derek was at their side in three long strides, pulling Irvin up to standing with one arm while reaching for handcuffs from Rhonda with the other.

"You have the right to remain silent," Rhonda began as Derek cuffed Irvin with an efficiency that came from years of practice. "Anything you say can and will be used against you in a court of law. You have the right to speak to an attorney, and to have an attorney present during any questioning," she continued as she hauled him out of the apartment.

"Ma'am, are you okay?" Derek asked Sylvia, who sat up on the couch in bewilderment.

With a disoriented look on her face, she replied, "Where are you taking my husband?"

"He's under arrest, ma'am, for hurting you. I need you to tell me what happened."

"Oh, no, no, please. I don't want to cause him any trouble. We told you everything was fine," she pleaded. "He just got so rattled by the police showing up…" Her voice trailed off.

"Is that why he was choking you? Has this ever happened before?"

Her eyes glazed over, and it was clear that silence was the only reply she was willing to give. She stared at the broken lamp on the ground while he continued to ask her questions that went unanswered. After several more minutes, she looked from the lamp to the door, and Derek wondered if she might try to make a break for it.

"I won't press charges against him," she said finally.

"We don't need you to. What we saw is enough to press charges," he bluffed, knowing it would be much harder to make it stick without her statement.

Natalie cleared her throat as she entered the apartment. "Detective Hartmann, may I speak with you a moment?"

Derek hesitantly left Sylvia to talk with Natalie outside.

"Please let me speak to her," Natalie began.

"What? No. You're interfering with police business, Natalie, and what's worse is you put yourself in danger to do it. I can't allow that to continue."

"I know, and I would say I'm sorry, except that I'm not. Because I was *right*." Natalie tucked a strand of hair that had fallen loose behind her ear. "I was right that she was in trouble, and I'm glad that my actions, even if reckless, helped her."

Derek couldn't tell if he was annoyed or aroused by her defiant determination. It seemed to be a bit of both. There was fire—and an intense burst of blended colors he hadn't noticed before—in her steel-gray eyes. Blue, green, and a hint of brown swirled together, making it difficult to discern her actual eye color—and impossible to look away. Speechless, he kept a stern face while she continued to argue her case.

"She's scared. You can't interrogate her the way you would a witness or a criminal."

"I know how to talk to victims," he rebutted in self-defense, feeling his annoyance level rise.

"She doesn't want to be treated like a victim, either." Her own annoyance came out in her voice. "She's just a woman that made the mistake of falling in love with the wrong man. She needs time to realize that, and to process it, before she'll be ready to talk about what happened."

Derek didn't know how to respond. The passion with which she spoke lead him to believe this case was personal for her. It was even more reason to not let her get involved, but something held him back from saying no. He felt as if he could never say no to her. At a loss for words, he motioned his hand toward the apartment door.

"Thank you… Alone, please," she said when he had started to follow her.

Derek waited outside for twenty minutes. He had instructed Rhonda to take Irvin into custody and send back a second patrol car, and that car had now arrived. *What was taking so long? Five more minutes, then he was going in there.* His anxiety dissipated at the sight of Natalie's smile when both women emerged from the apartment.

Sylvia stopped in front of him. "Um, Detective, I'd like to give you my statement now, if that's okay. But I don't want to go into the police station."

"That's fine, Mrs. Porter. I can take your statement right here." He pulled out his phone and got her permission to record the conversation.

Sylvia then described the events of that day in detail, as well as several past occurrences of abuse. Derek noticed Natalie kept her eyes on the ground, except when consoling Sylvia the few times she paused to cry. He couldn't help but wonder what she must have said to get Sylvia to open up like that.

"I'm not sure how long we'll be able to hold Mr. Porter. Can I give you a ride anywhere?" he asked once the statement was wrapped up.

Sylvia glanced awkwardly at Natalie, who responded on her behalf. "Actually, you can give both of us a lift back to my place. I've been looking for a roommate, so she's going to come see if it's a good fit."

Unbelievable. Derek took several steps away toward the patrol car. "Natalie, a word. Privately, please."

"It'll just be a minute. Why don't you go pack a bag with a few things?" Natalie smiled politely at Sylvia and then walked over to where Derek stood, waiting to explode.

"What do you think you're doing?" he yelled under his breath. "This is completely out of line. You can't take in this woman like some sort of stray."

"I'm a civilian in need of a roommate. There's nothing out of line about that. She needs a place to stay where her husband can't find her. We'll be helping each other out."

"And what if he *does* find her, Natalie? Don't you realize that puts you in danger too?"

"Highly improbable, but if he does, then I guess it's a good thing I have friends in law enforcement." Her face remained stoic against his sharp glare. "Look, I get that this is serious. But she's got nowhere else to go, and I promised to help her get back on her feet. It'll just be a temporary arrangement. I *want* to do this."

At least he now understood why Sylvia was willing to give her statement. He let out a sigh. "I still don't like it, but I assume there's no way I can change your mind?"

She shook her head.

"Fine. Let's go, then."

To his surprise, Natalie responded by wrapping her arms around his neck and hugging him tightly. When the embrace ended, he no longer remembered the reason for their argument. She smiled and ran back toward the apartment to get Sylvia.

CHAPTER EIGHT

2

Late June

It had been almost a month since the first victim, and there were still no leads. As each day passed, Derek secretly hoped it had been a random homicide all along—with the note left to throw them off, perhaps as a sick joke. That hope faded as he stared down at the number "2" left on the busty brunette.

"Pamela Sinclair, age thirty-eight. According to the man that found her, she was a single mom that worked at one of the department stores here," Carl began.

All the muscles in Derek's body tightened. He quickly bagged the note while Carl continued. "Cause of death appears to be asphyxiation. Based on the markings on her neck, she was likely strangled with a medium-gauge piece of twine or rope, although nothing like that has been found at the scene yet."

"Is it possible that her body was dumped here, and our real crime scene is elsewhere?" Derek questioned, looking around the busy mall parking structure blocked off with tape and surrounded by press. The cool night air buzzed with the sound of clicking cameras and huddled reporters speaking over each other. There wasn't any chance of keeping this one quiet. Clearly, the killer had wanted a more public display of his work.

Carl examined the bottom of the woman's feet. "Definitely possible. These scraps on her heels indicate she was dragged for some distance; whether dead or alive at the time, I can't tell yet."

"Okay, fill me in as soon as you know." Deep in thought, Derek lingered in silence an extra minute or two before walking over to the mall security guard that found the body. "Hi, sir, I'm Detective Hartmann. I need to ask you a few questions. Do you mind stepping over here with me?"

Evidently still in shock, the brawny man froze in place. His dark eyes held Derek in a wild stare for several moments before he replied. "Of course. Anything I can do to help. It was so awful finding her this way."

"What's your name, sir?" Derek asked, while guiding the dazed guard to a less crowded corner of the lot.

"James… uh, James Miller. I've only been working here for a few months. You expect to see some stuff as a security guard, ya know, but nothing like this. You never expect anything like this." Although he was built like a linebacker, there was fragility in the way he shook his head and gently rocked back and forth.

"I can understand what you must be feeling right now, Mr. Miller. I know it won't be easy, but please walk me through the details of when you found her. What time it was, who else may have been around, and anything else you can remember, even if it doesn't seem relevant."

Derek then jotted down everything that Mr. Miller relayed. Pamela's body had been found thirty minutes prior at eleven o'clock or twenty-three hundred hours, as Derek transcribed. James had been driving his cart through the parking lot, doing his normal rounds, when he saw a bare foot sticking out from behind a column. He had rushed over, thinking that someone had fallen and needed help.

Adrenaline had kicked in when the blue shade of her face told him she wasn't breathing. Using what little medical knowledge he had gained from a crash course in CPR, he immediately began chest compressions but could not remember for how long. After collapsing with exhaustion, he thought to check for a pulse but couldn't feel anything but his own pounding heart.

It was then that he first noticed the markings on her neck. He would never forget the horrific feeling of realizing the poor woman's fate was far from an accident. The feeling was only made worse when he later recognized her as the nice woman who would sometimes chat with him if he happened to be in the food court area during her lunch break. She had a teenage son that was about the same age as his own, and they had bonded over the struggles of being a single parent, James explained.

After Derek thanked James for his statement, he noticed Rhonda arrive at the scene and began crossing the parking lot toward her. Then something else caught his eye that had him halting in his tracks. He stood in disbelief while watching forensic photographers circle the premises, taking pictures at various angles and somehow still missing what he was seeing.

"Robatille! Follow me over here, please." Derek marched over to the opposite corner of the lot. "Tell me what you see."

Todd Robatille, a freckled redhead straight out of college, lowered his camera and walked over to meet Derek. "Uh, a security camera, sir. We've already requested all of today's footage from mall security."

Derek's scowl only deepened. "Have you taken any photos of this security camera yet? Does anything look off to you?"

Rhonda soon approached from behind, unaware of the conversation in progress. "Damn it. I guess we won't be getting any helpful footage from these cameras."

Todd blinked up at the security camera, *which was pointed directly up at the ceiling*, then dropped his head in justified shame. "Oh."

"I want all the security cameras photographed and dusted for prints," Derek hollered out so anyone within earshot could hear, "and I want all the footage they have, going back weeks, even months. This entire parking lot is part of the crime scene. I want every fiber, every piece of trash analyzed as potential evidence. Do you hear me?"

Without waiting for a response, Derek stormed off to his police-issued unmarked car. The sound of the engine starting rumbled through the near empty parking garage like thunder at the onset of a storm. It was nothing compared to the mounting anguish that reverberated through his chest. He stepped on the accelerator and sped past the thinning crowd of reporters that still congregated near the entrance of the parking structure.

His nondescript sedan hit the open road like a breath of fresh air. Thoughts raced by faster than he could gather them. Despite the late hour, he needed to talk to someone. And he knew the one person who would understand.

City limits were soon in the rearview mirror as Derek's car raced into the darkness toward Mount Hood.

***

Derek printed a photo of the second victim and pinned it next to Nicole Brook on the framed corkboard Marty had pulled out of a musty closet. The pushpins loosely clung to the material made friable from years of reuse, barely supporting the weight of the photos. Beneath them were evidence bags containing the numbers one and two. He stepped back, and both men stared at the board. The only sound was the hum of the antiquated fluorescent bulbs above them. It was an eerie quiet that Derek ascribed to being so far away from the steady flow of people and cars.

Marty's hunting cabin had become his full-time residence after his early retirement from the Hood River County Sheriff's Office. The old log walls were adorned with deer and elk antlers. More imposing were the stuffed cougar and black bear trophies that stood in their life-sized glory in opposite corners of the room. Death surrounded them, and there was a stillness in the air that made it both easier and harder to think. Derek focused on the board.

There were no patterns. The only thing he could be certain of was that there was purpose in the deceitful randomness. He had seen it before. He had studied it his whole career. The Hood River Killer—named after the county that housed all his ostensibly random victims—had numbered the women as well. Blondes, redheads, and brunettes. Tall and short. Plump and thin. Students, professionals, and mothers. It didn't seem to matter. Seven women had been killed before the spree ended and the case went cold. That was almost twenty-five years ago.

Marty was the first to break the silence, having not said a word since Derek had arrived and asked for the board. "So, you think he's back?"

"I don't know what I think," he said with an honesty that matched the rawness he felt inside. "I mean, it's possible, right? Except why now? And why start back at number one?" Derek paused, his eyes fluttering left and right, searching for answers to his own questions. "Could it be a copycat?"

Marty dismissed the idea with a wave of his hand. "A copycat would have mirrored the exact details of the previous killings. But these two…" He paused and motioned to the board. "These two are different."

Derek nodded. With twenty years on the force, followed by over two decades of consulting on cases since his retirement, Marty's opinion was backed by invaluable experience. Derek appreciated and respected that opinion.

Marty left the room and returned with a second board. Derek didn't need to look at it to see the contents. They were etched into the inner cavities of his brain after too many sleepless nights of willing them to transform into answers. But the answers never came. Marty flipped the board around and propped it against the sturdy coffee table. The lifeless eyes of seven women glared back at them.

"What similarities do you see?" Marty asked, as if teaching a class.

Derek looked directly at Marty, not sparing either board a glance as he spoke. "Caroline Meyers, victim number three, was a twenty-nine-year-old office assistant," he said, speaking of the Hood River cases. "Blond and exceptionally attractive. Just like Nicole Brook."

"Very good. What else?" There was pride in his voice, like that of a father passing down the reigns to the family business. When Derek faltered in his response, Marty added, "I know this is difficult."

Derek didn't need to be reminded that Marty understood well. He was the only other person who could. Marty had been the lead detective on the Hood River cases. Derek had witnessed firsthand how tormented Marty had been about not being able to catch the killer.

And now, Derek could unfortunately relate to the feeling that additional bloodshed would be on his conscience if he could not bring the killer to justice.

"Number seven was a single mom with dark hair, short and curvaceous, similar to Pamela Sinclair." Derek managed to get the words out, sounding only a fraction as dejected as he felt inside. Then the puzzle piece he had been struggling with clicked into place. "He's just going in a different order this time around. A do-over?"

"It would seem so, kid."

For the first time in weeks, he was invigorated by a feeling that had long eluded him. *Hope.* Even if but a glimmer, it was there. "Regardless of order, that means that we already know the profiles for his next five victims. And I'm going to do everything in my power to make sure he never gets that far."

Spurred into action, Derek began feverishly writing down every detail he knew about the five other Hood River Killer victims.

CHAPTER NINE

Sylvia Porter

"I'm told running releases endorphins that make you feel better, but if nothing else, the trail has an amazing view," Natalie said five minutes into the run, already sounding out of breath.

Sylvia hoped that meant the run would be short. Although she was grateful for everything Natalie had done to help her over the last few weeks, this was not her idea of a good time. And she missed Irvin. She knew she shouldn't, but she did. *He hadn't been all that bad*, she rationalized.

Wasn't unconditional love about accepting people's faults? He had made some mistakes, sure, *but didn't he deserve her forgiveness?* Her stomach clenched into a tight ball when she wondered if he could ever forgive *her* for reporting him to the police.

"Hey, Sylvia, what type of car does Irvin drive?"

The question startled her. *How had Natalie known she was thinking about him?* "Um, a blue pickup truck. Why?"

"Not a white van?" Natalie slowed her pace, eventually coming to a full stop.

"No, why?"

"It's probably nothing, but I could swear a white van has been following us since we left the apartment." Natalie looked up and down the street that ran parallel to the waterfront. "I don't see it now, though. To be honest, I've been feeling a little paranoid lately. I promised to help keep you safe, but I can't shake this feeling that Irvin might find out where you're staying and come for… retribution."

"He's not a psychopath, you know," Sylvia declared in his defense. "Just because he made *one* mistake, it doesn't mean he's going to come kill me or anything."

"I didn't say that. It was more than a mistake, though, Sylvia. He was violent on more than one occasion. He hurt you, and you don't deserve that. You know his actions were not your fault, right?"

Ignoring Natalie's question, Sylvia turned her gaze toward the river. The sky was bright, yet dull at the same time. For late June, it was an unusually hot day. Geese settled in under the shade of the cherry trees that wouldn't bloom again until March. Beachgoers swam off along the nearby riverbank. A kayak floated farther out, and, beyond that, an otter could be seen crossing the Willamette.

It was a beautiful scene all lost on her. Everything was dark and broken without Irvin. All she could think about was whether she would ever see him again.

"Irvin likes to fish sometimes. Back when we were dating, he brought me out to the river once and taught me how to fish. We caught a salmon that day, and Irvin cooked it later that night. He put candles on the dinner table and everything. It was so romantic." Her voice cracked as tears streamed down her face. "He's not a bad man."

Natalie placed her hand on Sylvia's shoulder. "I know it's hard. And it's natural to focus on all the good times when we miss someone, but right now, you need to focus on the reason you left."

"I left because of you! Because I let you talk me into filing a complaint! He's the only person who has ever loved me, and I abandoned him when he needed me the most. He lost his job, you know. That's why he had been so upset lately. He felt like the world had turned on him, and now I've turned on him too." She began sobbing into her hands.

Natalie moved in closer, as if she might hug her. "Sylvia, it'll be…"

"Stay away from me, please! You think you're helping, but you're not. I just want to go home." She then took off running back toward Natalie's apartment.

Considering it best not to follow, Natalie stood alone on the running trail. She'd give Sylvia space and time to cool down before trying to talk to her again. *But what else could she say?* After a moment of contemplation, she spotted Leah jogging toward her in the distance.

Despite Natalie's many sent texts and calls, she hadn't heard from Leah since the misunderstanding at the bar. Hoping to get the chance to talk things through, Natalie waved in her direction. Leah stopped when she saw her, then jogged away in the opposite direction.

Natalie had never felt so alone. Friendless in a new city, she wondered if she had made a mistake by leaving New York. It had been her home, although she doubted anywhere would ever feel like home again without Nick. Then it hit her. *Oh no!* The home Sylvia referred to wasn't Natalie's apartment. Sylvia was planning to go back to Irvin, *and she needed to stop her.*

Natalie sprinted back to her apartment to find Sylvia already heading out the door with her packed bag. "Sylvia, please, wait!"

"Look, I'm sorry I yelled at you before," Sylvia said calmly as she hauled her suitcase down the steps to the sidewalk. "I appreciate you letting me stay here for as long as you have and for helping me find a better job, but I belong back home with Irvin. I love him, and he needs me."

Still winded from her run, Natalie took a deep inhale and slowly exhaled. "I understand why you feel that way. Trust me, I do. But please think about yourself for a minute. He's probably still upset. And he *will* hurt you again."

"You don't know him like I do. He'll be happy to see me."

"Maybe he will at first, but I promise it will happen again. And you may not be so lucky to get out next time. *Please* reconsider this!"

"Even if you're right, why do you care so much?" Sylvia stepped forward to board the bus that screeched to a halt in front of the stop. "Take care of yourself, Natalie."

Watching the bus as it drove away, Natalie felt utterly helpless. She knew the abuse would continue, and there was nothing she could do to stop it. *But someone else could.* With renewed hope, she turned and ran toward the police station.

***

One week later

The chlorine stung her eyes, but she didn't care. It was a different type of sting than that from crying her eyes out for days, and different was good. They had been angry tears. Anger she still felt but channeled into her workout. Natalie was nearing her tenth lap in the fitness center pool when she heard a familiar voice.

"Good form."

She could hear the grin on Derek's face even before she lifted her head fully out of the water. The impulse to dive into the depths of the pool was immediate but fleeting. He was one of the last people she wanted to see, but there was no sense in trying to avoid him. She reached out for the edge of the pool at the end of her lap and finally surfaced, wiping the water away from her eyes before opening them. Goggles had never been her style.

His grin was as charming as expected, and it noticeably widened when she lifted herself out of the pool. Ignoring that fact, as well as the magnificence of his bare chest, she calmly wrapped herself in a towel. Her insides usually churned in his presence—part butterflies, and admittedly part hormones—but today there was something more.

"What are you doing here?" Her voice was intentionally curt, all business. She wasn't about to let her vulnerability show, even if she was half-naked and soaking wet.

"Believe it or not, I belong to this gym. I was planning to get in a quick swim before heading back to the bureau." Derek spoke in a strategically relaxed, friendly tone one might use to de-escalate a hostage situation.

It only incited Natalie further. She was not about to be backed down with kindness on this one. "Why rush? Is it so you can hurry back to all the people who need help and *not* save them?"

In the silence that followed, she remembered hearing of another woman's murder on the news. The second in a serial case. Derek's case. She also thought back to the sorrowful tone of his voice when he had told her about the first murder. It was like a window into his soul had opened that night. He would certainly feel responsible for any subsequent victims, guilty that he couldn't save them.

She was the smallest person on earth. "What I meant was…"

"I know you're upset about Sylvia," Derek said, graciously excusing her insensitive comment. "I actually wanted to talk to you about that."

"You did?"

"Yeah, the chief told me that Sylvia went back to her husband." He paused, as if choosing his next words carefully. "I've been keeping eyes on them. Unofficially."

"But he told me there was nothing the bureau could do." She had been so furious with the chief, and although she hadn't asked Derek for help directly, she assumed he would have given her the same reply.

"Correct. The bureau can't do anything. I'm just a concerned citizen," Derek said with a wink.

Natalie couldn't believe what she was hearing. Water from her drenched hair ran down her back and lightly tapped onto the tiled floor that surrounded the indoor pool. She tilted her head side-to-side to clear any residual water from her ears, which somehow also allowed her to process the information. An overwhelming surge of delayed emotion filled her chlorine-dried eyes with tears.

Without further thought, she wrapped Derek in her arms. "Thank you so much!"

His muscles immediately tightened against her. The soothing contrast of his hot skin against hers, which was now covered in goosebumps, had her clinging on longer than an average hug. She hadn't realized what she was doing, nor that her towel had dropped, until the warmth of him had fully permeated her body. Letting go, she stumbled back a step, only to be caught by his waiting arms before she could fall.

"Whoa, are you okay?" He leaned back and looked into her eyes. His were filled with concern... and something else.

Lust, she assumed. And she'd have been lying if she didn't admit she felt it too. Their bodies were still touching. He had arched back so that their faces were only inches apart, close enough to feel the heat of his steady breath. She imagined it was the part in a romance movie where they would kiss. *But this was real life.*

"Yes, sorry." She stepped back, more stable this time. "I don't know what came over me. I was just so… so…"

"Grateful?"

"Yes, extremely grateful. Thank you again. How is she?" Natalie asked, truly wanting to know but also eager to change the subject of the awkward hug.

"Well, I *accidentally* ran into her last night while she was out grocery shopping, and she seems to be doing fine. No visible marks or bruises, at least. We made small talk, and then I invited her to one of the self-defense classes I teach each week."

"And Sylvia agreed to go?"

"She was hesitant at first," Derek explained, "but once I clarified it was for protection from everyday predators, not her husband, she seemed more open to it. She's supposed to come to my next class at the Y on Tuesday night. You should come too."

"I would love to, but I wouldn't want to spook her. She would probably think the whole thing was a setup to talk her into leaving Irvin if she saw me there."

Derek nodded his understanding. "I teach the class on Thursday nights as well. You should come to that one, then."

"Sounds good. And listen… I'm sorry about what I said before. I know you're doing everything you can to protect… people." Her last word was intentional. *People* sounded less horrible than *unsuspecting women* or *future murder victims.*

He dismissed it with a wave of his hand, but the look on his face told her it hurt more than he cared to admit. "Don't worry about it."

"Okay, then… Bye." She hesitantly turned to leave and was suddenly aware of her attire. Although she had worn a one-piece rather than her usual bikini, the high-cut suit left her backside on full display.

The towel she had wrapped herself in earlier laid on the ground in front of her. She debated picking it up, but bending over was a far worse option. All she could do was walk away, as briskly as possible, and ignore her swimsuit creeping up her crack with each step. Pulling it out while she was certain he was watching was out of the question. She had almost reached the door that led into the gym locker rooms when she heard Derek call out to her.

"See you at the chief's Fourth of July barbecue tomorrow?"

Pivoting around, she took a few steps back toward the pool. "The chief put you up to watching over Sylvia, didn't he?"

"My actions are not bureau sanctioned." Derek's grin had returned. "But he may have implied that he'll look the other way if I get caught."

Of course. Natalie felt like a jerk again for having been so mad at the chief. She should have trusted that he would do the right thing, as she had always known him to do. It seemed she owed him an apology as well.

"Yes, I'll be there."

CHAPTER TEN

Independence Day

The heat wave continued unexpectedly, but Natalie wasn't complaining. She much preferred hot weather to the original forecast that had called for rain. *Shows what they know.* She pulled on a red tank top and cutoff blue jean shorts over her white bikini and then frowned at her reflection in the mirror.

The patriotic colors had seemed appropriate when she picked the outfit out. But now, the red top was too flashy… or the short shorts were too slutty… or maybe it was the combination of the two. Regardless of the reason, she felt like she was starring in *Pretty Woman* before the transformation. She let out an audible sigh and then walked over to her closet to keep looking.

The barbecue had already started an hour ago. *Fashionably late as always*—if only she could get the fashion part right. Her cell rang, and a quick glance at the display relieved her worry that it might be someone from the party wondering why she wasn't there yet.

"Hey!" she answered.

"Happy Fourth of July, bestie!" Jessica exclaimed through the phone. "How's it going?"

"Good. I'm actually getting ready to head over to your uncle's house for his annual barbecue… if I can ever figure out what to wear." Natalie emitted a low growl.

"Glad to hear you're going! I'm sure whatever you wear will be fine, Nat." Jessica paused. "Wait a minute! Is *Detective McHottie, or whatever,* going to be there?"

Natalie had to hold the phone away from her ear to escape Jessica's excitement. It was *Detective McSteamy,* she inwardly corrected but didn't dare add kindling to the flames. "His name is Derek, and yes, he'll probably be there," she said nonchalantly.

"Oh, that's right! Derek… Such a cute name. You better wear something hot, Natalya Elizabeth, and let loose a little today!"

"You're such a mom, middle-naming me. What are you and the family up to today?"

"Don't think that I don't know what you're doing," Jessica playfully scolded but, to Natalie's relief, allowed the subject to change anyway. "The kids and I are over at my parent's house right now, barbecuing and just hanging out. Brad stayed home to catch up on some sleep. He's exhausted from all the long hours he's been working lately. Poor guy."

"Sorry to hear about Brad, but tell your parents I say hello. I really miss them. And you! I better let you go, though. I'm already late."

"Okay, but have fun!"

"Yes, ma'am. Bye!" Natalie chuckled as she ended the call.

She looked at herself in the mirror again. "I guess I can make this work." She then grabbed her purse, slipped on a pair of sandals, and headed out the door.

***

The large backyard was filled with off-duty officers and their families. Some splashed around in the pool while others played ladder ball and bag toss games on the lawn. The air was heavy with the smell of hot dogs and smoke from the barbecue manned by the chief himself. He had dispelled anyone who offered to help, including Derek, who now sipped on a cold beer several feet away and scanned the crowd.

She had said she would be there but was nowhere to be seen. The uncertainty of her arrival made him jittery inside. *Why did it matter so much whether Natalie was there?* He had been to enough of these functions alone to know how to have a good time. He took a longer drink of his beer this time to calm his nerves and then scanned the area again.

There were lots of familiar faces, but none that he recognized as friends. Everyone seemed preoccupied either playing games, chasing their kids around, or engaging in conversations that involved laughing and backslapping. Derek wasn't in the mood for any of those things. He wasn't even sure why he came.

Circling a drain of self-pity, he finished his beer just as a rogue beach ball came straight toward his head. He reacted quickly, using his forearm to bunt it back to the giggling kids in the pool.

"Smooth move."

His heart swelled at the sound of a female voice that he could only hope was hers. Disappointment quickly set in when he turned to see Rhonda and another woman. *What was happening to him?* He shook it off and smiled politely.

"Derek, this is my friend, Sarah." Rhonda introduced the pretty brunette at her side. "Sarah, this my partner, Detective Derek Hartmann."

"Nice to meet you, Sarah." Derek extended his hand, which she met with a firm grip.

"Likewise. I'm glad Rhonda has someone watching her back."

"It's more like she's got mine. How do you two know each other?"

"We met at the gym. Rhonda here is an expert rock climber and offered to help me with my form," Sarah replied suggestively, smiling at Rhonda.

"I see. Well, you two ladies have fun with that." He added a wink in Rhonda's direction. "I'm going to go grab another beer. Can I get either one of you anything?"

"No thanks," Rhonda replied, appearing flustered. "We're going to go mingle some more. Talk to you later."

They were out of sight before he even reached the cooler, and a fresh wave of loneliness washed over him. It made no sense. He was surrounded by people he knew at a festive event, yet he had never felt more alone. He thought about sneaking out the back gate, retreating home. And then he saw her.

She was hugging the chief. Her golden-blond hair was pulled up into a messy bun, exposing the freckles on her back. He couldn't help but look her up and down, landing on her long, bare legs that disappeared under tight jean shorts.

"Are you going to open that?"

Startled back into the buzz of the party by Marty's taunting question, Derek looked down to see a new beer in one hand and a bottle opener in the other; both frozen in a statue-like pose. He opened the beer and handed it to Marty. "This one's for you."

"Mm-hmm. Thanks." Marty smirked knowingly and took the beer that Derek held out. "Just go talk to her."

"I'm planning on it. When did you get here?" Derek asked, stalling. He knew it was cowardly, but he needed to wait—at least until she was away from the chief. *Forbidden fruit*, Derek reminded himself.

"A few minutes ago. First beer." Marty raised his bottle to toast, which was quickly met by the new bottle Derek had opened for himself. "Cheers. To good health and the safe return of all our brave soldiers serving this country."

"Cheers to that!" Derek took a swig of his beer and thought back to Natalie's comment about him being a

Marine, *as if that was a bad thing.* Not knowing why still bothered him.

His eyes had not left her as she stood speaking to the chief. There were some hand gestures and then another hug before she started walking toward the house. He grabbed another beer from the cooler and swiftly intercepted her path before she could reach the kitchen door.

"Beer?" He put on his best smile despite the nervous churn of his stomach.

"Oh, no thank you. The last thing I want to be is drunk in front of a bunch of my future co-workers," Natalie replied.

Her easy smile and playful tone had him at a loss for words. He squinted to read the look in her eyes, but all he saw was his own reflection in her sunglasses. He pulled his own down from atop his head to mask his vulnerability.

With a light laugh, she held up the red plastic cup in her hand and motioned toward the beverage table. "I opted for the kiddie punch over there. I'm too much of a lightweight."

Humidity had caused the tan T-shirt he wore to cling to his chest, lightly coated in sweat. This, paired with his camo-print swim shorts, gave him the appearance of a solider who had just completed a workout. He supposed she'd be put off by that as well.

The esteemed lady of the house soon exited from the kitchen and engulfed Natalie in a warm embrace. "Oh, sweetheart, it's so good to see you!"

"You as well, Mrs. Serrano. Thanks for having me! You have such a lovely home here."

"Oh, pish-posh. It's about time! I've been hounding Victor to invite you over ever since you got into town. Work's been keeping him so busy, though, with everything going on."

"Yes, I can certainly understand that," Natalie said. Her smile had faded, and her head drooped.

Marjorie Serrano ran a hand through her silver pixie-cut hair, as if to wave away any bad thoughts. "And I see that you've already met Derek here, my favorite little charmer on the force," she said while wrapping him in a mother-like hug next.

Her presence instantly put Derek at ease. "Good to see you as always, Maggie."

"I was just headed to the kitchen to see if there was anything I could help with," Natalie offered.

"Not necessary, dear." Mrs. Serrano then turned back to Derek. "There are several platters of food on the kitchen counter ready to be brought out, if you will. Please set them over on that picnic table next to the plates. Natalie and I have some catching up to do," she added with a wink.

"You've got it." Derek headed into the kitchen, happy to make himself useful and even happier to be excused before making a fool of himself in front of Natalie. He didn't understand the effect she seemed to have on him. It would be best to calm his nerves before attempting to talk to her again.

The spacious country-style kitchen glistened as it usually did and smelled of warm apple pie. Perfectly spaced stainless-steel pots and pans hung from a rack over the stove, and a variety of fresh herbs lined the large windowsill above the sink. He peeked into the oven to confirm it contained several freshly baked pies being kept warm by residual heat. His mouth watered at the sight, but he quickly closed the oven door out of fear of getting his hand figuratively caught in the cookie jar. Marjorie Serrano would certainly reprimand him for snooping in her kitchen.

Overflowing platters of food covered the large marble countertop in the center of the kitchen. In honor of Independence Day, there was a red-white-and-blue platter of ripe strawberries and blueberries with a whipped-cream dipping sauce between them. Another platter contained homemade sugar cookies shaped like flags and stars. There were also various pasta salads, green salads, skewers of meats and cheeses, chips and dips, veggies and hummus, and, of course, Maggie's famous loaded potato skins.

Derek looked both ways before quickly sampling one and then headed back outside with two of the platters in hand. He scanned the crowd for Natalie while heading toward the picnic table and quickly spotted her chatting with Maggie under the shade of a maple tree. She seemed so relaxed, as if in her natural element, unlike their previous encounters. He could see her laughing and wondered what they were talking about, somewhat self-consciously.

After dropping off the first two platters, he headed back in for another round. It took several trips back and forth to bring out the cornucopia of food, which was already getting scooped up into the eager mouths of partygoers.

Marjorie approached the table as he was setting down the last of the platters. "Thank you so much, dear. You're such a good boy."

He hoped she had expressed such sentiments to Natalie, who he now noticed was nowhere in sight.

"Despite what he says, I think Victor could use some help over at the grill next, if you don't mind."

"Of course." Derek smiled at her effortless command of any situation. Chief Serrano only *thought* he was the one in charge.

He was soon bringing hot dogs, hamburgers, and chicken from the grill to the table, where a small line of officers had already formed. Like a pride of hungry lions with a zebra in sight, they salivated at the platter of meat he carried. He decided it was best to place the food down at the opposite end of the table and hurry away before they could mob him.

Pivoting on his heels to head back toward the grill, he collided squarely into Natalie and latched onto her shoulders to prevent either of them from tumbling over. "I'm so sorry. Are you okay?"

With her body pressed firmly against his, she replied, "It's my fault. I shouldn't have gotten in the way. Are you okay?"

Besides feeling his heart in his throat, he assumed he was fine. He relaxed his grip. "Yeah, of course. I'm just concerned about you. I bumped into you pretty hard."

"The amount of force exerted on us was the same. If you're fine, then why wouldn't I be?"

He could tell from her smirk she was toying with him, but her proximity prevented him from forming a cohesive argument. Instead, he said the first thing that came to mind. "I'm a lot bigger than you."

"Size isn't everything." She took a step back, slowly scrolling her eyes down his body. She no longer wore sunglasses, and he noticed her chameleon eyes looked more blue than gray that day.

Her smirk escalated into a deep laugh that melted into him like a hot knife through butter. He hadn't realized how tense his stance had been until, all at once, his muscles relaxed. Her laughter was infectious. For the first time in weeks, he found himself heartily laughing as well.

From across the lawn, Chief Serrano cleared his throat. Derek looked up to see him sternly watching them. "Right," he said to Natalie, still laughing. "I've got to go get the rest of the food."

She simply smiled and motioned him on his way. When he returned, balancing a third plate atop two others in his hands, she had disappeared again. *Was she being flirtatious and mysterious on purpose?* He certainly hoped so. In either case, he felt disarmingly out of his league.

Marty approached from the side. "Smells good."

"It sure does. Burger or dog?" Derek offered, knowing Marty would scoff at the idea of chicken despite his high cholesterol. There was no point in trying to steer him toward healthier options on a holiday.

"One of each, please," Marty replied with the grin of a child getting away with not eating his vegetables.

Derek served Marty and then placed a piece of chicken on his own plate before setting the rest down on the table. He again wondered where Natalie had gone. Since she didn't appear to be in line for food, he placed another piece of chicken and some additional sides on his plate, just in case, and then wandered over to a lounge chair near the pool to sit and eat.

The sun had dipped below the horizon, painting the rose gold sky in even more brilliant shades of pink and orange. Parents hollered at their children to get out of the pool and eat. Fireworks would soon be starting over the river from the nearby park, with prime viewing right from the backyard where they gathered. It was no coincidence that this barbecue had become an annual tradition for as long as Derek could remember. He imagined Marjorie had picked out their home along the Willamette with festivities such as this in mind. Being less than ten miles south of the bureau, it was a win-win for the chief as well.

Halfway into his plate, Derek caught sight of Natalie at the other end of the pool, walking toward another lounge chair. She seemed off balance. Punch sloshed out of the cup she held and ran down her leg, causing her to bend over and wipe it with her palm. He noticed nearby men gawking at the motion and felt tinges of jealousy previously unknown to him.

Ten long but speedy strides later, he was at her side, offering her his napkin and taking the cup that continued to spill from her hand. "Here, let me help you."

"I don't need help from men, especially not *you*," she slurred, dragging out the last word.

"Are you drunk?" He then answered his own question by sniffing her cup. "This isn't the kiddie punch."

She laughed and half-sat, half-stumbled into the lounge chair beside her. *This was a problem.*

"I bet you haven't eaten yet. I'm going to go grab you some food and water. Just stay right here and don't talk to anyone, okay?"

Instead of a reply, she slouched farther into the chair. He took that as a signal that she was going to stay put and dashed off to fetch the needed items. When he returned minutes later, she was standing, unsteadily, and talking with Marty.

"Here, have some water." Derek held out a cup but then noticed she already had one in her hand.

"I brought her some soda. It looked like she could use a little caffeine," Marty said.

"Thanks. Hey Natalie, why don't you try one of these potato skins. They're amazing."

Natalie pushed away the plate that Derek held out, instead leaning in to take a bite of the potato skin he had grabbed for himself. She gazed at him with sensual eyes as she ate from his hand. He knew she was too drunk to know what she was doing and that her behavior shouldn't turn him on, but he struggled to maintain his composure.

"I'll leave you two alone," Marty chuckled.

"Pie time!" Marjorie hollered from the open kitchen door. Her voice traveled as clearly across the lawn as if she had been right next to them. "Derek, can I borrow you for a few more minutes, dear?"

"Marty, wait," Derek said. "Can you please stay with Natalie while I'm gone?"

"Sure thing."

"Thanks! And try to keep her away from everyone else." He then darted over to the kitchen to help Maggie.

The chore of serving all the pies took about ten minutes. *It could not go quickly enough.* Derek was eager to get back to Natalie and make sure she was okay. Once the last pie was served, he carried three slices back to the pool area to find that Natalie and Marty were no longer there. *Where the hell were they?*

Derek weaved wildly through the crowd of partygoers gathering at the far end of the backyard. The fireworks would be starting any minute. Several mothers had laid out blankets for their tired children to sit on while others had pulled over various lawn chairs, all facing the direction of the river. He spotted Marty first. *Alone.*

"Where's Natalie?" Derek snapped, his panic escalating. He swallowed hard to suppress the pounding in his throat.

"I tried to keep her away from everyone, but she got excited by all the commotion and took off into the crowd. I couldn't keep up with her." Marty tapped his bum leg with his cane.

Derek let out a deep sigh. "Sorry, I don't feel like myself lately. Let's just find her before she gets into any trouble."

He and Marty spread out into the crowd as the first bursts of red and white flashed in the sky. The loud booms echoed over the patriotic music that filled the backyard. A moment later, an unexpected clap of thunder that could've easily been confused as a firework released an onslaught of water from the sky. *He needed to find her.*

CHAPTER ELEVEN

Jared

Natalie awoke disoriented, her head pounding. Sunlight beamed in through open window shades, causing her to squint and rub her eyes. As her blurred vision slowly came into focus, she rolled over to find herself in an unfamiliar bed with another sheet-covered body beside her. A small gasp escaped her lips. The sleeping body stirred but didn't wake.

She then quickly assessed the situation. She was wearing a man's T-shirt. Underneath was something less comfortable than underwear. *Her bikini from the day before*, she realized. She spotted her handbag and sandals on a chair in the corner of what was definitely *not* her bedroom. *Where was she?* And why couldn't she remember *anything* from the night before?

A sharp pain in her temple served as a clue to one probable reason, but she only remembered drinking fruit punch at the party. Her foggy brain slowly worked out the mystery. It must have been *spiked* punch. *But how drunk had she gotten, and what had she done?*

As her mind spiraled with possibilities, she inched her body toward the edge of the bed. She would try to get answers later, but right now, she needed to get out of there. She let one leg slip off the bed and then followed it stealthily with the other. Moving at a snail's pace, she gradually lifted off the bed and came to a standing position. Quietly as possible, she took a step toward her belongings.

"Good morning, Natalie."

She swiveled around to see Derek sitting up in bed, with a grin on his ridiculously handsome face. And shirtless. *Why did he always have to be shirtless?* "Oh, hi. I was just…"

"Trying to sneak out?"

Caught red-handed. Suddenly dizzy, she sat down at the foot of the bed. "Well, yeah, actually. What the hell happened last night?"

"You don't remember anything?"

"*Would I ask if I did?*" Her tone came across sharper than she intended. "Sorry, but I'm really confused about how I got here. I honestly don't remember anything after… playing bocce ball at the party. Why did I wake up in your bed?"

"Wow, you must have been even worse off than I thought. You played bocce ball at the party?" Derek asked, seemingly distracted by that minor detail. "Never mind. Let's get you something to eat, and we can discuss further." He rose from the bed, pulled on a fresh shirt from his dresser, and started toward the kitchen.

"Wait, why are you going to make me breakfast? *Oh god, did we sleep together?*"

"Sleep, yes. Sex, no. Food will help you feel better."

She followed him into the kitchen. It was impressively large, with modern appliances and a center island. "So, *nothing* happened between us? We really just slept?"

"I would never take advantage of a woman that was too drunk to consent. That would be rape."

His tone was serious, and his frankness caught her off guard. "Uh, I'm sorry. I wasn't trying to imply that you would… I just… for the record, not all men would see it that way."

"Well, I do. And all men should, for the record."

Her respect for him went up exponentially. "Well, what *did* happen last night?"

"Do you like French toast?" He pulled various items out of the cupboard as he spoke.

"Derek, seriously, tell me what happened!" Natalie snapped, her anxiety level rising.

"Okay, I will." He pulled out a chair for her at the breakfast table and set down a glass of water and some ibuprofen. "Here, take these at least. Are you sure I can't make you any food?"

She shook her head but gladly took the pills he offered.

"You had gotten drunk from spiked punch at the party."

She placed her throbbing head in her hands. "I had figured that much. But how did I get here?"

"Well, when I found you during the fireworks last night, you kind of freaked out and wanted to leave right away. So, I brought you here."

"What do you mean by 'freaked out'? What did I do?" Mortification was already building inside her.

"It's hard to explain exactly, but you seemed terrified and repeatedly begged me to get you out of there. It was like the fireworks triggered some type of PTSD episode." He paused for a moment and then asked, "Who's Jared?"

Her heart froze at the sound of his name. "What?"

"You kept saying that he was there and you needed to leave. Who is he?" Derek appeared to be studying her face, reading her tells, before he concluded, "Someone who hurt you. An ex-boyfriend?"

She looked down at the table and nodded. "I must have been such a wreck. I'm *so sorry* you had to see me like that."

"There's no need to apologize." Then, being the detective he was, he went into interrogation mode. "Natalie, what happened with Jared?"

"I can't. I can't." She put her face into her hands and rocked back and forth. "I still can't believe I got drunk and freaked out. Did anyone else see me like that last night? The chief?"

"No, only me. Everyone else seemed preoccupied with the fireworks. But Natalie, please tell me what happened." When she shook her head, he added, "Just start at the beginning."

After a couple more futile attempts to avoid telling him about Jared, she took a deep breath and then told him the entire story.

It was a long time ago, she emphasized. She was only twenty-two years old, and her self-esteem was at an all-time low due to a bad breakup with her college boyfriend. Besides cheating, her ex had constantly put her down throughout their four-year relationship. He had led her to believe that she wasn't good enough for him or anyone else.

Everything changed the night she met Jared. It had only been a couple of months since her breakup, so she hadn't felt like going out, but her friends insisted she join them at a new country-western dance club. Their eyes had locked across the room before he came over and introduced himself.

Jared was easily six foot two, extremely muscular, and carried himself with an air of confidence. He had dark-blond hair and piercing blue eyes that made her feel he could see into her soul. When he had approached and asked for her number, she couldn't believe that someone so gorgeous would be interested in her. She still remembered the way he looked at her that night, as if she were the only girl in the entire club.

She had been plainly dressed in jeans and a T-shirt, as compared to the plenitude of beautiful girls wearing next to nothing. And yet he chose her. It had made her feel like the luckiest girl in the world. So, she gave him her number, and they started dating right away.

Jared was a Marine living on base near her hometown of San Diego, she explained. He would drive over an hour round trip to see her whenever he could, and he would obsess over what she was doing every minute they were apart. She had attributed it to their intense connection and felt flattered that he would care so much. In hindsight, it had been a red flag. One she had been too blinded by passion to see.

Then, after less than two months of dating, he asked her to move in with him. It had felt too soon, but she wanted to make him happy. Plus, she had been staying at Jessica's parents' house while she was looking for work and didn't want to continue to impose. So, she moved onto the base.

He had apparently pulled some strings to make it possible. She distinctly remembered the conversation in which he told her that *normally* girlfriends were not allowed to live on base. But for her, he had gotten them to make an exception. She didn't know how and hadn't cared at the time. It had made her feel special. Looking back, she realized he had been bragging and making it intentionally difficult for her to say no.

Living together had been great, at first. They would cook meals together after he got off his shift, go for long walks along the beach, and make passionate love every day. She had also secured a part-time job at the credit union on base to earn herself a little money. Everything was seemingly perfect. But then things changed.

Jared came home late one night after he had been out drinking. She had waited up for him, and when she casually asked where he had been, he immediately got upset. He started tearing through their apartment, irrationally asking where she was hiding all the other men that she was sleeping with behind his back. Confused and scared by his behavior, she tried to explain that she didn't know what he was talking about, that she would never cheat on him. He called her a bitch and a liar, and then he hit her—hard. So hard that she didn't know how many times he hit her, because she had blacked out from the pain.

The next morning, her face was swollen and bloodied. Jared seemed horrified by what he had done. He was extremely apologetic, going on and on about how much he loved her and couldn't believe what had happened. He swore he would never have done such a thing if he had been sober. He even cried.

She had wanted so badly to believe him, to believe that he loved her. She couldn't stand the thought that it wasn't true. So, when he begged her not to leave, she agreed to stay.

Several weeks went by without incident, but things between them were beyond tense. He became increasingly controlling and obsessed with her whereabouts. She wasn't allowed to leave the apartment until her face healed, which he said was to spare her embarrassment. He had even called her boss at the credit union and said that she wouldn't be coming into work anymore, purporting that she couldn't handle the stress of the job.

Then one day, she couldn't find her cell phone. She asked Jared if he had seen it, and his flared temper let her know he had taken it. He asked her, "Why, who are you going to call? You're planning on leaving me, aren't you?" He then grabbed her by the neck and threatened to kill her if she ever thought about leaving. He nearly choked her to death right then and there before he eased off.

After that, her fear alone was enough to control her. She wasn't allowed to leave and had to do whatever he wanted out of fear for her life. He thrived off that control and took full advantage by demanding all sorts of sexual favors. If she tried to decline, he accused her of not loving him. And if she didn't love him, then he would have to kill her, because he couldn't bear the thought of her leaving him for someone else. She was trapped.

Natalie paused to wipe away her tears. Derek had been listening intently, and although her story was tearing him up on the inside, he managed to stay composed and calmly asked, "How did you get away? Were you able to go to the MP?"

MP was short for military police. She wiped away the last of her tears and then looked Derek sternly in the eyes. "He *was* the MP. I had no one to help me."

Derek couldn't believe what he was hearing. It appalled him that one of his own brethren, a fellow Marine *and* police officer, could do such unimaginable harm. Rage boiled inside him. He had to control his emotions, though, to keep her talking. He had to know everything. "Please, go on. What happened next?"

Natalie continued, "A few weeks later, I couldn't take it anymore. So, I snuck out in the middle of the night while he was sleeping. I had gone to bed that night in sweats and left shoes by the front door so I could slip out quickly. I knew I'd be dead if he caught me, but it felt worth the risk.

"Once I got outside, I ran as fast and as far as I could to the barracks at the other side of the base and pounded on a random door. A young Marine that I had never seen before answered. I told him I was in trouble and asked to please use his phone. He let me in and closed the door. Then I asked for the phone again, and he said I couldn't use it."

She trembled as she spoke. "He apparently knew Jared and said that he should call him to come pick me up instead. I begged him not to and explained that he would kill me if he did. Then he said I had a decision to make. He could either call Jared to come get me, or I could sleep with him and he would help me get off the base.

"He said that I had to decide, but it wasn't much of a choice at all. I was pretty sure he was going to do whatever he wanted even if I said no. So, I agreed to his deal. It was awful, but he held up his end after and drove me off the base. He dropped me off on the side of the highway, pretty much in the middle of nowhere, but I didn't care. I was free."

Tears burned down her cheeks once more. "Eventually, I got to a call box. Jessica picked me up, helped me with some cash, and took me to the airport. I bought a one-way ticket to New York and never looked back."

Natalie decided to leave out that she had lived in fear for years, always worrying Jared was going to find her somehow. It had all happened twelve years ago. She had moved on eventually and learned to trust again, thanks to Nick. She was fine now, or so she had thought.

What had triggered her fear at the party? She still couldn't believe that she would have freaked out in front of Derek. All those feelings had been suppressed for years, as good as gone. *Unless… had she actually seen Jared that night?* The mere possibility shook her to her core. But no, he couldn't have been there. It was likely just the patriotic holiday mixed with way too much spiked punch.

"What's his last name?" Derek's voice boomed, jerking her back into the present.

It took her a minute to comprehend what Derek was asking. "Jared's? No, no. I don't want to stir up any trouble, please! It was a long time ago." *Jared hadn't been able to find her in all these years. She certainly didn't want to give him any cause to find her now.*

Derek stared at her from across the table, his face the color of fresh blood, his nostrils flared. She couldn't tell if his intent eyes reflected pity or anger, or both, but she didn't like it either way. Her unsettled stomach stirred as she looked down at the table in shame.

"And before you ask, no, I didn't report any of it. I know I should have, but I was too scared and embarrassed. Trust me, it haunts me every day to think that he may have gone on to do the same thing to someone else. But it was twelve years ago, and it's way too late to press charges now, even if I wanted to. It was in the past, and I want it to stay there. *Please.*" Her last word came out as a wounded whisper.

Derek was overwhelmed by an emotion toward Natalie that he couldn't fully understand. He wanted so badly to take her in his arms, to make her feel safe. And he would, once he got the information he needed. Although there was nothing he could do to Jared *legally*, he could at least run a search for records, find out his current whereabouts, and make damn sure he could never hurt her again.

His gaze softened, but his voice held firm. "Natalie, I won't cause any trouble for you. Please, tell me his name."

After letting out a defeated sigh, she conceded. "Fletcher. Jared Fletcher."

"And the other guy?"

"I never knew his name." She looked down at the table again.

At that, Derek instinctively stood and walked around to her. He knelt near the table, gently tilted her face toward his, and looked her squarely in the eyes. "Thank you, Natalie, for sharing your story. I know that wasn't easy for you." He touched her face softly again when her eyes avoided his. "I also need you to know that you did nothing wrong, and you have no reason to be ashamed or embarrassed. You were in a horrible situation, through no fault of your own, and you were brave enough to get yourself out of it. That makes you strong. Do you understand?"

Natalie hesitantly nodded, and then a tidal wave of emotion came over her. She buried her face in Derek's shoulder, weeping uncontrollably as he wrapped his arms around her. Having always considered it a sign of weakness, she had never cried like that in front of another person before. As the tears poured out, she felt overdue solace.

For years she had blamed herself for everything—for being seduced by Jared in the first place, for moving in with him, for not seeing the truth sooner—even for choosing to knock on the wrong door after running away. She had replayed those events over and over again in her head, each time analyzing what she should have done differently. Not once had it occurred to her that she had done nothing wrong.

She also noted Derek's choice of words. She was grateful that he did not express any pity or say he was sorry for what had happened to her. He understood her somehow. He understood her need to feel strong, rather than weak and helpless.

Once the tears stopped, she pulled away from Derek and wiped her face. She glanced down at his T-shirt that she still wore over her bathing suit. "Can I use your restroom? I need to change."

"Of course." He went and grabbed her belongings for her and then showed her to the bathroom.

She changed, freshened up a bit, and then eyed herself in the mirror. Her face was red and blotchy from crying. She looked sickly and felt nauseous from drinking *only God knows how much* alcohol the day before. She had shared all the details of her most horrifying and humiliating experience with Derek—a practical stranger who had now seen her at her worse on several occasions. It didn't help that she was innately attracted to him, as much as she wished that wasn't the case. *She needed to get out of there.*

When she emerged from the bathroom, Derek was placing a freshly toasted bagel with cream cheese on the table for her. "I thought this might help settle your stomach."

"That's incredibly sweet of you, but I want to go home. Is it okay if I leave now?"

Her question took him by surprise. *Did she feel like he was keeping her there against her will? Had he been too forceful in his line of questioning?* He felt awful. "Of course. I'll walk you home."

"Thank you, but I'm fine on my own. I'm really sorry for… everything." And then she was out the door.

Derek sat down at his kitchen table, perplexed. While not sure how to help, he certainly didn't want to make things any worse for her. *But had he already by forcing her to tell him about her past?* He'd have to find a way to make that up to her, to level the playing field somehow. But for now, he decided, he'd go down to the station and search records for Jared Fletcher.

He took a bite of the bagel in front of him and stood to leave as his cell phone rang. It was work. "Detective Hartmann," he answered and then listened as the caller on the other end explained that there had been another murder. "I'll be right there."

CHAPTER TWELVE

 # 3

Natalie stepped out of Derek's building and took a deep breath. The brilliant blue sky was clear, in sharp contrast to her clouded head that still pounded. There was a high probability that she might get sick on the way home, and she'd be damned if she'd let Derek witness that again. An older model white van that sat parked outside the building started its engine and drove off as Natalie began swiftly walking toward her apartment.

As usual, she repeatedly replayed the recent events of the morning in her head while she walked. One of her darkest secrets was now exposed. It felt surreal and unnerving. She had never shared the full story before, not even with Jessica. And definitely not with Nick. She had never wanted him to look at her differently or to feel sorry for her.

With Jessica, she had minimized the horror, only telling her that Jared hit her once and that she needed to start fresh somewhere new. End of story. She preferred that version. It portrayed her as a stronger woman than she ever felt she was. Over time, her shame surrounding the secret had become her greatest weakness.

Feelings of guilt boiled at the surface as Natalie wondered if telling Sylvia would have stopped her from going back to Irvin. She had wanted to confide in her weeks ago but couldn't bring herself to do it. The thought of yet another preventable tragedy on her conscience was unbearable. She stopped in the middle of the busy sidewalk and fished for the phone in her purse.

Relieved that it hadn't been lost like her sunglasses and recollection of the previous night, she cradled her phone with great care as she scrolled to Sylvia's contact information and hit call. The phone rang three times before going to voicemail. Natalie left an imploring message for Sylvia to return the call, put the ringer volume on high, and then placed the phone back in her purse.

A passing skateboarder caused her to step aside—and back into consciousness of her surroundings. She willed herself to walk again, despite the dull ache in her gut. Her lips and mouth still tasted of salt as she fought back fresh tears. *Sylvia would not call her back.* Feeling that in her bones, Natalie made up her mind to go talk to her face-to-face instead. *But first, home.*

Only a couple more blocks to go, she reminded herself as the heat exacerbated her queasiness. She moved quickly, one foot in front of the other, and did her best to ignore the potent mixture of aromas that poured out of the local restaurants she passed. Coffee, bacon, and Chinese food—each normally an agreeable scent—but not all combined, and not today. She held her breath and increased her pace as she entered the final stretch.

Moments later, her apartment building was within view, and across from it was a parked white cargo van. She slowed as her brain struggled to make connections. *Was this the same van she had noticed while running weeks earlier? And the one that was in front of Derek's this morning? And if so, why was it now parked in front of her building?*

She pulled out her phone again and moved closer to take a picture. Once she got into position, however, the van drove off and the photo blurred. She squinted at the license plate of the moving van but couldn't make anything out, thanks to the distance and glare of the blinding sun.

The driver had been waiting in the van, *but waiting for what?* It seemed unreasonable and paranoid to assume it had been waiting for her. *But what if it had been?* She hurried inside her apartment, locked the deadbolt behind her, and then reopened the photo on her phone to see if anything was discernable. Unfortunately, it was merely a picture of white light with obscure objects, overexposed by the direct position of the sun.

Tux had come over to greet her at the door and was now loudly meowing for her attention. Stooping down to pet him, she immediately felt woozy.

***

At least she had made it home, Natalie told herself after spending the last hour hugging porcelain. She hadn't been that sick in a long time. The room spun as she laid face down on her bed. Tux jumped up and sniffed around, as if checking on her. It always amazed her how perceptive animals could be. He then nestled into the crook of her outstretched arm, offering a sense of reassurance as they both dozed off for a long nap.

Loud, melodic chimes jarred her awake. It was dark outside already, so she had apparently slept all day. Her pulse quickened as she reached for her phone, remembering that she had turned the volume up in case Sylvia called. But Derek's name flashed on the screen instead.

He had given her his number after the ride-along, saying she should call if she needed any help while Sylvia was staying with her, but she had never used it. How he had gotten *her* number was beyond her. Not wanting to deal with another interrogation, she silenced the call, sending it to voicemail.

A few seconds later, her phone buzzed with a text instead: *Natalie, this is Derek. You may be in danger. I'll be there in 10 minutes.*

Time stood still. Natalie agonized over all the possibilities but kept landing squarely on one. *Jared.* It had to be about Jared. She had told Derek about him earlier that morning, and now she was in danger.

Why had she given him his last name? Having known better, she mentally kicked herself for doing it. Derek must have looked him up, but then what? *Did he talk to him? Does Jared know where she is now?* It made no sense, but she was certain he was coming for her.

Fear she hadn't felt in years was suddenly back with a vengeance. Without thinking twice, she went to her closet, pulled out a suitcase, and began throwing essentials into it. A few changes of clothes, fresh underwear and socks, and the travel kit of toiletries she always kept under the sink— not to mention the large Zip-lock bag of important documents and cash already safely stowed in a hidden compartment of the suitcase. She had always been prepared for this moment, while hoping it would never come.

A loud knock on the door caused her to freeze. *He had gotten there before she could leave.* Acting on instinct alone, she opened her bedroom window and contemplated heading down the third-floor fire escape without the suitcase.

There was a second knock. "Natalie, it's Derek. Are you in there?"

With one leg already out her window, she froze again, this time remembering that Derek had said he was on his way over. *What was she doing? Jared couldn't be coming for her; it had been less than twenty-four hours since she revealed her secret. Derek's cryptic text most likely referred to something else. But what?* As if a spell had been lifted, she pulled herself back inside and rushed to answer the door.

"Can you hold your badge to the peephole, please?" When she peered through the door, she saw Derek holding up his badge as requested and, beyond him, another officer in uniform that she recognized as Rhonda. It occurred to her that this must be serious if he had felt the need for backup. She finally opened the door. "Sorry, just wanted to make sure it was you."

"That's fine. Is it okay if we come in?"

The apologetic look on his face told her it was bad news. She ushered them in and closed the door, locking the deadbolt once again.

"You should probably sit down," Derek said, pointing toward her couch.

Natalie didn't feel like sitting, but since arguing was even less appealing, she complied. Tux immediately jumped into her lap, comforting her more than he could have possibly known. She petted him calmly and waited for Derek to continue.

Derek stepped closer to the couch, resting one hand on the end. "Natalie, I'm sorry for what I'm about to tell you."

Rhonda stood about two feet from the entry with her back to the door and the entire apartment in her view. Her arms were stiff at her sides, where Natalie noticed her holstered gun. Natalie also watched her scan the apartment, as if looking for something or someone. She then saw Rhonda's gaze land in her bedroom.

"Going somewhere?" Rhonda asked, almost accusingly.

Derek turned to face Rhonda, looking momentarily confused until his eyes followed hers into Natalie's bedroom. The door was wide open, as was the window. The overhead light in the center of the room perfectly illuminated the packed suitcase open on her bed.

Natalie rushed to explain when Derek's eyes returned to her. "Um, you said I was in danger, so I started packing, just in case."

"It's okay," Derek said. "I shouldn't have scared you like that. It's about Sylvia Porter."

"What about her? Did Irvin hurt her again? Is she okay?" Her breath grew ragged as it struggled to keep up with her racing heart. *Sylvia had to be okay.*

Derek's hazel eyes turned somber. "We found her body this morning." He paused, allowing the gravity of that statement to be absorbed. "We have Irvin in custody for questioning, but I don't think it was him."

More taken aback by his second statement than the first, Natalie leapt off the couch. "What do you mean? It had to be him!" She began pacing her living room. "Oh my god. Oh my god. This is all my fault."

"It's not your fault, Natalie. Please sit back down."

She stopped pacing but couldn't sit. Her eyes silently pleaded for an explanation as she stood facing Derek.

"Sylvia was murdered," he said, his eyes never leaving hers, "most likely by the same person who killed the other two women. There was a note left with the number three."

"The serial killer?" Natalie looked at the ground, searching for answers. Puzzle pieces involuntarily pushed their way to the forefront of her memory as if trying to get her attention. *The van. The night she thought someone was in her apartment. But what did it all mean?*

Her thoughts were interrupted by Rhonda. "We're going to need you to think back to when Sylvia was staying with you. Did she meet anyone new? Was anyone watching her?"

The words sent chills down Natalie's spine. She glanced at Derek, who had taken a seat on the couch, and then turned back to Rhonda. "No, I don't think so. But I think someone has been watching me."

CHAPTER THIRTEEN

Live Bait

Several days later

"Learn how to merge, asshole." Leah hit her brakes to avoid hitting a pickup truck that abruptly cut in front of her car. Emergency vehicle lights blazed in the barely discernable distance, indicating an accident ahead. Her car crawled to a near stop. *Well, that figures.* She was already dreading facing her family. The traffic delay would allow her to agonize over the inevitable that much longer.

Sitting in the parking lot known as I-5 North, Leah questioned her decision to visit home. Her sister's call had come as a surprise, given it had been over a year since anyone in her family had spoken to her. When she had packed her bags for Portland to join the Academy, her mother had tearfully proclaimed that she only had one daughter left, referring to Latisha. Even though she tried to chalk it up to her mother's grief, the comment had cut Leah deeply. She was still grieving for her brother as well.

She wouldn't let anything deter her career goals, though. She couldn't. Not after how hard she had worked and everything she had given up. Coming out to her childhood friends and family had been difficult. It had left a wake of strained relationships and silent treatment. But pursuing her dream of becoming a police officer, *that* was unforgiveable to her family.

Now, her father was in the hospital. A heart attack, Latisha had said. Leah had always considered him in relatively good health. *A young sixty.* He had been athletic his entire life, a trait she gratefully inherited. She missed her father, but being there for him in his time of need would also mean facing her mother again.

The lane closure, now visible ahead, was a good sign that the worst of the traffic was over. Once everyone merged, the speed would pick up again. She could also now see the wreckage. There had apparently been three vehicles involved, each crunched beyond repair, and her stream of consciousness flowed to Natalie.

It had been over a month since the awkward confrontation with Rhonda that resulted in Natalie running out of the bar. She had understood Natalie's reaction, to an extent, but it didn't make it hurt any less. She had been rejected—and much worse, *humiliated*—in front of Rhonda. Although Natalie had called and texted countless times, Leah was in no mood to talk about it.

But that was her biggest problem, wasn't it? Her inability to talk about her feelings. It ended her relationship with Rhonda, was preventing a friendship with Natalie, and had long isolated her from her family. She let out a deep sigh as she accelerated past the carnage and mangled metal. Toward what she sped, she could only imagine would be worse.

Right on cue, the hands-free display in her car alerted her to a call from Natalie. Leah debated ignoring it, as she had been for weeks, but to her own surprise, she hit answer instead. "Hello."

Natalie's shocked voice projected clearly through the car speakers. "Oh my goodness, Leah! I'm so glad I finally got ahold of you! How are you doing?"

"I'm fine. Driving to see my family up in Seattle right now," Leah said, as if heading to a joyous event.

"That's good to hear that you're out of the city, actually."

Odd response, Leah thought, but she continued listening.

"There's so much I want to say to clear the air between us. But first, the reason I called. I think you could be in danger, Leah."

Natalie's words lingered in the air for a moment before Leah processed them. "*In danger?* What do you mean?"

"Have you heard about the serial murders in Portland?"

"Yes," she said hesitantly, unsettled by the question. "They're calling them the *City Sidewalk Killings*, because any woman you pass on the sidewalk could be next. It's horrible, but I don't understand why I would be in more danger than anyone else."

"I think whoever it is has been watching me. I don't know for how long. And more than that, they've been in my apartment. A knife was stolen…" Natalie paused, audibly steadying her shaky breath. "A woman I knew was murdered with it."

"*What?*" Leah said in disbelief.

"I know it's crazy, but it's true. There was also a white van I noticed following me a couple times, once when I had been running with Sylvia. And now she's gone." Quiet sobs broke up Natalie's voice.

"And so, you think she was murdered because she was seen with you?"

"I don't understand the 'why' yet, and may never, but yes, possibly. And you're the only other friend I have in the city—or had, at least. So, I'm worried about you."

"Natalie, I appreciate the concern, but none of this makes any sense. I mean, if a killer has been following you, then wouldn't *you* be the one in danger?"

Natalie was silent, and Leah, who had mostly been thinking aloud at that point, finally realized the graveness of the situation. *Natalie was obviously in danger. And terrified. What she needed most now was a friend, not someone holding a grudge.*

"I'm sorry. You must be pretty scared. Is there anything at all I can do to help?" Leah offered.

"It helps me to know that you are safe, so thanks for answering the phone and *please* be careful. I've had police detail outside my apartment building for the last couple of days, watching for anything suspicious. Mostly I'm grateful, but part of me feels like a fish in a shark tank. You know, live bait." The quiet sound of nervous laughter followed her statement.

"You'll be safe with the force watching over you. Who's on your detail?"

"They take shifts. Derek, Rhonda, Detective Gibson."

The familiarity with which Natalie said their names was a punch in the gut. "So, you're friends with Derek and Rhonda now?"

"Not friends, really. I've just been working with them a lot lately, you know, due to the case."

Tension built over the airwaves a moment longer before there was a loud knocking sound in the background.

"Sorry, someone's at the door. I've got to let you go, but let's talk again soon," Natalie said.

The phone disconnected before Leah had a chance to say goodbye. She turned up the music on the radio and stared at the blur of car lights ahead on the road, dots of white and red now moving quickly in opposite directions. Darkness had encroached, even though she hadn't yet entered Washington State. *This was going to be a long drive.*

***

Derek didn't like it one bit. True, it was the first lead they'd had so far, but staking out Natalie's apartment while she was inside felt like dangling bait. She should be somewhere else, somewhere safe. The least he could do was make sure she was okay.

"Hungry?" He held up the bag in his hand once Natalie opened the door. "I brought you some Chinese food. How are you doing?"

"I'm okay, I guess. Do you want to come in?"

"Thanks." Derek stepped inside and scanned the entire apartment out of habit before placing the food down on her kitchen table. The cut flowers in the center of the table had started to wilt, a subtle reminder that she hadn't left her apartment in days.

"You don't have to stay holed up in here, you know. We can get you a police escort if you want to get out, get some fresh air." At her indignant look, he changed the subject back to food. "I'm not sure what you like, so I picked up a few options. Sweet and sour chicken, spicy eggplant, shrimp chow mein… Any of that sound good? It's best to keep your strength up," he added, sensing her reluctance.

"Sweet and sour chicken sounds nice. Thanks."

He handed her the corresponding takeout container and then followed her over toward the inviting couch where she sat. He found it comforting that she chose to eat there, in a casual cross-legged position, rather than at the dining table. Although a bit unconventional, it was how he preferred to eat at home as well.

Natalie had already started digging in and was focused on grabbing a large chunk of glazed chicken with her chopsticks. Derek smiled as he watched her. If nothing else, at least he could assuage her hunger. But he wanted to do more.

"Mind if I take a seat?"

She shook her head without looking up, and he sank into the plush cushion next to her. A black-and-white cat hopped over from the adjacent chair to greet him.

"Hey there, buddy," he said, petting the purring feline that nestled into his lap.

"Sorry," Natalie mumbled between bites.

"No need. I like cats, remember?"

She nodded while chewing, and he felt his eyes drawn to her mouth like a tractor beam. Those plump, pink lips of hers were a dish far more delectable than the shrimp chow mein he chose for himself. Once she had swallowed her food, she said, "Cal, right?"

"Good memory," he said, trying to ignore his heart beating double time.

Damn, she was beautiful. Sweatpants and all. He let his eyes momentarily drop from her mouth while opening his chopsticks and then slid them slowly back up her body until they met her blue-gray eyes. When she peered back at him expectantly, he broke his stare and switched to business.

"We've pulled a list of all the white vans registered in Multnomah and surrounding counties, but it's slow-going, as you can imagine. Lots of records to go through," Derek explained while picking at his food. "I've enlisted Marty to help us narrow it down to likely suspects. He's great at profiling."

"Marty?"

"Marty Thompson. He's a retired detective and my mentor. Really knows his stuff. You met him at the barbecue on the Fourth, but… I take it you don't remember that?"

"Unfortunately not. About that night," she said, "I have some questions I wanted to ask you. Some things that don't make sense to me."

"Shoot," Derek said before carefully lowering a twirl of dangling noodles into his mouth.

"Well, for starters, you explained why I ended up back at your place that night, but I still don't understand why I woke up in your bed… *with you.* I mean, couldn't I have slept on your couch or vice versa?"

Grateful that his mouth was too full to reply immediately, he held up a hand and slowly chewed while he considered how to respond. The truth was, she had begged him to stay with her that night to make her feel safe. He had attempted to sleep on the couch, but she had clung to him like a child afraid to be left alone in the dark. He suspected she wouldn't like hearing that, though.

"Well, you were pretty rattled that night, so I thought it was best not to leave you alone." When she looked at him skeptically, he added, "There was nothing else to it, I assure you."

"Okay. Next question. Why was I wearing your T-shirt over my bathing suit and not my own clothes?"

Another sensitive topic. He was sure it would mortify her to learn that he had found her wearing only her bikini while still at the party, after she most likely stripped herself down. It had taken him another ten minutes to locate her clothes, which were soaking wet and strewn across the lawn.

"Your clothes had gotten wet in the rain. I put them in the dryer and gave you my shirt to wear in the meantime."

"Oh… I didn't realize it had rained. Well, thanks for that, then." She shook her head. "I don't mean to imply anything by my questions. It's just frustrating not being able to remember *anything.* I mean, I've certainly been drunk before, but never to the point of complete memory blackout. It's… unsettling."

"I understand, and I'm happy to answer any questions that I can."

"Aren't you supposed to be down on stakeout duty right now?"

"Rhonda's got it covered tonight. I thought you might want a little company in here… and Chinese food." He held up his takeout container. "August Moon is my favorite."

"Good to know," she said, and then her eyes glazed over as if lost in thought. While lifting another piece of chicken toward her mouth, she froze mid-bite.

"Is everything okay?"

"Nothing is," she replied after a brief silence. "Sylvia is dead. Whoever killed her is presumably watching me and broke into my apartment. They stole one of my knives but used it on Sylvia rather than me…" Her voice trailed off as if leading her somewhere she couldn't follow.

"We'll get whoever it is," Derek stated with more confidence than he felt.

Her eyes widened. "Does anyone at the bureau think I could have done it? Am I a suspect?"

"What? No, of course not. Besides, you have a solid alibi, since you were passed out in my bed when it happened."

"But others at the bureau don't know about that alibi, right?" Natalie lifted her eyebrow at him.

"No, they don't. But you're not a suspect, so it doesn't matter."

"It matters to me. I bet Rhonda suspects me. She was quick to question me when she thought I was skipping town."

Derek opened his mouth to defend Rhonda but was cut short by Natalie. "And she's smart to suspect me. I mean, my prints were on the knife, and she doesn't know I have an alibi. It would be narrow-minded not to consider me just because I'm a woman."

There was that feminist, independent spirit of hers that was both admirable and irritating. He considered himself fairly forward-thinking, but she continually raised the bar on what it meant to treat men and women equally. She challenged him, and he was still deciding if he liked it or not. "So, you're saying I'm narrow-minded and sexist not to have considered that the killer could be a woman?"

"I didn't say that. You already knew that it wasn't me, but you raise a good point… I don't think we can completely rule out the possibility of a female killer."

Derek was almost certain he hadn't raised the point, but her cleverness had him embracing the idea. "We can certainly widen the search. Man or woman, we're going to find this killer and keep you safe. I promise."

They both knew it was a promise outside of his control, but he fully intended to keep it. Her safety was his top priority.

"And while we're on the subject, I have an idea that I'd like to run past you. My only ask is that you consider it fully before shooting it down or assuming it to be sexist."

Natalie slowly nodded as he spoke, her worried eyes fixed on his.

"Since this search will probably take longer than any of us would like, and longer than the department will be able to staff twenty-four-hour surveillance, I'm wondering if you will consider moving in with me. Temporarily."

As if woken from a trance, Natalie's nodding head jerked to a halt. She blinked at him several times but remained quiet.

He continued, "My condo has a spare bedroom and state-of-the-art security system, and I'll be there at night. Your apartment isn't safe, Natalie. Not only due to ease of access, but he… or she… has been here before, meaning they know where to find you. I know it's a big decision but…"

"Okay," she said, interrupting his sales pitch.

"What?"

"I said okay. I'll move into your condo, temporarily, while you work on catching this killer. You make a valid point that it will be safer. You're sure it won't be an imposition, though?"

"Not at all," Derek replied, astounded that she had agreed so quickly.

"And also, a strictly professional living arrangement. I'll pay you rent, like a roommate."

"That's not necessary."

"It's one of my conditions."

"Okay. Any other conditions?"

"Like I said, a strictly *professional* arrangement. No funny business."

He chuckled at that and got a stern glare in return. "Okay, okay. Deal."

CHAPTER FOURTEEN

On the Case

Mid-July

Derek's palms were sweating, a phenomenon he didn't even know was possible. Chief Serrano had asked to see him first thing Monday morning. It had to be about Natalie moving into his place over the weekend. Derek had intended to clear it with the chief first, but he needed to act quickly to ensure her safety, or at least that was going to be his story. *How did the chief find out already?*

Mandy sat at the front reception desk, twirling a strand of her bleach-blond hair around her finger. Jolted into action when her phone buzzed, she answered it, nodded as if the caller on the other end could see her, and then motioned him into the chief's office.

"Good morning, Detective Hartmann. Please have a seat," Chief Serrano instructed.

"You wanted to see me, sir?"

"Yes. The *City Sidewalk Killer* case… I hate that they're calling it that, but they are. Any progress there?"

"Not as much as I would like, sir. As you are aware, Natalie gave us a firsthand account of the white van that we believe our suspect drives. But without a plate number, it's taking us a lot of time to sift through all the records. We also dusted her apartment for prints but came up empty-handed."

"About Natalie," the chief began.

Here it comes, he thought. "I was planning to tell you, Chief."

Chief Serrano nodded, allowing Derek to continue.

"Her apartment wasn't safe, sir, and prolonged surveillance would neither be practical nor fair to her. She values her independence, which I respect, but even she realized that moving into my place was her safest bet. It's only temporary… until we catch this bastard. And I understand you may be upset, but respectfully, it was the best option to keep her protected."

"Hmm." The chief leaned back in his office chair and clasped his fingers in front of his chest. "It would seem that problem is solved, then."

"I'm sorry. What do you mean?"

"I was going to ask you to get Natalie to move somewhere safer—although not necessarily to *your place*—and to keep a close eye on her. But I wasn't sure if you'd be able to get her to agree to that. As you said, she values her independence."

"You didn't already know." The tension in Derek's shoulders relaxed as he exhaled.

"No, I didn't, but I appreciate you keeping me updated, Detective. Still, I'm surprised she agreed to that arrangement."

Derek felt equally surprised that the chief was supportive of his plan. "Well, it's a strictly professional arrangement, sir, and she's a smart woman. It wasn't difficult for her to realize that she was in danger there."

"Very smart, indeed." Chief Serrano leaned forward, placing his large hands on the wooden desk that separated them. "That leads me to my next point. I'd like Natalie included on the task force. Maybe a fresh set of eyes will help uncover some connections we've missed."

After Derek hesitated for a beat too long, the chief asked, "Do you have a problem with that, Detective?"

"No, sir. But she's a civilian, and… well… she's extremely close to the case, having known the third victim. I'm worried it might be too personal for her."

"We have civilians consult all the time, and she'll be a strong addition to the team. I've read your reports on the first three victims. Do you really believe we're dealing with the Hood River Killer from almost twenty-five years ago?"

"I'm not sure, sir."

A moment of silence passed before the chief spoke again. "Is it too personal for you?"

"No, sir."

"Okay, then. Keep me updated on any new leads, and I'd like a written status report by the end of the week."

Derek perceived that as his cue to leave and stood from his chair. "Yes, sir. Will do."

Later that day, Derek sat across from Marty in the old break room that had been converted to a conference room. A new break room with a full kitchen had recently been built down the hall of the otherwise outdated police building.

"How's the narrowed-down list of vans coming along?"

"I have a partial list for you to get to work on, but there are still tons of records for me to review."

Derek nodded his understanding. "I appreciate your help. The chief wants a full report from me by the end of this week. I'm worried I won't have much more information to provide."

"These things take time. Chief Serrano understands that."

"There's more." Derek rose out of anxiousness and walked over to reheat his cold coffee. A perk of the converted conference room was that it still contained a coffee pot and microwave. "He wants Natalie added to the task force. Thinks she might bring a fresh perspective."

There was a long pause before Marty asked, "Are you taking it as a sign of lack of confidence?"

He hadn't. *Until now.* "Do you think that's what it is? The chief doesn't think I can handle this case?"

"No, I'm sure that's not it," Marty said unconvincingly.

"Well, she's planning to join the Academy in the fall. And she is his niece's best friend."

"Is that so?" Marty said, sounding surprised by the connection. "That makes sense, then. Probably just a favor to help her out."

"I'm not so sure I'd call being on this case a favor." Derek ran his fingers through his hair. "There's something else that's bothering me."

"What's that, kid?"

"Sylvia Porter. She doesn't fit the description of any of the Hood River victims. I was certain our killer was repeating the murders in a different order, but now I don't know."

"I'm with you," Marty said with a sigh. "Maybe we were looking for connections to the past that simply don't exist."

Derek paced the floor. "Maybe, but the first two women, and the numbering of victims. That can't all be a coincidence, could it? I mean, am I grasping at straws here?"

"Did I ever tell you about the case that Serrano and I worked on together years ago?"

"No, I don't think so."

"It was before he made chief and moved to Oregon. We were both detectives with the LAPD at the time, and we got assigned a homicide case that affected him. There had been reports of domestic violence before the murder, and he said he was worried about another family under similar circumstances. Someone his niece knew."

Derek pulled his coffee from the microwave and sipped it slowly. "Are you thinking it could have been Natalie's family?"

Marty shrugged his shoulders. "I'm just saying he knows what it feels like when a case hits too close to home. He was convinced that the victim had been killed by her husband, even though there wasn't any evidence pointing in that direction."

"Well, besides the history of violence," Derek corrected. "Was it him?"

"That's the thing. It ended up being a completely random murder by a junkie that had broken in to steal some money. He had gotten spooked when she arrived home in the middle of the day, and he killed her." Marty held up his coffee mug to accept a refill from the fresh pot Derek poured. "Thanks. So basically, we had wasted weeks trying to find evidence to confirm it was the husband, and we only got a break in the case when the junkie got busted breaking into another apartment in the same building. When they arrested him for burglary, the weapon that killed our victim was found on him."

Derek considered it for a moment. "Is that what you think I'm doing? Wasting time pursuing this angle?"

Marty shrugged again. "The lesson from that story is that we can't let our history bias us."

Back at his desk, Derek logged into the records system and began researching the short list of profiles Marty had given him. They were all registered owners of white vans, and all had had some type of run-in with the law before. It was like trying to find a needle in a haystack; if only he could find the right stack of hay to search.

A couple of hours later, he walked over and placed a stack of manila folders on Rhonda's desk. "Ready to go interview some potential murder suspects?"

Rhonda looked down at the folders and then back at Derek. "You bet!"

"Great. I'll drive so you can review those in the car," he said as they both exited the station.

***

When Derek returned home much later that evening, Natalie sat cross-legged in his favorite spot on the couch, entrenched in her work. The television played a movie that she hardly seemed to notice. Beside her, an almost indistinguishable heap of black, white, brown, and orange steadily inhaled and exhaled. Much to his surprise, Cal and Tux had gotten along instantly, with Cal assuming a big brother role to the younger cat. *No territorial behavior or warm-up period needed.*

Natalie was wearing a blue tank top that hugged her curves and gray sweatpants that served as a resting spot for her computer. A mass of golden hair sat loosely atop her head with a pencil through it, and the glasses on her face perfectly framed her large eyes. They made her look smart—*and sexy as hell*—but he pushed that feeling aside. Her intelligence still gnawed at him, opening insecurity like an old wound.

"Nice glasses." The comment came out more like a sneer than a compliment.

"Oh, hi, I didn't hear you come in," she said, looking up from her laptop. Her cheeks reddened as she removed her blue-framed glasses. "I only wear these when I work on the computer all day. Otherwise, I get bad headaches."

He nodded as if he understood perfectly, when in reality, she was an enigma to him. *How could someone so beautiful and boldly independent also be so timid and insecure at times?* He assumed her painful history probably played a role in that, but it didn't define her. She was not the type of woman that would ever let that be the case.

Feelings of admiration quickly replaced resentment, and he berated himself for ever being upset with her. It wasn't her fault that the chief wanted her on the case. Nor was it her fault that he had taken it personally. Still, it was all way too personal.

"How was your day?" He felt trite asking but truly wanted to know.

"It was good. After several hours of procrastination, I finally got a time-sensitive 'Quality of Earnings' summary report done for my client's diligence project back in New York. It was a huge relief. How about your day?" Natalie moved the computer from her lap to the coffee table, which caused both cats to stir. Tux jumped off the couch and headed toward the kitchen.

As if routine for years, Derek walked into the kitchen, knelt to pet Tux, and then opened the fridge to add some food to his bowl. "I wish I could say it was as productive. Rhonda and I interviewed a bunch of van owners today that fit the profiles Marty identified, but they all had pretty solid alibis for the dates of the murders."

The sound of the can opening had Cal running into the kitchen as well. Derek patted Cal's head and then stopped to muse at how easily the two cats had adapted to their new living arrangement. It had only been a few days, but he supposed he had acclimated to it as well. Having Natalie there when he got home felt normal somehow, nice even.

"How did Marty identify the profiles?"

Her question caught him off guard. "What do you mean?"

"You said the people you interviewed fit the profiles that Marty identified, so I'm curious how he went about narrowing the selection." Natalie pulled the pencil out, letting her hair down, and then twirled a strand around her finger. "What were the profiles based on?"

"They were based on years of experience and knowledge of traits and behavioral patterns that fit a serial killer." His response came off more defensive than he had intended. *But what gave her the right to question Marty's expertise?*

Her finger, now three twirls deep into her hair, tensed, and her whole body emitted an anxious energy. "I'm just trying to learn. What traits and behavioral patterns fit a serial killer, for instance?"

This caused Derek to take pause. He remembered learning about profiling in his criminal justice courses, but it occurred to him he'd never been through the process himself before. He had relied on Marty for years.

"Well, all the individuals questioned today were white males, between forty and fifty years old, with some minor offenses on their records." Noticing Natalie's face contort, he added, "It doesn't mean we're ruling out other demographics. We just start with the most probable group.

We think our perp is older than usual due to a likely connection to a string of murders years ago."

Natalie nodded, but Derek could tell she didn't agree.

"Go ahead. Tell me what you're thinking."

"Nothing. I mean, I'm probably naïve to how things actually work, given that my knowledge of criminal profiling is limited to what I've learned in movies and novels, but…"

"But what?"

"I always thought profiling was done by psychologists is all. But I'm sure Marty knows what he's doing."

Annoyance overtook admiration. Derek thought carefully before replying, knowing the conversation could easily escalate if he let it. "You're correct. That is often the case. All detectives are trained in forensic psychology though, both through coursework and the aforementioned on-the-job experience."

"I see. Thanks for explaining."

Derek searched for tones of sarcasm that weren't present and then let it go. "Anyway, I spoke with the chief today."

"Oh, how is Victor doing? Maggie said the stress has been taking a toll on his health lately. He hates dealing with the press, and this killer has certainly gotten their attention."

"He seemed fine." His annoyance level rose. Family friend or not, it was apparent that she did not have the same deference for authority as was so firmly ingrained in him. Another reason it was a mistake to include a civilian, but he was outranked. "He asked for you to be on the case, actually."

"Me?"

"Surprised me as well." From a messenger bag flung over the back of a chair, Derek took out several folders that he hadn't planned to share with Natalie and dropped them onto the mahogany coffee table in front of her. "These are the case files. Three victims so far. I should warn you that the photos are pretty gruesome, so I'd understand if you want to decline."

Natalie stared at the closed folders and slowly shook her head.

"No problem. It's probably best if you're not involved anyway. I'll let the chief know." Derek went to pick up the folders.

"No. Leave them. I'd be honored to help in any way that I can."

Derek froze. His scare tactic hadn't worked, and he hadn't thought it through well enough to have a backup plan. "Are you sure? This isn't something you have to do."

"Yes, it is. I owe it to Sylvia."

CHAPTER FIFTEEN

Damsel in Distress

The horror those poor women had experienced. Natalie could still see their terrified faces whenever she closed her eyes. She had stayed up all night reviewing the case files and needed to clear her head. Her breath was steady as she ran along the waterfront. The air was so fresh she could taste it with each inhale. Pine mixed with a tinge of salt from licking her lips.

Suddenly, she was being forced into a van. She hadn't seen it coming, hadn't heard the vehicle approach. Everything was dark, as if her head was wrapped in a bag. Her sense of reality was shrouded, muddled. There were voices that wouldn't register, words that couldn't be discerned. She wondered if she had been drugged. *But when?*

She laid perfectly still to hone her other senses and detected warmth next to her. She tried to feel around, but her hands were bound. *When had that happened?* She inched her body backward until her hands hit something solid. Tracing her fingers along the object, she felt skin and hair but none of the warmth from before. It was ice cold and stiff.

A dead body. She shuddered at the thought and squirmed forward again to escape it. Only now she realized the floor beneath her shifted as she moved and had a similar icy texture. This was not the floor of the van. *Where was she?*

She struggled to get the bag—or whatever was impairing her vision—off her head by sliding her face against the pliable floor. Once she was finally free of the appendage, the darkness of wherever she was still lurked. She blinked several times, willing her eyes to adjust faster to the dim lighting. Objects slowly came into view. And then faces. Sylvia's lifeless face gazed up at her from the pile of bodies that Natalie now found herself bound atop. She let out a bloodcurdling scream.

Within minutes, Derek burst into the room, his gun at the ready. He turned on the light and slowly lowered his weapon.

Disoriented, Natalie remained lying on her side, trying to piece together her whereabouts. "The bodies," she muttered as her eyes adjusted to the light and searched for evidence of what she had experienced. "I was in a van, and then somewhere else. Sylvia was there. Where did they take me?"

"It's okay. It was just a bad dream."

Her fists clenched onto something behind her—a bedsheet, she realized—rather than being bound. Natalie slowly released her grip on the sheet but remained on her side, shaking her head quietly, not yet believing she was safe. It had all felt so real.

Derek sat on the edge of the bed and tucked his gun away into the waistband of his unzipped jeans. "I never should've dumped all the case files on you like that. I was upset and reacted poorly. I'm sorry."

Natalie sat up, abruptly cognizant and engaged. "Why were you upset?"

"Because the chief asked for you to be on the case, I guess."

"And you don't want me on the case?"

"Well, I don't think it's a good idea, for your sake." He turned his face away once her eyes caught his. "And it's not because you're a woman, in case that's what you are thinking. No one should have to be exposed to this."

With his head turned, she shamelessly took in the view, scrolling her eyes from his sexy tousled hair to his bare tan chest, then down to the black underwear on display beneath his jeans. "But you're exposed… to the case, I mean."

"Trust me, I wish I wasn't." After a moment, he stood from the bed with his back to her and zipped his pants before turning to explain with a flushed face. "I threw these on and hurried in here as soon as I heard you scream."

"Yeah, I'm sorry I startled you for nothing." She couldn't help but gawk at his muscular chest as awkward tension filled the space between them. His left pec twitched under her watch. Not trusting her own judgment, she forced her eyes to the clock on the nightstand. It was almost four in the morning. "I should probably let you get back to sleep."

"Are you sure you're okay? I can stay up with you a while longer. I don't mind."

She wasn't sure that she was okay, or ever would be, but she needed his firm body out of her presence. It stirred things in her that were best kept beneath the surface. "I'll be fine. Thanks, though."

"Okay, but I'm just across the living room if you need anything at all."

Derek exited the room, and Natalie felt her body sigh. She hated the effect he had on her. *Damn hormones.*

Alone once again, she looked around the foreign bedroom. Details that had eluded her during move-in were now piquing her curiosity. A large painting of a Tuscan landscape hung above the rustic dresser. The rolling hills covered in grapevines were various shades of green that perfectly matched those in the curtains and bedspread, which she now realized had been kicked off onto the floor.

She crawled to the foot of the queen-size mahogany sleigh bed and leaned over to retrieve the quilted bedspread. It looked old, with certain patches more faded than others. The corner of the quilt, just out of her reach, was embroidered with the initials *DFH*. As she contemplated what the F in Derek's name might represent, she leaned a little farther to grasp the edge of the bedspread, gently tugged it toward her, and—in one swift movement—ended up on the floor.

She quickly covered her mouth to silence the curse that escaped and hoped the bedspread had muted the thud. Within seconds, Derek reappeared, weapon drawn, still shirtless. Stunned from the fall, Natalie felt glued to the floor on exhibit as she lay there in her boxer-like sleep shorts and coordinating magenta tank, wishing she had stuck with her sweatpants from earlier.

Derek lowered his gun, again, and cleared his throat. "Are you okay?"

There was that question again. She couldn't tell what was more badly bruised, her tailbone or ego. She wiggled her toes, decided she could move, and used her arms to press up to a seated position. "Embarrassed is all. The blanket had fallen off the bed." She pointed to it, considering that explanation enough.

He let out a small laugh. "That's not all that fell. Here, let me help you up."

She grabbed onto the strong hand he held out and was on her feet in seconds. "Thanks. Sorry to wake you… *again.*"

"I hadn't gone back to bed. I was sitting out on the couch, wide awake."

"Well, I'm sorry for that, too."

"No need. I'm usually up not much after now anyway. I like to get an early start on the day."

Natalie remembered waking up to the smell of coffee at five o'clock the previous morning and groaned. "Ugh, a morning person."

He laughed even harder at that. "I take it you're not."

"I believe humans were meant to be nocturnal, but modern society has ruined that for us." She sat down on the edge of the bed, a touch off-balance after the fall.

Derek seemed to consider her statement, then he tilted his head. "So, how come we don't have better night vision, then?"

"Our eyes adjust to darkness eventually. The lights and screens we stare at all day are what make it difficult for us."

"But wouldn't cavemen have gotten eaten by predators if they were out at night?"

"Even more reason to be awake. You'd be easier to pick off while asleep and cornered in a cave."

A wide smile spread across his face.

"What?"

"You've got an answer for everything."

"And that's a bad thing?"

"No, it's not bad at all." His eyes, which had been reasonably glued to hers, now slid slowly along her body, causing it to tingle.

She leaned back on the bed and rested on her elbows. A subconscious move that she now realized allowed him to take in a better view. Her conscious mind lingered on thoughts of cavemen as she gazed at his bare chest and imagined being thrown over it and carried back to his bed. She clenched her legs together in a vain attempt to hold back a rush of moisture. Her pulse quickened, sending a flash of heat to her face.

She sprang back upright, praying he hadn't noticed the carnal effect he was having on her. She wanted so badly to say something, to break the rising sexual tension, but feared her voice would fail her.

Luckily, Derek spoke first. His eyes were no longer on her when he moved a step closer. He bent over and lifted the faded quilt off the floor. "My mom made this for me when I was about ten. I had hated it at the time. Thought it was too girly." His voice, barely louder than a whisper, had a sadness in it as deep as life and death.

Natalie instinctively scooted over, inviting him next to her. He sat on the edge of the bed with the quilt on his lap. She traced her fingers over a patch that had grapevines and floral accents, similar to those in the painting on the wall. She assumed that was no coincidence.

"It was my mother's dream to visit Tuscany," he offered, as if reading her mind. "She would always say, 'Someday, mijo, someday.' But she never went."

Natalie slid her hand toward the corner where she had seen the initials. "What does the *F* stand for?"

"My middle name is my mother's surname."

"Which is?" Natalie regretted prying when Derek's shoulders tensed.

He looked at her and then back down at the quilt for a beat. "Fuertes."

"Strong like her, I bet."

Derek looked stunned. "You know Spanish?"

"A little. I grew up in San Diego and took a bunch of courses in school. I'm not as fluent as I would like, though. You know what they say, if you don't use it, you lose it." She laughed quietly, attempting to lighten the mood.

A small smile returned to Derek's otherwise solemn face. "I'm sure that's not true for everything."

Natalie wasn't sure what he meant by that, but her mind immediately went to the fact that she hadn't been with a man in almost a year. A fact she imagined was on display like a scarlet letter on her chest. She felt the heat rise in her cheeks once again. His strong hand rested mere inches from her bare thigh. She eyed it longingly, pretending to admire the quilt.

"I like the horses in this patch here."

"Stallions. Born to run free," Derek said with a wink.

She felt as if she might explode. Or worse, jump him right then and there. "Um, I should probably…" She stood to exit the room, to make a swift escape, but her foot hooked onto the portion of the quilt still on the ground. She spun around to avoid tumbling onto the floor and landed squarely on Derek's lap instead.

"Whoa, are you okay?" He grabbed her to break her fall, the warmth of his hands on her waist.

Similarly, she reached out to brace herself for impact. His firm, bare chest was rock solid yet smooth to the touch under her palms. Her legs straddled his left thigh, while her head rested on his right shoulder. Suddenly dizzy, she wasn't sure if it was from him or the fall. "I just need a minute."

"Wait, did you hit your head before? You could have a concussion." Concern laced his voice as he leaned her forward and looked into her eyes. Releasing one hand from her waist, he cradled her chin and then moved his head side-to-side. "Follow my eyes with yours."

"This is crazy. I'm fine," she said but involuntarily complied anyway.

As if on a warm beach staring out at tranquil waves washing ashore, she lost herself momentarily in the sea-like depths of his hazel eyes. Their swaying motion, their flecks of green dancing in the light; it was mesmerizing. She was grateful when it stopped.

He moved his hand from her chin to the back of her head. "No lumps, so that's good."

"I'm glad I don't have a lumpy head."

"I guess you *are* fine, but you should probably lie back down and get some rest. You seem a bit off balance." He leaned to one side, allowing her to dismount more easily.

Off balance was an understatement. She sighed as she plopped down into a fetal position on the bed. "I don't think I'll be able to fall back asleep."

"You don't have to, but at least try to rest your eyes. I'll stay right here. You'll be okay."

Natalie had already succumbed to the realization that she was *not okay*, and hearing that word yet again brought forth all the reasons: her childhood, Jared, Nick's death, Sylvia's murder, and the unshakeable feeling that she may be next. She had convinced herself that she wanted to become a police officer to help others. But as she lay there feeling as helpless as ever, she knew the real reason.

Her body trembled as she held back inevitable tears. "I'd rather be alone, please."

Derek slowly stood from the bed and walked to the door. "I'm really sorry, Natalie."

She waited for the door to close behind him, and then the floodgates opened.

***

Why had he shown her these? Derek sat at the kitchen table with the case files open in front of him. He felt awful. The images of those three women, and others from past cases, still haunted him and always would. It was the last thing he wanted for her.

He had hated leaving Natalie alone when she was so upset. Her sobs, although faint, had been audible when he stood outside her bedroom door, lingering longer than he knew he should, but unable to tear himself away. He had wanted nothing more than to hold her in his arms and make all her pain go away. *The pain he had caused*, he reminded himself.

She had every reason to be upset. Her brutally murdered friend had been partially skinned by the paring knife taken from Natalie's own kitchen. *And he had thought it was a good idea to show her the photos? To what? Scare her out of wanting to work on the case?* He shook his head at himself for being so idiotic. He'd be lucky to have her help.

The coffee was already brewing, filling the room with its strong, earthy aroma. Yearning for a cup of heaven, he momentarily closed his eyes to take in the scent. The deep inhale followed by an even longer exhale had a therapeutic effect. It had him taking several more, in and out slowly, savoring the coffee-soaked air before fully clearing his lungs. *If only he could clear his mind as well.* Since he was up, he figured he might as well get a jumpstart on some work.

Derek was on his fourth cup of coffee when Natalie emerged from her bedroom several hours later. "Hey, I'm glad you're up! I've been thinking a lot about what you said before, you know, about profiling. So, I got in touch with a behavioral analyst that has agreed to work with us on the case." He leaned down to pet Tux, who had immediately dashed from Natalie's bedroom to greet him. "His name is Benjamin Goyle. He's got lots of profiling experience with the FBI, and he was highly recommended by a buddy of mine that trained with him at Quantico."

Natalie took the seat across from him, at a noticeably lower energy level than his caffeine-induced buzz. "That's great. Um, work *with us?*"

"Yeah, listen, I'm really sorry about before. I let my ego get in the way of seeing how valuable your help would be. I'd be honored to work with you, if you're still interested."

He followed her eyes to the closed manila folder on the table and instinctively placed his hand over it, wanting to shield her from the glare of the unavenged women beneath its thin cover. "No more photos, though. You can still provide insight without needing to be involved in all the details."

Natalie slowly shook her head. "No, I want to know everything. It's okay. I'm all in."

"Are you sure?"

"Yes. Where do we start?"

Derek stared pensively for a moment, not at Natalie but through her, while he traveled to another place, another time. "We start at the beginning."

He then filled her in on the similarities to the Hood River cases.

CHAPTER SIXTEEN

4

One week later

The sky visible through the small window had gone from gray to pink. The last remnants of daylight threatened to disappear prematurely beyond moisture-laden clouds, dense and towering. Derek's stomach rumbled. He had lost track of time and feared they were running out of it.

The task force he had assembled sat in the "break room turned conference room," looking restless. It had been a week since the lifeless body of Sheena Greenwood, age twenty, had been found by her roommate. The clear plastic bag used to suffocate her could not conceal the expression of sheer terror that remained frozen on her face. And on her exposed pale chest, a note with the number four had been found.

Doctor Benjamin Goyle, the new behavioral analyst on the team, cleared his throat. "We've been at this all day with, unfortunately, no new insights. Perhaps we should start fresh tomorrow." His voice was calm, rational, and an octave deeper than one would expect from a man of his stature.

Derek felt far from calm. "You said it yourself, *Doctor.* This killer is getting less patient. He could be stalking his next victim as we speak. Time is critical."

"Well, that wasn't quite my assessment," Doctor Goyle corrected in a professor-like manner. "He was impatient with this last victim, likely incited by some event he viewed as a personal failure or setback. It spurred an intense need for him to kill, which he satiated. I don't believe his impatience is a trend or likely to intensify. In fact, it should subside now that he's gotten his fix."

Looking uncomfortable in his own skin, Ben Goyle ran a hand through his shaggy brown hair and turned his focus to Natalie, who sat across the table from him. "We might be able to think more clearly after some nourishment and rest. A dinner break, perhaps?"

The edges of Natalie's plump lips curved upward, and Derek could swear the room turned red. "Food is a great idea. I'll have something delivered so we can keep working. You're welcome to leave if you want, Doctor Goyle. Excuse me."

Derek exited into the hall to call in an order. He found it hard to admit that he could use a break as well. His nerves were already on edge, and there was something about Ben, or *Doctor Goyle* as he preferred to be called, that got under his skin even further. All his degrees and accolades, his matter-of-fact statements. He was pretentious at best, if not outright condescending. The way he and Natalie looked at each other certainly didn't help, either.

With her brains and beauty, Derek figured Natalie could have anyone she wanted, so why not Doctor Know-It-All? It made sense for her to end up with someone of equivalent intelligence. *He understood it, but it didn't mean he had to like it.* The best he could do was keep them within his sight.

Back in the conference room, an awkward silence fell over the team in Derek's absence. Natalie pensively observed each member while wondering how much longer they would all be there that night. Ben's gaze bounced nervously between the table and Natalie, and then back down at the table. He had kind eyes, similar to Nick's, she thought.

Rhonda, who had been unusually quiet during the meeting, squirmed in her seat as if deciding whether to stay or go. Marty let out a cough, a deep guttural sound that still failed to cut the hushed tension that permeated the shared space. Across from him sat Detective Gibson, another task force recruit with significant homicide experience.

Detective Michael Gibson, affectionately known as "Gibs," was the type of man that you could tell was handsome when he was younger, before life had taken its toll. Now in his late forties, he had the infamous *dad gut*, advanced male-pattern baldness, and deep circles around his eyes. His face looked markedly weary after the day's review of Sheena Greenwood's death. When the photos were first presented, he could be heard repeatedly saying, "she was so young" under his breath. It was probably because her red hair and pale freckled skin reminded him of his own college-aged daughter, whose picture at various childhood stages Natalie had seen proudly displayed all over his desk.

Natalie was the first to speak, directing her question to the whole room. "One thing I still don't understand is why take the risk of killing her in her own bed? I mean, her roommate could have come home at any time."

"Good thing she didn't. He probably would have killed her too," Gibs said solemnly.

"But if this murder was as spontaneous as it seemed, then the killer wouldn't have stalked her long enough to know whether she lived alone," Natalie continued. "She could have lived with several roommates or a boyfriend. Breaking in was an awfully risky move. Why not wait to grab her when she was out alone like the others?"

Ben timidly raised his hand, as if answering a question in class. "I don't mean to sound like a broken record, but I think whatever setback or negative event the killer experienced caused him to act in this illogical, impatient manner. And, therefore, he wasn't able to control himself long enough to wait."

Natalie stood and walked to the corkboard where various photos and pieces of evidence in clear plastic bags were pinned. "I don't disagree with the assessment that her killer was illogical and impatient. It's just that this one is so different from the first three murders, which seemed much more calculated and careful." She paced back and forth several times before addressing Derek as he re-entered the conference room. "This may be a dumb question, but has anyone analyzed the handwriting of all the numbered notes to determine if they're all written by the same person? There are experts that do that, right?"

"Yes, we have forensic document examiners in D.C. I could ask one of them to take a look for us," Ben offered quickly.

"Wait, what did I miss?" Derek walked over to where Natalie stood, his face displaying confusion mixed with genuine interest. "Do you think there could be more than one killer?"

"I'm sorry, but this is absurd." Marty stood, using his cane to hoist himself up. "We don't have time for far-fetched theories that will only divide our focus when the killer is out there, ready to strike again."

"Marty, you know I'm as eager to catch this killer as you are, but we brought Natalie onto the team to provide a fresh perspective. I think it's worth the time to explore all ideas further if there's even a chance we've overlooked something."

Natalie lifted her gaze from the floor to Derek, pleasantly surprised that he had defended her value as a team member.

"Well, let me know what you learn," Marty said as he began exiting the room. "I'm calling it a night."

The room was still after Marty left, with only the sound of the ancient coffee pot percolating in the background. "I'm sorry if I offended him," Natalie offered in a hushed voice.

"He's fine. He just gets cranky when he's hungry. Speaking of which, our food should be here in about fifteen minutes." Derek then turned to face the evidence board and crossed his arms. "Now what causes you to think there could be a second killer?"

"It makes a lot of sense, actually," Ben interjected before Natalie could speak. "It's highly unlikely that the killer from nearly twenty-five years ago would repeat his past crimes, because, in doing so, it would admit that he failed in some way the first time around."

Annoyance pinched at her temples. "That's not what I was thinking, actually. I'm no expert, but it seems to me this fourth murder might have been committed by a different person than the first three."

"Please, go on," Derek urged.

"Well, what if Sheena Greenwood's killer took the risk that he did, not just because he was so impatient, but because he couldn't physically remove her from the apartment?" Natalie resumed pacing the room, invigorated by the new connections forming in her brain. "The killer of the first three women was strong enough to transport the bodies to various locations. Sheena Greenwood was probably the lightest of all the victims, and yet her killer attacked her while she slept *and* left her body at the crime scene. It seems unnecessarily risky."

Rhonda rose from her chair, the energy building in the room. "Risky *and* cowardly at the same time. A confident man wouldn't need to target a sleeping woman."

"Exactly!" Natalie barely managed to keep her feet on the ground. She shot a look of gratitude in Rhonda's direction. "It would have been much easier to attack a woman out alone at night, *unless* the killer wasn't strong enough to risk a struggle."

Gibs also stood to speak, leaving only Ben still seated. "As risky as it all was, we still don't have any decent forensic evidence from the crime scene. While our guy might be weak and cowardly, it also tells me he's as sharp as a tack, possibly with some crime scene or law enforcement experience."

"Our guy or gal," Derek added, winking at Natalie. "We have to keep an open mind, cast a wider net."

"Right." Gibs nodded at Derek. "I'm gonna go pull some more records. Save me some food, will ya?" He turned to face Natalie before leaving. "Great work today."

Derek echoed the sentiment, the flecks of green in his eyes beaming at her. "That was great detective work, Natalie. I'm glad you're on the team."

CHAPTER SEVENTEEN

Leah Banks

Late July

Leah gripped the holds that protruded from the concave wall. Sweat dripped from her forehead into her eyes, adding to the challenge. She only hoped her hands remained dry enough to ascend to the top. A workout was exactly what she needed to clear her otherwise busy mind.

Thoughts of her family swirled around relentlessly. Her father had been discharged from the hospital to start a long recovery at home. She felt guilty for not staying to help him, but she could no longer bear her mother's cold treatment. It was as if Leah had been the one to pull the trigger herself, rather than the over-anxious cop that took her brother's life.

At only sixteen and having lost his house key yet again, Darren Banks had been climbing into the bedroom window he kept unlocked, despite their mother scolding against it. While hoisting himself up to the second-story rooftop, the icy water bottle stuffed in the waistband of his baggy pants had started to slide down his leg when the police officer ordered him to freeze. He instinctively grabbed at his leg to stop it, and the officer fatally shot him without further warning.

Another senseless victim of stereotyping, a cycle that needed to end. It had fueled Leah's passion to go into law enforcement, to fix the system from within. Leah's mother had seen it differently: consorting with the enemy, becoming one of *them*. She could not and would not understand how Leah could do that to her family.

A family that Leah no longer felt part of, all because she had followed her passion. For years, she had explored other career paths to keep the peace with her mother. She studied English and Philosophy in college—secretly squeezing in criminal justice coursework wherever she could—all the while preparing to become a high school English teacher like her father. It was a noble profession, but not the life she saw for herself.

Sweat caused her left hand to slip as she reached for the next hold with her right. Despite being out of practice, her quick reflexes and athletic prowess kicked into overdrive. Her right hand grabbed onto the next hold just in time, pulling her back into position.

"Nice save."

It took her only a split second to recognize the owner of the familiar voice. "Crap."

"Well, hello to you too."

Leah leaned back into her harness and pushed off the wall to descend to the floor. "You caught me off guard is all."

"Maybe that's better than, you know, having your guard up all the time." Rhonda stepped forward to help unhook Leah's harness.

Leah noted something different about Rhonda, something softer and less confrontational than usual. Butterflies mixed with anxiety in her stomach. "Did you come here for a reason?"

"Yes. I came here to apologize for the scene I made at the bar a couple of months ago. I guess you could say I was *caught off guard* that night and didn't handle it so well. I'm sorry about that."

"Don't worry about it. I kind of deserved it for the way I had ended things."

"*In a note*," Rhonda reminded her.

"I was thinking *abruptly*, but yeah, that too. I'm sorry for all of it."

"Why'd you do it, then?"

Leah stepped out of her climbing harness and picked it up off the ground. Her eyes wandered to the locker room entrance, willing her gym bag to magically appear from inside so she could make a quick escape. "Rhonda, you know I don't do well with these types of conversations."

"What is this *type of conversation*?" Rhonda gestured with air quotes.

"About feelings and stuff. Look, I know it's cowardly, but that was the reason for the note. I can't talk about how I feel."

"Can't or won't?"

Leah let out a sigh. "Do we have to do this here? How about I go get cleaned up and then we grab some lunch together? My treat." She wasn't sure having lunch with her ex was such a good idea, but her stomach grumbled at the prospect of food. And it bought her some time.

Rhonda looked at her skeptically. "Your treat?"

"Yeah, wherever you want to go."

"Okay, good, because I'm starving and don't want any of your health-food nonsense."

Leah laughed for what felt like the first time in forever. "My health-food nonsense is why I will outlive you."

"No, you'll outlive me because you're younger. Take it from someone older and wiser that a cheeseburger will be much more satisfying."

Leah laughed again. "So, we're settled on lunch, then. Let me go change, and then we can worry about how to spend the rest of our short lives."

"Sounds like a plan." Rhonda flashed one of her rare but beautiful ear-to-ear smiles. It wasn't until that moment that Leah realized how much she had truly missed her.

***

Derek returned home from work that afternoon to a surprisingly clean condo. Upbeat pop music blared from the radio, and he watched with amusement as Natalie danced and sang along while she scrubbed the stovetop. Finally, he cleared his throat to announce himself. "Hi there."

Natalie jumped like a cat startled by a loud noise. "Holy cow, you scared me!"

"Sorry," Derek chuckled.

She squinted at him with playful scorn in her eyes. "You don't look sorry. What are you doing home so early?"

"I left some files here that I wanted to go over again. What are *you* doing? I thought you had to catch up on some work of your own?"

"I'm procrastinating by cleaning up a bit first. I figured it's the least I could do, anyway, since I've been staying here for a few weeks now. Plus, it helps me to stay busy."

Derek peered into the living room. The area rug was freshly vacuumed, the floor was mopped, and piles of mail were neatly stacked on an end table. "You really didn't have to, but it looks great in here. Thank you!" Freshly cut flowers on the dining table caught his eye next. "Sunflowers?"

"Yeah, I thought they'd brighten up the place. I picked them up at the farmer's market earlier today. I hope that's okay."

Derek stared at the large yellow flowers, still reaching toward the sky. They reminded him of his childhood. "Yeah, of course it's okay. Thanks again for all your hard work. I feel like I should help clean something, though."

"No need. I'm almost finished. You should get your files."

"Right." Derek had already forgotten his reason for returning. "You seem to be in a particularly good mood, by the way. Any reason for that?"

Natalie tilted her head as if searching for the answer. "Yes, actually. I got a call from Leah today. You know, the friend I was with that night at Pete's?"

"Ah, you mean the night of the altercation with Rhonda?"

"That's the one. Anyway, she was pretty upset with me after that, but today she called to talk things through and wants to be friends again. Apparently, Rhonda and she have made amends as well."

"That sounds like good news."

"It is! I'm so happy to have my friend, slash workout partner, back! We're going rock climbing together tomorrow."

It was Derek's turn to tilt his head. "You enjoy rock climbing?"

"*Enjoy* is not the word I would use, but I do need all the help I can get preparing for the Academy."

"Well, I'm happy for you, then." Derek flashed a genuine smile while feeling a touch jealous that she wasn't going rock climbing with him. "Honestly, it's great to see you in such high spirits. I was a little worried about you after this past weekend."

Natalie thought back to her two-day binge fest, filled with wine and several seasons of old *Grey's Anatomy* episodes. Somehow, the suffering of fictional characters always made her feel better about her own. "Yeah, sorry about that. I was having a rough time. Saturday was… or would have been… my five-year wedding anniversary with Nick."

"Oh, I didn't realize. I'm sorry, Natalie."

"It's okay. I got through it." Lost in thought, she gazed at the flowers on the table and laughed weakly. "It's kinda crazy, though. I was with Nick for eight years, and he didn't even know me. Not really."

"What do you mean?"

She shook her head, not intending to overshare. "Oh, it's nothing. Stupid little things, mostly. He used to buy me red roses every year on our anniversary, for example, not knowing that I weirdly don't like them. And typical me, I never said anything, because I didn't want to seem ungrateful."

"You don't like roses?"

"I like rose *bushes*, just not cut ones. They're all thorny, and they wilt so quickly. And... I don't know... they remind me of death for some reason." She walked over and adjusted the arrangement on the table. "That's why I prefer sunflowers. They're happy flowers."

"Yes, they are." Derek sat down on the couch and stretched out his legs. "Well, I'm enjoying getting to know you better. You sing and dance when you clean. You're excited to go rock climbing even though you don't enjoy it. And you prefer sunflowers to roses. I'd ask if you were a cat or dog person, but I think I already know the answer there." Tux meowed as Derek reached down to pet him.

"Actually, I always wanted to get a dog, but my work schedule didn't make it practical. Cats are much more independent and okay with being left alone." She laughed weakly. "Ironically, I got Tux so I wouldn't have to be alone. It doesn't seem fair that he was by himself all day when I went to work."

"Cats don't mind it so much, like you said."

"Still, I'm glad I'm not working those insane hours anymore. It's nice that Tux has Cal now, too." Natalie joined Derek on the couch and gave attention to both cats when they jumped up to greet her.

"I can relate to wanting the company of a pet. I got Cal ten years ago, after my last tour in Afghanistan. He got me through some pretty rough times."

She nodded while wondering what war must have been like for him. Also, a decade was a long time to have only a cat for company. *A lonely cat man? Was that a thing?*

"So, you're a dog person, then?" he asked.

Natalie shrugged. "I'm a fan of all animals. Dogs are great because they're so loyal and full of joy, but they're also much more dependent, like young children. And I've never wanted *that* responsibility."

"You never want children?"

She shook her head. "I know it makes me sound like a sociopath, but no, I don't want kids. Babies, in particular, make me *extremely* uncomfortable. The sound of them crying..." Natalie cringed and then shrugged again. "I'd much rather get a dog. I've felt that way for as long as I can remember, despite everyone insisting that I'll change my mind someday. What about you?"

"Kids?" Derek stroked his jaw as if thinking. "I've honestly never considered them an option for me. *At least not on purpose.* I mean, if it happened by accident or something, I always assumed I would step up and be the best father possible—unlike the deadbeat that ran out on my mom when she got pregnant with me."

"It sounds like you were better off without him." *Fathers were overrated*, she thought.

"That's what my mom used to say." Derek rose from the couch, looking suddenly uncomfortable. "I better go grab the files I came home for before I forget them. Thanks again for cleaning up in here."

"Of course. It was my pleasure." She eyed Derek as he scurried away to his room.

A nerve had been struck. That much was clear. Understanding that family matters were often sensitive, she made a mental note to avoid the topic and then powered up her laptop. Her work had waited long enough.

CHAPTER EIGHTEEN

Muffins

"Oh, hi, I hope I wasn't making too much noise," Natalie said to Derek when he emerged from his bedroom. At nearly one in the morning, she wasn't expecting to have company.

"No, not at all. Just couldn't sleep. I'm guessing you had the same problem." He raked his fingers through his dark-brown hair, which she noticed had grown out a bit. Second- or maybe third-day stubble covered his sturdy jaw. He looked groggy yet gorgeous as ever. "What are you making?"

"Muffins!" The word came out awfully chipper for the early hour, surprising even herself. "Glorious Morning Muffins, to be exact. I don't bake often, but these muffins are one of the few things I think I make pretty well."

"I'm sure you do." His tone was flirtatious as his eyes scrolled over her.

Natalie glanced down at the simple black T-shirt she wore. White flour spotted her chest like carefully planned artwork and then trailed down her sides where she had wiped her hands. Her plaid pajama pants hung low on her hips, exposing a thin band of skin around her abdomen.

When she looked up, she found his gaze at her waistline and deflected, her heat level rising. "Well, it's hard to mess them up, at least. They've got shredded apples, carrots, and raisins in them, so they come out pretty moist even if I overcook them."

Derek walked over closer to the kitchen counter where she worked. "I like moist muffins."

Realizing the double entendre she had stepped into, Natalie blushed and shook her head. It had been years since simple banter had made her pulse race. While the sexual tension between them was difficult to ignore, she didn't like where it was headed.

"And why do you always do that, by the way?" he asked.

"Do what?"

"Put yourself down by minimizing your accomplishments." Derek's tone had changed from playful to serious, and his gaze lifted to her eyes as if searching for answers deep within them.

She reached for a kitchen towel to occupy her uneasy hands. "I don't do that. And I would hardly call baking muffins an accomplishment."

"It is if you do it well, and you're doing it again." Playfulness had returned to his voice as he leaned on the counter near her.

His proximity made her skin feel like it might steam. She pulled at the crewneck of her T-shirt, willing fresh air to cool her with only minor success. "You're wrong."

"About what?"

"About minimizing accomplishments. Just because I don't like to brag about being good at things, it doesn't mean I'm putting myself down. It's called being humble."

"Oh, I see. Thanks for explaining what it's called," Derek teased, slowly inching closer. "Tell me about some other things you're good at, then."

Against her better judgment, Natalie let her defenses drop and leaned in closer to him. "Well, for starters, I'm good at winning arguments."

"I didn't realize we were arguing. It must be because you make it so fun." Derek shifted so that he now stood directly in front of her, their bodies mere inches apart. "I bet you're good at lots of other things, too."

Natalie's lips parted, her mind temporarily going blank. His hazel irises, full of smoldering intensity, reeled her in like a fish on a hook. She closed her eyes upon feeling the warmth of his breath. Then an eternity later, his soft lips lightly brushed against hers, as if testing her acceptance before he took her mouth fully. Once he did, their tongues quickly entwined, moving in unison. Her neurons melted under his deep, passionate kiss.

But the mindless bliss only lasted a moment. Natalie suddenly felt boxed in by the counter behind her and Derek's muscular forearms, lightly squeezing into the sides of her waist. The weight of his body against her was heavy and unyielding. She couldn't think, couldn't breathe. Gasping for air, she leaned as far back as the counter would allow and shoved at Derek's chest. "Stop, please!"

Derek immediately took a full step back, raising his arms as if a weapon were pointed at him. "What's wrong? Are you okay?"

"No! I mean, I'm fine. But this can't happen. I shouldn't have let it. I'm sorry."

He lowered his hands slowly. "No, *I'm sorry*. I didn't mean to… I just thought… honestly, I thought you wanted me to kiss you, but I clearly misread the situation. I'm so sorry, Natalie. It won't happen again."

Her trembling breath gradually returned to a normal cadence. She *had* wanted him to kiss her—*and she badly wanted to keep kissing him*—but she couldn't allow it. Not when she found herself completely out of control in his presence. Not when her heart longed for something much deeper than the physical attraction between them. And not when he could so easily hurt her.

"I'm glad we're on the same page now." Natalie tugged on the bottom of her shirt that had crept up and then walked over to put the mixing bowl away in the fridge. "I'll finish these in the morning." She then escaped to her bedroom and turned before closing the door. "I'd really appreciate it if we could just forget this ever happened. Okay?"

He hesitated briefly and then said, "Sure, if that's what you want."

"It is. Good night, Derek."

After closing the door, Natalie slumped down with her back against it, still shaking. All her nerve endings felt unraveled and exposed. Holding back tears she knew would otherwise come, she shut her eyes tight as she replayed the kiss in her mind. The heat, the passion, and an intense connection she hadn't felt in years, if ever. It was as if his eyes had the ability to penetrate her soul, seeing her more clearly than she saw herself.

But hadn't she felt that way with Jared? Uncontrollably lured by his devilish good looks and charm. Blinded by passion. *No, she would not make that mistake again.* She pulled herself up off the floor and crawled into bed. She would sleep it off, and in the morning, she'd pretend nothing ever happened.

***

The sun glared in through the open window shade, forcing Derek to squint at the clock on his nightstand as he woke. Half past ten was much later than usual, but it had already been a long morning. His mind immediately traveled back to his kiss with Natalie. Her soft lips and tongue that he was certain had kissed him back. *Or had he been wrong about that too?*

He still couldn't get her reaction out of his head. He had never experienced anything like it before. The way she had pushed him away… *Had she been afraid of him?* He knew she had been through a lot in her past, but for her to believe he could ever hurt her was unfathomable. *Or had he already? By making an unwanted advance?*

He would have never kissed her if he hadn't felt confident it was what she wanted too, but her reaction made it perfectly clear that was not the case. The painful feeling of rejection, previously a foreign concept to him, had also spurred a counteraction. One that upon his recollection of the last few hours brought him guilt. Still squinting, he stretched his arm across the bed, alarmed to find it empty.

With all his senses shocked awake, Derek sprang from his bed at the sound of female chatter in the kitchen. *Oh, no, no, no.* He threw on his favorite weekend T-shirt and carefully inched open his bedroom door as if entering a war zone full of hostiles. At least he would know what to do in that situation. *This one, not so much.*

"Hey there, handsome." The cheery voice came from the redhead wearing boxer shorts and his T-shirt from the night before. "I didn't know you had a roommate. She baked the most delicious muffins! You've got to try one!"

Ignoring the emphatic offer, Derek quickly focused his attention on Natalie. He searched her face for any sign of emotion. *A hint of jealousy,* he thought hopefully. Her alluring eyes refused to meet his, though. She busied herself at the sink, washing a muffin pan he was sure he didn't own.

"Amber, this is Natalie. Natalie, Amber." Derek took a few steps closer to the kitchen, still maneuvering cautiously and wondering how well-acquainted the two women had become.

"We've met. Here, try this, seriously!" Amber waved a muffin in his direction.

"No muffin for me. I'm not hungry." That was a lie, but he didn't dare take anything else he didn't deserve. His eyes remained locked on Natalie, waiting for even the slightest reaction.

When Natalie had finished rinsing the pan, she looked up from the sink at Amber, still avoiding Derek's gaze. "I'm going to go for a run now and leave you two alone. It was nice meeting you, Amber."

"You as well. And I'll have to get that recipe from you! Seriously, the best muffins I have ever had!"

"You're too kind. I'll see you around." Natalie darted toward the front door, already dressed in her running gear, but Derek swiftly blocked her path.

"Wait up, Natalie. You shouldn't go out running alone. I'll change quick and go with you."

"No, I'm fine to go alone. *Plus, you've got company.*" Her hushed words came out in the sound of a low growl, and the awkward silence that followed reminded him they weren't alone.

"Amber, I'm sorry. Can I walk you home or something?" he asked.

More awkwardness followed as Amber looked from him to Natalie and then back to him. "Oh, I was kind of hoping we could hang out… but okay. I'm sure you have a busy day. Let me just go get changed."

"Amber, wait. Derek's not busy at all today. You should stay awhile. And when I get back, I'll write down my recipe for you. It'll be a quick run." Natalie was out the door before Derek could stop her.

He gave Amber an apologetic glance before heading back toward the kitchen. "Of course, you're welcome to stay. Can I make you some coffee?"

"Natalie made me some tea already, but thanks. I should get going, actually. I'll go get changed."

"Okay, sure." Derek struggled to keep the look of relief off his face. All he could think about was catching up to Natalie on her run, making sure she was okay, and explaining what happened. *How the hell was he going to do that?*

Ten minutes later, Derek had changed and was running full speed along the waterfront. He couldn't be sure which direction she had headed, so he had chosen to run downriver on a hunch that she wouldn't take her usual path this morning. At his pace, he figured he should catch up with her soon and was starting to worry that he had gone the wrong way when he saw her golden ponytail swaying back and forth in the distance. Motivated by the minor success, he increased his stride and caught up with her within a few minutes.

"Natalie, I'm glad I found you. We need to talk, please."

"No, we don't." Natalie slowed and then turned to run back in the opposite direction.

He followed her lead. "Yes, we do. I'm so sorry for what happened."

"Sorry for what exactly?" she snapped, stopping short in her tracks. "Sorry for proving me right? Sorry for being the type of guy that uses women to stoke his own ego? You should be apologizing to Amber, not me! That poor girl."

Derek stood dumbfounded while Natalie began running again. That wasn't the response he had expected at all. He had wanted to apologize for not respecting her wishes to keep things strictly professional between them.

It hadn't once crossed his mind that he had wronged Amber in some way. After processing that information, he ran after Natalie once again.

"Hey, wait! Please let me explain."

"There's nothing to explain."

Derek dodged a slow-moving couple pushing a stroller in the center of the path and increased his pace to catch up. "First off, Amber knows that she and I are just friends. I've been honest with her from the beginning about not wanting anything serious. I would never deceive a woman to get her into bed."

Natalie stopped running again, this time moving off the path to a grassy area under a tree. Her face was crimson red, her eyes full of fury. "Wow, you really are an egotistical bastard!"

"Excuse me?"

"You think just because you tell her you're only using her for sex, and she agrees to it, that makes it okay? Do you have any idea what that does to her?" She glared at him, waiting for a response he didn't have, and then continued waving her arms and wagging her finger at him as she spoke. "Of course not! But I can tell you. It crushes any shred of self-esteem she may have and makes her feel ashamed of herself. But she justifies continuing to sleep with you by telling herself that there's still a chance, that you'll someday see how wonderful she is and change your mind, if you just spend more time together. And then, you go and destroy that hope for her by kicking her out this morning! What is wrong with you?"

"I didn't think she… I never wanted to… I wasn't thinking." He looked at the ground in shame. Natalie was right, of course. He had unintentionally hurt Amber and was too dense to even realize it on his own. But there had to be more behind her rage toward him. "Natalie, I'm sorry and I'll apologize to Amber as well, but we should also talk about what happened between us in the kitchen."

"Nothing happened with us. You couldn't get what you wanted from me, so you turned to the next available option. Women are interchangeable to you."

"That's not true, or fair. I get that you are upset with me, but you haven't given me a chance to explain."

"Okay, go ahead." Natalie crossed her arms, her gaze stern.

Derek gulped involuntarily. *What could he possibly say to excuse his behavior?* Nothing came to mind, so he went with the truth. "I was a jerk. I acted on impulse, with you in the kitchen, and then again after you pushed me away. It was wrong. I realize that now and feel awful. But I need you to know that I never meant to hurt you, or Amber, or anyone."

"You didn't hurt me."

"Even so, Natalie, I'm truly sorry for my behavior. I thought there was a connection between us, and I acted on it, but I was wrong. You were upfront about wanting to keep things strictly professional, and I should have respected that. I was out of line. Can you forgive me?"

Her arms remained crossed. "No need. It never happened."

With the memory of their passionate kiss still fresh in his mind, her words seared through him like bullets. As if physically injured, his entire body stiffened and then relaxed to let all the pain go. It was a survival skill he had perfected over the years; one for which he couldn't be more grateful.

"Okay. We're good, then." Derek turned to leave but was stopped by Natalie's arm on his.

"You should date her."

"What? Who?"

"Amber. She seems like a sweet girl. You owe it to her to at least get to know her. Give her a chance."

Derek considered the idea, confused by the source. If he hadn't already realized he didn't stand a chance with Natalie, this confirmed it. He simply nodded and then walked away.

CHAPTER NINETEEN

It's a Date

Early August

Natalie sat across the table from Benjamin Goyle and pushed salad around on her plate. She had agreed to go out to lunch with him to talk more about the case. It felt less like a date that way, and lunch with Ben was much better than another day of catered sandwiches in the makeshift conference room. It didn't hurt that Derek seemed bothered by the two of them leaving together, *although certainly not the reason she did it.*

Ben was a nice guy, and not hard on the eyes either, Natalie mused. Under his designer-framed glasses, his face had a symmetrical structure with soft features that some might attribute to classic handsomeness. He was of average height and slightly lower than average weight. Not muscular, but not out of shape, either.

Attractive in a less obvious way. Like dining at an underrated local restaurant with amazing food, rather than a popular tourist trap with average food at exorbitant prices. Natalie always thought that was better. She quietly pondered this while Ben chattered on nervously about his decision to go into behavioral forensics.

"Sorry, I've been going on and on about myself. What about you, Natalie?"

"Oh, what about me?"

"Why are you interested in law enforcement? As a career, I mean." Ben's cheeks turned an endearing shade of red.

"Guilt, I guess." Her response seemed to surprise them both, and it was her turn to blush. "What I mean is… I don't feel like I'm doing enough with my life to help other people. I'm hoping to change that."

"Well, if I may say, you're already making valuable contributions to this case. I was going to wait until we were back at the station, but I got an email while we were waiting to be seated, and…" Ben looked over his shoulder and lowered his voice, "you were right about the note on Sheena Greenwood. It was deemed to be different handwriting than the first three."

"Are they sure?"

"These things are never a hundred percent certain. But statistically, it's highly improbable that the same person wrote all four notes. The handwriting on the fourth note had characteristics of being written by someone left-handed, whereas the first three did not. That's what the QDU wrote in their report."

"Uh, QDU?"

"Questioned Documents Unit. They're the forensic document examiners in our lab at the FBI."

"I see." Natalie didn't know whether to feel proud she was right, or terrified. "Wow, two killers, then. Probably."

"It seems so." Ben cleared his throat. "On another subject, I hear there's a lovely Peruvian restaurant near the Pearl District. Might you be interested in trying it with me sometime?"

Her mind still lingered on the previous subject. "I'm sorry. What?"

"Um, how's your lunch?"

"It's good, thank you." She looked down at the fork in her hand, carefully loaded with one of each ingredient from her seasonal vegetable salad, and couldn't remember if she had even taken a bite yet. She forced a smile and drove the contents into her mouth, hoping it would at least relieve her from further discussion until she could focus.

Two killers played on repeat in her brain. Ben continued talking, but she had tuned him out, unable to digest any more information. The crisp tastes of kale and lemon mixed with summer squash and quinoa on her tongue. The food wasn't bad, but everything seemed tainted by the prospect of two killers. She nodded mindlessly while chewing, trying to look like she was enjoying her meal.

"Great. How about tomorrow night? I can pick you up around seven o'clock, if that works?"

Natalie nearly choked. "Tomorrow?"

"Yes, dinner tomorrow or another night, if you prefer?"

Realization set in that she must have inadvertently agreed to a date. With his hopeful amber eyes awaiting her reply, Natalie decided she could do much worse than

Doctor Benjamin Goyle. "Tomorrow at seven works great."

***

Tomorrow came fast, too fast. Natalie paced her bedroom floor in the black cocktail dress she had purchased earlier that afternoon. Shopping had seemed easier than going back to her own apartment, where about a dozen similar dresses hung in her closet. She paused in front of the full-length mirror and sighed.

Not bringing her full selection of shoes to Derek's was an epic misstep. She should have stopped home for a few more options. Then she reminded herself: *Two killers, at least one of which had been inside her apartment.* Her worn-out, strappy, black satin heels would have to do.

Tux perked up at the sound of the automatic can opener coming from the kitchen. It was Friday night, which meant a can of tuna each for Cal and Tux. Derek said everyone needed a treat after a long, hard week. The thought made her smile before her nerves resumed their place on edge.

"I'll let you out in a minute," she said to Tux, crouching down to soothe him when he meowed at the door. "I'm just not ready to face him yet."

She had avoided time alone with Derek after her lunch with Ben and hadn't yet mentioned she was going out. While a courtesy notification to her roommate felt appropriate, it wasn't like she needed his permission. *She was a grown woman and could date whomever she wanted.* She gulped at that thought. It had been eight years since she'd last gone on a *first date*—with Nick—and less than a year since his passing.

Why did she ever agree to this? Maybe she could still get out of it. She looked in the mirror again, conjuring up excuses to cancel. Saying she felt ill would at least be a half truth, since her stomach was tied in knots. She grabbed her phone from the dresser and then jumped at the knock on her bedroom door.

"Natalie, you have a guest at the front door." Derek's voice boomed into the room as if he had been standing right next to her. There were traces of annoyance in it.

She glanced at the clock, which read 6:43. *Ben was early.* She took a deep breath and opened the bedroom door. Tux darted out between her legs to join Cal in the kitchen, late to the tuna party.

Natalie gripped onto the door frame for balance. "Sorry, I meant to tell you I was going out tonight."

Derek's expression, stern at first, melted when he saw her. His eyes widened. "You look beautiful."

"Um, thanks."

Ben cleared his throat from outside the open front door to make his presence known. "Good evening, Natalie. Ready to go?"

"Yes. Let me just grab my purse and I'll be right there."

Derek hadn't invited him in, she noted. She shot Ben a sympathetic look before heading back into the bedroom. After retrieving her handbag, she turned and practically bumped into Derek.

His expression had turned serious again, but his gaze was soft. "I hope you have a nice time tonight, but please, be careful."

"I will." Her knees felt weak as she slid past his rigid body to exit the room.

Ben stood patiently outside the front door. Her first full view of him had her stomach doing flips again. He looked sharp, wearing a light-blue button-down dress shirt and black slacks. It differed from his usual attire of a polo shirt and khakis. His chestnut brown hair also appeared to be styled with more effort tonight. And his expression was fraught with nervous anticipation—a familiar look that Natalie couldn't shake.

Her breath hitched in her throat, but she forced herself to keep walking toward the door. "Let's go eat."

***

How long did it take to share a meal? Derek hoped that was all they were sharing. It was after ten o'clock. The thought of them together was driving him crazy, even though he knew he had no right to be jealous. She had told him he should date Amber, making it crystal clear there was nothing between them.

And didn't Natalie deserve to be happy? Ben seemed like a nice enough guy, despite the animosity Derek felt toward him. He picked up his phone and debated texting Natalie to make sure she was okay. Shaking off that idea, he drafted a message to Amber instead.

Derek: *Dinner tomorrow night?*

His thumb lingered over the send button a moment before pressing it. The finality of that decision had him drawing in a sharp breath. He'd take Natalie's advice and give Amber a fair chance at an actual relationship. *He might even enjoy himself for a change. And wouldn't Natalie be pleased that he was following her wishes?* He was brooding over his desire to make Natalie happy when his phone buzzed in return.

Amber: *Sure! Where should I meet you?*

Derek sighed. Her eagerness made him realize, yet again, that Natalie was right. Amber wanted much more than a casual relationship, and a respectable date was the least he could give her. The concept of getting to know a woman that he'd been sleeping with for the past few months not only seemed like the most obvious and decent thing to do, but it opened his eyes to the deplorable way he had been treating women for years. As objects designed solely for his pleasure and distraction, they had been easily replaced if even a shred of attachment was detected.

His mother would be ashamed of the man he had become. He hung his head low and drafted his reply.

Derek: *I'll pick you up at 7 o'clock. We'll go somewhere nice. Have a good night, Amber.*

He'd bring her some flowers, he decided. Feeling marginally better, he headed into the kitchen to grab a beer. Cal and Tux both raced in behind him upon hearing the refrigerator door open.

"Not for you this time, guys." Derek opened his beer using the bottle opener attached to the side of the kitchen counter.

The sound of the metal cap falling into the bin below coincided perfectly with the rustling of keys outside the front door. Similar to the felines' reaction to the refrigerator, Derek rushed to the door, hoping to preclude any prolonged goodbyes in the hallway. Natalie was still searching for the keyhole when he pulled the door open wide. He was both relieved and shocked to find her alone.

"Where's Ben? The good doctor couldn't bother walking you to the door?" he asked before assessing Natalie's face. Her eyes were puffy, and faint red splotches were visible on her cheeks and under her nose. She had been crying, maybe hours earlier, but the signs were still there.

"What's wrong?" His blood boiled as Natalie pushed her way past him and toward her room. Thoughts of murdering Doctor Benjamin Goyle came easy. "If he hurt you, I swear I'll…"

"He didn't do anything, and I'm fine. I just want to go to bed now, if you don't mind. Good night," she said, cutting him short and closing the bedroom door behind her.

He placed his hand on the bronze knob and considered following her in but stopped himself. She deserved her privacy, and he needed to start respecting her wishes. It didn't sit right with him, though. She had left with Ben several hours ago and returned alone, clearly upset. *What the hell had happened?*

He paced the floor of the living room and debated knocking on her door to force the conversation. After several deep breaths, he decided it could wait until morning. But he was going to get to the bottom of it.

Since he knew he wouldn't be able to sleep anyway, he powered up his laptop, logged in using two-factor authentication, and began scouring the case files yet again. They had to be missing something. Some connection or pattern they hadn't seen yet. Nicole Brook, Pamela Sinclair, Sylvia Porter, and Sheena Greenwood all must have been chosen for some reason.

Although, the fourth victim may have been chosen by a second killer. Her death was different. Perhaps the key was in trying to understand all the differences rather than looking for a common pattern. This killer craved variety, and if there were a second killer, he used that knowledge to his advantage. *But how would a second killer know to follow the same M.O.?*

He clicked on the file folder for the Hood River cases. *With a fresh perspective, it was best to start from the beginning.*

CHAPTER TWENTY

5

Dawn's early light illuminated the empty square dubbed "Portland's living room" outside the window and made its way in through the vertical blinds, shining dimly on the kitchen table where Derek had fallen asleep. He rose to answer his phone as soon its vibrations against the granite countertop jolted him awake, intuitively knowing the bad news that would follow.

"Hartmann here." He rubbed his eyes and then listened as the details of the call were relayed to him. *Another body had been found. This time was different, though. And it was worse.* "I'll be right there."

Ten minutes later, Derek parked his car on the road across from the International Rose Test Garden in Washington Park. Public access to the park had been blocked off by physical barricades and multiple police vehicles, which he maneuvered around to cross the street. Stepping onto the edge of the hillside garden that housed over ten thousand roses, he took in the spectacular view and a deep breath to ready himself. The air had a stench of death mixed with fragrant roses and morning dew.

Golden fingers of light from the rising sun backlit the downtown skyline and Mount Hood in the distance, while a sea of color—in organized shades of red, pink, white, yellow, orange, and even purple—glimmered in the forefront of his field of vision. The *City of Roses* certainly held up to its name. For a fleeting moment, he wondered if Natalie had yet visited Washington Park. *She had said she liked rose bushes, just not cut ones. They reminded her of death.*

As he walked toward the center of the garden, he was greeted by a young officer in uniform that looked visibly shaken. "Detective Hartmann, sir?"

"Yes, that's me." He flashed his badge, more out of protocol than necessity. "What's the story, Officer…?"

"Colizzi, sir. Officer Gray and I were first on scene. We had been following up on a noise complaint in the neighboring area. The groundskeeper over there," he said while pointing to a portly man that appeared to be trembling, "arrived shortly before six this morning to tend to the roses and… well, he called nine-one-one after finding her."

"I see." Derek had already begun walking away from Officer Colizzi and toward the flashes and clicks of forensic photographers. His jaw dropped when he caught sight of what they were encircling. *Yes, much worse.*

The victim's body was face down in the dirt, between two of the numerous rows of roses that filled the popular public garden. Dark hair that draped down her back was the only thing covering her otherwise naked body. About twenty feet away, a large "5" had been written with a dark, fluid substance on the green lawn of the amphitheater overlooking the city. An all-too-familiar metallic scent melded with that of freshly cut grass.

"Dear God," he mumbled to himself.

"God had no part in this."

Startled, Derek turned around to find the medical examiner standing behind him. "Carl, what the hell happened here?"

"Meet Maria Velarde, age forty-six. Her arms and legs have multiple puncture wounds from needles. A more detailed exam is needed, but from the look of things, it appears our killer drained all of her blood to create that artwork down there."

Derek cringed. He had known Carl to be morbid at times, supposed it came with the job, but never crass. "I wouldn't call that *artwork*."

"Not from our perspective. But to our killer…" Carl shrugged his shoulders, which Derek noticed no longer sported the sling from the last time he saw him. *His shoulder sprain must have healed already.* "He clearly wanted this one on display."

Derek ruminated on that further as Carl walked back over to the victim's body. The killer had picked an extremely public location, and the message was loud and clear: This was his fifth kill, and he wanted everyone to know about it. What Derek couldn't understand, and feared he never would, was *why*. Holding his breath, he put on the pair of latex gloves he had been handed upon his arrival, ready to aid in the search for any evidence that would bring this bastard down.

***

Why on earth did he choose tonight of all nights to plan a date with Amber? He had considered canceling, but Natalie's reaction at the mention of it had reinforced it wasn't the right thing to do. Despite being exhausted after a long day of investigating yet another murder, he had made a commitment and needed to keep it.

Commitment was a construct Derek had avoided like the plague for as long as he could remember. He contemplated his reasons for changing course while twirling spaghetti around his fork. *Comfort food*, he thought. The restaurant buzzed with light conversation all around him. Amber had finished relaying the details of her childhood, and it was now time for him to engage.

"It sounds like you're close with your family."

Amber tucked a loose strand of her fiery hair behind her ear and smiled. "Yeah, I only wish I could get home to see them more often. What about your family? Are they local?"

"No, I grew up in California. It's just me here in Oregon. How's your salmon?"

"Delicious, thank you. At least California isn't too far. Do you visit home often?"

Derek shoveled a forkful of pasta into his mouth and shook his head while he chewed.

Amber continued, "Well, it must have been nice growing up with all that sunshine, unlike all the rain here. Did you move to Portland for work, then?"

He nodded, deciding it was technically true, and then glanced at his watch. It had been an hour since he picked up Amber. *How long were dates supposed to last?*

Dating, he was discovering, involved a lot of talking, and he was not in the mood. He hoped listening would be easier. "Tell me more about yourself. What do you do for work?"

There was a pause and then a moment of dread. *Had she already shared that information when his mind was elsewhere? This was not going well.* He should have canceled like he wanted to and stayed home with Natalie. It had killed him to leave her alone, especially as miserable as she had seemed.

Natalie was still mourning the loss of her husband and wasn't ready to date. He understood that now. Earlier that evening, she had shared that she hadn't gone through with her date. She had instead spent the evening at the chief's house, after fabricating a story that Maggie was upset and needed her.

Except it was Natalie that had needed Maggie. Derek could certainly relate. Despite being unable to have children of her own, Marjorie Serrano had a comforting maternal quality. He himself had often turned to her for guidance and emotional support over the years.

Amber had finished chewing her food and took a sip of her wine. "Oh my gosh, I can't believe I never told you! I'm a dental hygienist over at Doctor Boron's office off Eleventh Avenue. You know, over where they found that poor woman's body in the alley a couple months ago. It was so awful. Are you involved in that case at all?"

He focused in again, a bit caught off guard. "Yes, but I'm not at liberty to discuss any of the details."

"Oh goodness, I wouldn't want to know any of the details! I just hope you guys catch the killer. So, so awful." She was slowly shaking her head now. Her usual bubbly demeanor had disappeared.

"Wait, we interviewed all the dental office employees, in case anyone had seen something suspicious. I'm sure I would've noticed you there." Derek held his breath this time. *Had he seriously not recognized interviewing the woman he had been sleeping with for weeks?* Maybe Natalie was right about him being a jerk, or however she had put it.

"Oh, I had stayed home from work that day. A lot of the women in my office were shaken up by the whole ordeal. None of us walk home or go to our cars alone anymore."

"That's unfortunate, but smart. You can never be too careful." The mood had turned grim, and while not an expert, even he could tell this was not a good date. At least it gave him an out. "I'm sorry, Amber. With everything going on right now, I shouldn't have asked you out. Do you mind if we call it an early night?"

"Of course. I'm sorry for bringing up such a morbid topic. That was stupid of me."

"Please, don't blame yourself at all. It was already on my mind, so I apologize for being distracted tonight. You deserve better than that."

"So, another time, then?" Amber asked.

Derek sighed internally, realizing what he needed to do. "Amber, you're a great person, but I have to be honest with you. My work isn't the only thing distracting me, and I don't think it's going to change with time."

"I see," she said, lowering her head.

"I'm truly sorry if I've hurt you in any way. You deserve to be with someone who is going to give you their full attention. I hope you understand."

Amber quietly waited while Derek signed the bill the waiter had brought over to their table. As they both stood to leave, she asked, "It's Natalie, isn't it?"

"Excuse me?" he asked, taken by surprise.

"You're in love with her, aren't you?"

His honest reply was even more surprising to him. "Yes, I think I might be."

CHAPTER TWENTY-ONE

Dealing with Pain

Natalie woke to a pounding headache and immediately regretted her decision, albeit an unconscious one, to finish both bottles of wine. The last thing she remembered was watching Rose let go of Jack's hand, allowing him to slip away into the icy abyss. She had fallen asleep before the end of the movie with tears in her eyes, unsure if they were for Rose's loss or her own.

She now found herself supine on the couch, warm under a fleece blanket she didn't recognize. The television had been turned off, presumably by Derek after returning home from his date. She couldn't help but wonder how it had gone. *Not that she cared.* Amber seemed like a nice girl, someone that Derek could be happy with if he gave her a chance. It would be selfish to want him to stay as lonely as she was, and she was done being selfish.

Her thoughts were interrupted by Derek entering the room. "Hi there, you're awake. How are you feeling?"

"Fine." She sat up and then groaned at the sight of the coffee table; her blatant lie exposed. The empty bottles and half-eaten popcorn were equivalent to evidence at a crime scene. "Uh, I may have had too much wine."

"Can I get you anything? How about some food?"

"No, thank you. I'll be okay. Good morning, by the way." She forced a smile despite the drumbeat in her head.

"Good afternoon," he corrected.

Natalie squinted at the clock on the wall to confirm it was in fact quarter to one. She wondered when she had fallen asleep, or more likely, passed out. "Wow, I guess I slept in today. At least it's Sunday."

"I'm worried about you, Natalie. I get it, trust me, but alcohol is not a healthy way to deal with your pain." Derek's voice was soft but serious.

"I know, and I'm sorry. You shouldn't have to deal with this. I think it's time for me to get my own place again. One with better security, though."

"What? No, Natalie… I don't want you to leave. I want to help you."

She stood rebelliously, ignoring the head rush that immediately followed. "That's the problem."

"It's a problem that I care about you?"

"No, that you think I need your help. I'm not some damsel in distress that needs saving, Derek." She pointed her finger into his chest when he stepped closer—into the wine cloud surrounding her.

"I never said you were. But you are grieving, which is normal after loss, and I won't let you go through it alone."

"I'm perfectly fine alone." As soon as she said the words, she knew it wasn't true. *Why was she fighting his help?* The stench of wine emanated from her pores. She looked down at the sweatpants she had been wearing since she had gotten home from her failed date. "How was your date with Amber?" she asked.

"Not great, but you're changing the subject. Everyone needs someone to lean on at times. If you don't want my help, that's fine, but you should talk to someone."

As she slowly exhaled, her misplaced anger evanesced. "It helped a little when I talked to Maggie Friday night."

"That's good. Maybe keep that up."

"I don't want to burden her, or anyone for that matter. Maggie's great, but she doesn't understand what I'm going through."

Derek seemed to mull something over before he spoke again. "Do you feel up to going for a drive? There's somewhere I want to show you."

Fifty minutes later, they were headed out of the city toward a winding, mountainous road. The radio blared with the musical talent of One Republic. Natalie had turned up the volume to avoid talking. The black Jeep that Derek drove hummed with the music as it sped east along US-26. Once civilization was in the rear view, Natalie got curious about their destination. Derek had been annoyingly tight-lipped about it when they had left.

"So, where are we going, anyway?"

"You'll see," Derek said, same as he had before.

"Okay, then. Tell me why your date last night didn't go well."

"I was distracted. It's not a good time for me to be dating, so I ended things with Amber."

"Derek! That was meant to be your first date with her, not your last."

"Well, I guess it was both."

"But you didn't even give her a chance."

"It's not her, it's me… which I get is cliché, but it's also true. I need to focus on work right now."

Natalie sighed. It was hard to argue with the importance of his work. *Of their work,* she reminded herself. "I still can't believe the effort the killer made to send a message about victim number five. I thought for sure Sheena Greenwood had a different killer. It's like he knew somehow."

"It's like he knew," Derek repeated slowly.

"That's what I said."

"I know. I'm... processing."

She turned the radio down. "I don't know how, but... If Sheena Greenwood's killer knew, or even suspected, that we thought she wasn't victim number four, then intentionally making a statement with number five to prove otherwise would make sense."

"Maybe. Unless…"

"Unless what?"

Derek stared straight out over the steering wheel. His eyes had gone dark. "Unless you were right about a second killer."

"And that killer left the number five to keep throwing us off," Natalie added, following where she believed he was headed.

"Exactly. There's no handwritten note to analyze this time, just a bloody lawn, so no way to be sure."

Neither spoke again for several minutes. The sound of the gravelly road filled the void as the Jeep made its way up the winding mountain pass. Though the bumpy ride rattled Natalie's brain, the thoughts within were far more disturbed.

As the two neared the top, she decided to break the silence. "One killer or two, both theories share a common problem about why the number five was left."

"They both assume the killer knew details of the investigation that only our team would know." Derek finished her thought as if he had already been thinking the same. "It doesn't seem possible, though."

"Well," she said carefully, knowing his allegiance to the team was stronger than her own. "The federal agents that helped analyze the handwriting were also in the know. Maybe there was a leak of information. We could start there."

Without acknowledgement, Derek veered off the main road onto a far bumpier path. Thick woods enclosed them as he maneuvered around downed branches and boulders.

"Where are we going again?" Natalie asked, feeling uneasy. She vented her window for fresh air, letting in the strong scents of pine and moss. The tall evergreens were magnificent, and so close she could reach out and touch them.

"We're almost there."

His response offered no comfort at all. They had already been driving for two hours. A stoic gloom had washed over Derek, and she couldn't help but feel it was spurred by more than their previous conversation.

Derek drove the rest of the way in silence, occasionally dodging ruts and debris with seemingly little effort. *He knew this path well*, Natalie realized. Her gut clenched reflexively, as if trying to warn her of danger ahead. Her whitened knuckles gripped even more tightly around the faded gray handhold on the passenger door. It felt useless to continue asking where they were headed. *They would be there soon.*

Ten minutes later, dusty brakes screeched to a halt outside a dilapidated wooden building that blended in with its surroundings. The facade had the charm of a log cabin mixed with the ghastliness of a haunted mansion. Derek pulled on the parking brake but didn't move from the vehicle.

"This was a restaurant, built over fifty years ago, when this was a thriving resort town. People would come from all over, but mostly from the city, to hike, camp, fish—you know, *get away from it all*," Derek said, still looking straight ahead rather than at the building or Natalie. "And if they got tired of fish or didn't catch any, they'd eat here. Until one day, the restaurant owner's wife got real sick. They packed up in the middle of the night, presumably to drive to the nearest town for medical care, and never returned. That was thirty years ago."

"What happened to her?"

"It's rumored that she died during the car ride to get help and was buried somewhere in these woods, but no one knows. She wasn't checked into any hospitals in the county, and it later came out that she and her husband were undocumented immigrants from Guatemala. They were probably too afraid of being deported to go to a hospital." He shook his head and blew out a breath. "The restaurant had flown under the radar due to its desolate location and the fact that Mr. Munoz, as he was known, had built this structure all on his own. With no deed recorded or taxes to be missed, the government didn't know to escheat the property. It laid abandoned and unacknowledged for about five years."

"Then what happened? And how do you know all this?" Natalie asked, her curiosity heightening.

"This place is special to me." At that, Derek opened the Jeep door and stepped outside in his hiking boots.

Natalie exited the vehicle as well, wishing she had chosen any other footwear besides heels as all four inches plunged into the muddy ground. She looked down to see her black suede, ankle-high boots with stiletto heels completely covered in the forest floor. "I wish you would have told me we were going into the woods. I would have dressed differently."

She wore a sequined blouse under a black moto-style, vegan-leather jacket, paired with ankle-length jeans and the now ruined booties. *At least they weren't her favorite shoes.*

Derek replied without as much as a glance in her direction. "You look fine. Come, there's something I want to share with you."

She begrudgingly followed Derek away from the Jeep, beyond the abandoned restaurant, and toward the edge of the woods where one of the trees was encircled in stones. In one hand, he carried a bouquet of flowers that she hadn't noticed him pull from the back seat of the Jeep, and in the other, a case file. As the gravity of the place took hold, she felt ashamed for being upset over shoes. *Someone had died here, likely of unnatural causes.* Once she took Derek's side, she forced words from her mouth in the form of a whisper. "Mrs. Munoz?"

Derek shook his head. "Five years after the building was abandoned, there was a murder here. A new resort area had sprung up closer to the city, and no one came here anymore after the restaurant closed. So, it was the perfect spot." He knelt down to replace the flowers from a vase that was buried in the ground. Both the old and new bouquets contained bright-yellow sunflowers mixed with sprigs of jasmine and lavender. "Her name was Carmen Franco."

"One of the Hood River Killer victims?"

"Yes, the seventh and final before the case went cold." He audibly inhaled and then released it with a shudder. "She was my mother."

Natalie silenced her gasp and instinctively took his hand. "Oh, Derek! I had no idea."

"Few people do, and I prefer it that way." He glanced her way and she gently nodded, tacitly offering her discretion. "Sorry I lied to you before when you asked about my mother's surname."

She again nodded her understanding. The *F* in his initials stood for Franco, not Fuertes.

"We had moved to a small town about ten miles from here. I was sixteen at the time and had gotten myself into trouble back home in LA, carrying drugs for some guys that turned out to be gang members. My mom had found out, scrapped together all the money she had, and moved us here practically overnight." His hand now trembled in hers. "I told my mom I hated her for making me leave behind all my friends, even threatened to run away and go back on my own. I was too stupid to see that she was only protecting me. I never should have gotten mixed up with those guys in LA."

"You were a teenager. We all make mistakes when we're young."

Derek took a step back, pulling his hand from hers. His breath was shallow and shaky. "My mistake cost my mother her life!"

"Derek, no. You *cannot* blame yourself for the horrible actions of someone else." She persisted toward him, reclaiming his hand.

His voice grew quieter, heavy with grief. "She would have never been in Oregon if it weren't for me."

"The weekend that Nick died, I was supposed to be with him, but I'd left for a last-minute work trip instead. All I've been able to think about is how, if I had gone with him, he wouldn't have been at that exact spot when that SUV entered the highway in the wrong direction. We probably would have left earlier so I could get ready for work the next day." She lifted her gaze to look Derek in the eyes. "Do you think it's my fault Nick was killed?"

"Of course not. It was the drunk driver's fault, not yours."

Natalie nodded. "I've been blaming myself for his death this whole time, and I now see it's as absurd as you being responsible for your mother's murder. It's the Hood River Killer's fault, *not yours*."

"They're two completely different situations."

"True, but they both have a common element of being in the wrong place at the wrong time. A factor we both believe we had control over, but did we really? And even if we did, does that mean we killed them?"

"No, but," he started and then stopped.

"Think about it," she continued. "You said it yourself that you were upset to move away from your friends. It wasn't your choice to move to Oregon, and even if moving was the best way to protect you, the two of you could have ended up anywhere else. It wasn't your fault, or hers, that she happened to move to a place where she was later killed. And you're certainly not to blame for the heinous acts of a serial killer."

Derek's jaw clenched and then relaxed. He let out a breath. "It might seem weird, but I come here to think."

"I don't think that's weird."

"It's just that," he said shakily, "she didn't get a proper burial, so I feel like her spirit, or whatever is left after, is still here."

Natalie recalled the case file in her mind. The body of victim number seven had been burned to ash, identified only by dental records. It was unlike any of the other murders, and arguably worse, since the medical examiner couldn't conclusively determine the cause of death or how much she may have suffered. Carmen Franco had been missing for nearly a year before her remains were found.

A few moments of silence passed between them, both staring solemnly at the flowers encircled in stones. Natalie squeezed his hand tight before releasing it and taking a step back. "I should give you some time alone with her."

"No, it's nice having you here. Please stay." Derek reached for her hand, which she immediately placed back into his.

"Okay."

"She would have liked you, by the way." His hazel eyes momentarily took hold of hers. "She was a feminist, like you, and boy could she argue any point across flawlessly."

Natalie opened her mouth, planning to protest that she wouldn't call herself a feminist *per se*, but then she closed it. She supposed she had a tendency to argue any point as well.

He continued, "She always said, 'Find a woman that constantly proves you wrong. That way, you're always learning.'"

"I would have liked her as well." Her heart broke for the woman she'd never meet, and for the son she left behind. She gave his hand a gentle squeeze and then found her gaze shifting around to the ominous structure behind them. "Is it still abandoned?"

"The government technically owns this land, but yeah, they've left it pretty much neglected. About five years after it happened, the county planned a public auction to sell the restaurant, but it got shut down by the State of Oregon due to being the site of an unsolved case. So, they boarded it up and here it sits." Derek gritted out the last words through his teeth, his frustration thinly veiled.

"Have you ever been inside?"

He shook his head. "I've reviewed all the evidence probably a million times, and I come here often to feel closer to her, but I could never bring myself to go inside that god-awful building."

Natalie rubbed her thumb across his trembling hand, finally understanding everything. If it were her, she'd want to burn the place down to the ground. Given that he probably had the same thought at some point, she didn't bother suggesting it. Being a law-abiding citizen, nonetheless an officer of the law, certainly had its drawbacks.

Without thinking, she used her free hand to scoop up a sizeable rock that she eyed near her muddy shoes. "Here," she said, handing him the stone. "I won't say a thing."

It only took seconds for the confusion in his eyes to shift into grateful understanding. Derek dropped her hand and assumed a pitcher's position, first holding the large stone at his chest and then cocking his arm back as far as it went. When he released his hand, the stone flew with tremendous force toward the dilapidated structure. The loud bang it made upon contact with the wooden boards echoed in the stillness of the forest.

Natalie placed another stone, slightly bigger than the first, in the palm of his open hand when he reached back without taking his eyes off the building. He hurled the second stone at the same boards with equal force and garnered an evener louder response. Meanwhile, Natalie had quickly gathered a collection of jagged rocks on the ground and nudged them toward his feet. He didn't hesitate to pick them up one at a time, throwing each harder than the last in rapid succession.

After several solid hits, one of the boards fell to expose the clouded edge of a window pane. Derek targeted the vulnerability and then dropped to his knees at the sound of glass shattering. His hand rested atop another stone, but he didn't move to lift it. His chest heaved and his whole body noticeably quaked while he quietly wept. Then, after several minutes, his body stilled.

True to her word, Natalie remained silent as the two stared at the building that had been the site of pure evil.

CHAPTER TWENTY-TWO

Charity Ball

Early September

Derek put all his force into a punch that resulted in an echoing thud. He loved Friday nights at the gym. The Friday before a long holiday weekend was even better. While hipsters and couples filled the city's gastropubs and rooftop bars, he enjoyed working out with no distractions. He threw several short jabs at the red punching bag in front of him before looking over his shoulder to observe Natalie doing the same. Well, *almost* no distractions.

"Nice hit. Just be sure to keep your other arm up in block position as you land the punch," he instructed.

Natalie corrected her form. "Got it. Thanks!" She threw several more punches—right, left, then right again. "Ten more minutes of this and then Chinese takeout, right?"

"That's the deal." Derek smiled as he landed a solid right hook and followed it up with a roundhouse kick.

Showoff, Natalie thought. Still, she was grateful for his help with her training over the past few weeks. Summer had flown by, and she felt far from ready to be starting the Academy in less than a month.

It hadn't helped that her former workout partner had been preoccupied lately. Natalie wondered how the rekindled relationship between Leah and Rhonda was going until her meandering thoughts landed on her own pitiful love life. *Right, left, right*—harder that time.

Ben had headed back to D.C. shortly after their failed attempt at a date. He had claimed he was needed on a more pressing case, but she couldn't help but feel responsible. *What if she had inadvertently hurt their case by causing him to leave?* Her only saving grace was that even Ben couldn't seem to make sense of the killer's abhorrent display of the number five with the last victim.

It was only a matter of time before there would be a number six. A fact she knew weighed heavily on Derek. He couldn't save his mother from such a fate; he *had* to save others. Peeking around her own punching bag, she watched him land multiple jabs in quick succession. She mimicked his movements and then dwelled on the case some more while getting through the last few minutes of what she considered physical torture.

After the gym and a well-deserved meal with gratifying amounts of sodium, Natalie propped her feet up on a strategically placed sofa cushion and sighed. "Thanks again for motivating me to work out tonight, but honestly… I never want to get off this couch again."

"Oh, come on. It wasn't that bad, was it?"

She flexed her arm before dropping it in her lap. "Ask me tomorrow."

Derek laughed. "I'll ask you during our morning run."

Natalie groaned but didn't object. They had gotten into a solid routine of morning runs followed by some type of strength training most evenings. She had also started attending his self-defense classes on Tuesdays and Thursdays, and although she would never admit it to him, she found them empowering. Moreover, she secretly hoped that their new routine was helping him as well.

It had been three weeks since that somber day in the woods. Derek had unburied his painful past from the depths of the earth, shared it with her, and then quickly locked it away in an impermeable vault. They hadn't spoken of that day or his mother since. Well-hidden as it was, she felt the presence of his pain as they sat there on the couch.

He cleared his throat. "Speaking of tomorrow, I have a favor to ask."

"I hope it doesn't involve manual labor." She attempted flexing her arm again. "That reminds me, I noticed some Epsom salts under the cabinet in the bathroom. Do you mind if I use some for a bath tonight?"

"Sure, go ahead." His cheeks detectably blushed before he continued. "No manual labor, but you will need to move off this couch—and wear something other than sweats."

She tilted her head, contemplating whether to take issue with his clear mockery of her preferred attire. *Everyone has their own coping mechanisms.* His, as she had learned, had been casual encounters. Hers was drinking wine and wearing sweatpants twenty-four seven. If he could kick his vice, she supposed she should try to do the same.

"Okay, the suspense is killing me. What's the favor?"

"Tomorrow night is the annual charity ball that the Portland Police Bureau hosts to raise funds for victims' families. While it's for a great cause, fancy parties make me anxious." Derek stood from the couch and walked toward the kitchen, empty takeout containers in hand. "Anyway, I have to go and could use a plus-one."

"Are you asking me to go or to help you find a date?" She smirked in his direction. "Because the latter may be easier."

"I'm asking you to go." His face lacked any signs of playfulness. "As a friend," he added. "And no more matchmaking, please. I'm done with dating."

She matched his sober tone. "Well, as long as it's not a date, I'm in. We might need to swing by my apartment tomorrow, though, so I can pick up something to wear."

"Thank you, Natalie! I'll owe you one. The only thing worse than going to these events is going alone."

There was a sadness in his voice that hit home. "I'm happy I can help."

***

The Kridel Grand Ballroom at the Portland Art Museum buzzed with an energy that felt unnatural to Derek. White and gold linens covered round tables dimly lit with candles, while ritzy patrons from throughout the city mingled in tuxedos and gowns. Nearly a thousand guests filled this year's charity ball, and yet only one in an elegant blue dress seemed to matter. His usual anxiety in large crowds became a distant memory at the sight of her smile from across the room.

Natalie was engaged in lively discussion with Marjorie Serrano when Derek returned to their table. He waited for a break in the conversation and then chimed in, "One Shirley Temple with extra cherries, per the lady's request."

"Thank you very much, kind sir." Natalie laughed and then placed the drink down after a quick sip. "Oh here, let me straighten this for you."

He noted how comfortable she looked as she fixed the crooked bow tie around his neck. "Tuxes aren't my thing. You seem to be a natural at all this stuff, though."

"Well, I attended a bunch of fundraiser events like these back in New York. My company would often host a table for us to network with prospective clients. It could be exhausting at times, but all the free champagne and gourmet meals made up for it." Her smile looked forced as she finished straightening his necktie. "Perks of the job, I suppose."

"This is one perk I'd normally rather pass on, but having you here really helps. Thanks again."

"It's my pleasure. And you look great in a tux!" Her eyes, currently a deep shade of blue, beamed at him. "Maggie was telling me about last year's event. You *seriously* showed up in jeans?"

"Like I said, tuxes aren't my thing." He scanned the room out of habit, looking for threats. When none were found, he relaxed. "Care to dance?"

Natalie raised her eyebrow at him. "Not into tuxes, but you know how to dance?"

"I know a few moves, and, for the record, it's easier to dance in more comfortable clothes." Her expression made him laugh for the first time that evening. "Don't look so surprised!"

"You are full of surprises, Detective Hartmann." With that, she stood and took his hand to be led to the dance floor.

The party band had transitioned from dinner music to an upbeat cover of "Uptown Funk." Natalie's jaw dropped when he started dancing, swirling her effortlessly around him. He bit back a smile. He may have been underselling his skill when he said he knew *a few moves*. Once her initial shock had subsided, he noticed her body went with the flow, matching his energy level.

The loud music and swift movements made it impossible to talk, but the smile on her face spoke volumes. She was enjoying herself, and his heart swelled. He couldn't ask for anything more. Even if temporary, her happiness in that moment, rather than all the grief he had witnessed for weeks, was the best gift ever. He would do anything he could to make it last.

A lively salsa was up next, followed by a set of swing. Derek twirled Natalie under his arm and then back out again, noting how well she was keeping up with his pace. She was evidently no stranger to the dance floor herself.

He smiled and realized he wasn't only happy that she was having a good time. In an unexpected turn of events, he was having a great time himself.

When the band finally took a break, the melodic voices of Zayn and Taylor Swift singing "I Don't Wanna Live Forever" played from the sound system. Breathless and grateful for a slower song, he felt Natalie melt into his arms as they swayed. She rested her head against his beating chest. His hand firmly supported the small of her back, while his thumb traced small circles on the skin exposed by the backless dress she wore.

He thought back to earlier that evening when she had first emerged from her bedroom in that silky, high-neck gown. The sapphire color brought out the blue in her eyes, the depths of which he could be happily lost in forever. She was the epitome of both beauty and elegance.

Seeing her ready to leave had taken his breath away, but it wasn't until she turned her back to him that his heart nearly stopped. He had been waiting all evening for the opportunity to caress her smooth skin left bare by the deep-V that stopped just above her perfect ass.

Her voice was breathy when she lifted her head toward his ear to talk over the music. "A few moves, huh?"

The heat of her mouth near his ear made him stiffen. He pulled back to look her in the face, fighting every urge in his body to not kiss her. "You're not bad yourself."

"Thanks," she laughed, "but seriously, where'd you learn to dance like that?"

He hesitated only a split second before responding. "My mom was a choreographer. She used to make me practice her dances with her, saying that dancing was a necessary skill to find a wife someday."

"Smart woman." Natalie then rested her head on his shoulder, squeezed him a tad tighter, and caressed the back of his neck with her fingers while they continued to sway.

When the song ended, they reluctantly let each other go and headed back toward their table, rather than staying for the upbeat techno mashup that followed. An assortment of small desserts awaited them, though it seemed the rest of the table had long finished theirs and left. Derek pulled out Natalie's chair for her to be seated.

"I think we've earned these," he said while reaching for a mini cheesecake.

"Can all that dancing count as tomorrow's cardio instead?"

He laughed. "Just this once."

"Great. Hand me that chocolate mousse, please. I'm going to savor every bite."

***

"Oh, that's much better." Natalie bent down to pick up her strappy heels after immediately kicking them off at the front door. "My feet are killing me, but it was worth it. I had a fun time tonight, Derek. Thank you."

"It's me that should be thanking you. Honestly, I thought bringing you to the gala would help make the night tolerable. I never expected to have such an amazing evening." Derek kicked off his shoes as well and tossed down the bow tie that he'd promptly removed in the car.

They both moved toward the center of the living room. Tux and Cal ran out from Derek's bedroom to greet them by jumping on the couch and meowing until sufficiently petted.

"Aww, did you miss us?" Natalie asked in a higher than usual voice. Both cats responded by rubbing their heads against the hand she offered.

"They clearly missed *you*."

"Well, they sleep in your room for whatever reason. Not that it's a competition or anything." A nervous laugh escaped her lips. "Why are you so surprised that you had a good time tonight?"

"I never do at those things." He shrugged, then turned away and stroked Cal's back. "I don't enjoy being in large crowds of people. It's like… the more people I'm around, the more alone and insignificant I feel. Like I could just disappear, and no one would notice. It's stupid."

"It's not stupid." She reached for his shoulder. Her desire to comfort him was instinctual, but not out of pity. She felt a connection, a closeness, when he revealed small pieces of himself. And it left her wanting more.

"Well, I didn't feel that way tonight. So, thank you."

"Derek," she said softly, "I want you to know it meant a lot to me that you shared about your mother teaching you to dance. I'm sure that wasn't easy for you."

"Actually, it was nice to remember her doing something she had loved." He turned to face her, the tenderness in his hazel eyes tugging at her heart. "Too often I only think about how things ended, but she believed in living life to its fullest. She would be proud that I lived mine tonight, with you."

Her heart lost the tug-of-war that had been waging inside her for weeks. In the absence of words, she threw her arms around his neck in a long hug. When she finally pulled away, familiar feelings of guilt and fear overwhelmed her. "It's getting late… I should probably turn in for the night. Good night, Derek."

"Good night," he said as she rushed off to her bedroom.

She closed the door behind her and sank down against it. They were having a moment, and, *of course*, she felt the need to end it. *What was wrong with her?* The shoes in her hand mocked her. Tossing them into a pile in the closet, she groaned and pulled herself off the floor. As difficult as it would be, she knew she needed to go back out there and explain.

She turned the doorknob as slowly as possible and pulled the door open, expecting to see Derek still standing where she left him. Except he had gone into his bedroom already. She crossed the living room, turned back, hesitated, and then turned back again until she stood in front of his door. The fist she held up froze midair. *Just knock,* she told herself. *But what would she even say?*

Before she lost the nerve, her fist tapped on the door. The door flung inward, and Derek stood there with his white tuxedo shirt unbuttoned. His tan, muscular chest practically glistened.

"Natalie, is everything okay?"

"Yes. No. I'm sorry." She struggled to get out each word. "I shouldn't have run off like that."

"Was it something I said?"

"No, it's me. I was starting to feel things that…" Natalie trailed off, her mind going blank until she realized she was staring at his chest. She moved her focus to his eyes instead, which did not help. "It's hard to think straight with you looking like that. I should probably go again."

"Natalie, wait," he said after she had turned away. Then he laughed.

What the… Why was he laughing? She swung back around. "What's so funny?"

"Nothing. Sorry. I was just thinking how I can relate." When she squinted in confusion, he took a step forward into the doorframe. "I can't think straight any time I'm around you."

"Oh." The single syllable was all her mouth could manage. Their bodies were only inches apart, and when she angled her face up toward his, their lips were even closer. She felt his warm breath on hers, but he held steady. This was her move to make, and they both knew it.

Inhibitions be damned. She placed her hand on his bare chest, then dragged her fingers over the smooth yet firm surface. As if it had an agenda of its own, her hand traveled across both his pecs before making its way down along his ridiculous abs. His muscles tightened under her touch. All her self-restraint and worries disappeared. *This was happening.* Instinct took over as she closed her eyes and moved toward his waiting lips.

A knock on the door jolted them both back before their lips met. *Who in the hell could that be?*

CHAPTER TWENTY-THREE

The Unexpected Guest

"Hello, can I help you?" Derek asked as he opened the door wide after a quick check through the peephole.

"I sure hope you can." The bleach-blond woman standing in the hall drew out each word provocatively while eyeing his bare chest up and down.

Natalie, who was still standing in a daze by Derek's bedroom door, was alarmed by the familiar voice. "Mom?"

Linda Blackwood peeked her head in through the doorway. "Nattie! Oh, good. I found the right place. Wow, don't you look pretty. I hope I'm not *interrupting* anything." She smiled and ogled Derek again, prompting him to re-button his shirt.

"What? How did you…? Why are you…? It's the middle of the night, Mom. What are you doing here?"

"Please come in, ma'am." Derek stepped aside and then closed the door behind her.

"Oh, please call me Linda. Ma'am makes me sound like an old lady."

Natalie cleared her throat impatiently.

"I'm sorry to come so late. I was here earlier, but no one was home. Then I saw your lights on and thought I'd try again." Linda moved toward the living room and dropped a purse that looked like a bowling bag onto the couch. She tilted her head toward Natalie. "I like the blond hair, Nattie. It suits you! And now you look just like your mama."

Natalie groaned. "Please stop calling me Nattie. What are you doing here from California? And how did you even know where to find me?"

"Does a mother need a reason to want to see her daughter?" Linda pretended to take offense, *poorly.*

"Why aren't you answering my questions?" *And what is the boiling point of brain?* Natalie wondered.

Derek made his way into the kitchen. "Can I get you anything to drink or eat?"

"Oh, thank you. A glass of water would be great. It was a long drive. Can I use your bathroom too?"

"Of course. It's right over there."

"Thank you so much." Linda darted straight to the bathroom, avoiding Natalie's burning glare.

Once Linda was out of sight, Natalie pulled her own hair in anguish. "Oh my gosh, Derek. I am so sorry about this! I have no idea what she's doing here."

"Don't worry about it. It's fine." Derek took a drink of water that he had poured for himself and then held out a glass for Natalie, which she took absentmindedly.

Natalie felt as if she might implode. Her mother was finding novel ways of embarrassing her, even as an adult. "It is definitely *not* fine! I haven't seen her in years, and then she shows up here in the middle of the night out of nowhere. *Who does that?"*

"Natalie," Derek said in a hushed tone, "she's your mother and probably just misses you. She's welcome to stay here either way. I'll go put some fresh sheets on my bed for her."

"And where will you sleep?" She spoke before thinking and then blushed at the memory of their interrupted encounter.

"I'll take the couch," he said nonchalantly.

"No, no, no. If anyone is being put out by my mother, it's going to be me. I'll sleep on the couch, and she can use my room." *This was non-negotiable.*

Linda returned from the bathroom before Derek could argue. "Well, I feel *much better.* Nattie, honey, you might want to light a candle or something in there, though."

"Mom!" Natalie growled under her breath and shook her head.

Derek's tight grin appeared to be holding back laughter. "Here's that glass of water, ma'am."

"It's Linda, and thank you, handsome." She took the glass offered and drank the full contents in one gulp.

"Well, I should let you two catch up, but I'll be right in there if you need anything." Derek pointed to his bedroom before heading inside and closing the door behind him.

Natalie took a deep inhale and let it out slowly. "Please, just tell me why you're here, Mom."

"Well, I didn't want you to be upset, but if you must know, I got evicted from my apartment last week. Then I started thinkin' that since I'm not working right now, I should come up and see you."

"Last week? Where have you been staying this whole time?"

"In my car. It took me a few days to drive here anyway, so it really hasn't been that long. I'm just glad I kept my storage unit all those years, even though you always gave me a hard time about it."

"Oh no, Mom. Not again." Natalie sat on the couch to stabilize herself and put her face in her hands. "Why didn't you ask me for help?" Then she sat up straight. "Wait, I've been transferring rent money into your account each month. Why were you evicted?"

Linda looked apologetic for the first time since she arrived. "That's why I didn't want to tell you. I knew you would be upset."

"*Why, Mom?*" Natalie felt her limited patience wane.

"You know that guy Kenny I met a few months ago?"

Natalie had already heard more than she had cared to about Linda's latest conquest, Kenny, in painstaking detail. She nodded to get her mother to continue.

"Well, he introduced me to a friend of his that's a professional blackjack player. He guaranteed he could double my money in a single trip to Vegas, but he needed a minimum investment of ten thousand dollars. I saved up the rent money for five months to give it to him, and then he disappeared."

Natalie sprang from the couch, her blood pressure skyrocketing. "Mom! Are you kidding me? How could you fall for something so idiotic?"

Linda went on the defense. "Kenny told me he had seen him do it a bunch of times before. It was a solid investment! I figured he'd double the money, and then I could pay my past due rent *plus* pay you back. Win-win. How was I supposed to know he would cheat me?"

"First, blackjack is gambling, *not an investment.* Second, anyone with half a brain would know he was going to take your money! It's obvious he was a con man, Mom!" Natalie paced the living room, fighting back angry tears. "And you didn't have to pay me back. I wanted to help you out by paying your rent. I can't even...."

"Well, I'm sorry I'm not as smart as you."

"Clearly." Natalie regretted the comment as soon as it came out, but it was too late to take back. And she was too livid to apologize. *She'd add it to her long list of things to feel guilty about later.* "It's late. We should get some sleep and figure things out in the morning. I'll show you to my room."

***

Sleep was a joke, Natalie thought as she tossed and turned on the couch. *Why couldn't she have been born into a normal family? Why was life so unfair?*

Self-pity soon morphed into self-consciousness and embarrassment. *How much had Derek heard of their argument?*

It wasn't like she had been keeping her voice down. Her temper had felt out of her control.

Natalie obsessed over that for a while longer until she heard Derek emerge from his room. Pretending to be asleep, she discreetly peeked one eye open and watched him tiptoe toward the coffee machine. It was nice that he was trying not to wake her, she thought, which consequently helped her avoid another uncomfortable conversation. Or at least it would have, if not for her mother appearing next.

"Mmm, that coffee smells good."

"Good morning, ma'am. I mean, Linda," Derek said. "It's about ready. Did you sleep well?"

"Oh, yes. That bed was like sleepin' on a cloud. Thanks so much for having me."

Natalie yawned and stretched from the couch as if just waking up. "What time is it?"

"About six," Linda replied.

Right. Morning people, Natalie thought. She couldn't be more different from her mother, but she supposed that was a good thing. "I'm going to need some of that coffee, too."

Derek looked at her with a baffled face. "You don't drink coffee. Good morning, by the way."

His smile in her direction almost made her feel better about the situation with her mother. *Almost.* "Good morning, Derek. I hope we didn't keep you up last night with our talking."

"No, I was out like a light as soon as my head hit the pillow. Must have been all the dancing." Derek winked at her, and she wondered if that meant he had, in fact, heard them.

"Oh, Nattie *loves* to dance. Weren't you and Nick taking dance classes in New York, honey?" Linda asked cheerily.

"Yes, we had been. Nick had two left feet, but it was sweet that he tried." The memory made Natalie smile and feel uncomfortable at the same time.

"I wish I could have met him." Linda shook her head. "I would have flown out to New York for the wedding if you two hadn't decided to elope. But it is what it is."

"You eloped?" Derek asked, looking even more puzzled than he had when she asked for coffee.

Natalie looked away out of guilt, almost certain he had seen her watching the video footage of her large New York wedding. She stood from the couch, walked toward the kitchen, and accepted the mug he handed her. "It was just easier. Thanks for the coffee."

"So, how long have you two been together?" Linda motioned between them and then turned to Derek. "My daughter never tells me anything."

"We're not *together*, Mom." Her cheeks burned with embarrassment. "Derek's just helping me out while I prepare for the Police Academy."

"That's right. You're a detective." Linda smiled at Derek in her usual flirtatious manner. "Jessica mentioned that when she told me where to find you," she directed at Natalie.

Jessica. Of course, that's how her mother had found her. Natalie made a mental note to kill her later.

"Have you ever been to Portland before?" Derek asked Linda.

"Oh, no. I hardly go anywhere. This has already been quite the adventure."

"You'll have to check out the local sights while you're here. A buddy of mine runs jet boat tours on the Willamette. I can get us tickets." Excitement poured out of Derek's voice. "There should also be some fun Labor Day events going on this weekend."

Natalie spoke up before her mother could. "That sounds really nice, Derek, but my mom and I should probably spend today figuring out where she is going to stay."

Derek shrugged. "She's welcome to stay here. Besides, it's a holiday weekend. Hotels are likely booked."

"I meant an apartment, not a hotel, and there's a lot to figure out. I don't have time to be off gallivanting. I'm going to go take a shower." Natalie stormed out of the room to hide the bitter tears forming.

Once Natalie was in the bathroom, Linda placed her coffee mug down on the kitchen table and sat. "You'll have to excuse my daughter. She doesn't know how to have fun, but I suppose that's my fault. She was always the responsible one in the family."

"It's okay. I didn't realize you were moving here to Portland."

"Oh, I'm not. California is my home, always will be. I'm just living out of my car for the moment, and Natalie doesn't approve."

Derek was starting to understand the relationship between Natalie and her mother a little better. "Well, it's none of my business, but I'd have to agree it's not a safe option."

"I suppose that's true, especially here in Portland. I've been following those murders on the news. So horrible." Linda sipped her coffee. "I'm hopin' I can convince Nattie to come back home with me. She's been away too long."

"Oh, I see." His heart sank. He hadn't considered the possibility of Natalie leaving with her mom, but it made sense. She would be safer if she left Portland. *Shouldn't he want that for her?*

Natalie showered in record time, wanting to leave Derek alone with her mother for the shortest amount of time humanly possible. Her stress levels were elevated enough without also having to worry about the earful that Derek was likely getting. She patted her face with the towel to ensure her eyes were dry, quickly redressed, and reemerged into the living room. To her astonishment, the room was empty.

A note sat on the granite countertop: *Headed to Marty's to talk through the case. I saved you some extra coffee. Have a good day with your mom! I'll see you later tonight—Derek.*

Great, Natalie thought. *Linda scared him out of his own house.*

"Mom? Are you in there?" She peered through the partially open bedroom door. Empty as well. *Where the hell did she go?*

Natalie retrieved her phone from the coffee table near the couch where she had attempted to sleep. Memories of her restless night had her yawning. She hit 'Mom' from her favorites.

Linda's annoyingly chipper voice soon came through the other end. "Hi there, Nattie! You're probably wonderin' where I went."

"Yes, I am, and please stop calling me Nattie. That's not my name."

"I know your name, *Natalya*. We just called you Nattie ever since you were a little girl."

"Well, I'm not a little girl anymore, and I go by Natalie now. Anyway, where are you?"

"After your hunk left," Linda started.

"He's not my… never mind. You were saying?"

"I decided to get a quick bite to eat, since I know you're not much of a morning person. I'm havin' me an egg McMuffin and a second cup of coffee. If you wanna join me, I'm at the end of your block."

"No, thanks. I'll see you when you get back." Natalie hung up the phone and immediately felt guilty for being rude to her mother. Again.

She went into the kitchen and poured herself another cup of coffee. *It was going to be a long day.*

CHAPTER TWENTY-FOUR

Childhood Trauma

Derek walked along the riverfront path later that evening, soaking in the last rays of warmth. At seventy-five degrees and sunny during the afternoon hours, it had been a beautiful day. The city teemed with people, mostly local tourists from surrounding Oregon counties, enjoying the long weekend on and near the river. Tour boats sped up and down the Willamette, earning glares from fishermen in small metal boats jostled in their wake. Families picnicked in parks that dotted the shoreline. Couples dined on rooftop patios.

As he did on most holidays, Derek found himself alone. He quickly shook off the twinges of self-pity, though. There were more important matters worthy of his concern. Catching a killer that would surely strike again being at the top of that list. Three weeks had passed since the bloody display of the number five at the park, and yet they were no closer to identifying a suspect than when he held the first handwritten note.

He had spent the first half of the day rehashing all the details with Marty out at his cabin in the woods, but that didn't stop him from replaying it all again in his head.

The victims: *Nicole Brook, Pamela Sinclair, Sylvia Porter, Sheena Greenwood, Maria Velarde.*

Their ages: *29, 38, 34, 20, 46.*

Locations found: *Alley, parking garage, abandoned warehouse, bedroom, and Washington Park—all within Portland city limits.*

Murder weapons: *Box cutter, rope, paring knife…* Derek mentally recoiled and corrected himself. *Natalie's paring knife… a plastic bag, and… needles? Was that all that had been used to kill Maria Velarde?* The autopsy had confirmed that she had been heavily drugged with sedatives and blood thinners. Her arms and legs had multiple puncture wounds from the needles used to drain the blood from her body.

There was no apparent pattern to any of it. The first two victims had similar profiles to numbers three and seven in the Hood River killings, but Sylvia Porter and the rest that followed did not. Sheena Greenwood's murder broke the mold even further, both due to the nature of the attack and different handwriting on the note. And then there was Maria Velarde. Her raven black hair and kind face reminded Derek so much of his own mother. He couldn't shake that thought.

He was too close to it. He wondered if he should step down from the case. There must be someone better suited to lead the task force. He was failing at his job, and that meant another woman would pay the ultimate price— soon. Math wasn't Derek's strong suit, but he knew that five victims in less than three months meant that three weeks was already longer than the average time between murders. *The next killing was imminent.*

That last thought, combined with the growing chill in the air, sent shivers throughout his body. He zipped up the casual hooded sweatshirt he wore and squinted toward the west, where the cloud-filled sky was turning magnificent shades of red and pink.

A runner flew past him. Although she was moving like the wind, he recognized her as the woman who was at the bar with Natalie the night they had met. She turned left on the path and then became a distant shadow in the twilight. At the risk of sounding like a madman, Derek wanted to yell out for her to hurry home and lock her doors and windows, but she was gone.

Despite the constant media coverage, people were still going about their lives as if everything were normal. *Were they all that desensitized to death?* He wanted to warn everyone to shelter in place. He had pleaded with the Mayor's Office to issue a city-wide curfew but was told it would be too disruptive. The fact that it was an election year had nothing to do with it, they claimed. *Sure.*

A light drizzle began as Derek quickened his pace toward home. He had stayed away as long as possible to give Natalie the privacy he could tell she desired. He hoped she had at least enjoyed some of the beautiful day, but he could immediately tell that was not the case upon entering his condo.

Natalie was curled on the couch in her usual sweatpants with a cat on either side. Her hair was loosely piled atop her head with a pencil through it, and she held a glass of red wine in her hand. An empty wine bottle sat next to her laptop on the coffee table. "Hey, I wasn't sure when you'd be back. Sorry if my mom scared you off this morning."

"No, not at all. I just wanted to give you two a little time alone."

"Ha! I'm not sure time alone is what we needed. We spent the whole day fighting, and then she called it an early night. She's asleep in my room."

Derek walked over to the couch and sat at the other end. "Are you okay?"

"No, and I'm tired of pretending I am," she said, sounding as dejected as she looked.

"Is there anything I can do to help?"

Natalie shook her head, raised the glass of wine to her mouth, and then stopped. "I've spent my whole life trying not to be like my mother."

"And you're worried that you might be anyway?"

"No, with the exception of poor judgment in men, I could *not* be more different from her. I've succeeded there."

"Oh, okay." He waited for her to go on, confused as to what the issue might be.

"In trying to not be my mother, I'm afraid I've become someone much worse. I didn't realize it until today, but I'm a lot like my father. Cold, critical, selfish, short-tempered…"

"You're not any of those things," he interrupted. *Why couldn't she see herself the way he did?*

"You don't know me very well, then."

"I know you were warm and selfless when you helped Sylvia out of a bad situation."

"Some good my help did her." Natalie took a long drink.

"That wasn't your fault." Derek reached out for the wineglass in her hand. "Let's talk without this. You're a good person, Natalie. I mean, come on, you want to become a police officer to help people. That's pretty selfless."

She sighed and turned away from him. "I tell myself that I'm doing it to help people, but if I'm being honest, my true motive is completely selfish. I want to become a police officer so I can protect myself."

"It's natural to want to protect yourself. That's not selfish."

"It felt pretty selfish when I did it as a child." Natalie pulled the pencil out of her hair, rested her head on the arm of the couch, and curled into a fetal position with her feet pointed toward him. "My dad, Frank, used to beat up my brothers. It didn't happen often, but when it did, it was bad. I didn't do anything to help them… to protect myself."

Derek lifted his arm, wanting to reach out and hold her, but decided to give her some space instead. "That's awful that you were put in that position. But you were right to protect yourself. You were just a child. You couldn't have stopped it."

"My brothers and I were sitting at the dinner table the first time I remember it happening." Natalie spoke calmly, as if disconnected from her emotions. "I was ten years old, and my older brother, Corey, was twelve. Our younger brother, Ivan, was only a toddler at two years old, sitting in his high chair. My mom had been working that night, and Frank had been eating his meal in front of the TV while sorting through the mail. Then he got to the phone bill."

She lifted her head from the couch and looked at him with wide eyes. "You see, Corey had recently gotten back from summer camp, where he had met a girl that lived in northern California." Looking away again, she continued, "Anyway, there were some long-distance phone charges, as this was before the days of cell phones or unlimited calling plans. Frank accused Corey and quickly got enraged when my brother said it wasn't him that had made the calls. Things escalated so fast. Frank yelled, 'don't insult my intelligence' and something about lying being disrespectful. He had a crazy look in his eyes. Corey pushed away from the dinner table and ran through the kitchen and into the laundry room around the corner.

"I couldn't see them anymore, but I'll never forget the sound of my brother being slammed against the washing machine over and over. He cried for help, but I just sat there, frozen at the table, feeling like I would be invisible as long as I didn't move." She quickly wiped at her face.

Derek noted that she referred to her father as Frank, distancing herself from him by discarding their relation. It was a coping mechanism often exhibited by trauma victims in his experience. He sat quietly while she continued.

"The next major incident was a couple years later. Corey was a freshman in high school and had gotten a 'C' and some comments on his report card stating that he was the class clown. Frank was *furious*. It started off as a long lecture with him asking things like, 'Do you think you're a comedian?' and 'Why can't you be more like your sister?'

"Our mom was home this time, quiet at first, but she yelled for him to stop after the first couple of swings at Corey. That was the first time I saw him lay hands on my mother. He pulled her hair so hard that she fell to the ground, and then he went back to hitting my brother."

Derek reached out and took her hand in his. "Natalie, I'm so sorry that your family went through that."

"I had sneaked into my parents' room that time to use their phone and called the police. By the time they arrived, things had already calmed down. Frank answered the door, surprised to see them, and acted like nothing had happened. The officers then questioned my mother, who also lied and said everything was fine. They didn't even step inside the house or ask to talk to me or my brother. They took her word for it and left." Natalie swatted away more tears as she sat up on the couch. "I don't think I've ever forgiven my mother for that."

Without hesitation, Derek wrapped his arm around Natalie, wanting to block out the world for her. He thought back to her strong reaction on the ride-along that day with a new sense of clarity. The police had failed her family, just as he would have failed Sylvia if not for Natalie. He wanted to help her understand that she was already making a difference in the world, in his world, but the words eluded him.

"Things only got worse from there," she continued. "Corey was kicked out of the house at seventeen, after another beating. He starting couch surfing with various friends and soon got into the wrong crowd, drinking heavily and doing drugs. Meanwhile, Frank started focusing his anger on my younger brother, Ivan, who was only seven years old when Corey left. Ivan struggled in school from a young age and was often getting himself into trouble. I was a teenager at that point and avoided home as much as possible by hanging out with my friends. And even when I was home, I stayed in my room and kept to myself.

"Then I moved out as soon as I turned eighteen and didn't look back. Poor Ivan was left all on his own to deal with our father. I later learned that his beatings were more frequent than with Corey. My mother stepped in to break things up when she could, but she often worked when Frank was home. I had pleaded with her so many times to divorce him, but she wouldn't. She said that she wanted to wait until Ivan graduated high school."

Her shoulders lifted under his arm and then dropped with a sigh. "He never graduated, though. When Ivan was sixteen, Frank found yet another bad report card that he had hidden, not thinking that the school would call to follow-up. Frank had cornered my brother in his room, where Ivan had been keeping a gun under his bed. He had apparently gotten it off some kid at school, who had stolen it from his parents. According to Frank's statement to the police, Ivan pointed the gun at him first, but then he turned the gun on himself and pulled the trigger."

Natalie spoke matter-of-factly, an icy wall around her. "A few weeks later, after the funeral, Corey OD'd on ecstasy at a party. It was hard to say if it was intentional or not. I had moved to New York already and was too afraid to come back for any of the funerals, but all I had told my mother is that I didn't want to go.

"When we were fighting today, she brought up how much me not being there had hurt her. My response was, 'Good.'" Natalie pulled herself out from under his arm and looked him point blank. "You still think I'm not cold and selfish?"

He was still trying to process it all: an abusive father, a teenage suicide, another death by overdose, a grieving mother, and a traumatized daughter that had clearly not come to terms with any of it.

"I think you are angry, and understandably so, about everything that happened. And you're angry at your mother for her role in it."

"You know who else had anger issues?" Natalie asked rhetorically.

"When you were fighting with your mom earlier today, did you get physical with her?"

"No. Of course not!"

"Then you're not your father, Natalie. It's like you helped me to see, you can't blame yourself for the bad actions of another person."

"You don't understand. I could have done *something* to help Ivan, but I didn't even try." Tears rolled freely down her face. "I'm a horrible person. You're right that I'm angry at my mother, which is why I hurt her with my words, but I'm angriest at myself."

Derek intercepted the wineglass on the table when Natalie reached for it. "Alcohol is not the answer. It's self-destructive."

"Maybe I want to self-destruct. Did you ever think of that? Huh?" Natalie's voice cracked as she waved her arms in the air. "My existence isn't fair! Why did he hurt them but leave me alone? Why are they gone when I'm not?"

"Survivor's guilt is natural, but you *need* to forgive yourself, Natalie. Then, if you want, you can decide to forgive your mother and start to help each other move forward."

At that, Natalie collapsed back into his arms, her muffled sobs pouring into his chest. "I'm sorry I'm such a mess."

"There's no need to apologize to me." Derek stroked the back of her silky hair. "You should get some sleep, though, and we can talk more in the morning. Take my room tonight, and I'll take the couch."

She peeled herself out of his arms, wiping her face as she did. "I've inconvenienced you enough. I can't take your room too, unless…"

"Unless what?"

"Never mind. A good night's sleep sounds nice. Thanks." She half-stood and stumbled back onto the couch. "Do you mind helping me into bed?"

He braced her elbow as she stood again, then led her across the living room. Once in his bedroom, Natalie closed the door and leaned against it. "Stay with me."

"What?"

Before he could process what was happening, Natalie was kissing him. She had wrapped both of her arms around his neck and was running her hands through his hair. Her kiss was forceful at first, and then her lips became playful and gentle. Full of need, Derek kissed her back, even though he knew he shouldn't. *Would she even remember kissing him in the morning?*

Her hands soon moved from his hair to his chest and then slid down to fumble with the waistband of his jeans. Derek forced himself to take a step back. "Natalie, we can't. You're drunk and upset. You don't know what you're doing."

"*You* don't know what *you're* doing!" she slurred back. "Don't you want me?"

"Not like this."

"How about like this?" In an instant, she pulled the drawstring of her oversized sweatpants and kicked them away. She stood before him in full lighting wearing nothing but a lacy, hot pink thong and a black tank top.

"Natalie, please." He reached for her sweats on the ground to help her redress as she moved toward the bed.

"Oh, I forgot." She pulled the tank over her head and tossed it at him. "How's this?"

He was temporarily stunned when Natalie arched back against his mahogany bed post. She stared at him seductively while running her hands up her body to cup her exposed, perky breasts. "Do you want me now, Derek?"

He took a step forward and stopped. *She's drunk, she's drunk, she's drunk,* he reminded himself. *Did she have any idea how much she was torturing him?* He reached for the throw blanket at the foot of his bed. "Let's get you covered up."

At the same time, Natalie rolled on top of the blanket, and, before he knew it, he was stumbling on top of her. He immediately pushed himself up onto his forearms to avoid crushing her with his full weight. "I'm so sorry. Are you okay?"

Her sultry eyes stared up at him. "If you kiss me, it'll make it all better."

Derek felt the heat of her naked body pressed against him. He didn't know if he had the willpower to do what was necessary. But then he heard her voice in his head saying, 'Maybe I want to self-destruct.' *Not on his watch.* He pressed himself up and stepped away from the bed.

"Let's talk in the morning." He turned to leave the room and heard a loud scoff.

"I knew it!" Natalie proclaimed.

He stopped but kept his back to her to avoid further temptation. "Knew what?"

"I saw the way you looked at me after the charity ball. But now that you know my history, that look is gone. You don't want the *real* me." Soft cries followed her statement.

"That's not it at all. I'm trying to do the right thing, Natalie. *You're drunk.*"

"Say what you want, but I know the truth. It was a test, and you failed. You can turn around by the way, I've covered myself."

Derek spun around. "You were *testing* me? And how did I *fail* by doing the *right* thing? I can't believe we're even having this conversation." He reminded himself, yet again, that she was drunk. Arguing with her was pointless.

Natalie had pulled the bedspread over herself but was still lying on her back. Her eyes were fixed on the ceiling. "It's the same reason I told Nick I was an only child and never let him meet my mother. He also never knew about Jared, or anything bad that has ever happened to me. In his eyes, I was *perfect*.

"So, I put on fancy dresses, went to lavish galas, laughed, smiled, and pretended that I belonged up on that high pedestal. But that wasn't me. I didn't want to go to big parties and act like I was having fun when I was really a wreck inside." She glanced at him, and it pained him to think she might also be referring to the charity ball. "I don't even deserve to be alive, let alone enjoy myself. I've often thought about just ending it all, almost did once, but I can't even do that."

The vise around his heart tightened. "Natalie…"

"Nick didn't know that, either." She laughed weakly between sniffles. "I'm not even a natural blonde, but Nick had thought I was. I had dyed my hair to change my look when I first moved to New York and then kept up the lie. *That* was the Natalie that Nick loved. And now you've confirmed what I've always known: It's the only Natalie that anyone *could* love."

"That's not true." Derek softened his voice to match the sadness in hers. He could tell that she truly believed her words, and it broke his heart. He took several steps forward to peer down at her face.

Her eyes were closed. Her breath was shallow. She had fallen asleep.

Derek leaned down to place a kiss on her forehead. *He would have to tell her how wrong she was another time.*

CHAPTER TWENTY-FIVE

Labor Day

Derek plopped down on the couch with a beer and was greeted by Tux rubbing against his leg. Cal hadn't bothered to move from his spot on one of the kitchen chairs, but he vocalized his affection from across the room with several meows. Derek reached down to pet Tux. "At least I still have you, buddy."

He didn't think the day could get any worse. His heated interaction with Natalie that morning had begun with her apologizing for her drunken behavior the night before, *which she at least admitted remembering*, but then she quickly added how grateful she was that nothing had happened between them. He didn't consider their kiss *nothing*, but the real salt in the wound was how much she had stressed that them getting together would have been a *huge mistake*.

She had gone on and on about it, saying that it was for the best that her mother had interrupted them the night of the charity ball as well. A romantic relationship between them would be a disaster and was *never going to happen*. "They were better off as friends," she had said. The cherry on top was when she asked if he could please forget that night had ever happened, same as she did after their first kiss in the kitchen.

It had hurt him deeply, but not knowing how to tell her that, he had instead suggested the opposite of what he wanted—for her to go back to California with her mother. The shock on Natalie's face when he had said "it would be for the best" let him know she hadn't even been considering it before. He had attempted to explain by adding that he meant she should only go *temporarily* to help her mom get settled into a new apartment, but the damage had already been done.

Natalie had next asked him if he would mind caring for Tux, temporarily, until she could fly back for him. Then she packed up the rest of her belongings. Within an hour, she and her mother were headed south on I-5 toward San Diego. He missed her already. He sat alone with his thoughts for the next hour until his phone rang.

"Hey, Romeo, what do you and Natalie have going on for the holiday?" Marty asked. "I came into the city today to escape my fortress of solitude and enjoy the nice weather. Wouldn't mind some company if you're free, but I also don't want to impose."

"Oh, Marty, I really screwed things up."

"What's wrong?"

"It's Natalie. She's gone."

"What do you mean *she's gone?* Where did she go?"

"Back home to California with her mother. It's kind of a long story, but her mom had shown up here a couple of days ago unexpectedly. Natalie didn't take it so well, and then this morning I suggested, *like an idiot*, that she travel back with her."

"Is she coming back?"

"I don't know. I'm hoping it's just temporary until her mother is settled, but I really don't know. I was a total jerk, Marty. *How do I undo it?*" He sounded only half as desperate as he felt.

"Call her up and tell her you didn't mean it."

"I don't think that's going to be enough. She was pretty heated when she left."

"You love this girl, don't you?"

Derek paused for a moment, trying to decide how much truth to share. "Yeah, but how do *you* know that?"

Marty let out his signature chuckle, deep and raspy, with a hint of creepy to those that didn't know him as well. "I'm very perceptive. But it doesn't take a detective to crack that case. You've been head over heels since you first met her. Everyone knows it, except probably her, and it seems you, too."

"Good to know."

"My point is, lover boy," Marty continued, "you need to tell her how you feel."

"I don't know if I can do that, not yet at least. Besides, it's probably for the best… safer," he corrected, "for her to be out of Portland until this killer is caught."

"Where in California is she headed?"

"San Diego. It's where she's from, although she moved away years ago…" Derek's thoughts trailed off to the reason she had moved. *Oh no! Why hadn't he thought of it sooner?* He had pushed her out of the frying pan, straight into the fire. "Marty, sorry to spoil your holiday, but can you meet me at the station? I need to look into something… someone, I mean. Natalie might still be in danger."

Fifteen minutes later, Derek unlocked the door to the station and ushered Marty inside. The smell of Pine Sol and disinfectants assaulted their senses without the usual smell of burnt coffee to mask it. Derek intended to fix that by brewing a fresh pot immediately. He side-stepped a cart that the night cleaning crew had abandoned and made his way through the empty station toward the break room.

Marty coughed and fanned his hand at the fumes in the air. "Are you going to tell me what we are doing here while the rest of the city is out enjoying the holiday?"

"Thanks for coming. I wouldn't have asked you if it wasn't important. I need help searching location records for a man I believe to be dangerous. His name is Jared Fletcher. He was a Marine and MP, stationed near San Diego about twelve years ago." He searched his memory for any other details Natalie had shared. "Tall guy, blue eyes, I think. That's all we have, but I need to find out where he is now."

Derek scooped fresh coffee into the filter and hit brew on the machine while Marty eyed him suspiciously. When the water started percolating, Marty finally asked, "Ex-boyfriend?"

He nodded. "It's not what you're thinking, though. This isn't a jealousy thing. He had threatened to kill Natalie if she left him. He's a credible risk if he finds her."

"I see." Marty had a far-off look, as if still processing the information. "If he's military, he's probably moved several times by now. It's unlikely that he's still in California."

"Agreed, but I'll feel better confirming that fact."

"Let's get to work, then."

It was surprising how many Jared Fletchers were found. The archaic software only allowed them to filter by name, date of birth, race, and gender. Since Derek didn't know the date of birth, they were stuck sorting through a ton of white guys with the exact name. Military status and an estimated age range of thirty to forty would have to be checked manually for hundreds of records.

Two hours in, Derek rubbed his eyes as they blurred while looking at a Jared Fletcher in New Jersey that fit the age and physical description but had been in the Army rather than the Marines. *Not even close*, he thought. Any Marine would tell you it was like night and day. Derek looked over at Marty, thankful for the second set of eyes, and recalled his disappointment when he had told Marty he had planned to join the military.

Marty had said, "they raise obedient cattle, not men," and that he would be better off getting trained by Marty to hunt in the backwoods. It was the only time Derek could remember having a disagreement with Marty, and it was a big one. When he became a member of *The Few, The Proud*, he had expected Marty to be equally proud of him. But that was not the case.

They had lost contact during his years on tour. It wasn't until Derek was out of the service and joined the police force that Marty stepped back in to assume his role as mentor, as if no time had passed between them at all. Not one for holding grudges, Derek was extremely grateful to have Marty back in his life. The rest, as they say, was water under the bridge.

Derek blinked twice to make sure his eyes were not deceiving him. The Jared Fletcher on his screen was a thirty-seven-year-old ex-Marine, with blue eyes and dark-blond hair. He had served in the military police at a base in San Diego County twelve years prior, before being dishonorably discharged from service due to what the record labeled as *drunk and disorderly behavior while on duty.*

"Marty, I think I found him!" Nervous energy coursed through his veins. "This can't be right though."

"What is it?"

"His last known address is in Ridgefield. That's only twenty miles north of here."

"Let me take a look." Marty awkwardly maneuvered the right-handed mouse with his left hand and scrolled down the page. "Looks like, after San Diego, he lived in New York City for a couple of years. Must have hated it though, and I don't blame him, because it appears he's been in the Pacific Northwest ever since. He bounced around a lot. First, six months in Seattle, then shorter stays than that at a bunch of small towns along the Washington and Oregon coastlines. And look at that, he lived right here in Portland for a year." Marty pointed to the screen.

Derek was still trying to wrap his head around it. *He had followed her to New York. Had he known she was there? And why come search all over the Pacific Northwest next? Could it possibly be a coincidence that he lived in Portland before Natalie moved here years later?* His mind swirled while Marty continued clicking through the public record.

"There was a marriage license filed here in Multnomah County five years ago. Bride's name was Veronica Scarpino."

"Wait, Scarpino?" Derek's brain churned faster. "Why does that name sound familiar?"

Marty scratched his head. "Not sure. Pretty popular Italian surname, I believe."

No, that wasn't it, but nothing was coming to mind. *He'd have to figure it out later.* "More importantly, what the hell is this guy doing here in the Portland area? Can you see what he does for work now?"

"I'd have to pull his credit report, but I can call in a favor for that one." Marty walked back toward the scuffed-up desk he had long ago claimed as his own once he started consulting with the Portland PD. They were going to throw it out anyway during a remodel, so no one could complain that he was rarely at the station. He picked up his cell phone.

"Thanks, Marty. I really appreciate it." Derek grabbed his keys, tossed them to Marty. "You mind locking up when you're done here?"

"Wait, where are *you* going?"

"I'm going to go talk to that asshole."

"You sure that's a good idea?"

"No, but I'm going to do it anyway."

***

It was a quick drive to Ridgefield, even quicker the way Derek had been driving. The smell of backyard barbecues and swimming pools filled the air when he stepped out of his car into the blistering heat. He checked his watch, saw *1506* on the display. *Between meals was a good time for an unexpected visit,* he thought. Nerves boiled up in his stomach as he walked toward the Fletcher home. He had parked a block away for good measure.

All the two-story homes on the suburban block had a similar look. Two-car garages were adorned with sculpted shrubbery on either side. Wooden siding covered the exterior of the houses, alternating from shades of white, blue, gray, and tan. Derek stepped off the sidewalk to let a couple of kids pass on their bikes. As he stood in the street, several houses away from his destination, his phone vibrated in his pocket.

"Hey, Marty, I'm about to walk up to the house. What's up?"

"A couple things. First, he appears to work for a private security company. I did some digging and learned he's assigned to patrol a local storage facility up there."

"Okay, good to know."

"It gets better. I also looked into his DMV records. Guess who's the registered owner of a white utility van?"

"What? Son of a…" Derek dropped his phone, then caught it midair.

"I know, I know. Listen, you're going to have to play this one cool, though." Marty spoke in a calmer than usual voice, which was still raspy. "You don't want to spook him before you have any real evidence to bring him in. Plus, you don't have any backup. Do you hear me?"

A long silence passed on the phone before Derek spoke. "I hear you. I don't understand how we missed this, though. I went over all the van records a dozen times and would have recognized his name."

"Ridgefield is in Clark County, *Washington*, even though it's part of the Portland metropolitan area. All my records were from Multnomah County, Oregon. It was an oversight."

Oversight was an understatement. Derek actively worked to control his temper. "Thanks for the call, Marty. This could be the break we've needed. Meanwhile, let's widen the net to registered vehicles in all surrounding counties in case this lead falls short."

Marty must have sensed the frustration in his voice. "Kid, you've got motive and a matching vehicle description. I thought you'd be ecstatic about this?"

"I guess I'm still processing. I gotta go, but thanks again." Derek ended the call and slid the phone back into his pocket. More questions than answers ran through his mind. It made sense that Jared could be their killer, and yet it didn't at the same time. He walked past the Fletcher home, opting to take a lap around the block first to settle his thoughts.

His line of questioning would be different now. It needed to be. *He was here on official police business*, he reminded himself, stopping in front of the blue home with white shutters and trim. The green lawn was a bit overgrown, and there were faint oil stains on the driveway, but overall, it was a well-maintained home. A red pickup truck sat parked in front of the closed garage. *Was that where he was hiding the white van?*

He walked up the gray cobblestone pathway that led to the front door and knocked. The faint sound of voices could be heard through the door before it opened.

A muscular man, slightly taller than Derek, stood in the doorway. He had bags under his pale blue eyes and second-day scruff on his face. "Can I help you?"

"Jared Fletcher?"

"Uh, yes. Do I know you?"

"I'm Detective Hartmann with the Portland PD. Sorry to intrude on a holiday, but I'm hoping to ask you a couple of quick questions." Derek flashed his badge and did his best to fake a friendly demeanor, resisting a strong urge to deck the bastard. Without a warrant or probable cause to bring him in, he knew Jared could refuse to talk to him. *And worse, Jared would know that too.*

"What does this pertain to?"

"I think it might be best if we talk about that inside. May I?" Derek took a step forward, knowing it was less likely that he'd get asked to leave once he entered the house.

Jared stood firm in the doorway. "My wife and kids are in there. Baby just went down for a nap. I wouldn't want to disturb them. What is this about?"

"There's been a string of recent robberies in the area." Derek relayed the lie he had come up with on his walk. "I'm going door-to-door to learn if anyone may have heard or seen anything helpful. I understand not wanting to wake a sleeping baby, though. Can we talk privately somewhere else, such as your garage?" Beads of sweat were forming on his forehead. "It won't take long, I promise."

Jared eyed him suspiciously. "Let me see your badge again."

"Of course." Derek held it up at eye level.

"You're with the homicide department. Why would you be following up on a bunch of robberies?"

Shit. He hadn't thought his lie through well enough and would need to improvise. He lowered his voice to a near whisper. "Well, I didn't want to alarm the neighborhood, but there were some casualties involved in the robberies. That's why your cooperation is of utmost importance."

Jared still scowled at him. *He wasn't buying it. Hell, he wouldn't have bought it himself. The whole story stunk. What now?*

A softer, friendlier voice shot out from behind Jared. "Hey, honey, who's there?"

Jared turned to her, his own features softening. "Just a detective asking about some robberies in the area."

A curvy brunette with plump lips pushed her way into the doorway. "Well, what are you guys doing standing out here?" She motioned to Derek. "Come on in. I just made a fresh pitcher of lemonade, and it's about a zillion degrees out there."

"Thank you so much, ma'am. I'd love a glass." *Saved by the wife.* Derek squeezed past Jared, biting his lip to restrain a smile. "I hope I didn't disturb you or the baby."

She laughed and placed her hand below the small bump on her belly. "The baby is fine up in here."

"Oh, I didn't realize you were expecting another." Derek glanced between the kind woman and Jared when he saw confusion on her face.

Jared chimed in first. "I thought you and the baby were taking a nap, honey."

She laughed again in a relaxed way that seemed natural to her. "This kid already won't let me rest. I guess I better get used to all the sleepless nights ahead." Turning her attention back to Derek, she pointed him toward a floral sofa in the family room. "Please, have a seat. I had trouble getting pregnant, so my husband's a little protective. This is our first child," she explained.

Interesting. No kids in the house. Derek doubted that would be the last of Jared's lies. "Thank you, ma'am."

"Please, *ma'am* makes me feel a hundred years old. I'm Veronica."

He had already assumed she was Veronica Scarpino from the marriage license, but it was good to have confirmation. "Sorry, old military habit. It's hard for me to be so informal. May I call you Mrs. Fletcher at least?"

"Sure." She laughed again and turned toward Jared, who still lingered near the front door. "*Mr. Fletcher*, care to join us in the family room? I'm used to formalities anyway. My husband was in the military too," she added to Derek, who feigned surprise.

"Oh? What branch?"

Jared moved closer to his wife. "Marines, sir."

"Me too. Sempre Fi." Derek's stomach churned at the thought of relating to him, but he had to gain his trust. *Dishonorable discharge*, he reminded himself to feel better.

Jared nodded. "Semper Fi. Some of my best and worst years were spent with the Marines, but I wouldn't trade the experience for anything."

"Agreed." Derek felt his fist clench and forced it back open.

"Why don't you boys sit and talk while I go grab us some lemonade?" Veronica dashed into the kitchen before either could object.

"So," Jared began once Veronica was out of sight. "Why don't you tell me what this is really about?"

"Are you familiar with what the media is calling the *City Sidewalk Killings* in Portland?"

Calm and collected, Jared replied, "Of course. The murders are all over the news. I won't let Ronnie leave the house alone because of it. Too many sick bastards out there."

"Yes, unfortunately that's true." Too many sick bastards *in here*, Derek thought.

"What does it have to do with your visit, though?" Jared seemed genuinely confused by the line of questioning, but lying was also second nature to assholes like him.

"I'm following up on any and all leads received."

Veronica Fletcher returned with three glasses of lemonade, expertly balanced on a serving tray. "Here you go, boys. I meant to ask you, Detective, do you know an Officer Scarpino at the Portland Police Bureau?"

That's why he knew the name! "Yes, ma'am. I mean, Mrs. Fletcher... Sorry. I believe he's a newer recruit in Vice."

"That's my baby brother, and it's okay." She laughed again in the same relaxed way as before, and Derek wondered if she was truly as happy as she sounded. She didn't appear abused or afraid of her husband. *But how could he know for sure?*

Jared accepted the glass of lemonade she offered him. "Thanks, baby. Now why don't you go rest, please. I'll finish up with the detective here. I'm sure he needs to be on his way soon."

"Oh, sure." Veronica turned to Derek. "I'm sorry if I've been chatting off your ear. I'll just be upstairs if you boys need anything."

"No need to apologize. I'll have to say hello to your brother." *He would absolutely be talking to him.* "And you are more than welcome to stay if you would like. I just have a few questions to ask."

"She should rest," Jared cut in. "I can answer your questions."

"Okay, then. Nice meeting you, Mrs. Fletcher."

"You as well, Detective..." she waited for his reply.

"Hartmann, ma'am. I mean... Sorry."

Her hearty laugh echoed off the tiled floor. "On that note, off to bed for me. Husband's orders." She winked across the room at Jared, who looked uncomfortable on the small decorative chair next to the sofa.

After Veronica headed up the staircase, Jared exhaled what seemed like a breath of relief. "She's had three miscarriages. I'm a nervous wreck about the possibility of losing this one, too. Thank you for letting her rest."

There was a gentleness to his voice that surprised Derek. He cleared his throat. "Of course. I'll get right to my questions. Do you own a white van, Mr. Fletcher?"

"White? No. We recently bought a new minivan in anticipation of our new arrival, but it's a blue Toyota Sienna. It's in the garage if you want to take a look."

Derek mulled over the offer. *It would make more sense to keep it off property.* "That won't be necessary. Where do you work?"

"What does that have to do with anything? Am I suspected of something?" His cheeks reddened almost imperceptibly, but it was enough for Derek's trained eyes.

"Standard questions. Do you work locally or commute into the city?"

"My current assignment is only a few blocks from here. I provide security for the local U-Haul storage center. I know what you're probably thinking…" Jared raised his hands in the air. "*Lame rent-a-cop job*, right? At least that's what I used to think back when I was MP. But the pay is decent, and the work is relatively safe. Ronnie already worries sick about her brother. She doesn't need to worry about me too." His eyes bounced around the room. "You know, U-Haul was founded here in Ridgefield."

"Is that right?" Sensing Jared was nervous, Derek suppressed a smile and asked the next question to which he already knew the answer. "You mentioned your current assignment. Were you working elsewhere before?"

"Before moving to Ridgefield about five years ago, I lived in Portland. I worked for the same private security company but was assigned to a high-end apartment complex. That's where I met Ronnie, actually. She was a resident at the time."

Derek raised his eyebrow at the new information. "Mixing business with pleasure?"

Jared noticeably blushed. "It wasn't intentional, but, yeah, you could say that. When you know, you just know. Anyway, we got married pretty quickly after meeting and then moved here to start a family." *He seemed genuinely happy.*

Nausea formed in the pit of Derek's stomach. Jared's large hands caught his attention. He imagined them wrapping around Natalie's neck, hitting her face. *He didn't deserve happiness.* His fists clenched again. "Tell me, Mr. Fletcher, do you enjoy hurting women?"

Jared's blissful expression quickly morphed into one of shock. He leapt up from his chair. "What kind of question is that?"

"A simple one. Quick to temper, I see."

"I think you should leave. We're done here."

Derek remained seated and spoke calmly. "You haven't answered my question."

Jared threw his arms in the air. "No! I don't enjoy hurting women."

"Then why do you do it?"

"What? Look, I don't know where this is coming from, but I'm not going to ask you to leave again."

Derek rose from the sofa as Veronica poked her head into the family room, concern in her voice. "Is everything okay in here?"

"Yes, I was just leaving." With his eyes locked onto Jared's, he reached into his pocket, pulled out a business card, and handed it to Veronica. "If you're ever in any trouble, don't hesitate to contact me. You can never be too careful."

Jared walked across the foyer, opened the front door. "Have a nice day, Detective."

The door slammed behind Derek as he stepped out into the sweltering heat. *Pot sufficiently stirred.* He pulled out his phone on the walk to his car. "Hey, Jones, sorry to bother you on a holiday, but we have an unofficial suspect that requires surveillance for the next twenty-four hours. Can you put a couple uniforms on it today?" He waited for her reply. "Great. I'll text you the address. You're the best. Oh, also, I need the number of Officer Scarpino from Vice."

Before returning home, he'd driven over to the nearby U-Haul center for a quick visual inspection. No white vans parked in sight, but that didn't mean it wasn't stashed in one of the larger storage units. The office was closed for the holiday, so he planned to come back first thing the next morning to dig deeper. On his drive back into the city, he had also called Officer Scarpino, who only had good things to say about his apparent saint of a brother-in-law. Nonetheless, Derek had warned him to keep an eye out for any signs of abuse, citing evidence of past violence but concealing his source.

For the remainder of the drive home, he thought about Natalie. *How was she doing? How far had they gotten?* He also wondered how she would take the news that Jared was living within striking distance to Portland. As he neared his exit, he had half a mind to keep driving until he caught up with her so he could tell her in person. Instead, he reluctantly crossed the Morrison Bridge back into downtown Portland.

CHAPTER TWENTY-SIX

6

Leah didn't know Rhonda Jones to be the stretchy shorts and hot-pink sports bra type of girl, but she also didn't mind the view as she lagged shortly behind during their run. "Five miles down, five to go. How are you feeling?"

Beads of sweat rolled down Rhonda's ebony skin. "Great. You?"

Leah was better than great. She was doing one of her favorite things with her favorite person in the world. The last month with Rhonda had been a dream come true. A second chance at happiness that she would not throw away this time.

"Perfect. You know, if we pick up the pace, we should be able to watch the sunset from the bluffs at Mocks Crest before heading back to my place," Leah said, catching up to run at Rhonda's side.

"I *love* the idea of getting back to your place quicker." Rhonda smiled and increased her speed.

Leah sped up as well, passed Rhonda, and looked back into her warm brown eyes. "I love *you.*"

"Wait, what?" Rhonda came to a gradual stop.

Leah did the same. She hadn't meant to blurt out those words for the first time, but she didn't regret them. "Sorry, I know it's not the best moment, but it's something I should have said back when we were dating before. I felt it then, and I still feel it now. I love you, Rhonda."

Even more rare than her smile were the tears that formed in Rhonda's eyes. "I love you too. I always have, but I didn't think that you…"

Leah cut Rhonda's words short by pulling her into a passionate kiss. The salt on Rhonda's lips blended with her own as her tongue plunged deeply, wanting to taste all of her. Electricity surged through Leah's body, exciting every molecule of her being. She couldn't get enough of the woman she loved; the feel of her soft lips; the sound of her quiet moans as they kissed.

When Leah finally pulled away, they stood there on the running trail, staring into each other's eyes until Rhonda said, "Let's go watch that sunset."

After their run, and the satisfying shower that followed, Leah and Rhonda snuggled on the couch together. An older episode of *Law and Order* played on the television, but neither were paying any attention to the show.

Leah's one-bedroom apartment was bare bones but functional. It had tan carpeting and eggshell-white walls that she refused to decorate. The small kitchen opened up to the cozy living room where they sat, huddled under a single throw blanket.

"Have you warmed up yet?" Leah asked Rhonda. "The temperature dropped pretty sharply tonight. I can turn on the heat in here, if you want."

"That hot shower helped *immensely*. I'm good now." Rhonda's smile was suggestive as she slid her hand high up Leah's thigh. "But I'm always open to building some more heat."

Leah let out a soft moan of appreciation for the fire stoked between her legs. She was still sizzling from their last session and yearning for more. "Stay the night with me."

"I have an early morning," Rhonda said, but then changed her tune when Leah traced small circles up her inner thigh. "Mmm. But there's no place I'd rather be."

"Good." Leah kissed her deeply. They'd had sex plenty of times before, but tonight was different. *Tonight, they would make love.*

***

Leah woke to an empty bed the next day. Rhonda had warned her that she would have to slip out early, but the vacant space her body had previously warmed still caused Leah to ache. She wanted to wake up next to the woman she loved, and not just that morning, but for all mornings to come. In that moment, she decided she would ask Rhonda to marry her.

Giddy from the thought, she popped out of bed and threw on a fresh pair of running clothes. The display on her phone read 4:58 as she scrolled to her favorite playlist.

Nothing like an early morning run to start the day. Leah laced up shoes that matched the pearly white smile stuck on her face. She couldn't have stopped smiling if she had tried. The upbeat music that streamed into her wireless earbuds only elevated her mood further.

It was a beautiful day already, Leah thought as she stepped out into the brisk air. The sun wouldn't rise for another hour and a half, leaving the temperature in the low fifties. Having grown up in the Seattle area, she didn't mind the cold. In fact, she preferred it to the heat. Unless, of course, it was generated by Rhonda's curvaceous body. Her stride hit full speed while her mind raced with ideas for how to best propose.

Deep in thought, Leah didn't notice the white van that followed closely behind.

***

"You seem to be in a good mood," Derek said.

Rhonda sat at her desk in the near-empty station, combing through mountains of cell tower records. Why anything was still on paper rather than digital was mindboggling to her. And yet, her cheek muscles burned from the smile stuck on her face. "I am."

"Any particular reason?" he asked.

"I guess you could say that things are going my way."

They really were. Not only were things better than ever in her relationship with Leah, but she was making great strides in her career as well. They had an unofficial suspect for the *City Sidewalk Killer* case, and Derek was finally including her in a more meaningful way. He had asked her to interview the family of the fifth victim and was also thrilled with her idea of searching the cell tower records nearest to each of the five murder locations. Frankly, she had been surprised that no one else had thought of it.

Although they could not obtain Jared Fletcher's personal phone records without a warrant, they could search the cell tower records to see if his number had accessed service in those locations around the dates and times of the murders. The cell carriers had been opposed to sharing access to their vast databases, even with law enforcement, because of mounting privacy concerns. Hence, the burdensome stacks of paper, which she was at least able to get for the limited timeframes. Rhonda saw it as a win.

"Well, I'm glad to hear that. Thanks again for coming in so early to help look through these records. I know oh five hundred isn't your thing." Stacks of paper covered Derek's desk as well, organized in a system known only to him. He moved a page from the tallest stack to one of the shorter ones on the right.

"It'll be worth it if we can tie our suspect to even one location. That should be enough probable cause to get a warrant."

"Let's hope so. Great work obtaining this data, Jones, and thanks again for even thinking to request it. I'm lucky to have you as a partner."

Rhonda's smile spread even wider as they each continued going through their stacks of records in relative silence.

Three cups of coffee and two hours later, Marty sauntered into the station to join them. "What's going on here?"

It took a minute for Derek to break his concentration and register the question. "Oh, hey, Marty. Jones had the idea of searching cell tower records, so we're seeing if we can place Jared Fletcher near any of the murder locations when they occurred."

"That's not standard protocol," Marty said.

"I know. It was great out-of-the-box thinking!" Derek finally looked up from his desk to see the scowl on Marty's face. "I didn't want to trouble you again after all the work you did on Monday, but we have plenty more of these to go through if you want to help."

"Sure, why not… I'm a glutton for punishment." Marty accepted the stack of paper that Derek handed him before hobbling over to his own desk.

"Thanks, Marty. The number we are looking for is written there on the top page."

The tedious work should have provided a much-needed distraction for Derek, yet he couldn't help but think of Natalie as he scanned for Jared's number on the pages. She needed to know that he was living in the Portland area, and that they were considering him a person of interest. The call he'd been dreading could not wait much longer. Phone in hand, he thought about getting it over with when it rang instead. It was dispatch.

"Hello, Detective Hartmann speaking." He then listened closely to the voice on the line. "I'll be right there."

Derek stood from his desk. "Let's go, Jones. An unidentified body was found on the Duckworth Dock. I'll keep you updated, Marty."

"Don't worry, I'll keep myself busy with these." Marty motioned to the stacks on all three desks. "You do what you've got to do."

Rhonda followed behind Derek, who has already halfway to the door. "Do they think it's our killer?"

Derek stopped when he reached the door, held it open for her. "The number six was carved into her back."

A simple yes would have sufficed, Rhonda thought. "Thanks for letting me tag along to this one." She opened the passenger door of the unmarked police vehicle, realizing that this was the first time they'd traveled together to a crime scene.

"You've got what it takes to be a detective, Jones. A damn good one, too. You've proven that already, so now you just have to ask yourself whether that's the career path you really want."

Rhonda mulled the question over in her mind as they pulled out of the station, but she already knew the answer. She wanted it more than anything.

CHAPTER TWENTY-SEVEN

Birthday Surprise

Two and a half days on the road with her mother had put Natalie on the edge of her mental limits. The journey to her hometown after being away for over a decade had also stirred a sea of mixed emotions. Although it had been a beautiful drive, the circumstances had made it far from a joy ride. Natalie let out a deep breath as she flopped down on the hotel bed. They had finally made it to San Diego.

Bright sunlight poured into the posh hotel room, decorated in a nautical theme with blue walls and white linens. Sail boats and jet skis recreating in Mission Bay could be seen from her window. Despite the high price and unknown duration of their stay, she had opted for separate rooms. *Worth every penny,* she thought, as she sank farther into the pillow top mattress. Her mother and she had appointments to tour several apartments for the next two days, but the rest of that day belonged entirely to her.

A quick power nap and thirty minutes later, she was on her way to decorate Jessica's house. Arriving in time for her best friend's birthday was a serendipitous outcome of the unplanned trip. Not telling Jessica she was on her way to town had been challenging, but she knew seeing the surprise on her face would be worth the wait.

She had stopped to get everything she needed at a party supply store and bakery along the way—certain that Jessica's husband, Brad, had not thought to plan anything. He would be working all day, according to Jessica. When Natalie had called earlier that morning to wish her a happy birthday, she had also learned that Jessica was spending the day at Disneyland with her kids, Lucas and Chloe, as well as her mom and sister. The thought had crossed her mind to join them there, but she didn't want to impose on their plans, nor bring down the mood at the *happiest place on earth*.

Given her current energy level, decorating Jessica's house instead was the perfect idea. Natalie parked her mom's faded black Honda Civic in front of the pink house, complete with a white picket fence around an artfully landscaped yard. It had been Jessica's dream home when she and Brad bought it seven years prior, after the birth of Lucas. Natalie had only seen it in pictures, which she now realized had not done it justice.

The newly renovated, 1950s, single-story home was both grander and quainter in three dimensions. As she approached the door, balancing the cake in one hand and a bag of decorations in the other, she was greeted by a sweet floral scent. Soft yellow and white roses, pink hibiscus, and a variety of flowering succulents lined the walkway. A large bougainvillea plant covered the side of the house and arched over the doorway. Its crimson leaves littered the ground like potpourri. Careful not to drop the cake, Natalie reached behind the trellis, where she knew Jessica kept the "in case of emergency" spare house key.

If surprising her best friend on her birthday wasn't an emergency, she didn't know what was. She moved both the bag and cake into one hand to unlock the door, pushed it open with her foot, and headed straight toward where she imagined the kitchen would be to unload the items. As she rounded the corner of the arched entryway, the scene in the kitchen had her stopping short.

Bradley Clark was neither at work nor alone. Two twisted, naked bodies assaulted her eyes. The cake nearly dropped from her hand, but she caught it. Not knowing whether to interrupt or flee, she froze, unable to talk or move. The sounds of heavy breathing and flesh smacking filled the room. As if watching a train wreck unfold, she could not bring herself to look away.

The woman—also brunette, but definitely not Jessica—was bent over a chair in the dinette area of the kitchen. Brad's back was to Natalie as he gripped his companion by the hips and repeatedly rammed her from behind. The muscles in his "bubble butt," which she knew Jessica adored, clenched and released with every blow. Based on the force used, Natalie would have thought that he was hurting the woman if not for her voicing demands such as, "fuck me harder" and "don't stop."

Anger stirred in Natalie as she thought about the devastation this would cause. *How could he do this to Jessica? And to their family?* Yet, she still couldn't speak. Her eyes wandered to the woman's upended body, which, like Brad's, was out of shape and pudgy in the middle. Streaks of what appeared to be chocolate were visible on her thighs and breasts, which bounced up and down with every thrust received.

Their sticky foreplay before the act in progress was confirmed by the Hersey's syrup and Reddi-wip bottles that she spotted on the kitchen island. Natalie stood there in silence for what had felt like an eternity. In reality, she had watched the whole scene unfold for less than sixty seconds before she regained her ability to speak. The impetus was Brad's familiar voice shouting out, "I'm gonna come, baby!"

Not on her watch. Natalie shouted back, "What if Jessica and the kids come home early?"

Brad jumped and swung around. His weapon of betrayal pointed straight in her direction. "Natalie! What the hell?"

She finally averted her eyes by turning sharply away from the kitchen, clutching the cake against her chest. It was as if protecting it would somehow salvage Jessica's birthday from inevitable disaster. She winced when she felt the cake smash within the box. "I'd ask you the same, but I already saw *what the hell* you've been doing."

She heard some fumbling around the kitchen, which she hoped was them putting on their clothes. Brad clarified in an exasperated tone, "I mean, what are you doing in *my house?*"

"Last I checked, it's Jessica's house too, and I came here on *your wife's birthday* to surprise her. You did remember it's her birthday today, right?"

"Of course, I remembered!" The sound of a zipper followed his statement.

"I think your surprise for her tops mine, unfortunately." Still looking away, Natalie closed her eyes for extra protection.

"She can't find out. *Please, Natalie.*"

The woman, who had been quiet up to this point, chimed in, "I should go."

"I'm so sorry about this, Susan," Brad said.

Aware that she was blocking the exit, Natalie stepped aside to let *Susan* pass. *Home-wrecking whore* was Natalie's first thought as she watched her leave, but she quickly reminded herself that too often the other woman gets blamed. Brad was the one that stood in front of God and family over a decade earlier and vowed to be faithful to Jessica, and he was the one who broke that vow. *Brad was the home-wrecking whore.*

Natalie turned her glare toward Brad, grateful to see him fully dressed. She wasn't sure that she'd ever be able to erase the naked image from her brain. "You apologized to her, but are you even sorry about what you've done to your family?"

"I haven't done anything to them! They don't need to know. Please, Natalie, you can't tell Jessica! It would crush her."

She scoffed in disgust. "And you didn't think of that *before* screwing another woman? No, you are not going to put this on me, Brad. She deserves to know the truth, and it should come from you."

"This was all just one huge mistake. I promise it will never happen again. I don't want to lose my family over this! Can't you understand?" There was self-serving desperation in his voice.

She had so many questions, but they weren't hers to ask. "I'm not the one that needs to understand. You have until tomorrow night to tell Jessica, or else I will." Still holding the cake and supplies, Natalie turned and left Brad alone with the mess he had made.

***

Back at the hotel, Natalie picked at the smashed chocolate cake with a fork she had snagged from the lobby. She shoved a large piece of the cake into her mouth in a failed attempt to distract herself. Her private room felt less relaxing with Jessica's marital issues weighing on her mind. Her best friend would soon be devastated, thanks to her.

Was it a mistake to show up at the house unannounced? No, she decided. Brad deserved to get caught, and Jessica was better off knowing the truth. *So why couldn't she shake the feelings of guilt festering inside her?*

She needed to talk to someone about the situation. Ironically, Jessica was the one person she would normally consult with on such a dilemma. Her remaining options were limited. Her mother was out of the question due to her general lack of discretion; the news would travel back to Jessica in a heartbeat. She thought of several friends back in New York that she hadn't spoken with since

Nick's death, but calling any of them out of the blue to discuss an awkward situation would be far too uncomfortable. *Maybe Leah*, she thought.

Her cell phone vibrated on the nightstand right as she reached for it. Derek was calling. Given her tense departure, she thought of sending him to voicemail. He was the last person she wanted to drag into even more drama. Still, her heart raced at the prospect of hearing his voice.

Unsure of what to say, she answered the phone anyway. "Hey."

"Hey. I'm glad I caught you. Did you make it to San Diego safely?"

"Yeah, we got here earlier this afternoon. Thanks for checking."

"I'm relieved to hear that." Derek audibly exhaled on the other end of the line. "Listen, Natalie, I'm really sorry for suggesting you should leave. It's not what I wanted at all."

"Don't worry about it. I would have kicked me out too after my drunken behavior. Really, I understand."

"No, you don't. I wasn't upset about that night, and I definitely didn't intend to kick you out. I just thought your mom needed you. Plus, Portland isn't safe right now with this killer still at large. That's actually part of the reason I called."

"Oh, what's up? Has there been a development in the case?"

"I'm not sure how to tell you this exactly."

"What is it?" Concern creeping in, she put down the fork she had been mindlessly stabbing into the cake.

"Well, after you left on Monday, I started worrying that Jared could still be in San Diego and that you'd be in danger. So, I went into the station to look up his last known address."

"And?" Natalie held her breath. Thoughts of whether Jared might find her there had certainly crossed her mind, but she had mostly put them aside. *It was all a long, long time ago*, she reminded herself.

"He's no longer in San Diego."

All the air rushed out of her lungs in relief. "That's good to hear."

"Yes, it is, but…"

"But what?"

"He's in the Portland metro area now. Ridgefield, to be exact."

"*What?* Since when?"

"He's been here for about six years, after bouncing around various towns in the Pacific Northwest for a couple of years. Before that, he lived in New York City for two years." He waited as she slowly absorbed the information, then asked, "Are you okay?"

When she spoke next, she wasn't sure if it was aloud or to herself. "I used to talk about wanting to live in the Pacific Northwest if I ever left San Diego. He was looking for me."

"That seems to be the case."

"I can't believe he was in New York, though. I rented a room off the books until I got married. My name was never on a lease. How would he even know I had moved there?"

"I'm not sure, but there's more, Natalie." His voice softened, signaling bad news. "Marty helped look into some additional records for me and learned that he's the registered owner of a white van. It wasn't on our radar before, since it's a Washington plate."

"Wait. Are you trying to say you think he could be…?" She couldn't finish the sentence. *It wasn't possible.*

"I was considering him an unofficial suspect, or person of interest, until today."

"What happened today?" Her rattled nerves caused her voice to tremble.

"There was a sixth victim found at the Duckworth Dock early this morning. He's officially our prime suspect, and we'll be bringing him in for questioning tomorrow morning."

"What? Is there anything linking him to the murder?"

"Circumstantial at this point, but it's enough for me. I confirmed he was in the city this morning, apparently meeting someone to discuss a private security gig near the dock."

The idea of Jared being the killer filled her with horror, but she still couldn't believe it. "Well, that doesn't mean he… how do you know what he was doing there?"

"I called his house, talked to his wife."

"Oh," was all she could manage to say.

"I should also tell you that I went to his house on Monday to scope things out. It was hard not to want to take a shot at him, but I promise I didn't mention you at all."

Her whole body cringed at the thought of Derek talking to Jared. "Okay… What *did* you say to him?"

"I had a lame cover story about robberies in the area that he saw right through, but then his wife invited me in, so he didn't have a choice but to talk to me. I just asked him a few questions to stir the pot."

"Such as?"

"Such as… if he had heard of the *City Sidewalk Killings*, if he owned a white van, what he did for work, and… if he enjoyed hurting women."

"Oh, Derek! You didn't!"

"I did, and I was asked to leave, but I was hoping it would prompt him to move the van from wherever he had it stashed. I was only able to put surveillance on him for twenty-four hours, though, and we didn't have any luck during that time." Derek got quiet for a minute before speaking again. "I didn't think it would prompt more violent action."

"You don't know that's what happened, and you can't blame yourself!" Natalie waited to make sure her point registered, then asked, "What about his wife? Did she seem… well?"

"She did. There weren't any signs of abuse, that I could tell, at least. And I learned something else."

"What?" she asked hesitantly, unsure if she could handle any more surprises.

"She's the sister of a fellow Portland PD officer, who I also talked to after my visit."

When a long silence followed his statement, she felt the need to make sure the call hadn't dropped. "Derek?"

"Yeah, I'm still here. Natalie… she and Jared were at the chief's Fourth of July barbecue. You didn't imagine seeing him there."

Natalie stood from the hotel bed and starting pacing the room. "He was really there. I'm not crazy."

"No, you're not. I'm so sorry to have to dump all this on you. I just thought you should know."

She nodded as if he could see her. "No, yeah, I appreciate you telling me. I still can't believe…" Her thoughts trailed off before coming back to her. "Despite what he did to me, I honestly can't believe he could be a serial killer. It doesn't seem possible."

"He may or may not be our killer, but he's not getting out of our sight again until I can rule him out for sure. I've already requested authorization for round-the-clock surveillance."

She nodded again, remaining silent.

"Natalie, are you okay?"

"Yeah, it's just a lot to absorb." She rubbed her temples with her palms. "It puts my other problems in the right perspective, at least. So, thanks for that."

"What other problems? Are you still upset with your mom?"

"Yes, but that's not what I was thinking about." She stopped pacing and stared out her hotel window. The black sky was lit up with SeaWorld's nightly display of fireworks from across the bay. The booms were faint but could be felt in her bones. It brought back so many memories, good and bad.

"What were you thinking about?" There was both concern and hesitation in his voice, as if he thought it might be about him.

"It doesn't matter."

"It matters to me. You sound unhappy. It might help to talk about it," he said.

Talking to him did always make her feel better, she realized. "Well, there is one issue where I could use an objective opinion, but I feel like I should spare you the drama. Plus, you have more important things to deal with right now."

"There's nothing more I can do on the case tonight. I'm all ears."

"Are you sure?"

"Hearing your voice has already been the highlight of my day. I'm sure."

Unsure how to react to his admission, she mentally brushed it aside and then filled him in on her surprise visit to Jessica's house, leaving out the graphic details forever burned into her memory. "So, now, I have to decide whether I break my best friend's heart or keep this horrible secret from her, assuming Brad won't tell her himself. And I'm pretty sure he won't. He's a selfish bastard."

"Wow, that's a tough predicament. Hopefully, he'll come clean to her."

"And if not, what should I do? I mean, what would *you* do in this situation?"

"Well, I don't think you're going to like my answer, but if it were me, I'd try to stay out of the middle of it. I don't think anything good will come from you telling her—for either of you."

He was right; she didn't like that answer. Nonetheless, she appreciated his honest opinion. "That's probably true, but I don't know how I could possibly keep this from her. It'll eat me up inside every time we talk. Plus, if she found out later that I knew and didn't tell her, she would never forgive me."

"She wouldn't understand that you were trying to protect her?"

"Let me explain to you how girl friendships work." She let out a short laugh. "We tell each other *everything*, especially as it relates to our love lives. Jessica gets mad at me if I hold back even a little. For example, I told her about you two days after we had met, and she was upset that I hadn't called her sooner."

"What did you tell her about me?" Derek asked with a smile in his voice.

"Huh? Oh, um, just that I was mortified after I threw up in front of you." Her cheeks started burning. *How did she get on this topic?* "Anyway, my point is… she expected me to tell her every detail of how we met and what you look like. She wouldn't let it go until I did, because that's what we do—we share *everything*."

"I see. What else did you tell her about me?"

She picked up on his flirtatious tone and played along. "Oh, you mean how I can hardly control myself around you? Yes, she knows about our kiss in the kitchen, and then again in your bedroom. She also knows all about your rock-hard body and dreamy hazel eyes, and we refer to you as Detective McSteamy. Is that what you wanted to hear?"

"Um, I, well… thank you?"

"Come on, Derek. You don't need to fish for compliments. You already know you're gorgeous and can get any woman you want. But that's part of the problem."

"So that's why you keep pushing me away? You assume I would be unfaithful or something?" He sounded mildly offended, if not hurt.

"I think that's one of many possible outcomes. All I know is that love always ends in heartbreak. Even if you didn't cheat or leave me, and we were madly in love, I would still end up hurt somehow. You could die, for example." The brutal honesty she inadvertently shared had her trembling and lowering herself back onto the bed.

Derek's voice softened. "It's hard to argue with that last point. I would never intentionally hurt you, though. And you're wrong about the other thing, too."

"What other thing?"

"You're wrong that I can get any woman I want." After a sufficiently awkward silence had passed, he added, "I should probably let you go. It's getting late, and I plan to get an early start tomorrow. I'm hoping forensics will have something for me on the sixth victim. She's still a Jane Doe at this point."

"Oh, okay. Good luck there, and please keep me updated, especially after you question Jared."

"Will do. That reminds me… When do you think you'll be back home?"

"I'm not sure exactly. Being back in San Diego after all these years brings back a lot of memories, but it also reminds me of all the memories that I've missed out on building here. It kind of feels like… I finally *am* home, you know?"

"Got it." His words were short, clipped.

"But I'll be back soon for Tux, I promise. How's he doing, by the way?"

"He's good. He misses you."

"I miss him too. I'll keep you updated when I book my flight to come get him, probably within the next few days."

"Okay, good night." Derek hung up the phone before Natalie had a chance to reciprocate the sentiment.

Was he mad at her? He had agreed to watch Tux, and it wasn't like she'd even been gone that long. Plus, it had been *his idea* for her to come back to San Diego in the first place. "Good night to you too," she said to no one.

CHAPTER TWENTY-EIGHT

Revelations

The hotel rooftop bar was bustling with tourists and locals alike. Groups of friends clinked glasses in celebration at the larger VIP tables, while couples filled the more intimate seating area. Twentysomethings in short dresses did laps around the perimeter in hopes of being noticed by the hard-bodied guys standing around in clusters. Natalie sat at the bar, taking in the scene. A lifetime ago, she had done the same thing with her girlfriends to score free drinks.

Mentally rebuking herself for having once been so foolish, she took a sip of the apple martini that she proudly purchased with her own hard-earned money. It was nice not needing a man to buy her drinks, or for anything. *Empowering,* she thought. Natalie checked her phone for the time. Jessica was ten minutes late already. While typical, she wondered if there was another reason for her tardiness—a huge fight with Brad, perhaps.

Those thoughts subsided when she saw Jessica approaching the bar with an enormous smile on her face. *She didn't know yet.*

"Natalie! Oh my goodness, I can't believe you're actually here! It's so good to see you!" Jessica embraced her in a tight hug, swayed back and forth several times, and then released her. "I was so surprised and happy when you called earlier today to say you were in town. But seeing you here in person… This is so surreal!"

"I know. It's so good to see you too! Your hair looks great, by the way."

"Thanks! I had it cut and added highlights. My sister treated me for my birthday." Dark-blond streaks accented the curly brown strands that framed Jessica's face. Her hair was as bouncy and full of life as she was.

"Speaking of birthday treats, I ordered you a martini as well. It should be out any minute."

"Thanks, bestie. So sorry I was late!"

Natalie waved at the air. "No worries."

"At least there's a good reason *why* I was late." Jessica's already large smile grew even bigger. "Brad surprised me while I was in the shower, and, well, one thing led to another."

"You guys had sex? Tonight!"

"Don't sound so surprised! We *are* married, you know. We're allowed to have sex." Jessica laughed over the loud bar noise. "Although I must admit, it had been a while before tonight. Too long, if you ask me. But with the kids and our busy schedules, it's hard to find time alone sometimes. So… *sorry not sorry* for being late tonight." She picked up the martini that the bartender had sat down in front of her. "Cheers! I still can't believe we're both thirty-four now. That's like *mid-thirties*."

Natalie tapped Jessica's glass with her own, downed the rest of her drink, and placed the empty glass on the bar. "Ugh. Let's not talk about aging. Besides, thirty-four is still early thirties."

"I don't know about that, but *I do know* that thirty-four means I've officially been with Brad for *twenty years!* Can you believe that? We started dating when we were fourteen. Freshmen year in high school, remember?"

"Yes, I remember." She also remembered not liking him then. The hate she felt for him now was much stronger.

"Anyway, it's kinda crazy to think that Brad and I have been together that long. I mean, it's not always easy, trust me, but I feel so lucky to have married my high school sweetheart. Not too many people can say that these days. I only hope we'll stay as in love as my parents still are." Blissfully ignorant of her husband's transgressions, Jessica's whole being radiated unbridled happiness.

Natalie's heart ached. She couldn't stand the thought of anything taking that joy away from the cheeriest person she knew. *Maybe Derek was right. Maybe she should keep the truth to herself. But how?*

"Enough about my boring love life, though. I want to live vicariously through yours. What's going on with Detective McSteamy? We're still calling him that, right? I want to hear everything!"

"There's nothing more to tell there. Like I said on the phone, we weren't on the greatest terms when I left to drive down here. I had made the mistake of telling him everything that happened with my family—and then drunkenly tried to seduce him—so, I don't blame him for wanting me gone."

"Did he *actually* say he wanted you gone?"

"*Basically.* He said he thought it would be best if I came back to San Diego with my mom. He later said he only meant 'temporarily' to get her settled, but I could tell he was upset with me. And sick of all my drama."

"That sounds like a lot of assumptions to me. Has he tried to call you since you left?"

"Yeah, we talked last night."

"*And?*" Jessica lunged forward, nearly spilling her drink.

"And what?"

"What did the two of you talk about when he called? I can't believe you didn't mention it sooner!" Jessica playfully hit her in the arm with more force than she likely intended, sending a shock wave of pain up Natalie's shoulder.

Her point to Derek was being reinforced. *There was no way Jessica would forgive her for keeping such a secret.* She couldn't share *everything* she had discussed with Derek, though. "He wanted to make sure I made it here safely."

"Aw, see! That means he cares about you."

"More like being polite. Besides, I shut down any chance of us getting together by implying on the phone last night that I didn't trust him not to hurt me."

"Oh, he was probably crushed by that, Nat. I know you've been hurt before, but I wish you could let yourself love again."

Natalie hoped Jessica would remember her own advice someday. "I didn't mean to be so blunt. It just came out. But you're right, now that I think of it, he did seem kind of hurt. He also seemed upset when I told him I'm thinking of staying here."

"You're going to stay here in San Diego? Permanently!"

Natalie nodded. "I think so. It's my home, Jess. Plus, I've already missed out on so much, like the birth of both your children and getting to be cool Aunt Natalie. I want to stick around to spend more time with you, them, and my mom."

"Oh. Em. Gee! This is the best birthday surprise ever! I'm thrilled to hear that, but what about joining the Police Academy in Oregon?"

"Yeah, I know I'd need to give that idea up… and talk to your uncle. I think he had pulled some strings to get me in. He'll be disappointed, but I'm sure he'll understand."

"Wow, that's great, if that's what you really want. You were so excited about becoming a police officer, though. Would you regret quitting?"

"Honestly, I don't think so. I wasn't doing it for the right reasons anyway."

"What do you mean?"

Natalie sighed. "I'm so sick of feeling scared all the time, Jess. I thought I'd finally be able to protect myself if I were a police officer."

"Oh, honey, that makes total sense. As for being afraid all the time, I know you don't share my faith, but all you need to do is put your trust in God, Natalie. Believe it or not, He's always watching out for you. He has a plan for all of us, even if we can't understand it at times."

"Thanks. I want to believe that. *I really do.* It's just that… bad things are always happening."

"Yes, bad things happen, unfortunately. But God doesn't give us more than we can bear."

"What doesn't kill us makes us stronger?"

"Exactly!" Jessica took a swig of her drink, giving Natalie time to process her next move.

"So, what if something bad happened that would make you stronger, but you didn't know? Would you want to know?"

"Like what?"

"Like, I don't know… *hypothetically*, what if Brad was cheating on you? Would you want to know?"

Jessica sat her near-empty martini glass down on the bar, focusing her full attention on Natalie. "First off, not possible. Secondly, Natalya Elizabeth, you have got to learn to be more trusting. Not all guys are pigs, I promise you. Please, give Derek a chance at least."

"This isn't about Derek." Anxiety rising in her throat, she ran her fingers through her hair, twirling the ends around her fingers. "Just pretend it was true. Would you want to find out if Brad was cheating, or would you rather not know?"

"That's a hard question. I mean, on the one hand, it would destroy everything we have together and hurt our family, which is why I know Brad would *never* do that." Jessica motioned with her hands as she spoke. "On the other hand, I wouldn't want to go on living a lie. So, I would want to know." She paused as if considering her answer further. "Yeah, I would want to know."

"Are you sure?"

"Nat, what's going on? You're starting to freak me out."

Natalie leaned forward and placed her hand on Jessica's arm. "It's true, Jess. Brad cheated."

Jessica rose from her barstool. "Is this some kind of joke? Why would you say that?"

"I'm so sorry, Jess. It's not a joke. I saw him… yesterday… at your house." She moved in to hug Jessica but was pushed away.

"No! That doesn't make any sense. You didn't even get into town until today."

"I lied about that, and *I'm so sorry*. I actually got in yesterday afternoon and went over to your place to surprise you. I had bought a cake and a bunch of decorations that I planned to set up before you got home from Disneyland. I used the spare key you hid behind the trellis and walked in on Brad and another woman."

Jessica shook her head. Her body visibly quaked. "No, I don't believe you. You're lying about this."

"I realize you're in shock, but why would I lie to you? It kills me to have to be the one to tell you this."

"Then why are you?"

Natalie was the one shocked this time. "You said you'd want to know. I couldn't keep a secret like this from you! You're my best friend."

Jessica's brown eyes flicked from disbelief to anger. "Does Brad know you saw him?"

"Yes, he knows. I wanted you to hear it from him, but he must not have had the courage."

"So, he also knew that you were going to tell me?"

"I told him he had until tonight to tell you himself. Again, I'm so sorry, honey." She reached for Jessica and was pushed away. Again.

Anger, grief, and disgust were all written on Jessica's expressive face. "I don't understand why you couldn't just let me be happy! Is it because you want me to be miserable like you are?"

"What? Of course not!" Natalie's heart sank. *She had made the wrong decision.*

Jessica grabbed her handbag. "I need to be alone right now. This is all too much." She stormed off before Natalie could say anything else.

Natalie sat back down on her barstool, completely shaken. Running after Jessica didn't seem like a good idea. Their friendship would get through this, she told herself. *It had to.* She pulled out her phone and drafted a text.

I'm here for you whenever you are ready to talk. I'll always be here for you.

She added a heart emoji, hit send, and considered closing out her tab. After getting the bartender's attention, she ordered another drink instead.

***

Even with the window ajar, the city outside was mostly quiet as Derek tossed and turned in bed. Deep slumber would be a welcome respite from his spiraling thoughts, yet it evaded him. Despite his long workday, which had at least provided some distraction, he felt even further from solving the case. His interrogation of Jared had only left him feeling conflicted. While he'd enjoy nothing more than taking down a scumbag like Jared, it seemed almost too convenient that he was now their prime suspect.

The sixth victim had been identified as Joy Chen, a twenty-five-year-old Chinese American graduate student at Portland State University. Unfortunately, she would never get the chance to earn the doctorate that her parents had envisioned for her. Derek would never forget the horrified looks on their faces when they confirmed the identity of their daughter's beaten corpse. According to Joy's roommate, she had not returned home Monday night after Labor Day celebrations on the river. Initial estimates had the time of death being at least twenty-four hours prior to when her body was found at the dock.

Those details had occupied his mind for most of the day. But nightfall brought persistent thoughts of Natalie. The knowledge that she wasn't coming back caused a dull pain in his chest, which was worsened by the fact that he had driven her away himself. His heart and body both yearned for her as his mind lingered on the distance between them.

He rolled onto his back and stared at the ceiling. Dark shadows formed shapes that his mind automatically converted to memories of her. The images only intensified when he closed his eyes in a failed attempt to block them. Her naked body arching against his bedpost was one image he didn't mind recalling, even though it felt mildly wrong to fantasize. She had made it perfectly clear they would never be together. Still, picturing her in his bed was much more pleasurable than all the other painful thoughts in his head.

He decided to embrace the indulgence. *Oh, the things he would do with her.* He'd start by deeply kissing her ready mouth, as he had before. But neither of them would stop it this time. Instead, she would beg him for more. He'd oblige by planting a trail of kisses down her neck, across her collarbones, and around her perky breasts. Moving next to her rosy nipples, he'd tease one with his lips and the other with his thumb.

Only when she softly urged him would he travel south, running his fingers down the sides of her body while slowly kissing his way down her smooth abdomen to her creamy thighs. He'd watch her need build as he kissed down one leg and up the other at a snail's pace. Once at her fleshy center, he'd part her with his tongue, first tasting, then devouring until she moaned his name.

He imagined testing her moisture levels, probing his fingers in and out while licking her engorged clit. He wouldn't stop until he felt her body quiver beneath him. Only then would he roll her over onto all fours and mount her from behind. He'd savor every second with her, caressing her curves while plunging in deep. Rock hard at the thought, he slowly stroked himself, envisioning each thrust.

His rhythm would start slow and then increase in intensity. His hand followed suit, but he wouldn't allow himself to finish yet. He wanted to feel her bursting with pleasure for a second time before he let himself lose control. When he was mentally nearing that point, his phone rang.

Startled, he sat up in bed, still holding himself. He considered letting the call go to voicemail until he looked at the time. It was one o'clock in the morning. *Only work called this late, and it was never good news.* He swiftly released his hand and then used the other one to answer the phone.

"Hartmann speaking." He hoped that his elevated heart rate couldn't be heard on the other line.

A sultry voice replied, "Hey, Hartmann."

He couldn't believe his ears. "Natalie? Is everything okay?"

"Yes, sorry to startle you. I couldn't sleep. Did I wake you?"

"No, I couldn't sleep, either."

"Oh, good. I mean… not good that you couldn't sleep, but good that I didn't wake you. I'm not making any sense, sorry. I just wanted to talk to you."

Feeling vulnerable, Derek pulled the bedspread over his lap. "Sure, what's up?" *He certainly was.*

"Well, I keep thinking about our conversation last night, and I feel awful. I want to apologize for implying that I don't trust you not to hurt me… you know, if we were together. I'm sorry, Derek. That wasn't fair of me, and it's not how I actually feel."

"How *do* you feel?"

"Scared, in general… but with you, I weirdly feel safer than I have with anyone. And not just physically. I feel like

I can tell you anything, which is not typical for me. I trust you, Derek, and I needed you to know that."

"Well, thank you for your trust. I know that doesn't come easy."

"The crazy thing is… it does with you somehow. Just hearing your voice puts my mind at ease."

Her words alleviated the ache in his chest. "I feel the same. It's so good to hear from you."

"Jessica actually helped me see what a jerk I had been. You were right, by the way."

"Right about what?"

"I should have stayed out of the middle of things. Instead, I told her tonight that Brad had cheated on her, and she was furious with me. Brad wasn't man enough to tell her, so I'm the bad guy now." Natalie blew out a breath.

"I'm sure she'll cool off and realize you had her best interest at heart."

"Hopefully, but she flat out accused me of telling her because *I want her to be as miserable as I am.*' It cut deep that she thought I would hurt her intentionally. That's why I knew I needed to apologize to you. Words can be hurtful, too."

"Yes, they can. I'm sorry that you had to go through that tonight. No wonder you couldn't sleep."

"Well, since I'm being honest, I took a nap earlier tonight. Jess and I had met at my hotel bar. I had a couple of drinks before coming back to my room and wanted to sleep off the buzz before calling you. You deserved a sober apology."

"I appreciate that." Hope ping-ponged in his chest. "So, does that mean you'll be coming back to Portland?"

"I haven't figured it all out yet, but I think I need to stay here a while. Once Jess stops hating me, she's going to need a friend and probably some help getting back on her feet. My mom still needs me as well. I didn't realize before how lonely she's been."

"I see."

"And I know I'll need to talk to the chief about not joining the Academy this fall, but I'm hoping he'll understand."

He swallowed down the shards of his broken heart as they pressed their way through his chest and up his throat. *She wasn't coming back.* An unwilling tear escaped his eye, and his words came out in a whisper. "I'm going to miss you. I already do."

"I miss you too," Natalie said.

A brief time passed with only the faint sounds of their breath between them. Neither knew what else to say. There was an understanding in the silence. *This was goodbye.* Derek was about to tell her they should both get some rest when she surprised him.

"I think about you often," she said in a low, sensual whisper that made his heart flutter.

"You do?"

"Yeah. I imagine you holding me and caressing my skin the way you did the night of the gala. I also imagine what would have happened if we hadn't been interrupted that night. Do you ever think of me *in that way?*"

His mouth went bone-dry. He opened it to speak but only muttered noise. "I, um… you, all the… that way… time."

She giggled, but not mockingly. Her laugh sounded pleased, mischievous, and inviting all at once. "I'll tell you mine, if you tell me yours. What would you do if I were there with you now?"

"Kiss you." His words came easily now. "And I wouldn't stop at your lips."

Though she had asked for it, the heat from his words took Natalie by surprise. A tingling sensation all over her body left her yearning for more. "Where else would you kiss me?"

"*Everywhere.*"

She didn't know an ordinary word could be so hot. It was the way he said it that had her full of desire. A low moan escaped from her lips before she could speak again. "*Damn*, I wish you were here right now."

"I thought we were pretending you were here with me… in my bed." The flirtatious charm she was so fond of had returned to his voice. "Or at least I had been… before you called."

"*Oh really?*" Intrigued, she reclined on the hotel bed to get more comfortable.

"Yeah. I know I shouldn't have, but I can't get you out of my head. Your beautiful body on my bed is all I see when I close my eyes."

With a tinge of embarrassment, she remembered her drunken striptease. "Next time I'll be sober. I promise."

"I like the sound of *next time*."

The heat that already consumed her body rose to her cheeks. *Did she just offer to strip naked in his bed the next time she was there?* As much as she wanted him, her own forwardness made her eager to change the subject. "Anyway, you probably need to get some sleep. I'm glad we had a chance to talk."

"Wait a minute, I told you mine; you said you'd tell me yours. Fair is fair." There was teasing in his husky voice, but something else as well—something raw, something vulnerable.

And everything in her wanted to draw it out further. "It is only fair. Mine usually happens in the shower. There's something about the hot water running down my body… it makes me imagine you are there with me."

There was a low groan on his end of the line before he said, "I want you so fucking bad."

Encouraged and thoroughly turned on by him, she decided to take it to the next level. "In the shower, your hands glide up and down my body and you slip inside me." Throwing caution to the wind, she moved her own hand under her panties and gasped. "I'm so wet for you."

"Natalie." He growled her name like a tortured prayer. "You have no idea what you do to me, how hard I am for you. Only for you."

Only for you repeated in her head. She wouldn't have believed it before, but now, it shot straight to her heart, among other places.

He emitted another low groan that let her know he was touching himself. "You feel so good. I want to make you come."

"Let's come together," she managed to say between shallow breaths. She had never uttered such bold words before, but being with him, even if over the phone, felt natural. It felt right. And hot as hell.

"Tell me what you're doing right now." His request sounded more like a plea than a command, and the rough edge of his sexy voice cut through any inhibitions she may have had left.

"I'm rubbing myself while you're deep inside me. I wish you could feel me right now… so tight around your hard cock, gushing for you… I. Want. You. To…" Already on the brink of control, she closed her eyes, flicking her fingers even faster over the sensitive nub. Gasps of breath passed between them over the airwaves until she felt the muscles in her abdomen tighten and her legs tremble. "Oh, Derek!"

Her moan was met with his own cries of pleasure, but she couldn't make anything out over the sound of her galloping heart. After a minute or so of synchronized panting, he said, "That was… are you… I can't talk."

She laughed, partly from nerves, but mostly because she was in a state of complete ecstasy. "I'm good. That was good. Amazing, actually."

"You're amazing." He paused briefly before adding, "When can I see you?"

Something inside her slammed on the brakes, hurling the erotic moment they had just shared toward the windshield. It all suddenly felt too real. She skirted the subject. "I'm looking at apartments with my mom all day tomorrow, or today, I should say. I'll keep you updated on how that goes. Thanks for… taking my call."

"Any time."

"Sleep well, Derek," she said as casually as possible.

"Good night, Natalie."

CHAPTER TWENTY-NINE

Travel Plans

"Here's everything we have so far," Derek said, pointing at the evidence board. "Our sixth victim, Joy Chen, was likely killed Monday night and then dumped at the Duckworth Dock early Wednesday morning. Her face was badly smashed, implying a more violent attack than the others. There were no signs of sexual assault, but her body was stripped bare, and the number six was carved into her back."

Diluted light filtered in through a small window above where the task force huddled. Derek stood in front of the conference room that had become home base and looked at his team. Rhonda appeared to be drawing circles on the notepad in front of her. Gibs was eating a sandwich, slowly moving his jaw as he stared in Derek's direction, whereas Marty's gaze was fixed on the wall clock near the door. Only Natalie was notably missing.

Derek tried not to dwell on her absence, or their unbelievable phone call from earlier that morning; he failed on both counts. It had been magical the way his solo act had spontaneously erupted into a burning hot duet. After he had gotten off the phone with her, he'd had to pinch himself to make sure it wasn't all a dream. But it was real and wonderful, except that he had no idea when he would see her again.

Gibs finished chewing his sandwich and wiped his mouth. As if reading Derek's mind, he asked, "When is Natalie coming back? She always has something insightful to add."

Never, Derek thought. *Natalie is never coming back.* He swallowed hard, unable to admit the truth out loud. "I'm not sure when," he answered. Then he went back to addressing the room. "I went over the details with Doctor Goyle on the phone yesterday. He and another colleague at the FBI confirmed what I had been thinking as well. Our killer is angry. Something is not going according to his plan, and he is lashing out because of it."

Marty grunted. "That's all you got from Mr. Ph.D.? Why are you even bothering to still include the Feds? This isn't within their jurisdiction."

"Goyle may have been stating the obvious," Derek acknowledged, "but I needed to know that my own thoughts weren't biased. Jared Fletcher is our chief suspect, and I had given him cause for rage on Monday when I confronted him."

Marty settled back in his chair. "So, you think you caused this girl's death." His statement was matter-of-fact, lacking any hint of a question.

Derek glanced at Rhonda, who was still doodling on her notepad. She was the only other person who knew a police detail had watched Jared from Monday evening to Tuesday night. He hadn't felt it necessary to loop in the rest of the task force yet. It had been an unauthorized use of department resources, after all.

He leaned on the chair in front of her. "Jones, you've been awfully quiet. Do you have any thoughts to add?"

"Huh?" Rhonda looked up from her notepad, seemingly surprised to find Derek at eye level. "Sorry, my mind was somewhere else."

"Care to share?"

"Well…" She looked around the room sheepishly. "I know someone who was out running near the Duckworth Dock early Wednesday morning before the body was found. She didn't see anything, and luckily she wasn't alone after running into a friend from her gym, but it's still… unsettling… that she could have crossed paths with our killer."

Derek nodded, realizing that the *someone* she referred to was likely her lover—and Natalie's friend—Leah. He could only imagine how he'd feel if it were Natalie in that situation. "Unsettling is probably an understatement. I can understand you being distracted, but I'd like to talk to this person and their gym friend, in case they remember something that might be useful."

When Rhonda gulped, he added, "You can give me their names later. Do you have any other insights to add regarding the details of this last murder? We had been talking about the increased violence, likely caused by our killer being angry."

Rhonda tilted her head. "I'm not sure about the attacks getting more violent, but our killer does seem to be branching out."

"What do you mean?" Derek asked.

"I mean… the first four vics were white women. But number five, Maria Velarde, was Hispanic. And now we have Joy Chen, an Asian woman. It's just an observation, but he seems to be getting more… diverse in his selection."

"Interesting," Derek said while thumbing his chin. "I hadn't considered that angle." He walked back to the board. "We know our killer craves variety, and that craving seems to be growing stronger as well."

"Or," Gibs interjected, "he's just opportunistic, kills the first woman he sees. The diversity could be random, based on statistics."

"Maybe," Derek replied skeptically, "but the murders seem too premeditated to be random. With the probable exception of Sheena Greenwood, I think our killer stalks his victims first. And he most likely has specific criteria for who he chooses." *He or she*, Derek reminded himself, hearing Natalie's voice in his head. *He missed her so damn much.*

Marty used his cane to hoist himself up to standing. "Why don't we break for lunch, come back to it with clearer heads? Not all of us have eaten yet," he directed at Gibs, who had a piece of shredded lettuce hanging from his lip.

Derek rubbed the back of his neck, lost in his own thoughts. "Let's break for the day, actually. I have a status report to write for the chief." He turned to face Rhonda. "Jones, can you please follow up with Joy Chen's roommate? She was in shock when we spoke to her on

Wednesday. See if she remembers anything else at all, such as suspicious vehicles or people that may have been watching Joy."

"You got it, partner." Rhonda dashed out of the room.

Detective Gibson finished his last bite and slowly stood from his seat. "Anything I can help with?"

"Yes. Apply some pressure to the local businesses near the Duckworth Dock. I had asked several of them for their surveillance footage on Wednesday, and now no one is returning my calls. An in-person visit may help."

"No problem. Pressure is my middle name." Gibs tugged up the khaki pants that sagged below his gut and sauntered out of the room.

Derek faced the board again. Pictures of the women killed over the last three months stared back at him, but his mind's eye saw the faces of the Hood River Killer's victims instead. They had all been Caucasian women, with the notable exception of his Hispanic mother, Carmen Franco.

His mother's death had been different in other ways as well. She was the only victim that had been missing for nearly a year before being found. The ashes from her burnt body had been placed in a Ziploc bag with the numbered note attached. And she was the seventh and final victim, which apparently meant something special to the killer.

He felt Marty's silent presence. "I thought you were hungry for lunch?"

"I am. Just wanted to make sure you were okay first. Something's eatin' ya, besides the case. What is it?"

Derek kept his eyes on the board. "I'm trying to be impartial on this case, but I think I'm failing. It all feels very… personal."

"That's understandable, kid, given your history. And our suspect is the ex-boyfriend of the woman you love. That *is* personal."

Derek turned to face Marty. "Do you think I should remove myself from the case?"

Marty shrugged. "What I think doesn't matter. You have to do what you think is best."

After a long pause, Derek sighed. "I think I need to talk to the chief."

An hour later, Derek was back at his desk, typing up the weekly status report. Chief Serrano had listened to his concerns and then told him to take the weekend to think it over further. But he was sick of thinking about it. His indecision on whether to resign from the case, amidst everything else, gnawed at him. He thought of calling Natalie as Marty approached.

"You need to eat. A burger with fries makes everything better." Marty dropped a greasy paper bag on Derek's desk.

Derek took the bag but didn't open it. "Thanks."

"What's on your mind now?"

"Natalie," Derek replied honestly. "I think talking with her might help with my decision."

Marty's eyes lit up like a Christmas tree. "Talk to her in person! You should go to San Diego tonight!"

"What? That's crazy."

"No, it's perfect! I can't believe I didn't think of this sooner. Women love big romantic gestures. You need to go there and surprise her. Do you know what hotel she's staying at?"

Derek nodded. He had received the location via text from Natalie's mother as soon as they had arrived in San Diego. He knew texting with Linda would likely upset Natalie, but he had needed to know she was okay and hadn't known if she would be talking to him.

"So, go to her! What's stopping you?"

"I don't know... what if she's not happy with me showing up there unexpected? If I were to go, shouldn't I at least tell her I'm coming?"

"Absolutely not. It would ruin the gesture. It *needs* to be a surprise. Now go on, book your flight, and get out of here!"

Derek wasn't sure he had ever seen Marty so passionate about anything in his life. However, the thought of seeing Natalie had Derek equally excited, especially after their last conversation. "Okay, okay!" He reached toward an empty spot on his desk. "Have you seen my phone?"

"No, why? You're not going to call her and ruin the surprise, are you?"

"No," Derek conceded, "but I need my phone if I'm going to book a flight and get out of here."

"Attaboy!" Marty tapped his cane enthusiastically on the side of Derek's desk. "Maybe you left it in the conference room earlier."

Derek was reasonably sure he hadn't, but it was worth checking. Getting up from his desk, he walked down the hall and unlocked the door to the task force's conference room. The evidence board again greeted his gaze as he scanned the room. His phone wasn't in sight. He locked up, returned to his desk, and began shuffling items around. "Found it!"

Marty was seated at his own desk, elbow deep in his bag of fries. "Great. Where was it?"

"Under this stack of papers on my desk. Honestly, I must be out of it right now. It's not like me to misplace things."

"Even more reason for you to go clear your head." Marty winked at him. "Go see that girl of yours!"

Derek wasn't sure that she was *his girl*, but he knew he wanted that more than anything. He quickly searched flights on his phone and booked one that left in a few hours. He would arrive in San Diego at twenty hundred hours and tell Natalie exactly how he felt, face-to-face.

***

"This place looks nice." Natalie pulled her dark sunglasses down from atop her head as she exited the passenger side of the car.

Shade cast by the three-story building slowly retreated, exposing intense sunlight. Seagulls squawked nearby, providing a nice reminder that this option wasn't too far from the ocean. It somehow made up for the disconcerting fact that this was the same beach neighborhood whose bars she once frequented at the innocent age of twenty-one. Most self-respecting adults her age had long moved to the suburbs to raise their families in quaint neighborhoods like Bay Ho, where Jessica lived, or the upscale planned communities of North County. But here she was, back where she started.

Unsurprising to Natalie, her mother was in a world of her own. Linda fiddled with her phone and grumbled. "I miss the days when phones had buttons. Do I need to swipe up or down or press somethin'? I just wanna open the damn camera."

"Here, let me help you."

"I need a picture of the front of the building, same as the others, so I can remember which one it was later."

"I know, I know." Natalie took the phone offered by her mother. "See, from the lock screen you just need to press and hold the little camera icon in the bottom-right corner." She demonstrated how to bring up the camera and then handed the phone back.

"I didn't see that there when I was lookin' at it." Linda squinted at the screen, snapped the shot, then stuffed the phone back in her purse with a huff.

"Well, you had probably already opened the home page, in which case you have to open the camera app instead. Don't worry, though. I can spend more time going over it with you later." *They would have plenty of time together later,* Natalie thought. *Probably too much time.*

When Natalie stepped away from the car, Linda placed a hand on her arm. "Wait, before we go in there, I wanna clear the air first." She removed her hand and started fidgeting with a key chain that dangled from her suitcase-sized purse. "I know you're upset with me, Nattie, 'bout everything: the rent money, me living outta my car… what happened to your brothers."

Natalie opened her mouth, feeling the need to disagree out of politeness, but then closed it. *Why lie? Yes, she was furious about all of it.* She instead crossed her arms and waited for her mother to continue.

"And I don't blame you. I'm mad at me too. Not a day goes by that I don't think of them." Her face tilted toward the ground, and she suddenly appeared much older than Natalie had remembered her.

"I know you miss them."

"It's more than that." Her mother shook her head slowly, glazed eyes still looking down. "I was planning to divorce your father before Ivan… but I waited too long… I just waited too long."

Although Natalie didn't want to make her mother feel any worse, she had to ask, "Why did you wait at all, Mom?"

"You know how my mother raised us eight kids all alone?"

When Linda looked up at her, Natalie nodded at the question, well aware of her grandmother's lifestyle choices. *Eight children, each with different fathers. Never married. Died at sixty before Natalie was old enough to get to know her.*

"Well, what you don't know is that we were often homeless when I was a kid, off and on. I rarely knew where my next meal was comin' from and had to drop outta school to help make some money. We slept under a freeway overpass, not far from here, on cardboard and a pile of blankets that we stole from the thrift store."

Natalie blinked several times, not sure what to say. Her mother had never shared that history before.

"Anyway," Linda continued, "I guess that's why sleepin' in my car didn't feel like that big a deal to me. But I *never* wanted that life for you kids. I knew I wouldn't be able to provide for the three of you if I divorced your father, and that his child support would be unreliable. We would've ended up on the streets. Or, I dunno, maybe you kids would've been taken from me. That's what I thought, at least. So, my plan was to leave Frank as soon as Ivan graduated high school, but…" Her words trailed off as tears filled her eyes.

"Oh, Mom, I had no idea." Natalie hugged her mother for the first time in over a decade, not realizing until that moment how much she had needed it as well. Tears of her own spilled out as she buried her face into Linda's shoulder. A person walking past them in the parking lot craned their neck at the emotional display, but Natalie didn't care. Her mother had been suffering alone all those years from the consequences of a difficult decision—one that she thought would protect her children, but cost their lives instead. *She would not be alone anymore.*

After a few moments, they broke their embrace and composed themselves. Natalie spoke first. "I was going to wait to tell you this until we found an apartment, but I'm planning on staying in San Diego, Mom, to be closer to you. I'm moving back home."

The blue-green in Linda's eyes sparkled. "*Really?*"

"Yeah, really. Let's go check out this apartment."

Thirty minutes later, they were sitting at the office manager's desk filling out rental applications. The apartments viewed had been spacious as described, with large bedrooms and ample closet space, an extra vanity area outside of each bathroom, and a walk-in pantry in the kitchen. The open layout meant you could wash dishes and watch TV at the same time. Natalie was sold.

"Mom, are you sure you like it here? Because there are a couple others we can still go see if not," she asked when the office manager had stepped away to retrieve them some water.

"Yes, it's great, and I'm so excited we're gonna be roomies!" Linda beamed.

As they headed back to the car, Natalie's mind swirled. The lease had been signed. The apartment would be ready for move-in on Monday. She was officially moving back home to San Diego. *And she would be living with her mother… holy hell.*

She had planned on renting two apartments in the same building, which would have allowed them to be close while still having their own space. Yet, somehow, Linda had convinced her to rent the two-bedroom unit together instead, playing on her sensibility that it was more financially practical. Though she feared she may easily come to regret the decision, it warmed her heart to see her mother so happy. She wasn't sure she had ever witnessed such joy on her mother's face. It both broke her heart and confirmed her path.

With the apartment hunt over, she allowed her thoughts to drift to Derek. She still couldn't believe how things had *evolved* on their call earlier that morning. *Had she really initiated phone sex with him?* It was uncharacteristic of her to do something so bold and erotic, but the memory still warmed her. *Yes, that's exactly what happened, and it was incredible.*

But now she lived here, and he lived in Portland. A relationship between them, assuming that's even what she wanted, would be too difficult. *Why had she started something she couldn't finish?* And, of course, now it would be awkward when she returned to get Tux and the rest of her belongings.

"What's wrong, Nattie?" Linda asked, glancing sideways at her while driving. "You have that worried look you always used to get as a girl."

"What? Oh, it's nothing. I was just thinking of the move and everything I still need to do. Should we stop for some lunch before heading back to the hotel?"

"Sure, that sounds nice. And then you can tell me what's really goin' on in that big brain of yours."

Natalie sighed. Avoiding her mother's prying questions would be pointless. "I'm worried about facing Derek again when I go back for my things. There's some *unfinished business* between us, and my moving back here complicates things."

"I see." Linda smiled. "You two haven't had sex yet?"

"Mom!" Her mother's unreserved nature never ceased to amaze her.

"What? I tell you all about my sex life."

"Yes, and I desperately wish that you wouldn't."

Linda laughed easily. "It's the birds and the bees, honey. I noticed the way the two of you looked at each other, and he's obviously crazy 'bout you. There's no harm in havin' a little fun."

"I'm incredibly uncomfortable with this conversation, Mother." Natalie had never seen herself as the type of person that had one-night stands. *But could she with Derek?* Her tense, hunched shoulders caused pain in her neck until she consciously relaxed them. "It's complicated anyway."

"Do you love him?" Linda placed the car in park in front of a taco stand.

It wasn't the lunch that Natalie had envisioned, but she was too distracted by Linda's question to care. "What? Of course not!"

She stepped out of the car, wondering why her response had felt like a lie. *She couldn't be in love with Derek.* It hadn't even been a year since Nick's death, although the anniversary was approaching. Familiar feelings of guilt settled in her stomach.

The smell of fresh tortillas, onions, and spices filled the air as they walked up to the window and placed their order. Natalie opted for chicken rolled tacos with an extra side of guacamole, while Linda went for a classic California burrito filled with carne asada and French fries. Mexican food was another thing that she hadn't realized she had missed until being back home.

"So, are you worried about breaking his heart, then?" Linda asked as soon as they had taken a seat at a nearby picnic table.

Should she be? She hadn't even considered that possibility. This line of questioning was making her feel worse, not better. "Can we please change the subject?"

"Fine, fine… but I'm just sayin' that you deserve to enjoy yourself a little, Nattie bug. I worry about you being so stressed all the time." There was genuine concern on her mother's face. "You should just go up there and see what happens. Don't overthink it."

"Okay, Mom, maybe I will."

As was typical, Linda continued to nudge. "Actually, why don't you fly up there tonight? We can't move into the apartment until Monday anyway, so this weekend is perfect!"

"But I don't have a flight booked. It would be so last minute." Natalie tried to think of other reasons not to go but came up short.

"I hear you can get good deals that way sometimes. I know *you know* how to use that phone of yours. It don't hurt to try."

It doesn't hurt, Natalie corrected in her head. When it came to her mother, grammar lessons were about as effective as arguing with her. Knowing that Linda would not drop the subject, Natalie pulled out her phone and searched for flights from San Diego to Portland. The same-day fares were surprisingly reasonable, and there was a non-stop flight leaving in four hours.

With a flight time of only two and a half hours, she could be at Derek's condo before eight o'clock. Warming to the idea, Natalie found herself clicking "purchase" before she could talk herself out of it. Her next action was to let Derek know she was coming.

She drafted a text: *Sorry for the short notice, but I booked a flight there for the weekend. It arrives tonight at 7:30. Looking forward to seeing you.*

Before hitting send, she deleted the last sentence and added a link with her itinerary for good measure. Putting her phone away, she looked up at her smiling mother. "You win. Let's finish eating so I can go back to the hotel to check out. I'm going to Portland tonight."

CHAPTER THIRTY

Dual Journeys

The pilot announced the final descent into Portland right on schedule as her inflight movie ended. Natalie had selected a rom-com—a genre she found to be thoroughly entertaining, even if predictable. There was always some obstacle or misunderstanding, but everyone could rest assured that the two main characters would eventually end up together. Otherwise, it would be a depressing movie—the kind where one character tragically dies, usually right after professing their love. *Damn you, City of Angels.*

She briefly wondered if her moving to San Diego might be the obstacle Derek and she would somehow overcome so their "happily ever after" could begin. Shaking her head, she reminded herself that real life was not like the movies. Besides, distance was not their only roadblock. She was still too fragile to put her heart on the line again. And Derek undoubtedly had not been with a woman for more than a handful of nights. Her mind then lingered on the idea of sharing at least one passionate night with him.

When her rideshare driver dropped her off in front of Derek's building, she told herself she would not overthink it. *Whatever was meant to happen that night would happen.* She took a deep breath and lugged her suitcase up the short staircase to the entryway. Once inside the building, she opted to take the elevator up to the second floor. Her nerves hummed like electricity in her body while waiting for the painfully slow elevator to climb the one story to Derek's unit.

Feeling anxious that Derek had not responded to her text, she dug her phone out of her bag to check it again. *No missed messages or calls.* Disappointment crept in, same as it had when she arrived in baggage claim and he was nowhere to be seen. It had been stupid to think that he would show up at the airport to surprise her when she hadn't asked for a ride. *He was probably still working anyway.*

When the elevator doors finally opened, a handsome young man waited for her to exit, holding the door open while she maneuvered her luggage. She thanked him and made her way down the hall toward Derek's condo. Her heart pounded in anticipation, thumping in her ears and throat. She reminded herself that he might not even be home as she nervously fumbled for the keys in her purse at his door.

A strong hand pressed against her mouth before she could scream. She dropped her purse as the syringe entered her neck. Struggling against the arm that had her pinned against the door, she kicked and swung her arms behind her in vain before everything went black. It had all happened so fast.

She woke to the feeling of cold steel against her bare back. Coarse rope dug into her wrists and ankles when she tried to move. It only took her a moment to realize that she was naked and tied to some sort of metal table. Panic set in quickly. *Oh no. This can't be happening. No, no, no. It must be another horrible dream. Please, please, please.*

She blinked hard several times to force her eyes to adjust but couldn't make out any shapes in the darkness. Since she couldn't see, she focused on trying to calm her breath so she could listen to her surroundings. It was useless. Her head throbbed, and she had a slight metallic taste in her mouth. *Was she bleeding? What had happened to her?*

Soon, a light clicked on overhead. She struggled against the ropes, pulling hard despite the pain, as a blurred figure approached. When her eyes focused, she recognized the man that had held the elevator door for her. He was no longer smiling, though. And he held a small knife, or maybe a scalpel, in one hand.

"Wait, please! Why are you doing this?" Her hoarse voice begged.

He stopped in front of her, placed the knife or scalpel down on an adjacent table, picked up a syringe, and inserted it into her arm. "This will numb the pain."

His eyes had a familiar kindness to them, but they stared at her devoid of emotion. Tall and lean with dark hair and chiseled features, he was ruggedly handsome, albeit young. He appeared to be in his early twenties. Natalie blinked away tears and pleaded again. "I don't understand. Why are you doing this?"

He picked back up the scalpel—*it was definitely a scalpel*, she realized—and glanced away before responding. "I don't have a choice."

"Yes, you do! Please, don't do this!" she cried out as he used the scalpel to make several small incisions on her abdomen.

Blood pooled around her navel, temporarily warming her otherwise cold skin. The drugs he had administered must have successfully numbed her, as she only felt a mild tingling sensation. She looked down to see many similar incisions on her legs. *Death by a thousand cuts*, she thought. Her muscles tightened when she felt the cool edge of the blade against her breast. Seconds later, the tip plunged into her flesh.

When she flinched from the searing pain it brought, he looked down at her face with an eerie calmness. "I need you to scream."

Terrified, Natalie began to sob. If the sick bastard wanted to get off by hearing her scream, she wasn't going to afford him that pleasure. Her skin suddenly stung all over as if covered in paper cuts, although she knew her injuries were more severe. She was already feeling lightheaded from the loss of blood. When she looked back up at her attacker, she saw Derek's face instead, or at least she imagined she did.

The realization set in that she was going to die there on that table, and she wanted nothing more than to see Derek one last time—to hear his voice, to tell him everything would be okay. Same as his mother, she would be victim number seven. *It would kill him*. A pain deeper than her wounds settled in her chest. She sobbed even harder. "I don't want to die. Please, I don't want to die."

The young man placed the scalpel back down and took a step back. He eyed her from a distance as if admiring his work. "It won't be that bad. Not too much longer."

As he walked away from her, Natalie noticed that the room they were in had a wood-burning stove in the corner and large saloon doors that led to another room. It looked a lot like a kitchen. He turned the light off before exiting through the swinging doors. Her head felt fuzzy from all the drugs he had given her. Nothing made any sense. *Why numb her pain if he wanted her to scream? And why prolong her death if he didn't want her to suffer?*

Her eyelids drooped heavily as she laid there alone in the dark. It wasn't long before her body began to shiver, then quake. Cold, weak, and painfully aware that her life was slipping away, she mumbled Derek's name when she saw what looked like sunshine encircle her.

***

Twilight's last scattered rays had already faded into darkness when Derek arrived at the resort-style hotel in San Diego. He was more excited than nervous, although his stomach had been doing flips since he'd first decided to surprise Natalie. Hunger was one possible explanation. He hadn't eaten the burger that Marty had offered him and now wished that he had. *Perhaps he'd tell Natalie how he felt about her over a romantic dinner*, he mused.

He pulled out his phone and sent a text: *Linda, it's Derek. I'm hoping you can do me a favor by asking Natalie to meet you in the hotel lobby. I'm here and want to surprise her.*

His phone rang seconds later. "Hi, Linda. I hope it's not…"

Linda cut him off mid-sentence. "You can't be here!"

"Why not? Is everything okay?" Concern raced through his veins.

"Yes, but Natalie flew to Portland tonight *to see you.*"

"Oh no." He put his hand to his forehead and groaned. "I knew I should have let her know I was coming. When was she supposed to arrive in Portland?"

"I think she said she should be at your place by eight, and it's quarter past now. Well, at least it'll make for a good story someday," Linda said with a chuckle.

"Hopefully." Derek forced a light laugh despite the nausea building in his stomach. "I better call Natalie and let her know. Thanks for calling, Linda. Have a nice night."

He immediately dialed Natalie next. Her phone rang unanswered, then went to voicemail. "Hey, Natalie, it's Derek. So, it turns out we both had the same great idea to surprise each other tonight." He laughed again to push away the unease he felt. "I just arrived in San Diego, and I heard you went to Portland. Please call me as soon as you get this so I know you made it there safely. Okay, bye."

Derek sat down on a plush chair in the hotel lobby and ran his fingers through his hair. The idea of her in Portland alone had him worried sick. He searched his phone for flights back. The last non-stop flight of the day departed in less than twenty minutes. He'd never make it. Out of options, he tried calling Natalie again. *No answer.*

His thoughts might have seemed paranoid, but everything in his body told him something was wrong. A quick check found that there were three flights that arrived in Portland from San Diego earlier that evening; all had arrived safely and on time. *She should be there already, so why wasn't she answering her phone?*

Feeling desperate, he called Rhonda next. "Jones, I have a big favor to ask."

"You mean *besides* checking in on your cats this weekend? Because I was already borderline about that," Rhonda said over the sound of running water and clinking dishes. "Hold on, let me put you on speakerphone. I'm on cleanup duty after the amazing dinner Leah cooked tonight."

"Sorry to interrupt your evening, but it's Natalie. She flew to Portland tonight, and I'm not there, and she's not answering her phone." His voice quivered as he spoke. "Something terrible has happened. I know it sounds crazy, but I feel it in my bones."

"Okay, okay. Calm down. Her phone might be dead." The hissing of the faucet stopped. "What can I do to help?"

"Can you please swing by my place to make sure she made it there okay? And if you talk to her, let her know that I'm stuck in San Diego tonight, but I'll fly back tomorrow."

"You're in San Diego? You said you were going out of town for the weekend, but I didn't realize… and she flew here, so that means you were trying to surprise her. Wow, that backfired."

"Yeah, I know. I'm never taking advice from Marty again." He wrung his hands in frustration and then forced himself to soften his tone. "And I know what I'm asking is way outside of the line of duty, but I don't know what else to do. I'm asking as a friend, Rhonda. Will you please head over there?"

A voice gentler than Rhonda's replied, "Yes, Derek. Rhonda and I are heading over there right now, and we'll call you as soon as we confirm Natalie is fine."

That must be Leah, he thought. "Thank you both so much! Again, I'm sorry for disrupting your evening."

Estimating that it would take about fifteen minutes before they would arrive at his place, he walked across the lobby to the twenty-four-hour café and ordered a turkey sandwich while he waited. He was nearly finished eating when his phone rang. He answered immediately. "Hey, is she there?"

"She was, but… I don't know how to tell you this," Rhonda said with a shaky voice.

His heart was in his throat. "But what? Jones! What happened?"

"A suitcase and her purse are in the hallway outside of your door, but it doesn't look like she ever made it inside. Her phone and keys are on the ground. It appears there was some type of struggle."

"No, no, no. We need to find her!" Derek paced the hotel lobby.

"I've already called the chief, and he's putting all units in the city on high alert. They'll be stopping and searching all white vans, and we're working with local media to get Natalie's photo plastered on the news to aid in the search."

"And where's Jared Fletcher?"

"The officer on his detail says he's been home all evening. Unless he has an accomplice, he doesn't seem to be involved."

Derek wasn't ready to rule out an accomplice. "Let's put a second officer on watch as well. I don't want to risk someone blinking and missing a move."

"You got it. Hold on a sec," Rhonda mumbled something away from the phone, likely to another officer. Derek closed his eyes and inhaled. *His hallway was officially a crime scene.* "Hey, Hartmann?"

"Yeah?"

Rhonda spoke in a soft, steady tone. "We're going to find her. It's going to be okay."

"I know. I gotta go, but call me if anything changes." His nerves had miraculously calmed. A wall had formed between his emotions and his brain, which was entirely focused on next steps. *There was no margin for error.* As soon as he disconnected, he was making another call. "Lieutenant General Braxton, sir. This is former Sergeant Major Hartmann, calling in a favor."

Within thirty minutes, he was boarding a V-22 Osprey military aircraft from the Miramar air station. It would take a few hours, but he was going back to find Natalie himself. *Tonight.*

The Marine Corps pilot had coordinated with the Air Force to land at the Portland Air National Guard Base five miles outside of the city. Derek would have a police car waiting to pick him up, and the pilot would refuel before returning to San Diego. About halfway into the flight, Derek had a different idea. He had played out various scenarios in his head. The city was already being searched, but they wouldn't find her there.

Where he needed to go was clear once he listened to what his gut had been telling him for weeks. *This was personal.* Whoever had Natalie didn't want to hurt her; *they wanted to hurt him.* She would be number seven. She was special, just like his mother. *That meant something.* He was done ignoring the connection for the sake of trying to stay objective.

He gave the new location to the pilot, who voiced his concerns over the noise of the propellers. "There's not enough fuel to lift off again once we land. I won't be able to touch down there."

"That's okay, Captain." Derek looked around, grabbed a parachute off the wall. "I just need you to get me over the area, and then you can continue to the air base to refuel as planned."

The pilot nodded his agreement and changed course. Derek sent a message with the new rendezvous point to Rhonda. If he was wrong about this, he would need a ride back into the city. If he was right, he would need backup and medics there as soon as possible.

Derek prepared himself for the jump as the aircraft neared Hood River County. Rhonda had confirmed that she and several units were en route, about forty minutes out. He would get there first and go in without backup. There was no time to wait. On the captain's signal, he was out of the plane, free-falling for about sixty seconds through the dark sky before opening his chute. He pulled a flashlight from his pack, pointed it at the forest below, and readied himself for landing.

It was a familiar rush, after all his jumps into combat zones, but there was so much more at stake this time. He used the steering toggles to avoid the tall trees and hit the ground running. Quickly removing the parachute harness, he pulled his gun from the holster strapped around his chest and continued running toward the abandoned restaurant. The rumbling sound of an old portable generator could be heard through the woods. When he reached the building, there was a white van parked out front.

Pure adrenaline pumped through his veins as he burst through the door. A young man wearing hunting gear fled toward the kitchen through double swinging doors. Derek followed him with his weapon aimed to kill. "Portland PD. Freeze!"

The kitchen was pitch dark. Derek kept his gun pointed with one hand while feeling around for a light switch with the other. "We've got you surrounded. There's nowhere to run."

Derek's hand hit the switch. Bright light from an overhead fixture illuminated the room. The young man held a blade high above Natalie's body as if preparing to plunge it deeply. Derek pulled his trigger without hesitation, firing several rounds into the chest of her attacker until he fell to the ground with a resounding thud.

Derek rushed to Natalie's side, terrified to see her bloody and unconscious. "Natalie, please, wake up! You're safe now." He felt for her pulse, which was barely detectable but rapid. "You're going to be okay. You *have* to be okay."

He stripped off his jacket and placed it over her bare chest and abdomen, covering pools of blood. Setting his cell down on speakerphone, he called Rhonda while he removed the rope from Natalie's feet and hands. "Jones, she's here, but she's unconscious and has lost a lot of blood. How long before the medevac gets here?"

"The chopper will be there in five minutes. I just spoke with them, and they have plenty of units of blood ready to go."

"Thank you, Jones. Thank you so much." His voice cracked. "I don't know how long she's been like this. I'm afraid I got here too late. What if it's too late?"

"It's going to be okay. They'll be there any minute now, and we're right behind them. What about the perp?" Rhonda asked.

Derek glanced at the body on the floor. The blade was still in his hand. Four bullet holes dotted his chest, one of which was clean through his heart. "He's dead."

"Copy that," Rhonda said, and he figured she knew better than to ask more questions since she had left it at that.

"I'll see you when you get here." Derek hung up the phone and took Natalie's hand. Tears streamed down his face as he whispered, "Please stay with me, Natalie. I love you." He pressed his lips gently against hers and then pulled back at the chopping sound of the helicopter approaching. "If you can hear me, Natalie, please just hang in there a little longer. Help is on the way."

He kissed her again and then looked up as figures in flight suits rushed toward them.

CHAPTER THIRTY-ONE

Hopes and Prayers

The next forty-eight hours would come to be the longest of Derek's life. After forcing his way onto the helicopter with Natalie, he watched anxiously while paramedics applied gauze and pressure wraps to stop the bleeding. The deep wounds on her abdomen and chest were addressed first as the most critical, but smaller cuts covered her entire body. Even her underarms and the soles of her feet were sliced, along with her face, arms, and legs. Derek tried desperately to expel thoughts of the pain and suffering she endured.

He spoke to the medevac crew through the headset in the helmets they all wore, which helped block the shuddering roar of the chopper. "How can I help?"

"Apply two fingers of firm pressure here." The paramedic pointed to an area under Natalie's left breast covered in bandages. "That injury is severe, so don't let up until we get to the hospital."

Derek nodded and did as he was instructed.

"Her body is in hemorrhagic shock. We have to control the loss of blood before we can add more," the dutiful first responder explained while he reached for several units of packed red blood cells, platelets, and plasma.

Another paramedic wrapped a blood pressure cuff around Natalie's arm and then inserted an IV needle. "Her blood pressure is dangerously low. Heart rate is 247 bpm and increasing. We can't wait any longer." She grabbed the unit handed to her, attached it to the IV line, and then addressed Derek. "Do you know how long she's been unconscious?"

"I… I don't know. She was unconscious when I found her." His mind started spiraling. *Had it been minutes? Or had it been hours?*

Derek applied continuous pressure to her previously gushing chest wound while both paramedics continued wrapping bandages and checking vitals. All he could think about was being too late. He estimated the time aloud. "She was likely abducted in the city around twenty hundred hours. It would have taken at least two hours to drive here, so that's twenty-two hundred hours." He glanced at his watch, which displayed *2355*. "Assuming all the damage was inflicted here in the woods, which would have taken some time, she shouldn't have been in this state for more than an hour."

Dread set in that she still might not survive. With his free hand, he took hers and squeezed it gently. He quietly begged her to live, to keep holding on, *to stay with him*. He remained by her side, applying pressure as directed, until they touched down atop the hospital about thirty minutes later. Everything after that was a blur.

He was forced to pace the waiting room, as they would not allow him into the OR and various exam rooms where she was checked for internal bleeding, signs of sexual assault, and other injuries. Worry pulsed through his veins. *He should be there with her.* Not knowing how she was doing felt painfully familiar to the year his mother was missing.

But he was no longer the naïve sixteen-year-old boy that had held on to the belief she would be found alive. Finding his mother's remains had not only crushed his hopes of being reunited with her; it had stolen his ability to be hopeful at all.

Two hours later, Rhonda arrived at the hospital after leading efforts to secure the crime scene. "Hartmann! How is she?"

"I don't know. They won't let me back there!" He continued pacing the floor, grateful to no longer be alone, and especially grateful for his partner. She had stepped up when he needed her the most. He'd never forget that. "The last update I received was that they had sutured her wounds and hadn't found any internal bleeding."

"That sounds positive."

"But she's still not awake, Jones. That can't be good! I was reading on my phone that massive blood loss often results in not enough oxygen getting to the brain and other organs. She could easily be in a coma, if she's even still alive!"

"Hold on there, Internet M.D." Rhonda grabbed his arm and spoke in a soothing tone. "Let's not jump to any conclusions until we hear from her doctors, okay? She's in excellent care here, and from what I know about her, she's a fighter."

His anxiety was only somewhat abated by that fact. Natalie's strength was one of her many qualities that he had come to love. She was a survivor. *But how much could one person survive?* None of what she had been through in her past seemed fair, and now there was this. *And it was his fault.* If only he had been home, he could have gotten to her sooner, or prevented her abduction altogether. *He was supposed to protect her.*

"Why don't we sit down over here together until someone comes out with an update?" Rhonda held onto his elbow and motioned toward a row of depressing chairs—seats where loved ones had undoubtably received the worse news possible.

Before Rhonda could coax him into a chair, a woman in purple scrubs approached. "Detective? I'm Doctor Fitzgerald."

"Yes, I'm Detective Hartmann. How is she, Doctor? How's Natalie? Can I see her now?" He heard his own frantic voice but didn't care.

"She's stable but still in critical condition. We'll be monitoring her closely for the next couple of days." The doctor scanned Derek, as if assessing his condition. "She's not conscious yet, but I can take you back to see her if you'd like"

"Yes, yes, please! I need to see her." He looked to Rhonda. "She'll need continuous police protection as well. An accomplice may still be out there. We can't take any chances."

"I'm all over it." Rhonda reached for her phone and stepped aside while Derek pushed his way through the ICU door the doctor held open.

"Right this way." The kind doctor directed him down a long corridor to the third room on the right.

Natalie was lying in the hospital bed, surrounded by monitoring equipment. Her eyes were closed. He crumbled when he saw her.

"Natalie! I'm here, Natalie, and I'm not leaving your side again." He shot the doctor a look that he hoped conveyed it would be over someone's dead body if they forced him out again. Then he held Natalie's hand. "Everything is going to be okay now. I promise." Tears burned in his eyes. *He had promised to protect her.*

"She's under pretty heavy sedation for the pain," Doctor Fitzgerald explained from the open doorway where she stood. "Her labs showed that she was also administered strong sedatives and painkillers intravenously before she was admitted, likely by her attacker. I thought you'd want to know… for your police report."

"Uh, yes. Thank you." Derek didn't take his eyes off Natalie. She looked so fragile, yet he knew her body was mightily fighting to stay alive. Grateful for her strength, he pressed his lips to her forehead.

"I'll be back shortly to check on her," the doctor said before leaving.

An hour later, Rhonda appeared with two other armed officers. "Officers Colizzi and Gray will be stationed outside of this room. Hospital staff has been informed that no one comes or goes without being cleared by them first. I've also updated Chief Serrano, who will be here later this morning."

"Thanks, Jones. I really appreciate you taking care of everything." Derek still sat at Natalie's bedside with her hand in his.

"It's early. Why don't you go get some sleep? She'll be safe here."

"I'm not leaving her." *Never again.*

"Okay. Well, is there anything I can get for you?"

"No, thank you. I'm fine for now."

Rhonda walked over and sat across from him on the other side of the hospital bed. "So, I've been dying to ask… How in the hell did you know where to find her?"

Derek looked up into his partner's eyes. She had been essential to the rescue efforts and deserved the truth. "It was the same location my mother was murdered twenty-five years ago." When Rhonda looked shocked and confused, he continued to fill in the gaps. "She was Carmen Franco, the seventh victim of the Hood River Killer. I knew that Natalie being taken as number seven couldn't be a coincidence."

"Wow, Derek! This is all so…" She shook her head and ran her hands up and down her shocked face. "So, the two cases were connected, then, but I still don't understand… I mean, the perp you shot couldn't have been born more than twenty-five years ago. He definitely wasn't the killer back then."

"No, but he could be a copycat. For reasons I don't understand, I think this was all done to hurt me. Do we know anything more about him?"

"Not yet, unfortunately. He didn't have any ID on him, and his prints aren't in the system. The white van found was missing plates, and the VIN had been filed off as well. We'll be able to run his dental records against the local database on Monday, even though it's a long shot. And we'll be looking for matches to family members that may be in the system using his DNA."

Derek was impressed by Rhonda's thoroughness. "This guy has taken extreme measures to stay off our radar, but the family connection is our best bet. Be sure to cross-reference his DNA against our database of murder victims. Guys like him often get their start killing someone close to them."

Rhonda nodded her agreement before asking her next question. "Can you think of anyone that would want to hurt you?"

"Not specifically, but I've put away a lot of people. Maybe he blames me for something related to my job. Or, I don't know…" Derek rested his head in his hands and racked his brain. "Before this, I led Marines into battle for over a decade. Some didn't come home in the best shape, or at all. Our perp wasn't military, or else his prints would have been in the system, but maybe he lost someone close to him." Derek thought back to the air raid at the end of his last tour. He had done his best to get everyone to safety before the bombs dropped, but there hadn't been enough time. He lost half his men and countless civilians. It had been enough for him to want to leave the military at the end of his term.

Rhonda interrupted his thoughts. "That would be a long time to hold such a strong grudge."

"You never forget losing someone you loved." He looked at Natalie when he spoke. *Please God, don't let him lose her too.*

He nodded off briefly after Rhonda had left, only to be woken by the next visitor.

Victor Serrano's broad frame filled the doorway as fully as the worry spread across his face. "Hartmann, how is she?"

"Stable, but still being monitored closely, sir. She's under heavy sedation for the pain, so I haven't been able to talk with her yet."

When the chief entered the room, Derek stood to shake his hand and found himself in a tight embrace instead. "Thank God you found her when you did, son. Really great work."

"Thank you, sir." Derek's response was muffled by the chief's arm wrapped around his shoulder. Once released, Derek turned his focus back to Natalie. "I just hope she pulls through this."

"She will." Victor exuded confidence that Derek wished he felt. "Maggie already has her entire church group praying for her. She would have come with me to see Natalie herself, but she's been battling a cold the last few days and didn't want to bring any germs here."

Derek envied the chief's faith that everything would work out, whereas he would need to see it to believe it.

Victor cleared his throat. "Pertaining to matters of official business, I should tell you that IA is requesting that you turn in your badge and gun while they investigate the circumstances of the perp's death. They're questioning why it doesn't appear a non-lethal shot was attempted first." He held up his hand when Derek reached toward his holster to comply. "Keep them both. I told them where they can shove their investigation. If anyone approaches you, direct them to me."

Derek nodded his appreciation. Chief Serrano sat quietly with him while they both stared at the machines hooked up to Natalie. The monitors beeped periodically, a persistent reminder that her vitals were fragile; her life still hung in the balance.

Shortly after the chief left, Marty Thompson arrived. "I came as soon as I heard! How is she? And how are you doing, kid?"

"She's hanging in there. I'll be a lot better once she wakes up."

"So, she hasn't been awake?"

Derek picked up her hand, anchoring himself amid internal turbulence. "No. I should have never let her out of my sight. This is my fault, Marty."

"Well, she's safe now. And all thanks to you, I heard. Shooting that bastard dead must have felt great."

His eyes moved to Marty's. "It never feels good to take a life, but I did what needed to be done to save Natalie. I'd do it again in a heartbeat."

"Do they know anything about the guy yet?"

"No, not yet. He's a ghost for now, but I think we'll find something when we run his DNA. Everyone has relatives."

Marty nodded and hobbled closer to Natalie's bedside, using his cane for support. "You look like hell, kid. Why don't you run home to freshen up and rest a bit? She's safe with the two guards outside, and I can stay here and call you if she wakes up."

"Thanks, but I'm not leaving her ever again." He stroked her hand gently with his thumb.

"That's not realistic. You need a break at some point, and you'll be of better use to her if you're well rested. Trust me."

He didn't look up at Marty. Something in those words triggered him, and he knew better than to speak before it passed. It had been Marty's idea for him to surprise Natalie in San Diego. If he hadn't listened to him, he would have been home when she arrived. Logic told him it wasn't Marty's fault, but he still felt bitter. He bit his lip and remained silent.

After Marty reluctantly left, Derek let out a long breath. He was done listening to anyone else. His own intuition would be his guide, and right now it was telling him not to trust anyone but himself. He wouldn't fail Natalie again.

Morning crept into day, which brought with it new visitors. Linda and Jessica arrived at the hospital together from San Diego. Jessica thanked Derek profusely while tearfully embracing him in one of the tightest hugs he'd ever experienced. She next apologized to an unconscious Natalie for her hurtful words, sobbing uncontrollably, and then vocalized several prayers.

Linda was less emotional, visibly at least, but Derek could only imagine how she must have felt at the sight of her daughter in the hospital bed. She had already buried two children; losing Natalie as well would be unimaginable. Derek blocked the possibility from his mind to hold it together.

Hours later, he promised to call Linda if anything changed and insisted both women stay at his place for the evening. Rhonda had already confirmed that his hallway had been cleared, and there would be an officer stationed outside. He'd convinced them by mentioning that it would help if they could check on the cats while he stayed with Natalie. *It would be what she wanted.*

Once visiting hours had passed, only Derek remained by Natalie's side. Her cold hand felt lifeless in his. Fighting the strong urge to sleep, he stared at her closed eyes. One painful thought played on repeat in his brain: *What if she doesn't wake up?*

The next day was filled with even more visitors, and Natalie slept through them all. Linda and Jessica had returned in the morning and kept Derek company most of the day. Gibs made a brief appearance to offer his prayers for Natalie's speedy recovery. He also offered Derek unwarranted congratulations for the daring rescue. It had been nearly two full days, and Natalie was still unconscious. *He didn't deserve any praise.*

Captain McCarthy called several times throughout the day to check on Natalie's status rather than visiting, which was fine with Derek. His captain had seemed more concerned with being able to obtain Natalie's statement than with her actual wellbeing. *That guy has always been a dick*, he realized. It was best that McCarthy had stayed away. Otherwise, Derek may have decked him, the way he was feeling.

In the late afternoon, there was a short knock on the door before Officer Colizzi stuck his head in. "Detective, sir, there's another visitor out here that we need your clearance on first. He says his name is Jared Fletcher."

Unsure if his sleep-deprived brain had heard correctly, Derek blinked hard several times before he bolted out the door. "What the *fuck* are you doing here?" he shouted at the visibly shaken man in the hall.

Jared's eyes widened as he took several steps backward. "I didn't realize you…"

Burning rage took control of Derek's body as he pinned Jared against the wall, pressing his forearm against the coward's neck with more strength than he knew he had left. "If you *ever* come near her again, I will kill you! Do you understand?"

One of the officers placed a hand on Derek's shoulder. "Whoa, take it easy, Detective. Think about what you're doing."

"Trust me, I am." Derek waited a breath and then lowered his arm, keeping it at the ready. His blood was still on fire.

Jared rubbed his throat and gasped. "Calm down, man! I'm not here to hurt her."

"Damn right, you're not! Because you'll have to go through me first." Derek's hand dropped to his holster and rested on his gun.

Jared held his hands in the air as if surrendering. "Look, if you know Natalie, then I get why you came to my house asking all those questions that day. But I swear I'm not that guy anymore. I've changed."

"Sure," Derek said, not budging from his position.

"I was really messed up back then, when I was in the Marines. I was juicing to bulk up and drinking way too much. It's not an excuse, but I was roided out of my mind. Once I got clean, I searched for Natalie for years to apologize."

Derek took a step back, still debating whether to clock him. He held his glare but allowed Jared to continue.

"Anyway, I saw Natalie's picture all over the news and heard what happened. It's so awful." Jared shook his head in what Derek considered a bogus display of sorrow. "I came down here to see her and finally apologize for everything I had put her through."

"You're not going to see her. Not now, not ever."

Jared threw up his hands again and slowly slinked back down the hall. "Okay, I'll leave. But can you please just let her know I'm sorry?"

Derek's jaw clenched. There was a stabbing pain in his chest that radiated throughout his body. He didn't know if he'd ever get a chance to relay a message to Natalie, but if he did, it certainly wouldn't be from this douchebag.

Without responding, he turned on his heels and headed back into her room. He'd already been away too long.

Linda stood when he entered. "Is everything okay? I heard yelling."

"It's fine. I just had to get rid of someone that didn't belong here."

"I recognized the name," Jessica said quietly. "Thank you for that."

"Who was it?" Linda asked.

Derek looked from Jessica to Linda. It wasn't his story to share. "It doesn't matter. He won't be back."

"Amen," Jessica said while reaching for Derek's hand. In her other hand, she already held Linda's, who held onto Natalie's. "Let's all say a prayer for Natalie."

He accepted the hand offered from across the hospital bed, then gently took Natalie's other hand, closing the huddle around her as they all bowed their heads.

After all the visitors had left for the day, Derek closed his eyes and said a prayer of his own. Praying felt disingenuous, since he had lost his faith in his mother's ashes, but he did it anyway. There was nothing he wouldn't do, nothing he wouldn't give, if it helped Natalie survive. He stayed by her side all night once again, silently begging her to wake up.

At midnight, forty-eight hours after he had found Natalie at the abandoned restaurant in the woods, he heard the sweetest sound when she mumbled, "Derek."

CHAPTER THIRTY-TWO

The Climax

Mid-September

"Hey, how are you feeling? Do you need any more pain meds?"

Trying not to turn her head too much, Natalie looked over to where Derek sat at her bedside. It felt good to be back in her own bed. *And alive.* "Hi, I'm okay. No more pills for now, please. They make my head fuzzy, and I want to be able to think."

The last few days in the hospital had been a blur. There was so much that she had wanted to tell Derek, and still needed to, but couldn't. Not until her head was clear. Thankfully, she hadn't broken the lease on her old apartment yet. Although she'd given Derek other reasons, she couldn't handle the idea of seeing his hallway again, of reliving her attack. Someone may have stolen a knife from this apartment, but they hadn't stabbed a needle into her neck outside of it.

"Is there anything at all I can do to help you be more comfortable?" Derek asked.

"Well…" she started and then reconsidered.

"What is it? Please, let me help you." Derek looked at her with pleading eyes, and it reminded her of the despair on his face when he had told her that whoever tried to kill her had done so to hurt him.

She had argued that it wasn't his fault, but it had been like reasoning with a brick wall. They were still waiting on DNA matches to identify her attacker. Once they knew who he was, Derek could hopefully stop blaming himself. In the meantime, she knew he desperately needed to feel useful.

"It's my hair," she said. "They didn't wash it very well at the hospital, and I think there might still be some dried blood matted in there. It's gross, so I understand if…"

"How should we wash it?" Derek interrupted.

"That's the tricky part. One option would be for me to lean my head back into the sink, but I'm not sure I can maneuver that well yet. And while I technically can shower, it hurts too bad to lift my arms or stand. Plus, it would be a pain to get all these stupid bandages wet and have to redress them again." She referred to the patchwork of gauze dressings that covered the stitches all over her body. The dreaded scars that would be left behind were something she actively forced from her mind to avoid tears.

"Well, I believe I saw a detachable showerhead when I used your shower earlier today."

She almost swallowed her tongue. *Did he have any idea how many steamy thoughts that statement evoked? Mental pun intended.* The only response she could muster was, "And?"

"And," he replied, "if I put a stool or chair in the shower for you to sit on, I could use the showerhead to wash your hair without getting the rest of you wet."

It did sound practical. Although, just the idea of Derek in the shower with her was already making her wet. She wanted him so badly and wondered if it was obvious. Heat surged through her like a California wildfire. After months of pushing him away, she was finally ready to make that leap. But now, of course, her body was out of commission.

"So, what do you think?"

She had to blink a few times to come back to the conversation. "Uh, yeah, that should work. I have a small stool under my vanity that will fit nicely."

"Great," he said, dashing out of sight. When he returned, both his strong arms slid underneath her. "Here, let me help you up."

As he lifted her out of bed and headed toward the bathroom, Natalie was instantly and acutely aware of her unsightly attire—and the fact that she wasn't wearing any underwear. The oversized, cotton gown with snaps down the front was necessary due to her limited range of motion, but it didn't exactly scream "take me." If possible, it made her look even more injured and weak than she felt.

She also imagined it was difficult for Derek to see her like that, which only made her appreciate what he was doing even more. She had been wrong about his "type" and hadn't given him enough credit before. He was caring, sensitive, and kind—in addition to being amazingly gorgeous. *Damn her broken body.*

Once in the bathroom, he placed her on the stool in a seated position. "Um, awkward question… do you mind if I take off some of my clothes so they don't get wet? This is the only clean set I have here right now, but…"

"It's fine," she said, at the risk of incinerating her already burning loins.

"Are you sure? Because I can leave them on if it makes you feel more comfortable. I plan to ask Rhonda to swing by my place to pick up some stuff for me anyway, come to think of it." As he rambled, she realized he was as uncomfortable with the situation as she was.

"It's fine, Derek. I'm sure." *I'm sure this could not get any more awkward*, she thought. Then she did her best not to stare as he stripped down to his underwear. And failed.

His shirtless, sculpted upper body, which she had tried to ignore so many times before, had her captivated. Her eyes were glued to his rock-hard abs and lower oblique cuts that trailed down into a V-shape beneath his snug boxer briefs. When he turned to close the shower door, she noticed his lower body was equally sexy, with long, muscular legs that led up to a perfectly formed rear.

She forced herself to smile through the discomfort building in her body. "Thank you for doing this."

"Of course." Derek then grabbed the showerhead and turned on the water, using his hand as a shield to protect her from any overspray.

The shower stall soon became as humid as a tropical rainforest. Her back was to Derek, but his presence could be felt all around her. She tipped her head back as he directed the warm water at it, now shielding her face with his hand. It didn't take long for her hair to become heavy after soaking up the water like a sponge. Once it was completely saturated, he turned the water off and began lathering her head with shampoo.

Fragrant jasmine and vanilla danced in the heavy air, tickling her nostrils. She breathed in the intoxicating aroma as if it were an entirely new scent, rather than the same shampoo she had used for years. Maybe it was the intimacy of the moment. Maybe it was the near-death experience. But everything was better than she remembered. Smelled better, looked better, felt better.

It took Herculean effort to suppress a moan as Derek gently massaged her scalp. His warm fingers moved in small circles from her hairline, over the crown of her head, and down to the nape of her neck. She had no idea getting her hair washed could be so sensual. But then again, she had never had her hair washed by someone like Derek. She closed her eyes and savored every second of every touch.

After he had rinsed her hair clean and wrung out the excess water, Derek knelt so they were at eye level. Natalie studied his face intently while he began drying her hair with a towel. *He was perfect.* She wanted to memorize every detail: his kind hazel eyes she thought she'd never see again; his plump lips she thought she'd never kiss again; and his strong jaw she knew clenched when he was hurting. It was relaxed now, and she wanted it to stay that way forever.

Soon, his gaze met hers, and the longing in his eyes mirrored her own. He dropped the towel and wove his fingers into her wet hair, gently pulling her face toward his.

She leaned in the rest of the way and grabbed his lips with hers, tugging them closer, parting them with her tongue. His deep yet gentle kiss returned the passion she had craved for so long.

Heat built up between them before Derek pulled away. "Your body needs to heal. I don't want to hurt you."

"I know. Just kiss me, though. And don't stop kissing me." Natalie leaned forward to meet Derek's ready lips once more, placing her hands on his bare chest to steady herself.

Their mouths meshed perfectly, like his was the puzzle piece that had been missing all along. Sweet, tender kisses deepened into the breathtaking, soul-shaking kind where time stood still. After an indefinite duration, his lips moved downward to place soft kisses along her collarbone and then up the side of her neck toward her earlobes.

"I want to kiss you all over," he whispered into her ear while unfastening the snaps on the front of her gown.

She tipped her head back and quietly gasped when he delicately took one of her nipples into his warm mouth. "Oh, Derek. Please. Don't stop."

He traced kisses farther down her chest and abdomen, carefully avoiding her bandaged areas, and then skillfully lifted her into his arms. She gripped onto his strong shoulders as he carried her out of the shower and into the bedroom. When he gently laid her down, he knelt at the foot of the bed and spoke with the need of a man roaming the desert without food or water. "I want to taste you."

She spread her legs in acceptance and moaned at the sensation of his warm breath. Within seconds, he was completely engrossed in the act of pleasuring her. Gentle yet ravenous, his mouth left no area neglected. She felt her tightness open to him when he slid his fingers in as well. In complete awe of what was happening, she bit her lip to hold back more moans as he repeatedly found the right spot.

It wasn't long before his adept tongue brought her to the edge of control. She hoarsely called out his name, her throat having long gone dry. She clenched the bedspread in her fists and curled her toes as the overwhelming stimulation peaked in glorious release. But instead of letting her body writhe like it wanted to, she laid perfectly still to avoid aggravating her injuries. The restraint involved ultimately made her climax much more intense.

Derek crawled onto the bed and laid beside her. "Are you okay? Did I hurt you?"

She turned her head to face him, hardly able to keep her eyes open. "No, I'm great. That was… amazing."

He tenderly kissed her forehead. "You're amazing. Get some rest now."

Natalie smiled as her eyelids drooped shut. "You know, having an orgasm has a natural pain killing effect on the body. It's the endorphins, I think."

"Oh, well, in that case, I'm happily at your service." He kissed her cheek. "Your pleasure is *my natural painkiller*," he whispered.

"Hmm?" she murmured, already starting to doze.

His last words before she drifted off came through crystal clear. "I love you, Natalie. Sleep well."

***

Natalie woke to the smell of coffee and vanilla emanating from her kitchen. Knowing she shouldn't, she pushed herself to her feet anyway and held onto the bed for support. The not-quite-healed stitches on the soles of her feet shot out fresh doses of pain as she slowly made her way to the nearest wall. Once there, she leaned her weight against it and walked carefully around the perimeter of her bedroom toward the partially open door, stopping once to grab a silky black robe from her closet. *Much better than the white cotton gown*, she thought.

Bracing herself in the door frame, she slipped on the robe and gazed across the living room into her small kitchen, where Derek stood shirtless, tending to something on the stove. *She could get used to that view.* Her heart simultaneously smiled and cracked. She wondered if he would still love her if he knew the full truth.

There was so much she still needed to tell him. And she would. That was the thing about Derek, she realized. He made her want to open up and share things with him that she kept hidden away from everyone else. She trusted him with more than her life; she trusted him with her secrets.

"Hey, good morning," Derek said when he turned around. "You shouldn't be standing up, though. Let me help you to the couch." He rushed over to meet her at the door and immediately scooped her up into his arms.

If she hadn't felt like she would collapse without the support of the wall, the otherwise patronizing action would have annoyed her. But she truly needed his help. And, if she were being honest, it felt great to be held by him. Another thing about Derek was that he made it feel okay to receive help. All her life, that had not been the case.

"I need to tell you a few things," Natalie said as Derek lowered her onto the couch in a seated position.

"Okay, but first let me grab your breakfast. You must be starving." Derek jogged back into the kitchen to the sizzling stove.

Natalie contemplated protesting when her stomach churned. She couldn't deny that she was hungry, especially since her last meal had been unmemorable hospital food. "What are you making?"

"French toast with bacon and eggs. It was my favorite breakfast growing up." He stilled as if reliving the memory. "Does that sound good to you?"

"It sounds amazing." She blushed, thinking back to the previous night. "You're truly amazing, Derek. I didn't even have any food in my fridge."

"Rhonda helped with that. She stocked your fridge before we arrived. She's just outside if we need anything else."

"She is?"

"Um, yeah, I forgot to mention it earlier, but we have a couple of officers and a squad car covering your apartment for extra security."

Natalie nodded her grateful understanding as Derek walked over to her with two plates in his hands. She happily took one and didn't wait for him to sit before digging into her food. "Mmm! This may be the best French toast I've ever had!"

Derek and his big smile sat next to her on the couch. "It was my mom's secret recipe, but luckily she shared it with me."

Natalie forced a smile in return. It was going to be hard to tell him all that he needed to know. When they had both finished their last bites of breakfast, she handed her empty plate to Derek after he insisted on cleaning up and waited for him to return to the couch.

"Thanks again for that delicious breakfast… and for everything." Warmth again brushed across her cheeks. *Focus, Natalie.*

"My pleasure." Derek returned his signature smile. "You mentioned you needed to tell me something. I'm ready to listen."

Her heart beat like a drum in her throat. Shifting in her seat, she crossed her hands on her lap to steady herself. "It's about something that happened when I was… when I almost died."

"Okay." His smile disappeared, and she already regretted the conversation.

"The thing is, this will probably be difficult for you to hear, and I'm not sure you'll believe me, but…"

Derek put his hand up to stop her. "I will always believe you, Natalie. You can tell me anything. Please, trust me."

"I *do* trust you, and I love you. That's why I'm afraid, though. I don't want to cause you pain."

"Don't worry about me. I want to know everything that happened. But first, you love me?"

She smiled weakly. It was the first time she had said those words to him, but she was more concerned with all the words she knew must follow. "Yes. I think I have for some time, but I knew for sure when I thought I was dying." She paused for a long breath before continuing. "When I was lying there, feeling the life drain from my body, all I could think about was *you*, Derek. I knew you would blame yourself unjustly, and that there was nothing I could do about it. That thought alone was far more painful than any of my physical wounds. *It shattered my heart.*"

Derek reached for her hand but remained silent.

"But it was more than that. I also thought that I'd never see you again. It was unbearable to think that I'd never again hear your voice or see that charming smile that makes my heart skip a beat every time. And that's when I realized… I love you more deeply than I ever thought possible."

Tears threatened their way out as she forced them down her throat with a gulp. "In the past, it often felt like death would be the easy way out for me, so much so that I've had thoughts about ending my own life. But on that table, I desperately wanted to live, even if only to see you one last time. You gave me the strength to keep going."

"No, Natalie, you've always had the strength. It's one of the many things I love about you." He wrapped her into his arms. "I love you so much."

She pulled back from his embrace, fighting back more tears. "I'm not as strong as you think. I know I didn't want to die that night. And I know I never want to cause you pain. But I honestly can't promise that I'll never have those thoughts again. That's what scares me the most." She closed her eyes, unable to watch his heart break. "And that's why it would be best if you didn't love me."

Derek wiped a tear from her face. "Before I met you, I didn't want to love anyone. I thought I could avoid the pain of loss that way. But falling in love with you wasn't a choice. And you know what else it helped me realize?"

She slowly opened her eyes and shook her head.

"I realized I was dead inside before you. I was existing without living. Yes, watching you fight for your life in the hospital was the most excruciating experience of my life. But the joy I felt when you survived, and the joy I feel every time you smile, is unlike anything I've ever experienced before." He softly kissed her lips before continuing. "Life is about the highs and lows. They unfortunately come together in pairs, but the highs are worth it. *You are worth it.*"

More tears flowed down her face. "But I don't want to hurt you, Derek."

"And I trust that you won't intentionally. You let me worry about the rest, okay?"

She nodded. "So, you still love me?"

"Yes, very much. Nothing you could tell me will ever change how I feel about you." He went to hug her, but she held out an arm to block him.

"Wait, there's more." Sniffling, she wiped away the last of her tears. "It's about your mother."

"What about my mother?" His tone became anxious.

"Well, you see, this is the part that may be hard to believe. I'm still struggling with it myself, to be honest… Do you believe in an afterlife?"

"Yeah, I mean, my mom used to take me to church as a kid. My faith waned after her death, but I still like to believe our spirits live on longer than our bodies."

"I've always wanted to believe that, too. I just wasn't sure before."

"Before what?"

"Okay, the thing is, before you showed up and rescued me, I was in a beautiful garden… with your mother. I know it sounds crazy…"

"I don't think it's crazy." Derek's hazel eyes softened, prodding her to go on.

Her shoulders relaxed on an exhale. "I remember feeling so cold. And then all of a sudden, there was this brightness everywhere, like sunshine, but with none of the warmth. Tall sunflowers that reached for the sky surrounded the area, and within them, the most beautiful garden I've ever seen. I wandered through flowers of all different colors. It was like a dream, only much more vivid.

"And then I saw her. She was sitting on a bench in the center of the garden with a bunch of cut flowers in her hand. She was sniffing them, which made me realize I couldn't smell any of the flowers around me. It was like I was allowed to visit, but I didn't belong there."

When Natalie got quiet, Derek squeezed her hand. "Please, go on."

Gazing beyond him, she tried to recall as much detail as possible. "Your mother looked radiant and peaceful. Her dress was covered in sunflowers, similar to those that framed the garden. Her dark wavy hair framed a face so familiar that I remember reaching out as if it were you. Then she motioned for me to come sit next to her on the bench, and I did. At first, we sat in silence, just smiling at each other. Her smile looked like yours too. I don't know how much time passed, but it was enough that the silence should have felt awkward. Instead, it was calming."

She stopped and looked at Derek when she felt his hand trembling in hers. "I'm so sorry. I knew this would be too much. I don't even know if it was real or…"

"She loved sunflowers," he said, looking as if he were the one who saw a ghost. "Her favorite dress was covered in them. She wasn't wearing it when she went missing, but she said she wore it whenever she wanted to feel extra happy. You saw her, Natalie." He swiped at the corner of his eye. "I want to hear everything. What happened next?"

"Well, I remember your mom throwing her arms around me when I started to shiver. I was still so cold, but warmth immediately began transferring from her body to mine. She held me in silence for what felt like forever, and then she finally spoke. She said that she could tell that I wasn't ready to go yet. And then she said…" Natalie paused to study Derek's face a moment. She wanted to remember what it looked like before he was broken, *before she broke him.* "She said that we share a common past… except hers found and killed her."

Derek sprang from the couch. "Who killed her? What else did she say?"

"That was all she said. The next thing I knew, I was back on that awful table, and you were there. I heard your voice, even though I couldn't get my eyes to open." Tears again streamed down her face as she grabbed for Derek's hand, which was out of her reach. "I have some ideas about what she meant, though."

"You think she had an abusive ex-boyfriend? And that's who killed her?"

Natalie nodded. Her heart was splitting in two for him.

He slowly shook his head. "But I would have known. My mom hardly dated, and the few boyfriends she had when I was growing up all treated her great."

"It could have been before you were born." She shifted uncomfortably on the couch. "What do you know about your biological father?"

His head was still shaking. "I never knew who he was. My mom said that he had taken off when he found out she was pregnant, and that we were better off without him."

"What about Hartmann? Did that come from him?"

"No. Hartmann was a random surname my mom picked when she learned it could be anything. She said she wanted me to grow into a man that was known for his heart. She also sometimes talked about being treated differently when she immigrated here from Mexico, so I always assumed that's why she didn't want me to have her last name." Derek's eyes grew wide. "Or… she gave me a random last name so he couldn't find me after *she left him*… because he was abusive! How had I never thought of that possibility before?"

"I'm so sorry, Derek."

"Don't be sorry. This is the biggest break in her case that I've had in all the years I've searched for answers!" Excitement filled his voice and spurred her to respond before thinking.

"That's great! I thought you'd be more upset to learn that your own father may have killed your mother." She immediately covered her mouth. "I'm so sorry! I…" *I am an idiot. I don't think before I speak. I didn't mean to say that.* Not knowing how to best finish that sentence, she sat quietly as her careless comment dangled between them.

His face changed while registering her words. It tightened and then relaxed. "Whoever he was, he wasn't my father. He was just the asshole that got her pregnant."

"You're right." She nodded, grateful that he was taking everything much better than she expected. "Of course, you're right. Now what?"

"Now, I at least know where to start looking." Derek walked over to the kitchen counter and grabbed his phone. "Back in LA, we lived with my aunt. I had overheard her refer to him before as 'el diablo blanco' or the white devil."

"So, she knew who he was, then."

"Yes, but she unfortunately died of cancer shortly before we moved to Oregon. I'm hoping she might have told some of her friends who he was, though."

"And what about friends of your mother?"

"They were all questioned back when she died. No one seemed to know of anyone that would want to hurt her."

"Hmm."

"What is it?" Derek asked from across the room.

Natalie thought for a moment. "When you lived with your aunt, do you know whose name was on the place? Did mail come to the house in your mother's name at all?"

"My aunt rented the house we lived in. I'm not sure about the mail. Why are you asking?"

"Well, when I was afraid that Jared would find me, I was careful not to put my name or address on anything. But twenty-five years ago, it would have been harder for the average person to track someone down that way."

When Derek looked at her without a semblance of understanding in his expression, she continued to explain. "It's probably nothing, but I was just thinking that she would have needed to be careful if he was someone with more resources."

"You mean, like someone in law enforcement?"

"Possibly. It would explain your mother's friends being too afraid to come forward."

"I have some calls to make. Are you okay there on the couch, or would you like some help back into bed?"

"I'm fine here for now, thanks. Speaking of calls, though, do you know what happened to my phone by chance?"

"Oh, yeah. Rhonda brought back a box of your things from the evidence room. One sec." He went into the bedroom and emerged with her phone in his hand. "The screen is cracked, but it still works."

"Thanks," she said when he handed her the phone. "I have a bunch of missed calls from you, I see."

"Sorry, I was panicking when I was stuck in San Diego and couldn't reach you."

"Wait, what? You were in San Diego?"

"Yeah, I had gone there to surprise you without realizing that you had flown to Portland. Great minds think alike, apparently." His forced smile looked painful.

"But I had texted you that I was coming and sent my flight details." Doubting herself, she opened her text messages to confirm. "Yeah, it's right here. Did it not go through?"

Derek opened his phone and scrolled through his threaded messages. "That's weird. I don't have any texts from you... not even older ones. It's like our whole text history was deleted."

"Could you have done it by accident?"

"Son of a..." Derek dropped his phone on the floor. His jaw dropped practically as far before his face transformed from one of shock to an all-consuming fury. "I know who's behind all of this!"

CHAPTER THIRTY-THREE

Finally

Two weeks later

Derek waited as patiently as he could in the visitor's area of the Multnomah County Detention Center. He hadn't been allowed to take part in the arrest or any of the official process due to his personal connection, nor had he wanted to leave Natalie's side. But now, she was safely back in San Diego with her mother, and he was ready to finally face his mother's killer. The bastard was being held there to await trial, after which he would head straight to the state penitentiary. Derek only had one question for him.

A buzzer sounded before the door opened. Armed guards led the cuffed inmate to be seated across from Derek at the metal table. The jail-issued clothing suited him. He belonged in prison, though not punishment enough. Once he was seated, the officers stepped away and stood guard at the door.

"You here to kill me, kid?" Marty Thompson shot him a devilish grin.

It took everything that Derek had to restrain himself. The wretched betrayal stung even more as he faced him. "No, you're going to rot in prison. I'm not like you."

"You always were more your mother's child. That's why I needed Junior." Marty spoke in a raspier than usual voice. "Tell me, how does it feel knowing that you killed your own brother?"

The DNA tests had confirmed what Derek had suspected: Marty was his biological father. The fact that Natalie's attacker, Junior Thompson, was also a perfect DNA match with Derek had come as more of a surprise. All evidence of childbirth had been lost in his mother's burnt remains, but she had apparently carried another child during the year she had been missing. *Without a doubt, against her will.*

Derek held back the emotions burning inside him. He would *not* give Marty the pleasure. "I didn't kill him. You did, the second you turned him into you."

Marty scoffed. "You pulled the trigger, kid."

Derek slammed his hand on the table. "Stop calling me kid!"

Finally invoking the reaction that he obviously wanted, Marty smiled. "Sure thing, *Detective*. Why are you here, then?"

"I want to know *why*."

"Why I killed your mother?"

"No, I know the answer to that question well enough. It's because you're a psychotic asshole that gets off on controlling and hurting women. My mother left you, evaded you for years. It must have tormented you. That's probably why you killed all those other women before you found her."

"Wrong. I found her first. She had slipped up back in LA by putting her name on a lease. Then the stupid whore thought she could run away to the middle-of-nowhere Oregon and that I wouldn't find her. I must say, you unfortunately inherited her intelligence."

Uncontrollable anger launched Derek to his feet. "Fuck you!"

The guards motioned him back down into his seat. If he wasn't more careful, his visit would be over. Marty let out a demonic laugh. "The other women were meant to throw everyone off. Although, I'd be lying if I said I didn't enjoy it."

Derek worked hard to regain composure, speaking through gritted teeth. "I meant, why start killing again now after all these years? And why Natalie?"

"Oh, that. Well, I knew you'd be on the case, and Junior was of age to prove himself. Those women were his handiwork, so I can't take all the credit there. Except Sheena Greenwood, of course. I enjoyed handling that one myself. I also enjoyed watching you struggle to make sense of everything, always looking for patterns that didn't exist. Then, too-smart-for-her-own-good Natalie started interfering where she shouldn't."

"So, that's why you went after Natalie? Because she figured out there was more than one killer?"

"Wrong again, Romeo." Marty laughed and coughed concurrently. "I hand-selected Natalie that first night at Pete's after you couldn't stop staring at her."

"What?" Derek asked, confused. "*Why?*"

"You still don't get it? You should know better than anyone that the best way to hurt someone is by hurting someone they love."

"No, I get that! But *why* did you want to hurt me so bad?" Derek felt his voice falter and consciously steadied it. "What did I ever do to you?"

"It wasn't anything you did, kid. You can blame your mother. I told her I would leave you alone if she cooperated. We could have all been a family: me, your mother, you, and Junior. But she fought me every step of the way." Marty's face reddened. "The day of Junior's birth, she got a hold of the knife that I had used to cut the umbilical cord, stabbed it right through my leg." Marty glanced down at the leg that he had so often tapped with his cane. "After that, I vowed to her that I would destroy what she loved most. *You.*"

Derek was stunned, enraged, and heartbroken all at once. There were too many emotions to process any of them. It finally all made sense, and yet he couldn't believe it was true. Marty had positioned himself as a trusted father figure and mentor in his life for nearly twenty-five years—all to destroy him. "Well, you failed."

"Did I?" Marty asked with a grin.

Suddenly aware of the tears that ran down his face, Derek wiped at them and stood. "We're done here."

As Derek walked toward the guarded door, Marty called out. "One last thing… I burned her alive."

Derek exited without looking back. *Natalie survived*, he reminded himself. His mother's killer was finally behind bars. It was over. *All of it was finally over.*

***

Her stitches were out, and her wounds would continue to heal, but Natalie doubted she would ever be herself again. She looked in the mirror and thought maybe that was okay. A lot had changed in the year since Nick's death. Her old self had lived in guilt simply for existing. Her new self, she hoped, would live in gratitude.

She traced her fingers along the raised pink skin on her cheek. Her scars served as a reminder that she was lucky to be alive. Her life was a gift that she was finally ready to cherish. And it was okay to ask for help when she didn't feel that way. She realized that now.

As soon as she had gotten home, she scheduled weekly sessions with a therapist. It was a long overdue action that she had thought about doing for years, but for some inexplicable reason never could before. The first session had already helped her, and it felt good to know that her mental health struggles would no longer be hers alone to bear.

It also felt good to be back in San Diego. Living with her mother wasn't as bad as she had imagined, so far at least, and Jessica had already visited several times. She was truly grateful for their support and happy to be home. But she missed Derek. As if reading her mind, Tux rubbed against her leg and meowed.

"I know. You miss your buddy too, don't you?" Still sore, she carefully tied her robe and reached down to pet her purring companion. Then she hit off the bathroom light and made her way toward bed.

A quiet knock on her bedroom door was followed by Linda's voice. "Hi, honey, are you still awake?"

"Yeah, what's up?"

Linda swung the door open. "You've got a visitor."

Derek stood in the doorway in dark jeans and a gray T-shirt, holding a bouquet of sunflowers and looking handsome as hell. Overjoyed to see him and grateful to have her mobility back, Natalie rushed toward him and wrapped her arms around his neck. "You're here!"

"Yes, I am," he said, enveloping her body with his.

She breathed in his woody scent to reinforce it was true. "What a nice surprise! I thought you weren't coming until next week."

"I finished up what I needed to earlier than expected."

Knowing that meant he got the answers he had sought, she leaned back to study his jaw, his one tell on an otherwise poker face. "How are you doing?"

"Much better now that I'm here with you." He placed a kiss on her forehead, making it difficult to assess his condition.

"I'll leave you two lovebirds alone." Linda smiled at them before retreating to her own room.

"How are you really doing?" Natalie asked once they were alone. "That must have been awful."

"It was, but it's over now. His goal was to destroy me, so I'm not going to let him win. You're alive and here in my arms. That's all that matters now." He squeezed her closer and kissed the top of her head this time, blocking her view of his jaw entirely. *He was good at hiding his pain.*

She supposed it was from years of practice, which made her heart break even more for him. She wanted to tell him that it was okay to fall apart in front of her, that he could accept help the way he had taught her to, but then she got distracted by the sight of his luggage and cat carrier in the hallway.

"How long are you able to stay?" she asked.

"Well, that's something I was hoping to talk to you about." He brushed his hand through her hair. "How would you feel about me moving in here?"

"Here? With my mom and me?" She leaned back to look at him again. "Are you serious?"

He nodded. "I've already cleared it with Linda, but it's your call."

"You talked to my mom about this already?" she asked incredulously, raising an eyebrow at him.

His lips curved into an irresistibly charming smile. "We text."

"Oh, be careful with that," she laughed. "I would love to have you here, of course, but I don't think you know what you're getting yourself into! Maybe we should get our own place instead."

"Your mom is so happy to be living with you. I don't want to take that from her. I think it'll be fine." When she tilted her head and eyed him skeptically, he added, "And if it's not, we can look into getting our own place later."

"Deal!" She squeezed him tightly again before pulling away. "But what about your life in Portland? Your job?"

"My life is where you are, and I can get a job anywhere. The chief has already forwarded a letter of recommendation on my behalf to the SDPD. There's nothing left for me in Portland, Natalie. I want to be here with you. I love you."

"I love you too." She leaned in to meet his waiting lips. Any residual worries melted away with what she could tell was a much-needed kiss for them both. "Let's bring your stuff into *our* room, then."

After getting Derek settled, they sat on the edge of the bed together. He ran his hand down the side of her plush robe and then rested it on her bare thigh, warming her entire core with his touch. As if unsure what to do next, his hazel eyes scanned her face like they were searching for answers. His hand inched up her leg and then stopped again. Sensing his hesitation, Natalie took control of the situation.

She kissed him with urgency and ran her hands up and down his shirt, prompting him to remove it. When he complied, the feel of his smooth, muscular chest under her fingertips only drove her further. She quickly moved to unfasten his jeans, tugging at the waistband with voracious need. Unable to remove them fast enough, she reached inside to feel for her prize. They moaned in unison when she stroked the full length of him.

"Make love to me," she whispered against his mouth.

Derek pulled away and looked at her with concern. "How's your body?"

"You tell me." She leaned back onto the bed seductively and untied her robe.

"I'm serious. I don't want to hurt you."

"You could never hurt me." When he didn't look convinced, she added, "My body is fine, I swear. A little sore at times, but remember those natural painkillers we talked about?"

"How could I forget?" His smile returned as he kicked off his jeans. "Let's get you a fresh batch of those first, then."

He placed his elbows on either side of her reclined body and slowly lowered toward her. She felt the heat but not the weight of him, which she knew was intentional. As much as it drove her crazy, the care he took made her love him even more. He kissed her mouth before trailing kisses down her body, and in that moment, nothing else mattered.

His thoroughness impressed her as he dragged his lips along every spot on her torso, slowly sliding lower with each kiss before devoting extra attention to the ache between her thighs. His tongue teased her to the tipping point, then plunged in deeply. Not wanting it to end, she gripped onto the sheets and bit back a moan while he continued ravaging her in the best possible way. Ultimately, her body surrendered to the sensation. Her legs trembled. Her toes curled. She cried out in pleasure as waves of the first orgasm washed over her.

But he was not done. His lips caressed her super-sensitive flesh a while longer before sliding up her body. She was pleasantly surprised that he had managed to slip on a condom without her even noticing. Every nerve in her body was fully stimulated as he slid inside. She wasn't sure she'd have noticed the sky falling at that point. He filled every inch of her, body and soul.

"Is this okay?" he asked, catching her gaze with his.

Much better than okay. She nodded as their eyes locked in the moonlight. It illuminated the tantalizing flecks of green that she adored. There was love in his eyes… and something uncharacteristic. *Fear? Uncertainty?* It was her turn to ask, "Are you okay?"

"Yeah, sorry. Just nervous, I guess. This is my first time." When her confusion caused her head to tilt, he clarified, "I mean, not with sex. I've had plenty of sex." Even in the dim light, she could tell he was flustered. And blushing. *It was adorable.* "Sorry, I'm making it awkward. It's just… I've never made love before, because I've never loved anyone before you, and I want tonight to be perfect. But now I'm messing it up."

"You're not messing anything up." She grabbed his face with both her hands. "And it will be perfect, *because* we love each other." She kissed him and then continued speaking between kisses of escalating passion. "Also… I'll let you in… on a little secret. Sex… and love-making… are the same thing."

She deepened her kiss again and moaned when she felt him harden and pulse inside her. "The love makes everything better, but the mechanics are identical."

He kissed her back with a low groan in his throat. "You promise you'll stop me if anything hurts?"

"I pinky swear," she said without offering her finger. "Now, *please*, have your way with me."

Much to her pleasure, her words seemed to lift his confidence and spur him back into action. His rhythm started slow and gradually increased in both speed and force. He pressed up to his knees, gripping her hips as he drove in hard.

"You mean, this way?" he whisper-growled.

Holding his gaze, she spread her legs wider and tilted her hips up to welcome him in further. A breathless "mm-hmm" was all she could manage.

Completely in tune with her body, he leaned in deeper and then lowered his mouth to hers. His kiss was hot and hungry. His tongue thrusted as intensely as the rest of him in gratifying harmonization. He ran a hand up her body, stopping briefly to strum her already aroused nipples before weaving his fingers through her hair.

Only the sound of their breath in unison could be heard as he continued making love to her. She felt everything tighten as a second wave of pleasure rippled through her.

When he stopped, she was ready to plead for more until he whispered in her ear, "Roll over for me."

She happily obeyed, rolling onto all fours. He again held onto her hips and plunged even deeper. She arched her back and gasped with delight when she felt him high in her belly. The repeated smack of his muscular thighs had Natalie biting her lip. She didn't know she could be so wet, nor did she think it could get any better until the third wave pulled her under. He finished with her this time, crying out her name.

Breathless and sweaty, they both collapsed on their sides and again gazed into each other's eyes. Once she could, Natalie was the first to speak. "I could get used to that."

He smiled. "Good. Me too. I love you so much."

"I love you too, Derek."

"Be right back." He darted off to the bathroom. When he returned, she felt his arm wrap around her from behind as he assumed a spoon position. *Or was she the spoon?* Snuggling had never been her thing, but like everything else, it felt right with him.

She let out a satisfied sigh. "Honestly, I never thought it was possible to feel the way I do with you. To have both complete trust *and* intense passion. You're a dream come true."

"And you're everything I never knew I needed. You've made me happier than I ever thought possible, and my only dream is to do the same for you." He gently kissed her shoulder. "I'll never do anything to break your trust, I promise."

"I know. You would never hurt me." Finally believing it herself, her heart filled with joy. "I'm so glad you're here."

"There's no place I'd rather be."

"Good. Get some rest now, my love." She snuggled in closer, holding onto his arms wrapped around her. "Because in the morning, I'm totally going to jump you again. And it'll be *my turn* to be on top."

With little effort yet great care, he rolled her over and on top of him. "Why wait until the morning?"

Her cheeks lifted into a smile only he could conjure from her. One of genuine happiness. "Oh yes, I can definitely get used to this."

They then made love once more that night, as she suspected they would for many more nights to come. Whether they would live *happily ever after* was still to be seen, but fear of loss would no longer stop them from finding out. There was plenty of pleasure to be had in the *happily ever present.*

Epilogue

The following April

Jessica Serrano was always late. Dark clouds overhead threatened unexpected rain as Natalie sat on a park bench waiting patiently for her best friend. Since they had much to catch up on, their plan had been to go for a brisk walk around the bay before grabbing some lunch. She only hoped Jessica would arrive before the storm. The last six months had been a whirlwind, as it was.

Natalie had been beyond busy. With a renewed sense of purpose after recovering from her attack, she used the wealth that Nick had left her to establish the *Sylvia Porter Foundation*, dedicated to providing resources to women in need. Helping Jessica land a job after her trial separation from Brad had spurred the idea for Natalie. There were plenty of women that could benefit from similar assistance, and she was in a unique position to help.

The first act of the non-profit foundation was to set up a local women's resource center. It would be different from a shelter, with free offerings such as job placement assistance, counseling, legal advice, relocation services, and even temporary housing in protected apartments when needed. Natalie would need to host charity events to raise additional funds for ongoing operations, but her seed money was enough to open the first *Fresh Start Women's Center* in San Diego.

With the grand opening in less than a week, Natalie finally had time to come up for air after months of preparations. Lunch with her best friend was exactly what she needed. She glanced at her phone to check the time right as it rang.

"Hey, Leah, it's great to hear from you! I heard Rhonda made detective. Please pass along my congratulations to her! How's the Academy going?"

"Thanks. Yes, it was a well-deserved promotion, and she's over the moon ecstatic that it came sooner than expected," Leah said. "Academy is tiring—since I'm still working at the gym as well—but it's worth it. I'll be graduating soon and finally starting my dream job."

"That's so exciting! I'd love to come up there for your graduation, if that's okay?"

"Of course, that would be great! I'll send you the information. I'm calling to share some other exciting news, though."

"*Ooh*, what is it?" Natalie asked, full of curiosity.

"Well, I proposed to Rhonda last night… And she said yes!" Joy radiated from Leah's voice.

"I'm so happy for you both! Congratulations!"

"Thank you! We haven't set a date yet or anything, but we're obviously hoping you and Derek will make it to the wedding."

"We wouldn't miss it for the world! I'll let Derek know the good news right away."

"No need. Rhonda just called him as well. We're a couple of blushing brides, I guess! Who knew?" Leah's smile beamed through the phone. "I gotta make some more calls, but let's talk again soon. I know nothing about planning a wedding!"

"Sounds good. Talk to you soon!" Natalie hung up the phone, smiling for her dear friends. They had come such a long way in their relationship and were one of the happiest couples she knew. She couldn't think of two people more deserving.

Her heart smiled when her mind wandered to Derek. Things had been going amazingly well between them. This was despite still sharing an apartment with her mother, six months longer than she ever imagined possible. Derek had been offered a detective position with the SDPD shortly after his move and had opted to investigate petty crimes rather than homicide. He reasoned that he had seen enough death in his lifetime.

The lower stress role also gave him time to study for his LSAT, since he planned to enroll in law school that fall. Over the last few months, Derek spent most nights studying while she drafted plans for the women's center. They were both a great support system for each other, and she was incredibly proud that he had decided to pursue his dream of becoming a criminal prosecutor. She knew his mother would be proud, too.

Her mind shifted back to Jessica, who was running unusually late, even for her. She opened her phone and called Jessica's number. It rang four times before going to voicemail. She hung up, then tried again.

It rang three more times before a male voice answered. "Hello, is this Natalie?"

"Yes. *Who is this?*"

"I'm an EMT, ma'am. Your friend says she was on her way to meet you. She was in a car accident, and we're on our way to Scripps Mercy Hospital for scans."

"Oh my goodness! Is she okay? Can I talk to her?"

"She's conscious but may have a concussion and some broken bones. Our other technician is examining her now. I'm sorry, I need to let you go."

She could hear Jessica crying in the background before the call ended.

Poor Jessica! Natalie's heart raced with worry as she ran from the park bench to her car. She called Derek on her drive to the hospital to let him know what had happened and then said a prayer for her best friend. *Please God, she has to be okay.*

***

Stay tuned for Book Two of the Fresh Start Series, *When Love Heals*, to read more about Jessica's story.

P.S. If you've enjoyed this book, please leave a review! It really helps. Amazon, Goodreads, social media, or other online book sites are all great options. Thanks!

Acknowledgments

This book is dedicated to anyone that has had their heart broken before—and especially to those that have survived abuse of any kind. While the events in this book are entirely fictional, the realities of domestic violence, murder, and suicide are far too prevalent in our society. A short list of resources as of the time of this publication is given at the end of this note. Please seek help if you or anyone you know may be suffering.

I'd also like to briefly thank my husband and all my amazing friends that have supported me with patience and encouragement throughout my writing journey. It probably wasn't easy for them to listen to me blab about "my book" all the time, but I never would have found my passion for storytelling and the continued determination to finish this novel if not for their kind support.

I started writing this book as a creative outlet for my otherwise analytical brain, stealing time where I could on nights and weekends. Although it evolved significantly during the writing process, the story of Natalie and Derek originally came to me in a dream and then continued to play out in my head like a movie for years. I knew I needed to get the story out, but a big part of me never thought I'd finish doing so. (Not finishing personal projects was kind of *my thing*.)

So, what started as a new writing hobby soon became a resolution to break that nasty habit. I needed to prove to myself that, if I set my mind to it, I could finish something I started. Along the way, though, I discovered I absolutely *loved* the writing process, and it became less and less challenging to prioritize the time. Whenever I wasn't working, I couldn't wait to spend all my free time writing!

And that's when it happened… At the ripe age of thirty-eight, I not only finished my first novel that had been four years in the making, but I realized I had finally found my passion! Joining various writer and bookish communities on social media also helped me realize that I had found "my people" as well.

Therefore, I'd also like to thank all you avid romance readers, bookstagrammers, and fellow authors out there that have made nerding out over our mutual love of books so cool. Keep being you, because you're awesome!

Lots of love,
S. J. Greene

Resources in the United States:

- National Suicide Prevention Lifeline: 1-800-273-TALK (8255)
- National Domestic Violence Hotline: 1-800-799-SAFE (7233)
- A much longer list of resources from the National Coalition Against Domestic Violence can be found at: https://ncadv.org/resources

About the Author

S. J. Greene lives in San Diego, California with her husband and adorable rescue dog, both of whom are the loves of her life. She enjoys spending time in nature and, of course, reading romance novels! Working in the corporate world by day and writing novels at night, she dreams of a life where she can be a full-time writer and dog mom, perhaps opening a rescue of her own someday.

To stay in touch, please follow **@author.sjgreene** on Instagram.

www.ingramcontent.com/pod-product-compliance
Lightning Source LLC
Chambersburg PA
CBHW021408310726
48971CB00005B/1252